THE JORVIK PROPHECY

DEAN CORBYN

PIER HOUSE
PRESS

First paperback edition April 2024
10 9 8 7 6 5 4 3 2 1
Typeset in Garamond Pro
Typewriter font by Tomasz Skowroński
Poem script in Aquiline Two

Cover design by Dean Corbyn
Copy Editors: Annie Jenkinson, Brad Reynolds

ISBN: 979-8-9886253-8-4 (hardback)
ISBN: 979-8-9886253-7-7 (paperback)
ISBN: 979-8-9886253-4-6 (ebook)
www.deancorbyn.com

PIER HOUSE
PRESS

For my parents, Maureen and Melvyn.
Your belief in me propelled me towards my dreams.

THE SHAMBLES, YORK

Dear reader,

Welcome to my favorite place on Earth!

Whilst many of the locations mentioned in this novel hold personal meaning for me, only one city has a special place in my heart. York.

Nestled near my birthplace, it boasts a rich history stretching back to the Mesolithic period. Today, it's cobbled Shambles are bustling with tourists, thespians and ghost tours. Moreover, within its storied confines, resides The Jorvik Centre (p. Yorvik), Britain's most beloved Viking Museum. With over 20 million visitors and still counting, it stands as one of England's most visited attractions.

Jorvik derives its name from the ancient Nordic word for York, by which the city is now known. It not only lends its title to this book but also serves as an ancestral backdrop for the timeless tale that unfolds within these pages.

I sincerely hope my research and commitment to historical accuracy shine through the narrative, transporting you to a world of intrigue and mystery. May you find yourself captivated by the story and perhaps even contemplate the profound philosophical question that lingers deep within each of our minds:

Do the choices we make in our everyday lives truly shape the outcome, or are our futures already predetermined like assembled pieces in a grand cosmic puzzle?

To find out...

Látum byrja,

Dean Corbyn

CHAPTER 1

O' Darkness Keep

Baden-Baden, Germany, 1945.

Reginleif fled down the steep hillside lane that weaved mercilessly through the sleepy German hamlet. Her bare soles smacked against the icy cobblestones as she pinched up the hem of her tweed skirt. As if holding on for dear life, she clutched her leather satchel tightly under her arm, its strap chaffing at her neck.

Nearing the bottom of the lane, the moonless path took an unexpected curve, sharply winding back uphill. A distant streetlamp up ahead revealed the lane forking.

"Damn it!" she spat as she came to an abrupt halt, the warmth of her heaving breath misting the frigid air around her face.

She spun in a full circle.

Where the hell am I?

Her plan to keep to the main street, Sophienstraße, had disintegrated the moment she ducked into the shadows of this narrow lane. Sophienstraße led straight to the bridge, to her safe place on the other side of town.

But the night's unforeseen circumstances changed all that.

Of course they did.

At this hour, the vacant bay-windowed shops lining the deserted street loomed silently behind darkened glass. Then, as if responding to her presence, the one nearest her shone to life, bathing her in an amber spotlight. Its shop door creaked open, jingling a cheerful, tinny bell. A stout elderly man with a full head of silver hair stepped out, grappling with a basket of fragrant French loaves. Behind him, a young girl with golden pigtails held open the door while her tiny knuckle rubbed the remnants of sleep from her eye. From her young age, Reginleif suspected that she was the man's granddaughter, her father likely lost to the war, just like her own father. Though his, a very different war.

The baker leaned to set the basket on the outside stall but paused midway. His head poked forward into the street, eyes squinting trying to adjust to the lamp-lit figure. The heavy basket found its place on the stall, and he cast his eyes up again, no doubt having noticed the strange girl had not moved an inch. "Guten Morgen, young Fräulein," he said jovially, his handlebar mustache curling to his cheekbones as he offered a warm smile.

Reginleif remained rooted to the spot, eyes wide like those of a startled wild animal.

The baker's gaze dropped to her shoeless feet, his smile fading. "Fräulein, your shoes!" He pointed a jabbing finger toward her bare toes. "My dear girl, you must be quite frozen."

Still contemplating her options, she quickly scanned her surroundings.

"Are you lost, child?" the baker inquired.

"The river," she spluttered in flawless German. "Please, I need to get to the river."

"The river?" The baker's bushy brows scrunched together, almost touching.

"Please," she cried. "I—"

In the distance, echoes of leather soles slapped the pavement like a torrent of angry raindrops, intensifying with each step. She spun her head, inhaling a sharp breath.

The old baker also looked.

Sensing she was in trouble, he beckoned her towards his shop.

"Hurry, come inside!" he whispered. "Come, come!"

Her first step came easy.

The warmth of the cozy store invited her in. The scent of freshly baked dough teased her nose, making her mouth water. But this was far more than just an aroma. The baker and the little girl invoked memories of a life cruelly taken from her.

All she had ever wanted was a family life—ordinary and simple.

It was all she dreamed about: a remote, idyllic cottage with a family of children playing outside, and freshly harvested cornfields as far as the eye could see.

But sadly, that was all they were, long-forgotten fantasies that had met their deaths years ago, along with the only family she'd ever known. Her childhood sweetheart, too. They were all gone, brutally murdered before her innocent eyes.

Since then, she had been running, fighting tirelessly to survive. No end in sight. Worse was not knowing why. In fact, finding the 'why' had become her life's mission and the reason for tonight's covert operation.

Her knee half raised, Reginleif hesitated. Realizing the danger to the baker and child, she instead stepped back. Twice more, before turning to flee.

"Fräulein!" the baker called after her. "The river!" He waggled a finger at what appeared to be a dark doorway, only two storefronts down from his.

On closer inspection, she saw what it really was—a cut through the building, a kind of tunnel. Its entrance appeared ominous and black. But with the thundering footsteps now only seconds away, there was no choice. She quickly ducked inside. Although her feet compelled her to keep running, curiosity constrained them. She huddled in the shadow pressing her shoulders against the damp mossy wall, inhaling the scent of it, the moisture seeping through to her skin. And there, she stood, stock-still. Watching.

Remembering the gun, she reached into the leather satchel looped around her neck. Her hand brushed over the manila envelope she had just seized from the church. She hoped its precious contents would shed light on her mysterious past. Resisting the urge to examine its contents, she grabbed the pistol. It was still warm from firing.

The guilt of having just killed a man, even unintentionally, weighed heavily.

How did they find me? No one knew my plan. No one.

Hoping for a clue, she replayed the tumultuous events, frantically searching for answers. Fragments of memory returned to her like scattered pieces of a puzzle.

How she'd dragged a small bench under the church window, then climbed out clutching the stolen transcripts. How she'd heard those cold, chilling words, "Nicht bewegen…" *Don't move.* The cold steel barrel of a gun pressed into her back. The raw gut feeling telling her: *it's them!*

The events following were hazy, as was often the case when driven to react on instinct. Years of combat training had made her that way.

The struggle for his firearm was murky, but she remembered it firing—the moment everything had slowed. The recollection of shock painted across the large man's face as he crumpled onto his hefty rear end, before collapsing onto his back.

He had offered no resistance when she knelt beside him and plucked the weapon from his grip. However, when her fingers touched his hand, a perplexing vision flashed through her mind.

Despite the bullet only grazing his flesh, his life aura seemed to be flickering and fading like a small candle sputtering out.

Why did she possess this extraordinary ability? Ability? More like an agonizing curse. The visions foretelling of someone's death had forever haunted her.

His wound was merely a graze. Why would he be dying from it?

Curious about his gun, Reginleif remembered how she examined it closely, hoping it might provide an answer. Unremarkable, it seemed like any other Luger P08.

She unclipped the magazine, examining the remaining bullets. Immediately, she noticed they were not the typical lead gray she had expected. No, these were most unusual, custom-made: blue, crystal-like. And when she tilted the clip in the faint light, they sparkled like gemstones.

What the—?

"Verzeihen Sie mir," the dying man cried out, startling her and setting her back on her hind. His bloodied hand reached up. Reginleif stood, backing away.

Forgive me? Why would he be begging me, of all people, for forgiveness? Unless, she wondered, *those dying words and the reaching out are meant for someone or something else?*

If the tables were turned, she knew the same compassion would not be afforded to her. And yet, as she backed away, she whispered to the dying man, "Ich vergebe Sie,"—*I forgive you*—then kicked off her burdensome heels, turned, and ran.

From the shadows, a hauntingly deep voice spoke out. "Guten Morgen, mein Herr."

Pulled from her reverie, Reginleif shifted her focus to the dimly lit street beyond the dark tunnel. She inched her head forward, raising the gun to eye level. Peering around the corner, eight men emerged into the bakery's light, each one panting and catching their breath. All sported cloth caps and wore slate-gray, austere suits, just like the man she had shot.

The baker cleared his throat then forced a cheerful smile. "Guten Morgen," he replied, nervously.

One man, distinguished by his gaunt countenance, a slender mustache, and a black patch concealing his left eye, stepped ahead of the rest. Reginleif's initial assumption was that he must be the one in charge.

However, her attention was soon drawn to the last to arrive. This man was middle-aged, with handsomely chiseled features, pale blue eyes, and light blond hair peeking from under his cap. His gait was slow, exuding a quiet confidence that commanded respect. The others instinctively gave him space, subtly acknowledging his authority. Despite having good looks and a deceptively honest demeanor, something about him unsettled her more than the others.

The one-eyed man pinched the peak of his cap, politely nodding at the baker. "Are you the owner?" She now knew who the deep sinister voice belonged.

"Yes, of course. How can I be of service?"

It was clear they hadn't raced there for the bread.

"By chance, have you seen a young Fräulein come by this way?"

The baker answered without giving it a thought. "Indeed, I have not."

The one-eyed man smiled, his head in a constant bob. Sizing. He dipped his pointy chin, eyeing the girl. "And you, sweet child? Have you seen anyone this morning?"

Before she could answer, the baker pulled her in toward his thigh, giving a nervous laugh.

"Oh, come now, gentlemen, you're scaring my poor girl half to death. I can assure you, she has seen nothing. She has been inside, cleaning."

Reginleif watched from the shadows as the baker reached his trembling hand to the basket, duly offering the men a length of loaf. "Here. Fresh from the oven. No charge for my first punters."

Ignoring him, the man squatted, glaring his one eye at the child. Simultaneously, Reginleif narrowed her sights on the side of his head, squinting down the barrel.

Touch even a lock of her hair, and you'll be the first to go.
I promise you.

"Does my patch scare you?" the man asked the girl.

Not daring to look him in the face, the little girl shrugged.

"It scares me, too," he said, attempting to sound relatable. "The war took it. Payment for trying to protect my country, my people, my family. And now…" He waved shamefully at his face. "Now I'm maimed for life. Ugly."

His saddened words encouraged the little girl to look up.

With her attention locked, the man's tone turned serious.

"This girl we seek, she is in great danger. I…" He indicated with a slight nudge of his head to the men behind, persisting in addressing his words only to the child. "*We,* I mean, are trying to protect her. Please think. She's a little taller than your…" He thumbed toward the baker. "He's your grandfather?"

She nodded proudly, hugging the baker's leg tighter.

The one-eyed man chuckled. "Thought so. She's a little taller than your grandfather, I'd say. Barely a grown-up herself, with a full head of black hair, shiny like a raven's coat. And her eyes. *Beautiful* eyes. Unmistakable. So blue they blaze from the darkness like polished sapphires." The girl's chin perked. The man concentrated his stare further. "You want her to be safe, yes?"

The little girl thought, then nodded.

"Me, too. So, she came by here, yes?"

Another pause, then another nod.

"Good, good." Shifting to the side to reveal the forking lane beyond, he finally asked, "Tell me child, which way did she go?"

From the shadowy cut, Reginleif could see the innocence in the girl's eyes as she stared right back. Pulling from her grandfather's grip, she bravely stepped beside the one-eyed man, promptly swinging her arm horizontally, finger pointing.

A surge of relief thrilled through Reginleif upon witnessing the small girl pointing to the leftmost lane, the one climbing more steeply uphill and away from the river.

Five of the eight men immediately took off in that direction, Reginleif pulled herself deeper into the shadows as they sped by the cut.

Bidding the baker and his granddaughter another good morning, the one-eyed man joined the remaining two before all three marched away in the direction of the forked road. The blond man in charge had a shrewd look about him. "We'll take the other lane," he commanded.

"But Herr Karl," the one-eyed man contested. "The girl, she said ..."

The leader slanted his cleft chin at his naïve comrade. "The girl was lying, you fool."

SURE ENOUGH, THE tunnel led to the river just as the baker's kind eyes had promised. As Reginleif briskly walked its banks toward the bridge, tears came. The baker's generosity and his granddaughter's valor had left her deeply moved. Without their help, she may have suffered a fate worse than capture.

Her safe house was close, and there, she could hide, and lie low for a day until everything quietened. Perhaps then, before she returned to France, she would stop by the bakery to thank them.

Midway across the stone bridge, she idled her stride as she passed under a streetlamp. Unable to resist, she lifted the leather flap, plucking the manila envelope from inside her satchel. With an eager gaze, she drank in the typed label.

```
CONFIDENTIAL
NORDIC GLYPH TRANSLATIONS
RECOVERED FROM AHNENERBE EXPEDITION, 1935-6
BOHUSLÄN, GÖTALAND PROVINCE, SWEDEN
APPROXIMATE AGE: 4,000 YEARS
CATALOGUE REF: A011291969BD
```

Just two weeks prior, she had been unaware this existed. She had been having her usual morning tea at Le Café de Flore in Paris when she first read about the glyph tracings.

Discovered in a Nazi bunker amidst a hoard of stolen masterpieces, the ancient texts had earned headline news. What intrigued Reginleif most was their Nordic origin. They traced right back to her own ancestral lineage and predated any others on record.

Answers awaited.

The *Le Figaro* morning newspaper also stated that philologists had since succeeded in decoding much of the writing at a collegiate church in Baden-Baden. Though the article shed no light on their context, it did disclose the religious texts were 'nothing short of *incroyable*'.

Fiendishly, she tore off the seal, sliding the thin stack of pages free. Immediately, confusion etched across her face as she read the front page. With worrisome fingers, she rifled through the remaining pages until reaching the end. She stopped dead.

No!

Apart from a four-lined poem on the front page, handwritten in blood-red cursive script, all the pages were blank.

What the hell is this?

She reread the poem, trying to decipher its cryptic, archaic English. The final line, however, jumped from the page. Reginleif found herself fixating on it, its ominous undertone sending shivers down her spine, transforming initial confusion into unbridled terror.

J Niht O' Light Will Darkness Keep

While studying it, a thunderous clap echoed from behind. A button-sized hole pierced through the poem's script, spraying a creepily sanguine red across the crisp white page. Reginleif stumbled forward, all the wind emptying from her lungs. She quickly regained her balance as a burning pain enveloped her upper chest. She looked down—and shrieked. Blood seeped through her chartreuse blouse, the stain rapidly expanding.

Gathering her might, she fled for her life toward the streets beyond the wide bridge. Then all hell broke loose. Gunfire erupted from behind, propelling her steps. Bullets ricocheted off the bridge's stone wall, breaking off dust and flying debris. She shielded her face with her arm as she ran.

One bullet grazed her calf, adding a painful limp to an already difficult stride.

Though her refuge was near, escape now seemed impossible. Once again, she withdrew the pistol, this time with practiced ease, spinning on her heel before dropping to one knee. With the precision of a marksman, she aimed at the nearest target, the one-eyed man running and firing.

Her first shot hit its mark, piercing his only good eye, and dropping him where he stood. The next shot fired a split second later.

This one struck another man's shoulder, forcefully hurling him back.

As for her third, it zeroed in on Karl, the leader, who aimlessly strolled to the middle of the road and came to a cool halt, casually gripping his firearm by his side.

She fired.

Missing by a fraction of an inch, his jacket flared at the hip as if catching a gust of wind.

Karl nonchalantly lifted his pocket flap, inspecting its perfectly shaped new hole, seemingly unfazed by the prospect of another round whizzing towards him.

Then, calmly, he turned his eyes on hers. Reginleif's pulse raced as she watched him raise his arm, and slowly tilt his head to spy down the barrel of his Luger.

In one last-ditch effort, using the bridge wall for support, she heaved herself to her feet, hobbling away. With each painful step, her head grew woozier, her feet heavier, and the distance to her safe house appeared to stretch farther. After only a few steps, she was forced to accept the harsh reality. *I can't make it.* Few times in her life had she allowed someone to take her captive. However much she hated the idea, surrender was the only remaining option.

That's if she wanted to survive.

With defeated shoulders, she turned to face Karl.

He was still posed, arm outstretched, gun aimed—motionless. With a clatter, her weapon rattled as it hit the concrete next to her feet, striking her toes en route. The agonizing wound on her upper chest limited all movements, allowing only her uninjured arm to rise in surrender.

The streets behind Karl flooded with more men all racing to the bridge, waving their guns. This time, there was no tunnel for escape. No shadows in which to hide.

Surrounded by insurmountable odds, a heavy blanket of desolate solitude descended upon her. Her bottom jaw quivered from the cold, from the adrenaline, from fear and abject misery. Hopeless tears welled, her trembling lips whispering the only question that had ever mattered. "Why?" Then, as hard as her drowning lung could allow, she screamed it. "WHY?"

The white flash from Karl's muzzle felt surreal.

Perhaps it was nature's mercy that the winter's night had chilled her to the bone, now numbing her from the bullet tearing into her upper left chest, arching her backward over the bridge wall.

The remaining air wheezed from her lungs as she dangled precariously over the stone plinth. Those pages she had dared to retrieve slipped from her fingers and fluttered to the pavement like autumn leaves. After a momentary spasm, her limbs gave out, exhausted from their struggle.

Her head lolled back, eyes closed against this tormenting world.

It had only ever brought her suffering and loss.

As her life flashed before her, she held onto a precious childhood memory of her father holding her hands as they skipped in a circle, dancing and singing. Around her, the air was sweet with evening primrose and thyme growing wild outside their simple thatched cottage. Beyond the rolling hills, a retiring sun was busy setting the sky ablaze with hues of orange and pink, poking shimmering golden holes through verdant English oak branches.

Then came the darkness, creeping in with measured stealth from all sides. The thunderous thump of her heart tamed, its tempo slowing, until finally—silence. As her head fell back, her limp body gave way and she slid from the wall into the dark, wintry grave of the river below.

KARL STOOD WITH his arm outstretched in front, smoke rising from the barrel, wrestling with his conscience, and hoping—praying—to have made the right choice.

Choice? It was a word absent from any soldier's vocabulary.

Only ever orders.

Either way, as honorable soldiers did, he felt a remarkable sense of respect and admiration for a brave adversary. As he lowered his pistol, others raced past him toward the bridge wall.

Face down, Reginleif's lifeless body drifted with the current, disappearing from the golden glow of the bridge lamps. Even now, the men offered no peace as they opened fire. Perhaps from anger for their fallen comrades, or because they selfishly competed to earn credit for the kill. Or perhaps they just wanted to ensure the job was done. Whatever the reason, none let up until their rounds were spent.

Karl stepped through the cloud of gun smoke toward the scattered pages whispering in the wind. He reached down, collecting several lying together. Bright blood spattered across the uppermost page and its ominous four-lined poem.

It was a good plan, he told himself.

Behind him by the edge of the bridge, two civilian Volkswagens screeched to a halt, all four doors on each vehicle springing open, emptying more men. Guns drawn, they posed ready to shoot. To fight.

All except for one, the youngest.

He sprinted toward Karl, almost plowing into his back as his feet hammered to an abrupt stop. His face was pallid and sweaty. In German, he panted, "What have you to report, Herr Hoffmann? Is she dead?"

Karl stood stoic with his back turned. "Yes, my brother; it is over."

"Herr Hoffmann, you will receive the Edles Ritterkreuz for this," the courier said in excited admiration, proclaiming news of the Knight's Cross as if it were his very own to give away. It was an accolade of the highest honor, mostly bestowed posthumously for bravery.

Yet the young courier's spirited words incensed Karl. Although the mission had been a success, he would be answerable to a higher power for what he had done.

God will never forgive this. Damn the Ritterkreuz; I don't want it.

The courier glanced at the men by the wall, staring into the river below.

"Where is she? Is she in the river?" His words rattled, the voice growing ever more nervous. "We need to find the body. Our orders were…"

"You forget who you're talking to, Dummkopf," Karl barked, cutting him short.

"Vergeben Sie mir," the courier said humbly—*please, forgive me*—snapping his heels to attention and pushing out his chest, a habit from his years assigned to the Wehrmacht High Command. "And what would be my orders, Herr Hoffmann?"

Finally, Karl turned to face the erect courier whose eyes avoided contact. New to the Order and with much to learn, the young postulant clearly had no idea of the gravity of what they had just done. Nevertheless, he raised an accomplished chin to command his instructions.

"Inform the High Priest at once that she is dead. Their prophecy has failed."

CHAPTER 2

The Philanthropist

Present Day.

"Mr. Goodwin, how long do you plan to fund the shelter?" asked a British Tribune reporter.

"How much did the renovations cost?" shouted another.

"Is resolving the homeless situation in the UK your number one priority?"

"Can you tell us about your next project?"

"Will it be in York, too?"

Cameras flashed repeatedly, the deluge of questions hounding the English aristocrat.

Scissors in hand, he was poised, ready to cut the giant red ribbon blocking the entrance to the newly renovated homeless shelter. City official Silvia Lang stood beside him, accompanied by an entourage of the council's top brass, prominent members of the foundation, and other dignitaries.

Amidst this distinguished assembly, two figures stood out.

Each standing six foot two and flanking on either side, they surveyed the crowd with steely gazes. Ever vigilant and prepared to risk everything for the man they were sworn to protect, these were his bodyguards.

"Ever considered running for MP?" screamed a reporter over the din of chatter and camera clicks. The question grabbed the educated Englishman's attention.

Laughing, he answered, "Maybe I should, old boy. Instead of paying to fix the problems our government has created, maybe I *should* run for election to fix this country's impoverished constituencies." With the style of a seasoned entertainer, he rallied, "What do *you* all think?"

His quip ignited a clamor of further questions and enthusiastic cheers from the public onlookers. After savoring the adulation of his devotees and their lively banter, he turned to the awaiting ribbon, pausing his cut to grant the eager reporters their snapshots. A snip later, the new shelter was officially open for business.

"Now, who's ready for a tour?" the Englishman exclaimed with fervent flair and panache, his welcoming wave beckoning the reporters inside as he opened the door and stepped in first.

Mr. Goodwin was Britain's most renowned philanthropist. More than that, he was a celebrity, every week making headlines or featuring on covers of popular magazines, the press adoring him. And it was not because he was so ostentatious, or because everything he did was flashy and extravagant. It was because he sold newspapers and magazines, lots of them.

Although a publicly well-known figure, the aristocrat avoided live events, or any place there was a crowd. His audiences and fans usually read about him and his projects—also of his wild ventures—the same as they would any star, via the media.

And seldom, if ever, could they set eyes on him in person, the reason today's event was so special. On this occasion, a hand-picked gathering of vetted spectators and select press were allowed to attend. Inside, he escorted his entourage from room to room, divulging every aspect of his project. And every finger point triggered an onslaught of camera flashes and clicks.

They visited every room. Eager to show off his accomplishments, Mr. Goodwin, never short for words, described the renovation's every aspect, especially acclaiming his personal involvements and grandiose ideas.

Among the bombardment of questions, one journalist from a rather unknown paper—new to the usual hand-selected team of hacks—screeched over the others. Her voice, high-pitched and shrill, stood out amongst her male correspondents.

But it was not the voice hooking his attention; rather, it was her accusatory tone. "Let's cut to the real story; why don't you explain exactly how you achieved such wealth?"

Mr. Goodwin razored his eyes, finding her in the crowd, the usual Cheshire Cat grin shrinking, a frown forming. He almost retorted a response he'd have come to regret. Instead, he bounced downward palms, commanding the room to silence, the flashes to a halt. In a split second, he composed himself, both frown and pursed lips dissolving into a pleasant smile.

He singled her out. "My dear... um?"

"Ms. Rothstein, Huntington Herald," she politely provided.

"Ms. Rothstein?" He pondered the name, massaging his chin. Not recalling it, he moved on to the paper. "The Huntington Herald?"

"Yes."

"You are new to this press corps, are you not?"

"Um... yes, but I don't see what difference that makes, Mr. Goodwin." Her voice trembled. Clearing her throat, she hoisted a single page above her head. "Regarding your fortune, this record shows—"

"Huntington, ah yes. Now I remember," Mr. Goodwin said, cutting her off. He turned to George, his right-hand man. "We built a war memorial in Huntington, did we not? I seem to recall we did."

George nodded as did many of the reporters.

"Yes, I thought so," Mr. Goodwin continued, laboring an already dulled point.

Again, not letting up, Ms. Rothstein pressed, "Sir, will you please answer the question? Prior to twenty years ago, your inheritance indicated—"

"Yes, yes, Ms. Rothstein…" His tone became sharper, more impatient.

He paused, taking her in, studying her, a young woman fresh off the line, with platinum blonde hair and dressed in a fashionable yet masculine pantsuit. She projected a pretense of confidence, yet Mr. Goodwin's uncanny intuition quickly gathered it was forced.

Extreme nerves hid behind her stern expression.

In some small way, Mr. Goodwin admired her tenacity, her vigor. She was smart. Certainly, she had done her homework. While she may have been on the lowest rung of the ladder with her largely unknown local paper, she would go far. Given different circumstances, he may even have offered her a position on his own staff. But not today. Today, he wanted her gone. Gone, gone.

"I will answer that question by saying this: As I have said time and time again, my wealth was inherited from my uncle. But I have also been wise with that inheritance, building my company and amassing a greater fortune than he bequeathed. I have since channeled a significant portion of that wealth back into the community. Millions of pounds, dozens of projects." He pointed over his shoulder to a twenty-foot banner sprawling the full width of the room. It prominently displayed the bold-lettered title, The Goodwin Shelter – Now Open! Below it, he read aloud his quoted campaign slogan, "I am committed to helping the less advantaged."

His response had captured everyone's hearts, that much was clear. From the expressions filling the room, the only character up for debate was Ms. Rothstein's. At this point, she was probably already regretting her ill-timed ambush.

"Is that all you had prepared for today's opening, Ms. Rothstein? A frivolous and baseless screed of slanderous propaganda? Or did you have another question for me? Hopefully, a better one, a meaningful one for all the people here? A question relating to the renovation of this homeless shelter, perhaps? Or one of my other charitable ventures?"

His head tipped to one side in the manner of a loyal hound listening to his master. It was, of course, put on for show, as if he cared to hear what she had to say.

Ms. Rothstein appeared lost in thought. Several of her colleagues had now turned their cameras on her. With each flash, her cheeks grew a shade redder.

"I... err, no. No more questions. Thank you."

She took a small step back, trying desperately to fade from the spotlight she had unwittingly created for herself. Fortunately, she did not have long to wait. The remaining press corps returned their lenses to Mr. Goodwin, their subsequent hoard of mundane questions breaking the few seconds of silence.

Before addressing them, Mr. Goodwin glanced at George. One simple look, eye to eye, no expression. That was all it took to convey everything needing to be said. In a similar fashion, relaying the information forward, George bowed a slight nod to his nearest guard who acknowledged similarly. Tasked with a mission, the guard ducked from the room.

The tour complete, the press corps returned to the front of the building for the formal meet-and-greet and final presentation.

Outside, the small group of spectators lined in single file behind a swagged red velvet stanchion rope, anxiously awaiting their host's return. Directly opposite, like a military firing squad, the press aimed their cameras. Finally, the man of the hour exited to a thundering ovation.

As if royalty, he trooped the line shaking the hands of each spectator and dignitary poised to meet him. Camera flashes exploded, capturing every moment, ready for tomorrow's newspapers. Except for the *Huntington Herald*. Ms. Rothstein was nowhere in sight.

CHAPTER 3

The Dentist and the Professor

Saturday night.

Dr. Theia McDormand sat cross-legged on the plush upholstered bar stool, her stilettoed foot bouncing with irritation as she thumbed a message into her iPhone:

I'm going to kill you!

Punching 'send,' she then slapped her phone onto the counter face up, chugging the last of her vodka tonic.

An attentive barman heisted her empty glass before she docked it on its napkin coaster. "Another?" he asked.

"Why the hell not!"

When the barman stepped aside, the wall of antique mirrors behind him, partially obscured by dozens of liquor bottles, reflected her emerald eyes. Like freshly polished gemstones, they were the only features she recognized. The hair, the make-up, and the glitzy black outfit all seemed foreign, over the top. Especially the hair. She hadn't worn it up in years, but now it was all bundled into a weaved coiffure, single blonde ringlets curling in front of her ears.

Garnishing her drink with a lemon slice, the barman set it down on a fresh napkin.

She sipped from it, confirming with a nod that it was to her taste. Ready to return to her assigned seat, she initially stretched a foot to the floor but found herself settling back.

What's the hurry? she mused. Besides, no one would miss her. No one here even knew her. Especially not her date. Tempted by the allure of the mirror, Theia stole another glance. However, this time, her gaze shifted over her shoulder to the far end of the ballroom. A tall man stood with his back shadowing the wall, his gaze fixed on her with intense scrutiny.

Ping! Buzz!

The screen on her iPhone lit up. Four little words from Audree Shaw:

Please don't kill me!!!

It posed a short distraction, but when her eyes returned to the mirror, the tall man had vanished. Her stomach cramped.

Get a grip!

Another incoming message pinged, this time, a praying hands emoji. Theia hovered her finger over the reply button. Deciding against it, she reached for her glass, swirling the ice.

She can sweat a little.

Remembering her meditation videos, she closed her eyes, inhaled a deep breath through her nose, held it, and then let it out slowly from her mouth. *I can do this. I can do this*, she chanted to herself.

Theia's next deep inhalation took in a whiff of cologne, its aroma undeniably masculine with rich earthy notes combined with a subtle blend of citrus, musk, and black pepper. Its potency masked the new carpeting smell previously dominating the room, even after the savoury five-course meal had been served. A tingle ran down her spine, signaling a presence closing in behind her right shoulder. She opened her eyes as he ordered a double bourbon, straight-up, then settled onto the stool beside her.

"Anyone sitting here?" he asked.

"No. Go right ahead." Though she preferred he didn't. The seat was probably still warm from the last *gentleman* who sat there. An optometrist. For ten minutes straight she had listened to him brag about himself. That, out of the hundreds of optometrists in New York City, he was the one being awarded at tonight's gala. Even more intolerable was his not-so-subtle flirting, and the fact he appeared at least twice her age—and married. "Doctors! Ugh!" she had cursed inwardly, forgetting altogether that she was one.

Being propositioned all night was reason alone to kill her friend. Slowly!

Ping. Buzz!

Speaking of the devil... She snatched her phone from the counter, swiping its screen. However, the text was not from Audree. Worse, it was spam—an image of some suave Englishman accompanied by a corny tagline: 'What's next for Britain's Favorite Philanthropist?'

"Ugh," she growled, aloud this time, then did the same as always—deleted it.

"Everything okay?" the man next to her asked.

"Yes, thank you. Hunky-dory!"

"Hey," he said as if he knew her. "You're the, um, dentist, right?"

Her gaze steered toward him, her head following a moment later. For some reason, she had expected an older man, like the vast majority in attendance tonight. Instead, he was in his late twenties, perhaps early thirties, with gorgeous brown eyes in which any woman could lose herself. Of course, looks were not everything in a man.

But they were *something*.

"Um, yes," she said, puzzling over his unfamiliar tanned face. "I'm sorry, do I know you?"

"Not exactly. We're sitting at the same table."

His thick New Jersey accent and coal-black mop of wavy hair hinted at New York Italian. "I read your place card, is all. McDonald Dentistry or something?"

She forced a smile, albeit against her better judgment. Smiles always invited more questions. His question invited a correction. "*McDormand*," she stressed. Yet somehow, she felt certain he had made that mistake on purpose.

Not recalling him, she glanced over her shoulder, beyond the busy waiters to her round table near the Grand Ballroom's center. "Are you sure you're seated at my table?"

"Yep!" His finger singled out two vacant seats, one of them being Theia's. "I'm seated right next to you. That's my aunt, with the gray hair, and pale blue dress." She happened to be looking back and waved. Theia found herself waving back, joined by her new, tanned friend. He added, "I see I made a strong impression on you! And to think, I even offered you my dessert!"

Her cheeks flushed. "I'm sorry. I'm not having the best of nights. I've been miles away." *I wish I really were miles away.* "Forgive my rudeness. I'm Theia. Obviously, you know my last name."

He stood, stretching out his hand. "Colombo, Matthew Colombo. A pleasure to—"

"Columbo? Seriously?" Instantly, she snatched her hand back.

Columbo was a hugely successful television series airing for over thirty years, beginning in the 1970s. In every episode, a famous, cigar-smoking, one-eyed detective would solve seemingly unsolvable murders. Spielberg himself had directed the first show.

"Is this some kind of a line?" she spouted. "Because I'm in no mood for…"

"I promise you," he vowed, hand on heart. "No line. Check my place card. Although it will say Doctor William Colombo, my uncle. I'm filling in last minute as he was called away." He tugged at his informal navy lapel, appearing ten years outdated. "Hence the lack of tuxedo."

"You're not a doctor?"

"God, no!" He recoiled from the insult and then appeared embarrassed. "Uh, no offense. I'm sure dentists are much less, how shall I say, nauseating."

She smirked. "Sometimes. So, what is it you do, then? Other than escort middle-aged ladies to medical award galas." *Damn it. A simple 'What is it you do?' would've sufficed.*

Without answering, he withdrew from his wallet an off-white recycled business card, handing it across to her.

Prof. M. A. Colombo,
Executive Assistant Curator,
American Museum of Natural History.

Examining it, she emphasized the words, sounding impressed. "Professor! Executive!"

Matthew shrugged. "Dime-a-dozen to be honest. Our New York office has twenty-seven E.A.s alone. Though I *am* working on a promotion. I'm so close." He crossed his fingers on both hands. "If I get it, I'll be the youngest ever holding that position."

"Really? Good for you." She motioned to hand back his card.

"Keep it," he said. "If you or your… *boyfriend* ever want a personal tour, or are interested in how the dating process works, I'm your man."

"Excuse me!" she cried.

Matthew seemed confused by her puzzled reaction, but that gave way to a bashful chuckle. "Oh, I see," he clarified, his voice softening. "Not that kind of dating! Let me start over. Mea culpa." He shifted on his stool as if gearing up to share an interesting story. "We date artifacts, relics for cataloging, things like that. Very interesting stuff. Well, it is if you're into it, like anything else in life, I suppose. Perhaps deadly dull otherwise… if it's not your thing." His words trailed off towards the end, losing both cadence and volume. He wore the expression of someone cautioning himself to desist lest he bore the pants off them. A vocational habit, perhaps.

On the contrary, Theia hadn't found it dull. She half-turned to face him, a million questions running through her mind. Ancient history happened to be her favorite subject too. An obsession really.

Just then, a soft hand touched her left shoulder, and though the tap was delicate, she lunged half off the seat and yelped like a small dog.

That made Matthew jump too, clumsily spilling half his bourbon onto his paisley green tie.

Theia's timid date glared at her. "I'm sorry," he stuttered. "Um, the toasts are starting shortly. I thought maybe you'd wanna, you know, take a seat?"

"Oh, right. Yes. Um, I'll just get the tab." Theia pointed at her drink. "I'll be over in a sec."

A moment of awkward silence followed before the young man returned to his seat.

Theia's shoulders drooped.

Out of courtesy to her friend, she had promised herself she would at least finish out the evening. Having sat through a five-course dinner already, the thought of returning to that table with what's-his-face was becoming unbearable.

"You know what?" she said to Matthew as she signaled the barman for the check. "I'm just gonna bug out."

Matthew was wiping his tie with a wet napkin, speckling it with white paper morsels, but her comment made his eyes go wide, like the look of a lost child. "What? Why?"

"I'm not even supposed to be here."

"What do you mean?"

"My best friend set this up." The barman swooped in with the bill. She leaned in to sign it. "Against my better judgment, she convinced me to come to some swanky do, which she knows I hate. Then, after I arrive all made up like some Christmas tree, she texts saying, 'Surprise! You're on a blind date'."

Matthew tried hard not to laugh. "Is it that bad?" He wafted his hand, directing her eyes around the opulent room brimming with black and white tuxes and elegant ball gowns. "They have ice sculptures, incredible food, an eighties' disco later. It could be worse. Besides, it would be a shame to waste a five-hundred-dollar ticket and leave early. Wouldn't it?"

"Five hundred dollars!" Theia jerked upright. *Audree can't afford that! I'm really going to kill her now!* She huffed, shaking her head. "I'll have to pay her back in that case."

"Look, I don't know you or your friend," Matthew reasoned, "but it seems like she went to great lengths to set this up. Maybe you should—"

"Yeah, well," Theia interrupted sharply. "I didn't ask her to." She gathered her purse, preparing to leave.

Matthew stood up alongside her, his eyes filled with disappointment. "I can't convince you to stay?" His words sounded less hopeful.

The idea of quizzing his intelligent mind was tempting, even if it merely served to advance her own research. But as she'd learned, it was impossible to ask questions without revealing something about herself. And that she could not do.

Rules were rules, even if they were her own.

"Sorry. I'm not a big social person." She glanced at the luxuries to which he had just alluded. "All this, you know? It's just not me. I have to go."

Before leaving, she found herself drawn once more into his heavenly eyes, deep and swirling like whirlpools draining a vast ocean. If she came too close to them, they would suck her in beyond the point of no return. She managed to force a formal smile. "Good luck with the promotion." Somehow, no matter how kind the words themselves ought to be, she always managed to make well wishes sound begrudging.

Matthew's mouth opened, but before he could speak, her back was already turned.

Theia was targeting the entrance now, heading away at speed, unwilling to slow or stop for anyone or anything.

Except… she did stop; the tall man had returned, the one who'd watched her earlier. Yes, he was back at the same spot right near the ballroom entrance, and she would have to walk right by him. His emotionless eyes again locked on hers.

A young waiter waltzed by, carrying a small tray of empty Champagne glasses. "Excuse me!" she called, stalling him. "Do you have security working tonight?"

"Yes, ma'am. Always. Is everything okay?"

She stepped closer, her chin lower. "Is he one of them?"

A subtle, double side nod sent the clear message she was trying to be discreet.

The waiter cornered his eye on the obvious candidate. Square-jawed, standing six-four with his back against the wall, he certainly appeared like security. "Um, I believe so."

"You've seen him before?"

"Um, no ma'am. But we use a third-party security company. We have new faces all the time." His duties beckoning, he turned.

"Sir! Is there another exit?" she called.

"Yes, of course. An emergency stairwell." When his arm gestured to point, she glared.

No, no, no, no. Don't point, show me.

CHAPTER 4

The Stranger

After an especially tiresome week, Dr. Theia McDormand was eager to get home and beat the notorious Friday afternoon New York City traffic. One final task remained—to check the following week's schedule. With a sense of dread, she brought her screen to life again. The curved office monitor had a split-screen configuration, schedule on one side and email on the other.

A click of her mouse advanced the calendar to the following week. It appeared no different from the chaotic one she'd just had. She forced a deflated breath through tightly pursed lips, sounding out a fluttering trill of disappointment.

There'd been a time long ago when a thriving dentistry practice and a busy schedule would have delighted her. Of late, she had been yearning for change, for a new life.

But for now, she would gladly settle for a quiet week.

Blip. A pop-up email alert centered on her screen.

"Ugh!" she groaned the instant it opened.

Yet another article about Mr. Goodwin, the 'debonair British philanthropist.' This time, his image sprawled across a magazine cover, standing pretentiously in front of his rural English castle.

A single click later, her junk mail had increased by one.

When Theia entered the reception area after shutting down, Stacy and Charlotte were diligently typing at their computer stations. Stacy expertly held the office phone between her ear and shoulder, showcasing her remarkable ability to talk and type at a blinding speed. If there were a gold medal for multitasking, Stacy would be the undisputed champion.

Theia began sifting through her incoming mail neatly slotted into a stacked tray, pre-sorted and screened from marketing flyers by her attentive staff. She wished the same could be true of her email inbox.

"Charlotte," Theia asked. "Do you know if Stacy contacted that network company yet?"

Before Charlotte could answer, Stacy covered her mouthpiece and whispered, "Yes, Barracuda came by and did their stuff. You're all set."

Theia slouched her shoulders, having hoped the expensive security firewall hadn't yet been installed. "Well in that case, it didn't work. I'm still getting those spam emails."

Stacy rolled her eyes, sighing. "Okay. I'll call them," she said, then unblocked the mouthpiece. "I understand, Mrs. Atkins, but we're totally slammed next week. That Thursday is the first available. I can put you on our waitlist if you prefer?"

Mail in hand, Theia grabbed her raincoat from the coat hanger and signaled her busy staff a good night, then made a swift escape through the patients' exit.

In the hall, her eyes fixated on the floor indicator above the elevator door.

After years of driving the same route, she knew if she didn't make it to Broadway and Columbus by four thirty, it would add at least thirty minutes to her drive home.

She tapped her toe, willing the numbers to descend faster, and without pausing on another floor.

14-13-12-11-*ting! Yes!*

The doors opened to reveal a half-dozen people with predictable dreary Friday faces.

They bunched closer, allowing Theia to squeeze in on the farthest right.

The only floor selected was level one.

Nowadays, almost everyone invariably exited at the street level, herding toward the Seventy-Second Street subway just a block away. Running every four minutes with easy access to the whole city, it was the quickest and most obvious choice for transport.

Yet, Theia always chose to drive herself, even if it meant paying the ridiculous annual premium that the management of her high-rise building demanded for her privileged underground parking space. The mere thought of roaming the crowded subway, of being crammed into tight spaces amidst a throng of strangers and enduring the incessant noise of the bustling underground was simply not an option. She would be exposed, an easy target.

As the doors closed, a hand thrust in between, causing them to reopen at the last second. A tidily dressed, middle-aged gentleman entered, taking up position on the opposite side.

For no reason, an uneasiness began to crawl across her skin.

She tightened her arms across her torso as if warding off a chill or holding her soul captive within her body. As the doors closed, the faint whirr of the elevator motor echoed from the shaft above, signaling its slow descent. Realizing she hadn't selected her floor, she stepped forward, maneuvering around a young woman, likely an intern, and extended her pointed finger towards the panel.

"Sorry," she said, brushing past the woman. "I just need to—"

"Allow me," a voice interjected.

The gentleman smiled, selecting the basement floor for her. Theia stepped back, her thankful expression forming into a confused frown. *How did he know what floor I'd select?*

Her eyes looked sideways to study him, his creepy vibe reminding her of the man at the gala from a week earlier. Though similar in height, this man was pencil-thin.

At first glance, he appeared no different from the thousand other middle-aged office workers frequenting her building. Except, he seemed more refined, way too crisp for a Friday afternoon, corporate New Yorker. His black leather shoes, buffed to a military sheen, appeared expensive and untarnished as if they had never been worn. His suit, black with a subtle pinstripe, was well-tailored and firmly pressed.

The elevator approached level one and eased to a stop, its doors sliding open.

Everyone except Theia and the gentleman exited.

Theia's jaw tensed. *Why isn't he getting out?*

The basement accommodated only a dozen or so cars. Most of their owners she knew. The man sharing the elevator with her wasn't one of them. The doors closed, and the elevator moved on to the basement, the garage level.

When the door reopened, the gentleman pushed his arm against the sliding doors, preventing them from closing. Waving her through, he kindly offered, "After you."

Hesitant to move, she gave a momentary back-and-forth rock on her heels, before darting from the elevator. She walked briskly toward her vehicle. Her eyes shifted to the side as if trying to see behind. She heard nothing, saw nothing, yet she sensed the man close on her heels, following. She increased her pace with a skip.

Now in sight, her vehicle was only yards away. She foraged inside her purse for her keys, while fumbling to hang onto her mail under her arm.

Suddenly, her grip loosened. The mail slipped from her armpit. Attempting to recapture the envelopes, she dropped her purse. Her mail hit the ground, fanning out like fallen dominoes, while her purse spewed forth everything but the kitchen sink. Lightweight items made a bid for freedom. Immediately, she sank to her knees, feverishly gathering. Without regard for order, she stuffed everything back into her purse, managing in a few seconds flat.

Then jumping to her feet, she raced the final steps to her vehicle.

Once again, frantic fingers rummaged for her keys. *Where the hell are they?*

Just then, the man's reflection appeared in the passenger window. She whirled, recoiling against the driver's door. The man drew near, his hand rising toward her face. Instinctively, she crossed her wrists in front of her. Expecting the worst, she clenched her eyes shut.

But to Theia's surprise, only the sound of jingling metal ensued. Curious, she peeled open her eyes one at a time to find her car keys dangling inches from her face, suspended from the skinny man's fingers.

The stranger grinned. "I think you dropped these?"

Gingerly, she took them from him, noticing a tattoo on the underside of his wrist. Though partially hidden by his suit sleeve, it resembled a double cross.

Smirking, he declared, "You wouldn't get far without those keys."

Theia stood motionless.

His smile and brows narrowed. "Are you all right?"

"Yes, yes, I'm fine. Thank you."

Thumbing her remote, the clunk of her car doors unlocking echoed off the barren gray concrete walls. She spun around, climbing inside, locking the door behind her. The man hovered by her vehicle, peering through her driver-side window.

Without hesitation, she hit start, reversed, and screeched away.

Only when the steep tunneled ramp leveled onto Columbus Avenue and daylight flooded her windows, did she stop to check her rear-view mirror, allowing herself to breathe.

Finding only the dark entrance to the basement garage behind her, she targeted the mirror on herself. A wall of tears had formed over her green eyes, the mildest fluttering of her eyelashes sending a single stream cascading down her cheek, trailing mascara in its wake.

Pathetic little girl. What on earth's happened to you?

Her head shook in disgust.

You used to be stronger than this, much stronger.

The emotions of fear and vulnerability felt despicable even though she lived with them every single day. If anything, it was getting worse, as if terror had burrowed inside her like some small animal with an insatiable appetite, feeding on her, growing with each bite. Soon, she'd be an empty shell, terrified of her own shadow, locked away in a room at home, curtains closed.

Having lost track of time, she checked her watch. "Ugh!"

It'll take a miracle to make Broadway in the next six minutes.

She wiped the tear from her cheek and, with one gigantic sigh, eased into a sea of red brake lights.

CHAPTER 5

The Wilsons

Friday Afternoon.

Sheila Wilson flinched as the ceramic bowl shattered on the kitchen floor, sending glass shards scattering over the slick linoleum in every direction. Her mitted hands, still warm from the hot dish, extended motionless in front of her.

 Allowing herself a moment for her nerves to calm, she dared to peek through one eye at the carnage below. *Argh!* Perfectly formed just moments ago, her meatloaf now lay in a shapeless heap, half covering her favorite fluffy pink slippers.

Ruined. The meatloaf and the slippers.

David, her nine-year-old son, leaped from his chair, heading for the kitchenette. Though tiny for his age, he moved like a whippet.

"No!" Sheila screamed. "There's glass everywhere. Just stay where you are."

He froze on the spot as if in a game of freeze tag, allowing only his eyes to move. It would have been funny if the situation wasn't so perilous. Sheila glanced at the dustpan and long-handled brush by the trashcan. Getting to them, she thought, would be like navigating a minefield.

She crouched, still wearing her maroon oven mitts, and gathered the broken glass and minced mess into a neat pile. Tears brewed behind her eyes. These days, tears seemed all too common for Mrs. Wilson, though normally they came at night when she lay alone in her bed. Fortunately, the breakfast counter shielded her mottled crimson face from view; allowing David to see her this upset was the last thing she needed.

Doctor Marudas, David's psychiatrist, had warned any further stress could set his progress back, perhaps permanently. *Progress,* she thought. *What progress?*

Post-traumatic mutism, the doctor had explained, was common in children who had suffered the tragic loss of a parent at an early age. A child having this challenging syndrome for over two years without improvement, however, was rare.

At the end of each session, the psychiatrist would whisper words of encouragement, 'Love, positive reinforcement, and optimism.' His voice was a gentle balm, his hand a comforting pat on hers as they shook goodbye. She always responded with a grateful smile and a heartfelt thanks, but a part of her longed to scream. Optimism in *his* upper-middle-class world, she was sure, came easily. In abundance.

In her world, it was as rationed as the necessities in her refrigerator.

But the psychiatrist was right. For her son's sake—to get him talking—she vowed to exude positivity as best she could, even if she faked it. Without her son, she had nothing. He was her entire world, every word he spoke was a milestone.

Still sniffling, Sheila swept the remaining pieces onto the dustpan, taking mental stock of her unburdened cupboards. This meatloaf was supposed to feed them for the next two or three days, and by then, she hoped she would have secured a job and, God willing, an advance. Her remaining cash from her last job had been paid out yesterday for rent.

And now, the meatloaf, their only savior, had abandoned them in their time of need.

At least we have a roof over our heads for the next four weeks.

She blustered a sigh as she scraped her culinary calamity to the bottom of the trashcan. By now, David had returned to his five-hundred-piece jigsaw puzzle by the living room window. With a motherly gaze, she watched as he inserted the last piece with immense pride, all it took to lift her somber mood. A dozen or more times she had watched him complete that same puzzle, always beaming the same smile. Not for having completed it, or because Captain Universe was his favorite superhero, but rather because the puzzle had been his father's last gift on his seventh birthday. The first time they'd completed it together was also their last.

"David, I'm so sorry, honey, but I've made a bit of a mess of lunch and dinner." She mustered a fake smile, a practiced gesture that had become all too familiar in recent weeks. "How about some peanut butter on toast, eh? I know how much you like that too."

David's silent nod and shallow smile did little to mask his disappointment, especially with the mouth-watering smell of freshly cooked onions lingering in the air.

When the two slices of toast ejected a few minutes later, it was as if an alarm clock had awoken her.

Oh, my God, I'm going to be late.

Now moving at twice the speed, she prepared the plate and then raced it to David, now kneeling on the living room floor playing with miniature figurines.

Turning for the bedroom, she scurried along the hall, untying her apron as she went. Being late for her interview would not be a good start.

Though she lacked the experience they needed, she was a fast learner with a knack for adapting. At least, that was the pitch she rehearsed in her mind as she lashed on mascara.

Fifteen minutes later, Sheila emerged from the bedroom completely made up. The curlers were removed and her thick black hair bobbed with fullness on her shoulders.

She collected her coat and purse at the door. "Okay, I'm heading out. Wish me luck."

David perked his chin. Then a thumb. Then returned to his playing.

Halfway out the door, she gazed back, knots twisting in her stomach for leaving him alone in the empty apartment. "Hey. Why not play with your ball outside? It's a beautiful day."

He actually agreed, though unenthusiastic, slipping on his shoes and moving to collect his black-and-white-checkered soccer ball.

As usual, the street was lined bumper to bumper with parked cars on both sides.

Most of their owners lived on Sheila's side in the triplet-tower apartments known as the Soledad Buildings, #1, #2, and #3. Sheila's was building #1. The majority of the accommodations on the opposite side of the street were equipped with private parking in drive-in garages. Those apartments were also considerably more affluent inside and out.

Unlike her building, their façades were beautifully integrated with carved and ornate stone copings, their entrances framed with Romanesque columns, crowned with giant capitals. She had never stepped a foot inside, leaving her to only imagine their niceties and splendors within.

Not that she ever complained; every day, she counted her blessings for her Greenwich Village apartment. Whereas the square footage was a trifle small compared to others, this location in The Village was where she desperately sought to raise a child, and this was the only good coming from her husband's former employer. To attract workers and their families, Chadwick & Stern offered subsidies for housing and moving expenses.

And while they could have chosen less expensive lodging on the New Jersey side of the river closer to Ben's work at the docks, they'd instead elected to go with Manhattan for its far superior school system and much safer streets.

At the foot of the building, Marc, another child from Sheila's tower, played on the pavement. Slightly older than David, perhaps ten or eleven, he was running around, jumping off park benches, holding an imaginary machine gun amid a wartime battle. He wielded his imaginary weapon, acting out being hit by multiple bullets from an invisible enemy and falling to the ground knees first in slow-motion in a dramatic death scene worthy of an Oscar.

Sheila was relieved to see him.

Another piece of advice from Doctor Marudas: 'Have David interact with other children as much as possible; interaction is the key to progression. Such children confine themselves to their own worlds. Show David other options, and in due course, he may see benefits to these. It will take time, so do not lose patience. Having him do things habitually will make them feel easier for him. They'll hopefully become routine for him.'

It seemed like sound advice.

Sheila pointed. "Oh look, it's Marc. Why don't you ask him to play, sweetie?"

At first, David stepped behind her, clinging to her thigh.

"Hey, hey, sweetheart, it's okay." Peeling away from his arm, she squatted. His eyes were down, partially hidden by his chestnut hair. With motherly fingers, she gently lifted his chin and brushed his hair aside. "Dear me, we need to get this mop trimmed." She pinched his freckled nose, fetching a smile to his lips. "Listen, I know it's hard." She sighed. "If you don't want to play, fine. I'm not forcing you. But I think it would be really good for you. And..." her voice grew excited, "we get to tell Doctor Marudas you played with Marc again. I bet he might even let you have an extra lollipop. Except this time, I want the red one; the one that looks just like your nose!"

She punched his nose again, then dug her fingers into his ribs, causing him to flinch and giggle.

After a moment, David timidly turned, starting toward Marc.

"Hey, young man, don't I get a hug first?"

He returned to his mother, and she hugged him tightly, then held him at arm's length by his narrow shoulders. "And remember, stay off the roads. Okay? Promise me."

He gave a single exaggerated nod.

"Okay. I'll only be two blocks away and back in an hour or so." After receiving a quick peck on his forehead, he walked away.

"Have fun, sweetie!" she shouted. "I love you."

CHAPTER 6

Kowalski P.I.

The 1930s cradle-style telephone rang incessantly on Bill's cluttered desk. Across the room, Audree Shaw sat at her station, feverishly sifting through an inch-thick open file. For the past ten minutes, the glossy red phone, wedged between her shoulder and glistening cheek, persistently slipped—like a slick bar of soap eluding a firm grasp.

She adjusted it for the umpteenth time. "Of course, Mrs. Faraday, I completely understand. Don't you worry your pretty little self. We'll find it. Yes, ma'am," she said, the guise of her certitude so undeniable that she almost convinced herself.

Kowalski P.I.'s third-floor office sat on the southwestern corner of a small five-story building in Chinatown on the Lower East Side. Although its two large windows brightened the otherwise dreary office, the mid-afternoon sun radiated heat through the west-facing window like a magnifying glass. Normally, she welcomed the warming afternoon rays. But not today.

Today was a scorcher, way too hot for the window air conditioning unit to manage. A few hours earlier, its hypnotic hum had ceased with a violent clunk followed by a dwindling death rattle, then silence. Opening the windows hadn't helped.

More to her annoyance, sweat beaded under her silky-black hair, frizzing it at the roots, undoing all her fastidious efforts to straighten it. Worse still, her favorite lime-green, paper-thin summer dress, apparently not as breathable as she'd hoped, clung to her chocolate skin like a paper towel to a damp surface. Wet t-shirt was not her look! Thirty years ago, maybe.

Born in Jamaica to native parents, she had never really caught up with the fast life of New York City, even after five decades of living here since age five. She was an island girl through and through, right down to the DNA. Even her accent refused to let go of her roots, being a mishmash of old and new—a kind of island Jamaican drawl with a sharp New York twang. She called it *Ja-New-Yorkan*. Given the choice over the fast-paced New York vibe with its unremitting ringing phones and urgent deadlines, she would take a limbo dance on the beach and a rum cocktail any day.

She loved life, and it was for living.

Yet, amidst the city's hustle, Audree had carved a niche, her easy-going charm and gift of gab proving invaluable assets. This calmness, ironically, was what now soothed their most tempestuous client—Angela Faraday, the Chief Prosecutor from the District Attorney's Office. Accounting for nearly half their business, Angela wasn't someone they could afford to lose. While emails flew between their offices daily, personal calls from Angela herself usually spelled trouble. And today's predicament? A missing affidavit that was crucial to her case.

A case being tried in court that very afternoon.

Already halfway through the stack with no sign of the document in question, Audree's doubt as to its whereabouts escalated, as did her veiled positivity. "Okay, we've got ya covered. Yes, indeed. We're getting there, sugar. Don't you worry."

Another trait of Audree's—she talked ceaselessly, especially when nervous, and with scant regard whether anyone paid attention. She was akin to some kind of wind-up doll, walking and jabbering until she slammed into a wall. Even then, her mouth was likely to keep going.

Audree paused on a page, snatched it from the stack, and scanned it top to bottom in a half second. Her words sang as she spoke. "Found it! Yessiree! I told you we'd get you covered, Mrs. Faraday." For a moment, Audree rejoiced, tapping her toes and waving the page as if it were a winning lottery ticket. But finding the document was only half the battle.

Now, she had to get it over to the courthouse lickety-split.

As she blathered to Angela, page in hand, she paced out of the office with her heels clicking against the tile of the floor and walked to another office midway along the corridor Here, like a woman possessed, she banged on the frosted glass and barged in. Perched over his side-facing corner desk, the startled boy in his late teens whipped his head up to stare big-eyed at the bright-green, curvy mass charging toward him on four-inch heels.

Tim was an odd-looking fellow, scrawny with a small head and petite features, except for bulbous round eyes and stiffly bridged nose. Although he worked for his father, a financial consultant, he often performed odd jobs for Audree, most notably as a courier.

Audree flashed the page in front of his face and with the toss of her chin, summoned him to follow, which he did unquestioningly. "No, no, no, I've got you taken care of, girl," Audree said to the D.A. insistently. "Don't be sending anybody, you hear? You've got too much on your plate. This one's on us."

Back in her office at her desk, Audree slid the document into a manila envelope marked 'CONFIDENTIAL' in printed, bold red, and scribbled 'ATTN: Angela Faraday, D.A.' on the front.

Handing it to Tim, she continued on the phone, "My boy here will have it to you in…" She glanced at her watch, nodding toward the door. "…about ten or eleven minutes."

Tim's eyes bulged even more from their sockets. The court building took an easy fifteen minutes each way. To make it in ten, or even eleven, he would have to sprint the entire journey *and* be blessed with uninterrupted green pedestrian lights at each intersection. Tim checked his own watch and then, snatching the envelope, sprinted from the room.

At this point, the D.A. was finally taming. In fact, she commended Audree, applauding her efforts, forgetting altogether that the oversight had been caused by Kowalski's office to begin with.

Accepting the compliment, Audree rounded the call. "Okay, you're welcome, Mrs. Faraday. Call me anytime." The phone back at its station, she wafted the squared neckline of her dress, fanning what little air there was onto her sweltering, sizeable bust and collapsing hefty hips into her blood-orange office chair.

A rum cocktail on the beach is sounding good about now.

For the first time in an hour, the vintage phone on Bill's desk ceased ringing. Knowing how much he loved the old black-and-white detective shows, she had bought the phone as a gift, thinking it a cute idea. Until she'd heard it ring.

In the newfound quiet, only the distant honking and bustle of New York traffic rose from the street below. For a New Yorker, that meant silence. Audree closed her eyes and sank into a peaceful slumber.

When the office door rattled open, waking her, she had no idea whether five or fifty minutes had passed. Bill Kowalski entered first with Zac Hudson, his apprentice, trailing close behind.

"Damn, it's like an oven in here!" Bill griped. As if already forming a sweat, he wiped his heavy brow, then scratched the back of his bald head. "Why are the goddamn windows open? Don't tell me; you need fresh air?"

Still rousing from her quiet meditation, Audree gradually focused on him. He hobbled past toward the window behind his desk, his short, stout frame skipping with a limp as he went.

He was lucky it was just a limp. By all accounts, he should have been dead.

Two and a half years ago, when Bill had first formed the agency, he'd walked with a cane. Before that it was crutches, which he loathed almost as much as the two months spent in a wheelchair. And while doctors would preach 'slow and steady wins the race,' Bill was simply too pig-headed to wait. No bullet was going to keep him down.

Or two bullets, in Bill's case.

He would get on with life as best he could. Because honestly, what choice did he have? Sitting around moping wouldn't win back his legs, would it?

When Bill was discharged from the hospital, his first call of business surprised everyone, especially Ronin O'Malley, his captain and former partner. He'd turned in his badge and gun.

But who could blame him? Having been shot three times on two occasions, he dared not tempt death a third time. Besides, at sixty-one years old, with aching joints and an ever-expanding waistline, he was becoming too long in the tooth to be chasing down arrests. Instead, he decided to put his detective skills to another use. And with his legal contacts already in place and a reputation for getting his man, business flooded in from the get-go.

Bill pulled the window closed with a loud exhale, then turned his eye to the air conditioning unit adjacent. Not hearing its usual hum, he momentarily placed an ear directly against it. Then, wiggling the on/off switch repeatedly and thumping the side, he finally concluded, "The air con's not working!"

"No shit, Sherlock," Audree cussed, springing to life. "I've been sweating my ass off all damn day, and *that's* why the 'goddamn window' was open."

Rising to her feet, she cocked her hip to one side, propping a hand on it: her laying-down-the-law pose. "And, honey, we're getting a damn answering machine. It was the biggest mistake ever buying you that old phone."

"Has it been busy?" Bill asked.

"Busy?" Audree huffed a laugh, pointing at Bill's desk, the vintage phone now innocently quiet. "That goddamn phone has been *ringing* its ass off all afternoon. I'm about to *ring* its ass out that window."

Zac, not yet thirty or possessing the maturity to know when to stay quiet, piped up, handing Audree a pale blue folder. "These are the depositions from the Gardner case. Can you get them…"

Before he could finish, she snatched the folder from his grip, tossing it onto her desk. "Yes sirree!" Her head scornfully jiggled side to side, eyes rolling. One thing could be said for Audree—she wasn't shy about making her feelings known. "I'll get right on it. As soon as I wring out this dress!" Then Zac's comment regarding the Gardner files sank in. She knew exactly where they had been to collect them.

She spoke as a mother would to her mischievous young boys. "Oh, so you boys have been down at Faraday's today, have you?"

"Yeah," Bill replied. "We took the Fire Marshal's report and the um… the… umm…" Forgetting, he snapped his fingers.

Zac interjected, "The suspect's GPS tracking records."

Bill's snapping fingers switched to a pointed index at Zac. "Yeah, those. And while we were there, we picked up those Gardner deps, too." He dipped his head at the new folder now on Audree's desk. "I wanted to talk to Angela about the case, but they said she's in court today."

Audree's volume toned down, sounding innocent and sweet. "Mmm-hmm, we were just chatting on the phone, actually."

"With the D.A.'s office?" Bill asked.

"No, with Angela Faraday herself."

Bill stepped back. "Oh yeah? What did she want?"

"She called to invite us over for dinner at her house. Champagne and all."

Bill, not knowing whether to smile or frown, did both. "Really?"

Her testy tone returned. "No! She called because *you* forgot to drop off the nightwatchman affidavit from the Leary case. The signed original."

"Uh! I dropped that off yesterday." Bill's heavy eyebrows became heavier.

"Well, I guess you didn't because it was sitting right there in that case file." Her inch-long glittered nails pointed at the thick file still open on her desk. "And on a day like today, I had to get poor Tim to *Jimmy Ryun* his ass across town to the courthouse. Eleven minutes he had. Mrs. Faraday wasn't too pleased, I can tell you." She bobbed her hair and examined her nails, holding her hands at a distance, then close up as if showing off a humongous new rock on her engagement finger. "It's a good thing you got me to save the day and keep our number one client happy."

Bill's expression remained poker-faced as usual, his body language still. His only emotional tell was that his empathy carried a slight stutter and slowed speech. He eyed the wall clock. "I, um, tell you what, Audree? Um, why don't you head off home? There's nothing that can't wait till Monday, and it sounds like you've already had a hell of a day."

"Damn right, I've had one hell of a day."

Not needing to be asked twice, she collected her purse and beelined for the mahogany coat rack by the door. Lifting off her sparkly raincoat, she slid her arm into a sleeve and cast Zac a pleasant smile.

"Goodnight, Zac. Have a wonderful weekend. Say hi to Cloe for me." She frowned at Bill. "And you… You better not stiff me on my two hours' pay for leaving early—I know what you're like."

Bill offered no response, absorbing the insult as if it had never occurred.

Now half out the door, Audree popped her head back in, addressing Bill again, "Oh, are you still picking me up at seven for dinner at Harlequins?"

"Yup," Bill said with a wink, easing back into his oversized leather chair. "Got the reservations all set up. It's a date. See you at seven."

Audree beamed her white teeth. "Okay, sounds good. Love you, hun. Byeee."

"Bye, babe," Bill replied.

CHAPTER 7

The Village

As usual, the Lincoln Tunnel traffic was backed up a mile along Ninth Avenue.

Theia had hoped to avoid that very thing, but her garage encounter with the tattooed stranger had delayed her departure. To her surprise, she'd made it past the Broadway intersection inside the four-thirty deadline, albeit by seconds.

She should have escaped the trickling molasses of New York's worst traffic, but the glorious sunshiny weather had brought out the tourists in hordes.

Why couldn't they take the subway? Or a cab? At least cab drivers knew how to drive in this crazy city.

The traffic and tourists provided a convenient diversion from the unsettling thoughts lurking in the recesses of Theia's consciousness. Those thoughts revolved around the stranger from the elevator, the image of the double-cross tattoo. The sight of that cross emblem triggered a faint recognition within her. She knew she had seen it before, but where? And when?

And although the gentleman's actions appeared charming, his vibe rang a different tune. Deep within her, a clouded memory refused to surface. Whatever it was, something told her it was better left forgotten.

An annoying yet familiar accompaniment of Calypso steel drums and maracas interrupted her classical Mascagni playing through the car's multiple Harmon Kardon speakers.

Only one contact in her phone had that ringtone. She pressed the answer button on the touchscreen display. "Hey, Audree."

"Hey, girl! Have you forgiven me yet?"

"Nope!"

"Sorry, hun! I thought he'd be perfect for you. He's always been sweet in the years I've known him. Obviously, I'd never set you up with someone I didn't know well. I'm not that stupid. I just hate that you're always alone in that apartment of yours. It was an honest attempt to find you someone nice. I'm sorry."

"I know, Audree, and I appreciate the thoughtfulness, but I'm not interested in a relationship right now. Trust me; when I am, I'll let you know. Okay?"

"Are you driving? You sound funny."

"Hmm, define driving. Right now, I'm sitting in my car with the engine running, stuck in traffic on Twenty-Third and Ninth." Theia sighed. "At this rate, I might be home for Christmas."

"Well, hun, you better get home in time for tomorrow. Haven't forgotten our little shindig, have you?"

She *had* forgotten. All she'd thought about while persevering through her grueling week was the tranquil weekend ahead. Right now, the last thing she needed was a night on the town. She spoke with a guilt-ridden tone. "Uhhh, noo!" Then wincingly, she tried to renege. "Listen, girl, I don't think I'm gonna make it. I've had one hell of a week…"

"Mm-mm-mm, you're not backing out now, missy. Come on. I've had a hell of a day too." Then, turning it around on Theia, Audree pressed, "You need this, girl. You can't live the way you've been living.

All work, no play. Mm-mm. You need a break, some fun. *That's* what you need." Audree's voice deepened to a whisper as if sharing a secret, "Anyway, I have interesting and exciting news. So, you're coming; we're celebrating."

Intrigued, Theia couldn't help but guess. "Bill broke down and gave you a raise."

"As if!"

"He finally asked you to marry him."

"Ha, that'll be the day! Ooh, but he is taking me to dinner tonight. At Harlequins too. You know, he gave me that wink when he mentioned dinner. Hmm, the only other time we ate at Harlequins was on our first anniversary. We *never* eat there. He's too much of a cheap ass. I wonder if—" The upgraded car speakers went silent. For a moment, Theia thought they had been cut off but then Audree spoke, "Anyway, nope, that wasn't it either."

"So, what's the big news?"

"I'm not telling. You're coming out, and that's that. Pick me up at eight. I'll give you the scoop then." When silence befell the line, Audree stormed in for the kill with her pathetic child-begging-for-ice-cream whine. "Come on, hun. Please, please, please. It'll be fun. I promise!"

Theia could almost envision Audree's pouting bottom lip protruding from her LCD display.

As many could testify, arguing with Audree was a pointless endeavor. Not that she was smarter than everyone else, or more articulate. It was nothing like that. She simply had an uncanny knack of swinging any debate her way. It was her gift.

"Okay, fine," Theia reluctantly agreed. "See you at eight tomorrow night. If I ever get home!"

Audree giggled. "Okay, hun. Be careful. Oh, oh, almost forgot. I actually have two surprises! So, you need to pick me up earlier—say around six?"

"Six! Why so early?"

"Because we need to make a pit-stop first. To the… you know… first surprise thingy."

"A pit-stop?" Theia's monotone intonation boomed with pessimism. "Where're we going, Audree?"

"Look, if I told you, then it wouldn't be a surprise, would it?"

"Why is it every time you say *surprise,* I get cramps? I know you, Audree. You're not telling me because you know I'll say no. It better not be another blind date."

"No, nothing like that. Look, it'll be fun. So, six o'clock?"

"Ugh. Fine! I'll grab us an Uber."

"Yay! See ya tomorrow, babe! Luv ya. Byeee!"

"Bye Audree." Theia hung up.

AN HOUR LATER, Theia finally arrived at Greenwich Village, or simply The Village as the locals called it. Originally called Greenwijck by the Dutch who'd first colonized the area, its translation was literally 'Green Village.' During that time, Manhattan's buildings had sprouted quickly, surrounding an area that had remained heavily forested.

Today, though the forests had been replaced by mortar and bricks, the streets still enjoyed a complement of trees rooted along both edges of every road. The mature evergreens bestowed a unique rural appeal, buried in the concrete jungle of one of the world's busiest cities.

Crowned in the center of the west-facing side of the street, the luxurious frontage of Theia's home was now aglow with warm sienna oranges and garnet reds; the retiring sun cast its last light from a harvest sky. Finally, she was home.

As Theia pulled to her garage entrance on the main street, she slowed to a stop.

Blocking her path were two young boys who had commandeered the road to play a game of pass with their soccer ball. To make way, the younger boy, David Wilson, collected his ball and then scuttled between two parked cars. Recognizing Theia, David threw her a welcoming wave and his usual timid smile.

Occasionally, David reminded her of her own childhood. As a motherless only child, she'd had to learn new and inventive ways to entertain herself. Seeing David play with other children brought her a sense of contentment.

Many afternoons from her townhouse window, she would find David kneeling at a wall across the street, robotically playing with his action figures neatly aligned on top. Yet, he always seemed so withdrawn, his mind carried off to another place. Playing never seemed to bring him joy, just passing the time, occupying his mind.

She remembered David's father carrying him on his shoulders, tossing him high into the air, the only time she'd seen young David giggle as a child should. But that seemed so long ago. She hadn't seen his father for quite some time. What had happened to him? It concerned her, but it wasn't her place to pry.

AS THE EVENING rolled on, Theia sat on her oversized white couch holding a large glass of Sauvignon Blanc in one hand and a stapled document in the other. Her apartment's interior was simplistic in style. Sparsely furnished, it had the appearance of a modern art gallery and was much larger than one would expect for such prized real estate in The Village. The three long couches formed a U-shaped seating area around a large contemporary-styled pearl-white coffee table. Theia sat on the couch opposite the wall of windows overlooking the main street three stories below.

Four deco lamps positioned on corner tables warmly lit the room's center, the surrounding walls gradually dissolving into darkness. It was quiet, the way she liked it. On the coffee table, a pile of faded envelopes and folders towered several inches high, their aged paper worn and frayed, making it impossible for them to lie flat.

A few of the folders lay spread across the tabletop in a disorganized fashion. Books of all sizes lay around them, some opened to pages revealing images of various symbols. This made up but a fraction of Theia's research. Probably for the hundredth time, she studied the page in her hand, the stemmed wine glass hovering at her lips, forever waiting to be sipped.

She sighed.

What am I missing? The document slumped to her lap.

Her other arm stretched to the coffee table, setting her wine glass next to an open leatherbound book. Presented across its pages were various thumbnail symbols lined up row after row—thirty to a page—resembling a cross in varying designs and configurations.

One of the symbols stole her interest.

The volume felt heavy as she lugged it off the table, setting it onto her knees. Then, dragging her forefinger, she scanned every line. When she flipped to the next page, her finger immediately pulled to a central symbol, a double cross, similar to the one on the man's tattooed wrist. She leaned in closer to examine it. After making a mental note of the page title, *Symbols of Christ,* she dog-eared the page corner.

Then—

Ping! Buzz!

Theia jumped at the incoming phone message.

She retrieved the device from the corner table, opening it with a swipe. An amusing cartoon animation of two girls disco-dancing popped up. Superimposed on their cartoon bodies were Audree's and Theia's heads, wobbling side to side.

'Girls' Night!' read the caption, the meme bringing a smile to Theia's face. It diminished quickly. *What on earth have I signed up for this time?*

CHAPTER 8

Grave Danger

The Following Night.

Somewhere in the heart of Chinatown, the luxury Uber eased to a stop at a traffic light. In the back seat, dressed to the nines, Theia and Audree sat gossiping. Theia's half of the conversation became more reserved the farther east they traveled.

With the number of pedestrians and tourists growing fewer and the surrounding buildings looking far less inviting, Theia's attention was glued to the outside.

"Isn't this the way to your office?" Theia asked, interrupting Audree's story.

"Um, kinda. But we're not going there. It *is* on the Lower East Side though."

"*Where* on the Lower East Side?"

"Just off Delancey, but that's all you're getting. You really don't like surprises, do you?"

"No. Not a lot. Delancey? Mostly residential blocks, isn't it?" Theia shifted nervously in the backseat. "Why am I already regretting this, Audree?"

"It'll be fine. I promise." Without skipping a beat, Audree quickly returned to her recap of her night out with Bill. "Anyway, I shouldn't have built my hopes up."

"If he didn't take you to Harlequins to propose, then what *was* the occasion?"

"Get this. Zac boasted to Bill that he'd taken Cloe to some fancy restaurant to make a fuss of her, just coz, I guess. So, Bill, with his enormous frigging ego, decided to outdo his ass and take me somewhere more uppity. He even laughed about it over dinner." She huffed. "Men and their damn egos."

"I'm so sorry, Audree." Theia prodded her with an encouraging elbow. "He'll come through one day."

Just then, the Uber pulled off Delancey Street, ducking under the Williamsburg Bridge into a depressing square surrounded by grungy, high-rise apartments. It slowed to a stop at the foot of the first tower. Theia's face neared the window, her breath fogging up the glass. Her eyes traced the concrete walls of the desolate structure, seeming to melt into the gray, overcast sky.

"Audree, why have we stopped outside a block of flats?"

"You'll see!" Audree thanked the driver and they exited. "Let's go."

Only when the Uber's taillights faded from view did Audree confess, "You're right. If I told you about this, you would've said no."

Immediately, Theia rolled her eyes, huffing.

"Just hear me out. You know how we've spent hours and hours at the library searching for information about you and your family history? Not to mention endless internet searches, hiring genealogists, nd even those scary visits to cult meetings. Well, you know everything we've tried."

"Yes. All your ideas, all leading nowhere."

Audree wiggled her hips, excited as she unveiled 'her first surprise. "Well, I've found something we haven't tried! And here we are."

"Oh, my God. What, Audree?" Theia's hand covered her eyes as if somehow being blind would soften the blow of what she was about to hear.

"A medium."

Theia lowered her hand. "A fortune teller?"

"No, don't be silly. Those are the ones called *Madame Zaza* that you visit at the fair, lurking in dark tents with crystal balls. No. This is the real deal. Totally legit."

"Legit? The real deal? Really, Audree? *She* told you that?"

"No, thank you very much. I heard she was the *real deal* from work, even worked with the police, solving cases. That's how I found her, from a case Bill's working on."

Theia's eyes climbed the dismal dark gray concrete of the high-rise tower, wrestling with the idea. "And she really helped with the case?"

"Well, not exactly, not on Bill's case. She can't be right all the time. But Bill said her reputation speaks volumes and he doesn't even believe in all that mumbo jumbo." She linked her arm with Theia's, escorting her toward the crooked double-glass doors of the main entrance. "Oh, come on, we're here now. Let's do it. It'll be fun! Plus, I want my reading done, too."

On the fourteenth floor, Audree and Theia stood near the end of a dark corridor outside apartment 1404. The fluorescent hallway light flickered intermittently. Audree clamped onto Theia's arm tighter, then made a ghostly 'ooh' while chuckling.

Theia grudgingly smirked. "I feel ridiculous!"

Audree rapped on the door. "She better tell me I'm friggin' getting married, or I'll beat the crap out of her. Maybe you should go first." The remark sent them both into girly giggles, quickly suppressing into nasally snorts as they tried to subdue it like children in a classroom.

When the door opened, they straightened their faces, coming to attention as if a military officer had just approached. Theia's eyes went wide. The lady opening the door to them was not an old crone. Nor was she stooped forward, with warts or a veil covering her face.

Theia had watched too many TV shows, she thought. Instead, the woman was in her late thirties, sturdily built, decidedly ordinary. Without enquiring who they were, the lady stepped back with a welcoming smile.

"Please, come in." She closed the door behind them and led them down a short corridor passing by an open door.

The sound of gunfire from an old cowboy Western ricocheted off the walls, along with the reflection of the black and white flashing screen, capturing a middle-aged balding man sitting on the couch, sipping a can of beer.

Raising his drink, he gave a brief, uninterested glance before returning his eyes to the screen.

In the kitchen, the lady filled a large glass of water from the faucet. "Sometimes, I talk fast, and my mouth gets dry. Didn't used to. Maybe it's just a part of getting older. I don't know. Thought about seeing a doctor but seriously, who goes to a doctor for a dry mouth? This'll do the trick."

After chugging some water, she refilled her glass. Audree and Theia shared wide-eyed glances. Audree tried to suppress a smirk as her eyes bulged.

The lady turned to face them, her glass brimming. "So, which one of you is first?"

Audree immediately thumbed at Theia as though it were a race.

The woman eyed Theia, sizing her up, then nodding to herself as if understanding something. "You ever had a reading before? A real reading, not from one of those phony cranks?"

Theia almost said no when she suddenly remembered she'd had one. "Yes. Though a very long time ago. And I couldn't tell you if she was a crank."

She'd been living in England back then, and the medium was, in fact, an old crone with a stoop, warts, and a veil. And nothing she'd told her proved to be of any real value. "Probably was a crank," she concluded finally. "So no, never seen a proper one."

The proud smile forming on the woman's face spoke volumes; you're about to see what a real reading's like. "Follow me." The woman gestured with a wave. Then referring to Audree, she called from the hallway, "Make yourself at home. Just don't drink any of Ralph's beer."

Theia squeezed into the room behind the lady, the space barely larger than a cupboard and made smaller by eye-level stacked boxes lining all four walls. In the middle, with just enough room to walk around, was a small round table, a single ceiling lamp hanging over it.

"Please excuse the mess. We just moved in and we're still unpacking." She positioned herself at the table, adding, "Actually, that's not true. We've lived here for almost fifteen years. That's just something I tell people, so they don't judge me. But I see you already did."

Theia frowned. "What? No, I didn't…"

"It's okay. You're a skeptic. I see it a mile away."

Theia's effort to hide her skepticism dropped along with her shoulders. Then a guilty smile joined her blushing cheeks. "Look, I'm sorry. This was Audree's idea—"

"No names!" the medium yelled, thrusting her palm forward and turning her head away with closed eyes, as if trying to unhear it.

An uneasy silence followed before Theia gained the courage to speak.

Being told off by a crank wasn't exactly high on her list of fun nights out. "Um, look, my *friend* set all this up and I'm here to appease her. Though you have an incredible reputation, I'm told." Theia's attempt to soften the mood failed.

The stone-faced medium eased into her chair, clearing her throat, huffing and puffing. "Well then, sit there." She wafted her arm toward the only remaining chair.

Theia sat and stared at the stack of oversized Tarot cards. "So how does this work? Do I cut the deck or something?"

"It depends. Sometimes I use cards, sometimes palms. Sometimes, I just close my eyes."

Well, that didn't explain a thing. Why would she have gotten the cards out if she wasn't intending to use them?

The medium narrowed on Theia, concentrating her stare.

It was hard to decide which made Theia more uncomfortable, the intense stare or the long silence. Growing anxious, she reached to scratch the figment of an itch on her cheek then combed her fingers through the back of her hair.

"Do you have any questions before we get started?" the lady finally asked.

Theia lowered an eyebrow.

"Most people ask about money, marriage, promotions, things like that. You know, usual everyday things, looking to see what's in store."

Theia's skeptical mind churned. Indeed, she did have questions. Her entire life was one long string of them. But the more information she provided, the more questions she asked, the more this so-called medium could *guess* at her life's issues. Join a few dots and fill in the blanks so to speak.

That was how fakes operated.

She decided not to be an easy target. "No. No questions. As I said, it was her idea. Surprise me. Call it a mystery reading!" She grinned, giggling.

The woman sighed. She picked up the cards, as if about to shuffle them, but then changed her mind and placed them back on the table. She reached out and said, "Just give me your hand."

Reluctantly, Theia extended her hand to the woman, wearing a scowl as if afraid of contracting a contagious skin disease. Her hand felt unnervingly warm and slightly clammy, though her own hand must have felt no different. The lady closed her eyes, inhaling deeply, their moment of silence seeming to pass like minutes. And then… "You are searching for something," the medium croaked, her head tilting. The nonspecific statement was not a good start.

Who isn't searching for something? Theia rolled her eyes, remaining quiet.

"Are you from New York originally?" the medium asked.

Some medium! Without information, she was fishing for clues. Theia answered with as few indicators as she could. "No, not originally. I'm from… farther east."

"England. Yes. I see it now."

Another roll of Theia's eyes. The British Isles would be the first piece of land you would hit heading east from New York. Plus, she'd probably picked up a tinge of an accent.

"You came here to escape something."

Again, the statement was very general. Although she *was* escaping something, she lied, "No, not really. I came here for a business opportunity."

The medium moved on. "Not married, I see. Correct?"

Nice observation. No ring. Out with a girlfriend on a Saturday night.

How many other women had sat here paying for this fake to tell them when they would meet Mr. Right? Again, she lied. "Actually, I am married. We're spending some time apart. He loves his work too much, whereas I'm concentrating on…"

"A child."

Finally, the medium had blown it, falling right into Theia's trap.

She's a fake. I knew it!

"No. Didn't have any kids the last time I checked."

But the lady seemed unfazed. "The child… is in danger. Grave danger."

Her grip tightened on Theia's hand.

What a thing to say, Theia thought. "What child? Like I said, we don't have a child." If she did have a child, she'd have been scared out of her wits by this crank's proclamation!

She tugged to take back her hand, but the medium's stout fingers only squeezed tighter. Behind her closed eyelids, her eyes flitted to and fro, her head twitching. Next, her arms and shoulders jerked as if experiencing a terrible nightmare.

Then her jaw fell wide, her breath irregular and sharp. Gasping. Panting.

Theia tugged harder. "Please, let go. It's been very interesting, but I'm done here." Using her other hand, Theia pried the medium's fingers free. "You're hurting me."

"Things are not as they appear," the medium groaned, melodramatic. "Beware the wolf in sheep's clothing." Suddenly, she sucked in a deep gasp and finally released her grip, pulling her hand from Theia's with a sharp, unforgiving tug.

Now, the medium was behaving as if *she* had caught something from the holding of hands! Something dreadful and frightening. She gazed ahead, as if replaying a vision, her hazel irises shrinking amongst the white. She picked up her glass of water, chugging half in one go, then wiping dribble from her chin with the back of her hand. Her panting calmed.

Theia stood, nursing the blood back into her hand.

Snatching her jacket from the chairback, she cried out, "This is bullshit! I knew I shouldn't have come. And to think you make a living doing this!"

The medium ignored the comment. Still speaking as if entranced, she droned out a warning. "The man you love… more than life itself… will…"

"The man I love?" Theia growled, adjusting her jacket collar. "Guess what, lady. I lied. I'm not married. Or have a man for that matter. And I *certainly* don't have kids." Leaning, she whispered, "I'm infertile. You're way off on this con." She shook her head, speaking under her breath. "I should've never listened to Audree. Ugh!"

She stomped for the door, reached out for the handle, and then…

"He will die! I'm… I'm so sorry."

The medium's voice was louder this time, more urgent, stopping Theia in her tracks. Over her shoulder, the lady still sat with her hands resting on the table, her head shaking.

"He will die in your arms, and you, *you* cannot save him. If you try, you will die too."

"You're crazy!" Theia said. "You need help. And you *are* a crank. You're all the same." As she stormed from the room, she yelled for Audree who promptly ran into the corridor from the kitchen. "We're leaving," Theia barked. "Get your coat."

At the door, Audree slid her arms hurriedly into her jacket. "What happened? Is everything all right? You look like you've seen a ghost."

"Let's just leave. We'll talk about it later."

"Okay, hun, okay."

Theia's hand was on the external door handle now, and the medium's voice yelled, "Wait!"

Both turned to find her standing at the end of the hallway. She walked toward them, her hands unclasping a necklace from around her neck. As she approached them, she held the necklace out in front. "It's a Saint Christopher. For protection. Please, take it. You must."

"Lady," Theia said as she scowled, "I don't want your damn necklace."

"It's not for you. It's for her."

CHAPTER 9

Stars Aligning

Hell's Kitchen seemed a fitting end to their already infernal night. Located on Manhattan's west side, the neighborhood was home to Musica, New York's largest, most infamous nightclub.

It was not exactly the tranquil setting Theia had hoped for but compared to Lower East Side…

Once they had climbed the LED-lit stairs and looked out over masses of raving heads, Theia couldn't help but wonder if Audree had intentionally chosen these bustling venues to force her out of her comfort zone and confront her social anxieties head-on.

However, if that was Audree's true motive, it hadn't worked.

After migrating to one of the many bars in the quietest corner of the room, Theia couldn't shake off the persistent sensation of being watched, the unnerving feeling of prickling skin, and the irresistible urge to glance around, searching for the source of the scrutiny. It was making her uneasy, restless.

As the night progressed, Audree sat catty-corner, inspecting her new Saint Christopher necklace over the glowing bar counter. The whites of her eyes and her teeth luminesced a bluish-white against her brown skin, now midnight black in the ultraviolet light. Two nearly empty cocktail glasses adorned with umbrellas, cherries, and smudged rouge rims perched beside her on the bar.

"Think this is real?" Audree asked, examining it closely. "Aren't Saint Christophers supposed to be sterling silver? Here, what do you think?" She offered it across.

"No thanks, it's for you. To protect you from… whatever. But I'm not sure if they're all silver anyway; I don't believe in all that nonsense."

Truth be told, the moment they'd left the flats, Theia imagined the medium rushing to her stockpile under her bed, clasping another Saint Christopher around her neck, ready for the next unsuspecting customer. It was nothing more than a simple, yet effective, gimmick to make her appear more genuine. Judging by Audree's fascination, it had worked on her.

"I hope you didn't shell out too much for that crap, Audree."

"It was supposed to be fifty bucks, but she wouldn't take a dime." Then, to Theia's disgust, Audree bit down on it.

"Eww! Don't put it in your mouth. You don't know where she's had that thing—I mean, it was around her neck, among all that hair for one thing! Eww."

Removing it as you would a lollipop, Audree sucked the remnants off her tongue.

"It *tastes* like silver."

"Oh, really, Miss Marple? I should have let you go first. You seem well suited."

The barman loitered nearby. Audree waved, signaling his attention. "Hey, can we get two Sand in the Cracks?"

"Oh, my God! What did you just order?" asked Theia, not believing her ears.

"You know," Audree said, as if common knowledge. "after you've had 'Sex on the Beach,' you get 'Sand in the Crack!'"

Theia chuckled finally, Audree dangling the necklace around her own throat. "What do you think? Do you like it? Does it suit me?"

Theia kept her feelings on the subject personal. "It's pretty, I suppose. Are you honestly going to wear it?"

Audree gently dragged her fingers across her yellow string pearl necklace. "Not tonight, it'll clash. Maybe later. We'll see."

As Audree coiled the necklace inside her purse, Theia threw another suspicious eye around the room. Audree followed.

"What's up?" Audree's perception was astute.

"Nothing." Theia sat straight, hugging her arms. "I just feel…" She leaned to whisper, Audree meeting her halfway. "I feel as though someone's watching me."

"Well of course. *I'm* watching you. I'm not sitting here talking to myself, am I? And it'd be a bit weird if I were talking to you but looking at someone else."

"No, not you… Don't be silly." Theia leaned closer. "Don't look now, but I feel like—"

Audree immediately spun her head, causing Theia to scream inwardly. *Oh, my God, Audree. Seriously!*

"Hun, hate to break it to you," Audree said, "but half the room's staring at you." Just then, their freshly made cocktails arrived. Audree quickly grabbed hers, swirling it.

"It's not just tonight either," Theia went on. "Yesterday at work, a man followed me to my car, and for a moment, I thought he was going to attack me."

"Oh, my God." Audree reached for Theia's leg. "Are you okay? Did he hurt you? Why didn't you say something?"

"No, no he didn't. I mean, he seemed charming enough. And it turned out he was just handing me my car keys that I'd dropped. But there was something else." She pointed to her wrist. "He had a tattoo. Right here."

"So? Lots of people have tattoos." Audree gave her hips a cheeky wiggle. "Even I've got some in places you wouldn't believe! But I wouldn't be showing them off in a car lot. Well, not very often, anyway. The last time was—"

"It's not that," Theia explained gravely. "It's just… he wore a suit like a business executive, was older, refined. Doesn't that seem off to you?"

"Girl, what century are you living in? Even one of the judges I know has a tattoo, an anniversary date, I think. Plus, you said it yourself, he was nice, right? He probably just wanted your number, but was too shy to ask?" She rubbed Theia's shoulder. "I'm sure you were safe, hun. Those underground parking garages are enough to give anyone the heebie-jeebies. I'm sure it was all completely harmless."

"But a creepy wrist tattoo of a cross?" Theia contested. "On a guy like that? That doesn't scream 'cult' to you? How many times have I said these men are all part of some weird religious thing?"

"The tattoo was a cross, you say?" Audree asked, her face lighting up.

Given the seriousness of their conversation, Theia found the excitement on Audree's face disturbing.

"You're gonna love me then!" From her purse, Audree pulled out something small enough to conceal behind her palm, flattening it against her chest.

"What's that?" Theia leaned away, dreading the answer.

"Your second surprise!" Audree's teasing smile appeared almost prideful.

Recalling Audree's last two surprises—the blind date, and tonight's visit with the psycho medium—Theia's stomach twisted at the thought of a third. "Audree, you've exceeded your quota for surprises this month," she said, her angst palpable.

"You sure?" Audree twirled her hips like a five-year-old girl in a new dress. "Even if it means getting closer to discovering all about this *cult*?"

Theia ignored the baiting.

The chance of Audree making such progress was slim at best. After all, Audree didn't even believe in any of this; to her, this was all a bit of fun, something more entertaining than belting out tunes at Radio Star Karaoke. Of course, if she knew the truth, even if only in part, that perception would change dramatically.

Unable to contain her surprise any longer, Audree blurted, "Okay, I'm just going to tell you. So... remember when I invited that guy over, the one with the beard; the historian dude—Richard?"

Theia furrowed her brow. "Robert, the genealogist?"

"Right, Robert. And he was gonna help you find out... you know, all that ancestry stuff."

Once again, Theia's trepidation mounted. *Where is this going?* "Yeah, I remember it didn't lead anywhere!"

"And whose fault was that?" Audree fired back. "He knew all about your little knickknacks, the histories, dates, and what have you. But as soon as he mentioned your McDormand family line, you shut him down. It was embarrassing."

"Yes, but!" Theia's voice rose. "It was a pointless exercise."

"Pointless?" Audree looked genuinely baffled, though Theia knew she had every right.

For years, Theia had reported how she spent every minute of her spare time researching her family's history, specifically, a tragic event purportedly occurring long ago when a female relative had been hunted by a mysterious group and then brutally killed. Fearing the same group might now be after her, Theia hoped to find a link before it was too late.

Audree, however, was convinced the story was fueling Theia's paranoia, promising to help her disprove it. Although her intentions were good when she sought out a genealogist and lured him to her townhouse, Theia couldn't bear to let the poor fellow waste any more of his precious time. It was indeed a pointless endeavor; McDormand was not her real name.

Audree regained her posture from Theia's surprising remark. "Since you seem very protective of your ancestry, I decided to seek out an expert in cults instead." She became excited suddenly. "When you mentioned the wrist tattoo being a religious cross, I almost died! A few days ago, I actually spoke with a specialist in religious cults and symbology, and that's exactly his area of expertise."

"Wait, you spoke with a specialist?"

"Yeah, on the phone. He was really nice."

"Audree, you think *everyone's* really nice!"

"He sounded cute too!"

"Oh well, in that case, we should call him right now; invite him over!"

"I already did. He's coming on Thursday."

"What!" Theia spun on her stool. "Are you serious? Audree, there's no way I'm letting some cult freak into my house."

"He's not a freak," Audree defended as if she had known him for years. Finally, she revealed her palmed business card. She slid it across the bar counter in front of Theia. "See. He works at the Natural History Museum."

Theia almost swallowed her tongue when she saw it. Immediately, she ransacked her purse. *I think it's still in here.* A moment later, she pulled out an off-white linen business card, given to her by Professor Matthew Colombo a week earlier. She slid it next to Audree's.

An exact match.

"How the…" Audree snatched both cards, her glazed eyes darting between them. "I don't understand. When did you…"

"Blind date night," Theia voiced in a trance-like state, calm, yet her mind racing. "The one *you* sent me on!"

"Graeme gave you this? The blind date?"

"No," she said, pointing at the card. *"He* did!"

After Theia recounted her chance meeting with the professor at last week's gala and listening to Audree drone on about fate, she conceded to speak with him, though for different reasons than Audree's. Audree's inner guru believed in providence and stars aligning. Theia believed in her gut. And it was telling her that just maybe, a meeting with Matthew might not be a disastrous idea.

Pleased with herself, Audree pressed, "So, was he cute? He sounded cute on the phone."

Theia lowered her chin, her eyebrows arching. "Is that all you ever think about?"

Audree slid off her stool. "Nope. Right now, I'm thinking... dancing!" Nodding her head and twisting her hips to the rhythm, she pushed her palms toward the ceiling. "C'mon." She dragged Theia off her stool toward the dance floor. "No more depressing talk."

After shouldering their way through the packed dance floor to an open space near the center, Audree unleashed a frenzied mess of clunky moves. While Theia, shy at first, began gently swaying her hips, slowly surrendering to the rhythm. Her eyes closed, head tilting back, she ran her hands through her hair, reaching upwards as if worshiping the strobing sun gods above.

Each booming beat drowned out the harmony of the music until all she could see behind closed eyes was a vast darkness, an infinity of black. And the only sound was the thumping rhythm exploding in the night, a sound like gunfire.

BEHIND HER CLOSED eyes, she was transported to a distant memory, to a place far from here. A place of utter darkness, so cold and empty that none of her senses existed, except for hearing. And the only sound she heard was gunfire.

Even that faded to silence, to nothingness, an unbearable void.

In that memory, she was dead.

CHAPTER 10

Mortal Recoil

Baden-Baden, 1945.

Reginleif's sight had returned. From total darkness, a winding tunnel of swirling light whizzed by as she fired through, slow at first, then faster, brighter. Sharp, unexpected turns with steep dives and climbs wove like a shimmering Schwarzschild wormhole. A breathtaking spectacle. Otherworldly. Also returning was her sense of touch. Growing ever intense, the electrical charge buzzed and crackled around her, its vibrating hum becoming deafeningly loud. Now terrifying, there was no escaping it. She tried closing her eyes, only to realize she had none to close. Not in this world.

The swirling light became a blur, so swift it was almost still, sound and sensation merging into one continuous surge of intensifying electromagnetic frenzy. Everything was white. Blinding white. And then, in an instant, it was black. Silent. And bitingly cold.

The first sign of mortality was always pain. And with a vengeance, it had returned to her bullet-ridden body. But the numbing, icy cold water of the Oos subdued its agonizing sting.

Finally, she heaved a breath, but face-down in the river, her lungs surged with water. Instinctively, she poked her head above the waterline. Through the coughing and the choking she managed to wheeze a long, lifesaving breath. Life now in her limbs, she treaded desperately to stay afloat. Spying a riverbank, she kicked her leaden legs, arms outreaching, splashing, fighting the relentless current.

She swallowed water, then more. Her head submerging, she anchored her hand to a tuft of grass, gripping on tight for dear life. But the river was too selfish to let go.

In a cruel game of tug-of-war, it swept her parallel, tugging mercilessly at her feet, testing her grip and the roots of the grass. With both hands, she grabbed at the muddy bank, finally dragging her sodden mass from that watery grave. The river still lapping at her ankles, she collapsed onto her stomach, mud squelching into her ear.

Gathering her energy and thoughts, questions flooded her mind.

Where the hell am I?

Who am I?

What happened?

And why am I in so much pain?

Her memories began piecemealing obscure images into a stuttering slideshow.

The church!

The translations!

It's a trap! Run! Bridge! Bullets!

Recalling the fatal bullet, her body shuddered as if reliving the impact. It jolted her awake, her mind snapping into sharp focus. Her instinct was to flee. To get to her apartment. To safety. But how long had she been out? Were they still chasing her? She glanced beyond the river to the bridge. Off in the distance, through the veil of low-lying mist that danced over the icy water, she discerned the hazy silhouette of a stone bridge. Bathed in the soft glow of a half dozen streetlamps, it shimmered like a mirage.

Men jostled on top, peering over its wall to the river below.

Her heart raced.

Blood pulsed through her veins, seeping too from open wounds. As she rolled onto her back, pain engorged her left shoulder. She inched her hand toward it. Even the slightest touch caused unbearable pain; a kind she had never experienced.

She managed to silence a scream, and then, with a clasped hand over her mouth, wept.

Her shivering body lay trembling with despair and hopelessness.

As she gazed up into the night sky, she focused on a patch of stars through a tear in the luminescent blanket of low-hanging clouds. As if a moth to light, they captivated her, their twinkling as bright as diamonds on a black velvet cloth. In that moment, all her troubles vanished. She almost forgot about her numbed torso, her aching wounds, and her relentless pursuers undoubtedly only minutes from finding her.

Maybe I could just rest for a while?

After a lifetime of running, of not belonging, she wished this time she'd remained dead. It was, after all, more peaceful. Certainly, better than this. There was a serenity and stillness at the end of life, a sense of release and letting everything go.

She sighed deeply as hope dwindled, but then, a shooting star catapulted across the stark night sky, and she found herself immersed in the tears cascading over her cheeks.

Not from the pain, but from a memory.

When she'd been a child, her father would tell her stories about her mother each night before bed, often describing how she would lie beneath the stars with unblinking eyes, waiting to catch sight of a falling star. She believed it would bring good fortune to those lucky enough to see it.

But in this moment, pain-ridden, cold, defeated, Theia believed it was her mother telling her to get up, that she mustn't give in. She must push on regardless; the message was as real as life. Not wanting to disappoint, she rallied her remaining energy.

"Okay, Mom," she whispered. "Okay."

Toughening herself up, she labored to her feet with a visceral howl of pain.

The act stripped her of strength. Hand on a knee, she doubled over, panting. Unlike her other wounds, the pain from her shoulder was not easing as it should. Something was seriously amiss. With one last glance at the distant bridge, she turned to look ahead, to the dark unlit streets ascending from the bank.

Her sense of hope returning and the thought of freedom reawakening, she took her bearing, then trudged wearily toward what she believed must be salvation.

The half-mile walk to her studio apartment building was grueling, though that was a cakewalk compared to the final hike. This one was a three-story climb which she cursed with each step.

Now at the final stretch and fueled by willpower alone, she dragged her feet along the narrow corridor, leaning against the wall.

The meagerly furnished apartment was only temporary, rented solely for this mission. Fortunately, she had eleven more nights remaining. Hoping it would prove unnecessary but erring on caution, she'd stocked the cupboards with a two-week supply of bread, cheese, and other necessities. What she hadn't stocked was a first aid kit.

Before tonight, she'd never needed one.

Despite her numbed fingers and shaky hands, she unlocked the door, limping inside. In total darkness, she felt her way toward the bathroom, bumping into unfamiliar furniture and knocking a lamp to the floor, its bulb shattering.

She flicked on the bathroom light and stood before the vanity mirror. She stared, reeling. Her gray woolen jacket sagged heavy with river water, appearing extra-large on her petite frame. Tattered hair streaked across her pallid face, half obscuring it. She brushed it aside to reveal sapphire-blue eyes encircled by hollowed shadows.

The running mascara, like black tears, added to her ghastly appearance.

She gasped at her appearance. "Theia Reginleif, you look awful."

Though admittedly, this was not bad for someone who had been shot multiple times, half-drowned, and... killed. At least now, there was warmth in her veins.

Carefully, she unbuttoned her jacket and slowly slid it from her shoulders. Her chartreuse blouse beneath was bullet-torn and stained red with blood. *So much blood.* With one hand, she unfastened it. Trying to slide free, she saw it had glued to the encrusted blood on her chest.

Like removing a stubborn Band-Aid, she carefully peeled her blouse from her skin, gritting her teeth against the pain. She could have counted to three, tearing it off in one quick movement. But the wounds were so deep she feared passing out and causing more damage. However, regardless of her tender efforts, the wound reopened.

Warm blood trickled down her chest.

Next, she unzipped her skirt. With a few sharp tugs, she wriggled free, and it slopped to the puddled tile around her ankles.

Standing in her white underwear, she surveyed the extent of her injuries. She checked her calf, finding the grazed gash had almost completely healed. Likewise, the wound on her chest that had punctured her lung was already forming a smooth mound of maroon skin. She leaned into the mirror to examine it more closely. The maroon faded to a pale pink before her eyes, matching her surrounding skin tone. Soon, any evidence of a wound would be gone.

While leaning in, she studied her reflection, turning her head from side to side. Her skin, as white as porcelain, bore the history of each blemish, each scratch, yet each had healed to a flawless finish. But her shoulder told a different story. The wound there remained open, oozing blood. More worrying were the fine bruised-blue, capillary-like lines creeping from the entry hole like shattered glass.

Was it infected? Never in all her years had she seen a wound like this. Not on herself, anyway.

Nor had she suffered such stinging pain that continued to intensify.

She cautiously touched the skin around the hole. Instantly, her knees buckled, pain engulfing her entire upper body. She inhaled sharply. Unlike the bullet wound on her chest where the round had passed straight through, this bullet was lodged firmly inside.

Normally, her body would simply work to expel the foreign object, but obviously that was not happening. For the first time in her life, she would have to extract it—manually.

In search of a suitable instrument, Theia rummaged through the only two drawers on the vanity, finding a small pair of scissors. Not ideal but they would have to do.

About to delve in, she paused, examining the wound closer. *Hmm.*

She scowled. Never having been sick, nor ever having suffered an infection, she wondered, *should I take extra precautions? Sanitize the wound before performing surgery?*

She dashed from the room, only to return a moment later brandishing a quarter bottle of Courvoisier Cognac, brought from France. This was the preferred brandy of Napoléon—it wasn't cheap—and somewhat hard to source during these times of rationing.

Tonight, she had hoped she'd be raising a glass to celebrate the end of a lifelong search. Instead, this rare and valued commodity, fit for royalty, was now disinfectant.

She flipped over a small glass, filled it half full of Cognac then swirled the scissors inside before leaving them to sanitize. She hovered the bottle an inch over her shoulder wound, ready to pour. Knowing the pain to follow, she stared her reflection in the eye, a last glance of self-pity and moral support. *You can do it.* She inhaled a deep breath. After holding it in for a few seconds, but ultimately not finding the nerve, she finally resorted to 'Dutch courage.' She gulped a giant swig from the bottle. Before she could talk herself out of it, she splashed a triple shot over the gaping hole.

"Holy Mother of God!" she exclaimed, the pain searing deep.

Panting heavily, she danced foot-to-foot until the eye-watering sting subsided.

Unfortunately, as painful as that was, the worst was yet to come.

Like a swimmer preparing to dive, she took three powerful breaths, grabbed the scissors pointing inward, and plunged them deep into her chest hole.

Almost fully inserted, the scissors hit metal. Carefully, she secured a hold on the bullet. Her world began to tunnel. Unconsciousness was fast approaching.

She had to hurry. But she was facing another problem. To grip the bullet, the scissors had to widen their jaws larger than the bullet hole. The withdrawal would be even more excruciating.

After several attempts, her scissors bit down with resistance.

She had hold of the invasive object, but would the grasp be sufficient for the extraction? Closing her eyes, she strengthened her grip on the sink.

"Come on! Come on!" With one final breath, she carefully eased the bullet to the surface, trying desperately not to let it slip. Tears pooled behind her eyelids as a high-pitched whimper escaped from behind clenched teeth.

Finally, a sharp yank released the bullet. As it tore through the skin, she let out an almighty scream. Unconsciousness swiftly followed and she slumped to the white tiled floor, now swimming in a pond of river water and blood.

While she lay motionless, the infection lines around the wound gradually disappeared. The hole began to close, healing with fresh pink skin. Her hand rested on the floor with her index finger and thumb still looped on the scissors. A few feet away lay the responsible bullet. Beneath the spotted blood, it glimmered a sparkling blue.

CHAPTER 11

The Research

New York, Present Day.

The blinding flash from the Luger's muzzle sent Theia's heart racing.

"No!" she cried, awakening with a start. Her eyes flew open, her right hand thrusting forward as she bolted up, peeling matted hair from the damp pillow. The disarray of her soaked bed sheets and the gallop in her chest proved this nightmare was more intense than the others. It had been years since one had shaken her so abruptly from her sleep.

Her hand drifted to her left shoulder.

There, her fingertips nursed the penny-sized circle of skin between her chest and shoulder. Several shades darker than the surrounding area, it was a constant reminder of that fateful night.

Fear, pain, and the experience of death itself came rushing back.

But the greatest woe was regret—for failing to uncover her reason for being.

A life without purpose was no life at all. So pointless, so empty. Akin to riding a tedious train to an unknown destination, an unknown distance ahead, never knowing when it would ever stop or when she would ever get off.

She would watch the countless passengers boarding, sharing their busy stories, their marriages, promotions, anniversaries, breakups, and then disembarking to live out meaningful lives.

But not her. Even when pushed off, as in the nightmare she'd just had, she would awaken back on board. *Clickety-clack, clickety-clack.*

As she did most mornings, she recited by heart the poem from the translated texts she had stolen from the old Bavarian church. For three-quarters of a century, she had clearly remembered every word, especially its ominous final line: *T'Niht O' Light Will Darkness Keep.* Those words and that sparkling, near near-fatal bullet, changed the course of her life. They turned her from warrior to recluse, from fugitive to immigrant. They boarded with her on the ship to the Americas.

And she never looked back.

In America, her research ceased. Not by choice, but by lack of means. The English village where it all began was far away. So too were the ancient records. Europe held all the answers, and access from across the Atlantic was impossible. That was until technology developed.

As the decades rolled by and New York City grew, library books and church records shipped from European countries became readily available and publicly accessible.

Then came the internet and with that, the exponential multiplying of resources. Each year, more and more records were digitized and uploaded. Having such resources at the click of her fingertips was overwhelming. The information was out there, simply waiting to be found. It was just a matter of finding it, a binary needle amongst the web's vast googolplex haystack.

Perhaps today will be the day?

Groomed and refreshed from her invigorating shower, she emerged from her bedroom.

Dressed in light-gray jogging pants and a black, loose-fitting sweat-shirt with a giant white 'NYU' on the front, she shuffled in red flip-flop slippers down the floating Acacia wood staircase to the kitchen. In a similar style to the rest of her apartment, it was simple in design.

Everything was white. White cabinets, white countertops. Even the double ovens were white.

Theia browsed through her office mail, her tea brewing in the pot. Tea was still her drink of choice. Seven decades of living with coffee-drinking Americans hadn't been enough to change her centuries-long habit of morning tea. Besides, the British took their tea drinking seriously.

It was more than just a hot beverage; this was a cure-all. No matter what ailed, tea was the age-old cure for homemakers across all the British Isles.

My husband left me—one lump or two?
I just got fired—I'll make us a cuppa.
I've severed my hand—I'll put the kettle on.

Two and a half minutes later, her brew was ready. With a splash of milk, two cubes of sugar, and with a quick clockwise stir of the spoon, it was perfected.

There it was, the elixir to fix all ills.

With the mug cupped in both hands, she took a loud slurp, another habit she hadn't broken. Nowadays, slurping would be considered rude.

But in England of those times, slurping your tea was a compliment to the brewer.

Tea was meant to be consumed at near boiling temperature and the only way to do it was to pour it onto the saucer or to suck air with it—hence, the slurp!

The first item on her mind? Research. She headed from the kitchen to the long hall.

Here, the wall on her left separated the hall from the main living room. It was clad with dark wooden panels, decorated with dozens of framed photographs of varying sizes.

The photographs were mainly of people, but none of Theia alone.

One photograph, slightly sepia from age, was of Audree and Theia hugging each other cheek to cheek. Apart from having auburn hair,

Theia appeared unchanged in it, ageless. Unlike Audree, who appeared much slimmer and in her early twenties.

Like a museum, various unique pieces of wall art and floor arti-facts were scattered throughout the apartment, though mainly in the living room.

The antique appearance of the pieces oddly seemed at home in the modern-style townhouse.

At the end of the hall, she stopped in front of the enameled, black-paneled entrance door to her apartment. Immediately to her left, propped against whitewashed walls, stood an eight-foot-tall, four-foot-wide bookcase sparsely filled with decorative books and ornaments. She perched her cup on top of a book lying on its side, grabbing the right side of the bookcase with both hands.

With almost no effort, the entire bookcase slid to her left, stealthily gliding on hidden wheels. Now open, she grabbed her tea, then entered her secret room.

In stark contrast to the other townhouse rooms which were neurot-ically neat and minimally appointed, this one was—a mess. Cluttered and disorganized

This was her research room and no one, not even Audree, knew it existed.

Within the room, the west wall had a tall window overlooking the front street. The wall to its left bore four pinboards stacked tight together in a grid. Covering every square inch were photographs, documents, hand-written notes, pages torn from books, and dozens of multicolored sticky notes, all pinned side by side or overlapping at varying angles.

The center of the room boasted a makeshift conference table formed by a series of rectangular foldable white plastic picnic tables, the adjoining legs fixed using white zip ties.

Edge to edge, the top was covered with scattered papers, several piles of documents, and a half-empty file box in the middle of the table. The documents were wrapped in long elastic bands, grouping them by region. To save table space, some were stacked on top of each other, the top folder on each pile bearing a rectangular white label with a handwritten title. The ones stacked topmost read, *The Montpellier Files*, *The Strasbourg Files*, and *The Jorvik Files*.

Theia moved to the table's far end near the west wall, sitting in the farthest chair. Holding the cup with both hands, she sipped her tea, examining her pinup wall. To any other eye, the wall would appear as a disorganized jumble of randomness. But to Theia, it made perfect sense.

The pinboard was structured into various categories, a few of which were religions, symbols, organizations, and governments. The paper titles pinned above each section used to be visible, but they had since become buried beneath layers of newer research material pinned on top and above. Some titles were still visible: 'Paganism,' 'Constantine,' 'The Holy Trinity,' and the one on which Theia focused today, 'Symbols of Christ.'

With barely an inch of space remaining on the littered table, she placed her mug atop a pile of papers, then picked up the closed book next to it, the same book of symbols she examined two days earlier. She opened it to the dog-eared page, her finger tapping on the center image as she studied it. Then carefully tearing the page from the binding, she approached the four-piece pinboard. Below it, a small plastic tray, attached with Velcro, held an open box of various colored plastic pins.

She pinched one between her finger and thumb, then pinned the page next to the others.

Uncapping a nearby red marker, she encircled the center symbol— the double cross—the one she believed had been on the mysterious man's wrist.

Out of the adjacent window, she caught sight of her neighbor, the young boy, David. White as a sheet, he stood terrified in the middle of the street below, a tall gentleman dressed in a pinstriped suit looming over him. He was balancing David's black and white soccer ball in one hand, while the other sat inappropriately on David's trembling shoulder.

The man in black!

Theia gasped.

Repeatedly, she screamed David's name, striking the window with the flat of her hands. When neither of them reacted, she banged harder. Screamed louder. "Hey! Hey!" But it was useless. Her double-paned windows were vacuum sealed, insulating her from the busy Village traffic and frequently honking horns.

Especially from this height, there was no chance they would hear.

She spun around, darting toward the door, clumsily tripping as she went. Kicking off her whimsical flip-flops, she sped barefoot from her apartment. Descending the six half-flights of stairs two steps at a time, she prayed David would still be there when she arrived at the street.

CHAPTER 12

Mr. Philips and David Wilson

Theia burst into the street. To her relief, David was still there. So too was the tall, suited gentleman, his hand still resting on David's shoulder as he villainously leaned over him.

From street level, the man appeared even lankier.

"Hello, can I help you?" Theia called out as she charged toward them. The man glanced over his shoulder, revealing an odd array of peculiar features. Most notable was the crown of his head. Bulbous and round, it seemed unusually large for his long, slender face which narrowed sharply to a pointed chin. The receding hairline made it worse, retreating so far back he appeared completely bald from the front. At least, he did to those shorter than him.

Which, from his height, was probably everyone.

Theia recognized him immediately. *Lurch.*

His rawboned face and lanky frame had earned him that nickname from the other kids on the street, adults too. Together with his creepy stare, she could see why.

But to Theia, she knew him as…

"Mr. Philips, I didn't realize it was you." Now only a few feet away, Theia eyed David standing frozen in position, chin tight to his chest. "Hello, David."

Only his eyes rose in acknowledgement.

Mr. Philips was a resident of her building, his apartment sitting directly beneath hers. He was not a threatening man by any means; annoying, maybe, but definitely no threat. He worked in the financial district for some investment company and from what she could tell, had done quite well for himself. For the years she had known him, he had always been alone: no partner, no visitors, not even a date as far as she knew. This was an assumption, judging by the dust collecting on his expensive sports car in their shared garage.

As harmless as he was, he was still Lurch to the kids. And she could see from poor David's eyes, he was petrified. Looking back to Mr. Philips, Theia asked, "Is there a problem?"

"No, no problem," Mr. Philips answered, patting David's shoulder. "I was just telling the boy, our street's no place to be kicking a ball. There are lots of expensive cars parked here, as you know." He leaned again, shadowing over David. "You wouldn't want to break any, would you?"

David shook his head, his glazed, Basset Hound eyes stretching up to meet Lurch's.

Mr. Philips straightened. "He needs to find a field to play in. Surely there's one close by?"

Finding the remark insensitive, Theia pressed out an artificial smile. She perched on her tiptoes to look over the parked cars lined bumper to bumper down both sides of the street.

Theatrically, with the ridge of her hand pressed to her eyebrows, she scanned left and right as if searching for a field. Having lived there for many years, she knew precisely where each one of the parks and squares was situated. And none were in their street, or close enough for a small child to wander off to. Mr. Philips knew that too.

"Well, as you can see, there aren't many fields around here, Mr. Philips." Theia's tone and body language communicated a not-so-hidden sarcasm. "And from what I recall, you park your car in there, along with mine."

She pointed behind her toward the garage of the apartment building, adjacent to the entrance.

"Quite right. But I'm not only concerned about myself. It's other people. And there's the boy's safety to consider, too. I mean, where are his parents? If it were me—"

"Yes, yes, okay. Thank you, Mr. Philips. I've got this."

There was another reputation for which he was known, for being a busybody, a nosey parker. Always observing and interfering in other people's affairs, he was happy to share his opinions and complaints.

No wonder he never married or had friends.

"Yes… well." Mr. Philips handed the ball back to young David, smiling as he did so. "You be careful. Okay, young man?" He gestured a farewell nod to Theia. "Miss McDormand," he said, then sauntered his gangly frame back toward the apartment building.

Theia escorted David from the street to the sidewalk nearest her townhouse. She squatted as low as she could. Although they'd been neighbors for years, she had never really spoken to him. Not recently anyway. Just the occasional niceties as she hollered from an open car window or passed by on one of her walks. Even then, the conversation was always one-sided.

Theia would shout "Hello David," or voice a complimentary white lie, "You're getting good with that ball!" David only ever smiled or waved in return.

"Hey! Are you okay?"

David hugged his precious ball, nodding.

"Where is your friend today?" Theia looked around.

David shrugged.

"Which apartment do you live in, sweetheart?"

David pointed diagonally behind him across the street to the first Soledad Tower.

Although both sides of the street were considered high-end housing, the three towers were commonly touted as *affordable living*. Some neighbors, however, had a less polite term for these imposing properties. Although they shared a similar aesthetic to the neighboring buildings, many of the wealthier neighbors complained about the towers' presence, motioning to have the buildings repurposed only because they provided meager accommodation, far less upmarket.

No doubt they were afraid of attracting lower-class tenants, reducing their own property values.

"Is your mother home?"

David shook his head.

"Is she at work?"

Finally, he spoke. A soft, whisper-like tone. "She's at another job interview."

"And your dad, is he home?"

David didn't respond. His eyes moved to the pavement.

Theia straightened from her squat, searching the street. Perhaps she could find him a safer place to play. During her scan, she noticed a figure sitting in the driver's seat of a parked car on the distant north side. It was difficult to discern any details other than the shape of a person just sitting there. The car also seemed out of place. She didn't know cars well, but this was an older model, the style atypical for her neighbors. Of course, they could be waiting for someone.

But once again, her gut instinct informed her this was off somehow.

Trusting it, she turned to David, extending her hand, palm down. "How about we wait for your mom inside? Come on, bring your ball too."

With the ball tucked under his arm, David's tiny free hand clasped hers as a smile stretched across his face. That idea obviously appealed to him.

She led him toward her apartment entrance. "I bet you like hot chocolate?" she said.

David's eyes lit up. From his expression, Theia guessed he hadn't enjoyed comfort foods in a while. She leaned to whisper, "I have some. All the way from England. And it's the best! What do you say?"

David's step picked up.

A short while later, he was sitting on the couch, gulping from an oversized purple mug with the words 'Cadbury' emblazoned in white. He needed both hands to hold it.

Theia savored his enjoyment. Living a solitary existence herself, she rarely spent time around anyone, especially children. She had forgotten the heartwarming joy of simply watching a child glug down a cup of hot chocolate.

Dwarfed by the large, white couch, David's little legs hung off its edge. His tarnished brown shoes appeared to be Sunday's best-turned-soccer shoe, marred and scuffed beyond the recognition of their former glory. He wore red shorts and a black t-shirt with Captain Universe silkscreened to the front in an explosion of color.

"How's the chocolate? Best ever?"

David looked over the top of the mug, nodding.

"You said your mother was at an interview? Doesn't she already have a job?" David continued chugging another gulp when she added, "I thought she worked at the co-op on the corner. I've seen her there."

David nodded again, allowing a moment to savor the rich, smooth chocolate on his tongue before swallowing. "She did," he said shyly, "but Mr. Tilman said business was quiet, and he doesn't need her anymore."

Theia sat half perched on the windowsill, peering down to the north end of the street. From her vantage point, she could still see the suspiciously parked car, long and boxy, painted a golden brown with a white leather roof.

The windshield reflected the sunlight, making it impossible for her to see inside.

"I don't mean to pry, David," Theia said, her gaze still on the car. "But what about your dad? Is he at work?" Not having seen him in a long time, she suggested that out of politeness. In reality, she assumed his parents had most likely divorced.

"No." David's voice lowered, "He died."

Theia's lips parted as she sucked in a breath, only for it to gag in her throat.

The weight of guilt for now having pressed poor David for an answer crushed her from all sides, especially hearing the sorrow in his timid voice.

Suffering the loss of a father at such an early age was something she understood all too well. And like the nightmare to which she had awoken that morning that unleashed long-forgotten emotions, David's words again reignited the mournful memory of her own father's death.

Her interest in the golden-brown car evaporated in an instant, her focus now switched to the boy partially hidden behind the giant Cadbury mug.

David's head wilted, facing into his lap. To comfort him, she went to the couch and sat next to him, her mind grappling for consoling words. She wanted to offer assurance that all would be okay, while also not wishing to promise false hope. After her father had been killed, she'd spent the next two years shackled and imprisoned in solitude. She was just a child.

Those dark two years haunted her still. Undoubtedly, her firm sense of independence and untrusting nature stemmed from that lonely time.

Sometimes, the simplest words were the best. "I'm so sorry, David."

"Yeah," David sniffled. "Me too." He ran his sleeveless arm the full length under his nose from the crook of his elbow to the end of his pointed finger.

Theia jumped to her feet, quickly grabbing a tissue from the opposite side table and handing it to him. "Here, take this." As he wiped his nose, his eyes were seeking, finally planting themselves on something behind her. He leaned sideways for a better look.

Theia twisted her neck to see what had captured his attention.

In the room's corner stood a mannequin body garbed in the entire regalia of a Samurai Warrior, complete with weapons. Theia glanced back at David, who was in total awe, mouth open, eyes agaze. "You like that?" Theia asked, moving aside.

Without blinking, David slowly nodded.

"That is a very rare piece. Do you know what it is?"

David shook his head.

Theia strolled over to it and, as if presenting a history class, began lecturing, "During the Shogun era of Tokugawa, many women became Onna-Bugeisha—*female* warriors. They were ferocious fighters. Fearless. The most famous was Nakano Takeko who became a prominent leader." Theia's animated storytelling began to dwindle, her eyes drifting, her mind seeming to wander to an ancient memory. "She led a great army at only twenty-one years old."

Leaning against the armor was a long pole with a sword attached. Theia pointed to it. "The ko-naginata—slightly smaller than the o-naginata and used by women—was her weapon of choice. Many a soldier died by that blade."

By now, David had moseyed over to the mannequin. Barely touching, his fingers ran across the dulled steel armor. "Whoa! Was this hers? How is it here?"

Theia chuckled at his excitement. "Um no," she said, taking in the armor with great pride. "This belonged to another warrior." She winked at David. "*She* kicked some butt too, though!"

David's interest in her favorite piece had brought him out of his shell. At the very least, it had lightened the heavy mood she had mistakenly set. She bent forward, resting her hands on her knees, leveling her face with David's. As low as possible, she deepened her voice and with a ridiculously fake British accent likened to Oliver Twist, asked, "Shall I give you the grand tour, sir? There's so much to see and so much to learn."

David's face was beaming!

As promised, she threw herself into the task, escorting him around the room and showing the various artifacts. Stopping at each one, she provided a more than detailed account of their origin and history, relishing the trip down memory lane as much as he loved hearing it.

Soon, Theia had made her way to the coin wall, and most notably, the least interesting. Regurgitating their histories, she paid more attention to the framed coins than she did David. "And *these* coins date back to a period, even before…"

She turned to see if David was listening, only to find him gone.

"David? David?" she called out, but no response. After frantically searching every inch of the room, she ran into the empty hallway. "David, where are you?"

The bookshelf door to her secret room was wide open, and she gasped. Normally, she would close it when leaving, but in racing to rescue David from *Lurch,* she had completely forgotten. Probably too focused on the hot chocolate, she also hadn't noticed the door being open when she and David entered her apartment and walked right by it.

She charged in, then came to an abrupt stop.

To her relief, and annoyance, she found David standing in front of her pin-up wall at the far side of the room, his hand reaching to a page.

"David!" she scolded. "I'm sorry, this room is off-limits. Please, we need to leave."

David remained, his fingertips drawing over the double cross encircled with a red marker. Theia stormed from the door to escort him out. Nearing the window, she peered out, across the street.

"Oh, your mother's home." Her voice sounded less cross now. Her hand pressing against David's back, she steered him to the door. "Come on. Let's go say hi."

Theia opened her apartment door to leave but then hesitated. She looked into David's big brown eyes, scanning to his scuffed shoes and soccer ball, proudly propped under his arm. She tried to imagine how difficult it must be for a single mother to be raising a young boy in

New York City. Especially jobless. The vision of him gulping his hot chocolate as if it were his first weighed heavily.

Their cupboards surely must be bare.

Over her shoulder, she glanced across her hallway to the kitchen, pausing in thought.

"Hold on a sec, David. Okay?" She raced down the hall, raising her voice. "I'll be right back." A few minutes later, she returned carrying six plastic grocery bags, three in each hand.

"Phew!" she gasped. "Okay, *now* I'm ready. Let's go see your mom!"

CHAPTER 13

Mrs. Wilson's Christmas

Fifteen minutes earlier, Mrs. Wilson was on her way home from her latest interview. Her hair was drawn into a tight ponytail for *a more professional style*, item number seven from the online article, 'The Top Ten Best Interview Tips.'

Following the same advice, she also made the effort to sit straight, smile, and make good eye contact. Other than padding her experience, especially when they had asked about her silver service skills, which she planned on Googling the second she got home, her answers were concise and *mostly* accurate. However, keeping her hand gestures to a minimum was by far her biggest struggle.

It felt unnatural and robotic not to use them.

Not that any of this advice had made a blind bit of difference. Though they had not informed her of their decision, the awkward moment at the end along with their spurious expressions informed her she had blown it.

That's two interviews in three days, both dead ends.

The rent was taken care of, but eating for the next three days would be a struggle.

Knowing she had lost this job opportunity, she focused only on the positive, just as her son's psychiatrist preached during every visit. With two of the shifts requiring late evenings, it would never have worked anyway for a single mother. The loss would prove to be a blessing, no doubt.

Besides, she had an application in with Thompson's Grocery. They offered much better hours and were far closer, meaning more time spent with David. She'd also heard that employees there receive a discount on in-store purchases. *That* was something she could use.

Now turning the corner onto her street, she stretched her neck, searching for her son.

Before her interview, she had told him to get some exercise and to play outside with his ball. At the time, Marc had been there too, providing David with some much-needed interaction. Not finding him anywhere, she assumed he must have ignored that advice. No doubt she'd find him still kneeling in the living room playing with his action figures.

As she passed by a golden-brown car with a white top, she noticed a man sitting in the driver's seat. Although his face was shadowed by the daylight, she could still make out his outline, the burning end of a cigarette glowing red against the darkness of his face. Then a hand plucked it from his lips as he exhaled a cloud of black, silhouetted smoke. She walked on.

When Mrs. Wilson entered her apartment, she blindly announced she was home. There was no answer from David, though that was typical. First, she checked the living room—no David—then the bedroom, the bathroom, and the pavement below from the living room window, wondering if maybe she had walked right by, just not seeing him. But he was nowhere.

Just as her panic was setting in, a double rap sounded at the front door. *David has a key! He wouldn't knock*. Her panic escalated.

She scrambled to the door, yanking it open, the aggressiveness of her swing surprising the woman in her hallway. When she saw David standing next to her, she let out a gasp of relief, planting a hand over her heart. She cocked her head to one side. "Hey, where have you been, young man? I was getting a little worried. And why didn't you use your key? Come here. Let's see you."

The woman lugging what appeared to be groceries answered, "Hi, I'm Theia. That was my fault. I told him to knock. I'm sorry, I didn't want to barge in unannounced." Mrs. Wilson opened her mouth, but confusion held her tongue. Theia added, "I live across the street. David was just... he was playing and... anyway, I just wanted to make sure he got home safe."

"Oh." Mrs. Wilson smiled, still appearing a little confused. "Um, Thank you."

As best she could, Theia hoisted the heavy grocery bags in each hand.

"I think somebody delivered groceries to the wrong address. They were outside my door, and I couldn't find who they belonged to. I've been trying all morning and didn't want them going to waste. I thought maybe...?"

Mrs. Wilson hesitated, the offer sinking in. Offers sounding too good to be true often were. There was always a catch. But then she thought... *hallelujah!* The timing was perfect. Maybe her luck was changing after all. She moved aside to allow Theia in.

"Oh, sure. Thank you. Where are my manners? I'm sorry. Come in, come in." As Theia entered, Sheila ventured, "I'm David's mom, Sheila Wilson."

When Theia entered the living room, her first thought was how cramped it was, though it didn't take long before she felt more at home than in her own apartment. Surveying the room, her eyes paused on the unfamiliar things she wasn't accustomed to seeing.

The completed *Captain Universe* puzzle centered on a modest table by the window; the miniature set of action hero figurines neatly aligned into a battle formation on the floor for which only a young boy would have the patience; the child-sized, scuffed shoes removed by the front door; the soccer ball next to them; the size 'Sml' jacket haphazardly thrown onto the couch instead of hanging in its place. The evidence of a child absent from her townhome.

Something else rather odd was the green and gold tinsel wrapped around each of the windows.

The kitchenette was separated from the living room by a narrow countertop. After filling the kettle with fresh water and then camping it on the lit stove, Sheila immediately began to delve into her new harvest. "I should really try to find out whose these are," she mumbled aloud, examining every piece before deciding its place in her kitchen. "I'll store it for now just in case the owner shows up." She glanced at Theia. "Um, Tia, was it?"

"Theia, actually."

"*Theia*, that's a beautiful name. Well, Theia, can I get you anything? Coffee perhaps? Though we're completely out of milk. Sorry."

"Um…" Theia took a seat at the kitchen counter. "You might want to look inside one of those other bags. You never know, there might be a carton in there. But no thank you, I'm fine. As I said, I've asked through the neighborhood already and no one claimed them. So, I guess they're yours now."

While Sheila rustled the bags in search of milk, Theia asked, "So, David tells me you had a job interview today? How did that go?"

"He said I had an interview?" Sheila asked, snapping straight. "Well, that's fantastic news. He normally doesn't speak to strangers. I'm lucky if *I* can get a word. So, you're privileged." She sighed with relief. "Finally, we're making progress. About time too."

Returning to the bag, a look of surprise perked her face when she pulled out a half gallon of two percent milk, presenting it to Theia as would a salesperson from the shopping channel. "Yay! With a bit of luck, there might be some cereal for David in the morning."

"In that last bag…" Theia's pointed finger quickly withdrew into her fist. "Probably!"

"Oh, the interview," Sheila's voice went up an octave. "Yes, it went… it went… quite well actually." But then, halfway through emptying the last bag, she paused. Her shoulders dropped, her head shaking. "I'm sorry, Theia. I don't know why I lied to you just now. Honestly, it was a disaster. But there's always tomorrow, right?"

"I'm so sorry, Sheila. I'm sure you'll find another one soon. A better one."

Sheila lowered her eyes, squeezing out a miserable smile.

The kettle spat and squealed.

As Sheila slid it to the neighboring hob, she unexpectedly broke into a muffled sob. For a brief second, both hands covered her bowed face before she quickly regained her composure, wiping her eyes and blowing her nose on a tissue. Her face blotchy and shameful, she regarded Theia. "I'm sorry. I hardly know you. You must think I'm a right mess. I'm not usually this—"

"No, not at all. It's not easy raising a child…" Theia almost added, 'as a single mother,' but instead, left it short, her sentence sounding unfinished.

To Theia, hardship was no stranger either. Her life was very comfortable but it hadn't always been that way. Not for most of it, in fact. Nevertheless, as familiar as she was with disappointment and despair, the moment was still awkward.

Spying a framed family photo on the wall next to her, Theia leaned across the kitchen counter on her elbows. Standing shoulder to shoulder behind David was Sheila, and—she assumed—David's father. Half cropped in the background, a Ferris wheel towered skyward. David appeared younger. His face frecklier. A sky-blue furry hippo, almost as big as he was, scrunched between his tiny arms. The ridiculous smile rumpling his cheeks, laying bare his missing front teeth, appeared as if a second earlier someone had wailed, 'Say cheese!'

"That was a wonderful day," Sheila offered. "The Long Island Annual FunFest."

"Is that your husband?" Theia was careful not to phrase him in the past tense.

"Yes, um, it was. He died. It'll be two years this January. An accident at work."

"Oh my gosh, that's terrible." Though Theia hated to sound surprised when she wasn't, the sorrow in Sheila's voice made it easy. "What happened?"

"Ben worked the docks over in New Jersey as a forklift driver. He'd only been there about six months or so. Anyway, to cut labor costs, the company decided to downsize its workforce. For a while, we were worried about his job, but I guess they liked him 'cause they kept him on. We were so relieved. So happy they did." Sheila huffed in disgust. "It meant a lot of overtime, too; that was part of the deal to stay on. Sort of taking on part of another's workload. But it suited us. More money and he was young and healthy enough for extra hours. One afternoon though, minutes before his shift ended, a crane driver had fallen asleep, or so they say—we don't actually know for sure as he died as well. His load snagged with a smaller crane, a crawler I think they said it was, or something like that. The big one toppled first, pulling the smaller one with it. Ben could have gotten clear, as many others did, but instead, he chose to warn the others in its path."

Theia reached for her hand. "How awful. He was a brave man. A hero."

"He was. And not just to me and David. In my nightstand drawer, I have half a dozen letters from wives thanking me for what he did that day. Grateful for still having their husbands." Her tears of sadness morphed into tears of anger. Her tone seething. "You know, only two people died that day, all because of my Ben. You'd think that would merit some sort of compensation. But no. All I got was a crystal placard for his 'loyal and dedicated service' and an extra month of pay, which barely covered his funeral. When I took the matter further with management, they responded with a letter stating, and I quote, 'his death was not accidental'." She air-quoted the statement with her fingers. "Oh, and my favorite, 'he violated company policy by knowingly putting himself in danger.'"

"What? Surely, they can't get away with that. There must be something you can do. An appeal, perhaps. Or a lawyer?"

"Oh, I contacted a lawyer, and while he said we had a strong case, Chadwick & Stern is a mammoth company with top lawyers and a history of winning lawsuits. So…" She flailed her arms. "Here we are. No job and filling the cupboards with someone else's food."

"I'm so sorry, Sheila. I know how you must feel. I've suffered my own losses. And I wish I could say it gets easier, but…"

Appreciating the honesty, Sheila nodded, smiling.

"Well, I should be getting back," Theia added, eyeing her watch and then turning to David still kneeling on the floor, playing with his action figures. "Bye, David."

He waved a hand, flapping his fingers.

As she neared the front door she spotted a teeny Christmas tree on the hall table, not more than a foot tall. She hadn't noticed it coming in. It too was wrapped with metallic tinsel. She lowered an eyebrow. "If you don't mind me asking, Sheila: what's with the Christmas decorations? The tree and the tinsel around the windows? It's a little early, isn't it?"

"Our pockets are empty, but not our spirits!" Sheila announced as though it was a slogan she often used. Approaching Theia, she brought her voice to a whisper, "You see, it was only two weeks after Christmas when Ben died, and that previous year had been such a wonderful time for our family. Such joyful memories. Christmas reminds David of his dad." She peered lovingly through the doorway at him playing. "It's his favorite time of the year, you see. So," she vowed staunchly, "in the Wilson household, it's Christmas Day every day."

Theia fought back the tears, imitating a smile, her empathy welling; right then, she just wanted to leave lest she succumb to tears herself. "Right. Well. Nice to meet you. Bye, Sheila."

She let herself out.

CHAPTER 14

Just One More Thing...

Thursday Night.

When Theia opened her apartment door, she was struck by Matthew's warm, inviting eyes that seemed to pull her into the hallway. He looked disheveled in his green corduroys, woolen sweater, and a lusterless brown leather jacket that had seen better days. As he flattened his windswept curly hair, a pang of regret washed over her for not having fixed her own tangled mess.

"Hello again," Matthew said, fidgeting with his brown leather satchel. "Miss McDonald, wasn't it?"

Suppressing a laugh, Theia responded with equal wit, snapping her fingers and pointing at him. "And you must be Lieutenant Columbo if I'm not mistaken."

"Yes, ma'am," Matthew replied, one eye squinting and his voice deep and croaky. The likeness to Peter Falk, the actor who played the TV detective, was uncanny. "May I come in, ma'am? I have a few questions if you don't mind."

Theia stepped aside, continuing to play along with his detective act. "Come on in, Lieutenant. It's nice to see you again." She caught a whiff of his musky aftershave as he entered.

"I have to admit," Matthew confessed, his voice returning to its normal timbre, "I was surprised when Audree called me back, dropping this bombshell on me. It's quite a coincidence that *you're* the one involved in such an intriguing mystery."

Intriguing mystery? Theia cringed at whatever spurious yarn Audree must have spun to get him here. "Yes, well, shall we?" she said, leading him down the hall toward the living room.

As they entered, Audree sprang from the couch to greet their new guest. "Hellooo, I'm Audree. We talked on the phone."

"Right." Matthew nodded. "I recognize the accent. Nice to meet you." He shook her hand, removing his brown leather jacket and scarf in the process.

"Here, I'll take those," Theia kindly offered.

As she did, Audree stepped from Matthew's eyeshot, miming three distinct words to Theia. "He. Is. Hot!" She fanned her face.

Theia held back a smile, averting her gaze, aware of the blush creeping up her cheeks. "Can I get you anything, Matthew?"

"Um, do you have any bourbon?"

"Sorry, I should have said. All I have is water, white wine, or tea," Theia replied, feeling a little self-conscious. "I'm not used to entertaining. Not much of a liquor cabinet, is it?"

Matthew surveyed the room, his eyes darting from artifact to artifact. "Whoa!" he exclaimed, obviously impressed by her extraordinary collection.

"Oh, and I have milk too," Theia offered, just now recalling the half-pint kept on hand for her own tea. But then she instantly regretted the offer, realizing how childish it sounded.

Yet, to her surprise, Matthew accepted. Focused on her samurai warrior armor in the room's corner, his gaze slowly steered his body towards it. Too terrified to leave her valuables unattended, Theia's feet took her no farther than the kitchen door.

Nervously, she turned her eyes back inside the room, spying on Matthew's every action.

With a well-guided hand, he delicately rubbed the tunic's leather sleeve between his thumb and fingers, scrutinizing every detail. "Japanese. Eighteenth century, I'm guessing. From the style, I'd say Tokugawa Period."

When Matthew spoke to himself, Theia couldn't resist a small chuckle. She could tell he was truly passionate about history, and his professional handling and accurate account restored her confidence. At least, enough to race to the kitchen and pour a glass of milk.

By the time she returned, Matthew was already facing the south wall behind the couch. Both hands reaching, he cautiously lifted the Japanese sword from its wall mount. Theia opened her mouth but managed to hold her tongue. It killed her to remain silent, watching him bounce her precious sword in his hands as if taking a stab at the weight. Then, careful and painfully slow, he unsheathed the blade about six inches from its scabbard.

Audree, unaware Theia was standing behind her, chuckled. "Ooh, she ain't gonna be happy with you. I'm not even allowed to touch her sh—stuff."

Matthew continued his examination, unfazed. Eyeing the Japanese symbology etched into the steel, he pulled it closer to his face. "Oh wow," he said, recognizing the markings. "This is a Katana. Of the same period, I think. Extremely rare, and in such excellent condition." He began to unsheathe it further. "It's probably worth—"

"A lot!" Theia cautioned, before finally entering. "And it's extremely personal to me."

Handing Matthew his milk, she exchanged it for the sword.

"Thank you," Matthew said.

After returning the sword to its rightful place, Theia noticed Matthew now drifting toward something else, a silver and gold chalice perched on a floating shelf.

Seemingly entranced by it, he crossed the room with his gaze fixed, even placing his glass of milk down without ever breaking eye contact with the chalice.

By now, Theia felt as though shadowing a small child, wondering if she would have to call a time-out. *Decree the 'no touching rule.'*

Too late.

He was already reaching for the chalice but to her relief, stopped himself just inches from it.

"May I?" he asked, turning his head to Theia.

Though hesitant, she conceded a nod, reminding herself this was an interview of sorts. A test. *Let's see how he fares.*

Matthew cradled the chalice in both hands, examining it, rolling it, then flipping it over. He seemed to recognize it. Suspiciously, he eyed Theia. "Is this… this is a pagan chalice. This should be in a museum. It's probably… I'd say a thousand years old."

It was pagan, and he was close on the age too. *Quite impressive.* So far, Matthew was three-for-three, including his accurate account of the katana sword and the armor. But for Matthew, the real test was yet to come.

Carefully, Matthew placed the chalice back on its floating shelf. Underneath it, running along the wall, was a long side table. Displayed on top were several artifacts, each from various periods. He ambled the length, pausing on each piece.

Finally, he turned to Theia, his tone suspect. "You say you're a dentist? How on earth did you come by all this? These pieces are truly remarkable. And to see them all in one place." He pointed at the artifacts he'd already examined. "None of these are in any journal or any listing I've seen." His eyes continuing to flit between each piece, he raised his eyebrows, forming a shocking conclusion. "Are these… did you buy these on the black market?"

Theia found his innocence charming, chuckling. "I can assure you, Matthew, none of these items are stolen. They're… heirlooms."

"Heirlooms? But—"

"Yes."

"There would still be supporting records. So, how come I haven't heard of you?" He mumbled *McDormand* over and over, trying to place it. "With a collection like this, you should be… this should all be documented, cataloged. I'm… honestly, I'm stuck for words."

Theia approached Matthew, her eyes meeting his as she reached out to touch his shoulder. "Because I'm a very private person. I've gone through a lifetime of trouble to hold onto this collection, to keep it private. And Matthew, I'd like to keep it that way. Okay?"

"Yes, yes, of course. I understand. I'm very discrete."

Theia made her way back to the couch and sat. "So, Audree tells me you also specialize in… other areas?"

With an insatiable curiosity, Matthew was already pacing the row of artifacts, pressing his nose up to each one. "Yes. As I mentioned, I have my doctorate in history, of course, but um, I minored in theology. Plus, I have a special interest in some of the more—obscure religions and ancient cults."

Getting right to the point, Theia picked up a single page from the coffee table, extending it to him. "Then what can you tell me about this?"

Matthew approached and held the page up to the light.

His eyes immediately drew to the centered image.

The one circled in red.

In a single glance, he dismissively concluded, "It's just a double cross. Nothing unusual." He gestured to hand the page back, but Theia was not finished.

Instead, she leaned back, crossing her legs. "That's it? Nothing more? Just a double cross? Audree tells me you're an expert in symbology, cults, and religion. One of the most brilliant minds in the field. Please, Matthew, take another look. And this time, tell me exactly what you see."

CHAPTER 15

The Double Cross

Matthew sighed with disappointment, re-examining the page in his hand. When Audree had called him a week earlier, she'd hinted at a historical mystery passing unresolved. A mystery of ancient cults, of secret symbols, and clandestine men in black.

A story worthy of a Pulitzer. Flattering his ego, she'd also described how other historians had attempted to piece the puzzle but had failed at it.

To him, this was his opportunity to make a name for himself. To further his static career. To gain the notoriety and respect of his fellow historians. To say nothing of the advancement from the lowly assistant archivist room in the museum's basement to the spacious, well-appointed Head Curator's office on the first floor. But now, holding this single page in his hand, he wondered, was this the big mystery—a double cross? Hopefully not.

As trivial as the subject matter was, he brushed off the disappointment, studying the symbol in more detail. "Although it's quite common, its origins are somewhat of a mystery to be honest," Matthew remarked. He sat on the center couch, placing the page face up on the coffee table. The first detail he noted was that the double bars were not the same width.

That ruled out the Cross of Lorraine.

"See here." He pointed at the picture. Theia and Audree leaned in. "Notice how the top bar is narrower than the lower bar. That tells me it's more likely the Patriarchal cross, which is also referred to as the archiepiscopal Cross or less commonly, the Crux Gemina."

"Crux Gemina?" Theia asked.

"Yes, but not many relate to it as such."

A true history buff, Matthew's excitement grew with every word he spoke. "Some believe the shorter cross on top is where the Romans placed the sign with the initials INRI."

Iesvs Nazarenvs Rex Ivdaeorvm
'Jesus of Nazareth, King of the Jews.'

"Many scholars consider the Patriarchal cross a more accurate depiction of the crucifixion of Christ. More so than the customary Latin cross found in every Catholic church around the world."

"Go on," Theia asked, hanging on his every word.

"Another theory is that it denotes seniority in an archdiocese. The bars—single, double, triple—like the stripes on a military jacket." Referring again to the page of symbols, his finger underlined another cross, left of the one encircled. "Take this one here. The papal cross, for example, has three bars and is usually reserved for his most high."

"Jesus?" Audree spouted; her voice filled with enthusiasm.

"The Pope," Matthew corrected.

Theia slumped back on the couch, collapsing her hands in her lap. "So, it's just a Catholic cross? Nothing more?"

"Basically, yes." *What was she expecting?* Matthew wondered.

His curiosity piqued.

A genius he was, though it didn't take one to figure there was something more to this story than either of them were letting on. Given the limited information to go on, he was confident he had provided a thorough context of such a prosaic symbol.

"The double cross has been used as a symbol by several religious organizations," Matthew concluded, "including the Knights Templar and the Hospitaller of the Holy Spirit. As far as I can remember, all are associated with Catholicism. So, it's linked in a way."

There was a long silence before Audree spoke up tentatively, "What about the occult?" she asked, her voice low. "Could it belong to one of those organizations?"

Theia's shoulders tensed as she shot Audree a disapproving head shake, her eyes like daggers. Despite Theia's reaction, Audree's question hung in the air, all eyes turning to Matthew, waiting.

"The occult? Um, possibly. But I would think—doubtful. There is nothing I'm aware of, anyway. Why do you ask?"

Theia and Audree glanced at each other, rousing his suspicion further. A slow smile crept across Matthew's face. "Double crosses? Cults? What's this all about? If you give me more to play with, then maybe I can… I don't know, steer you in the right direction. Or maybe there are more specific questions you'd like to ask?"

Pressing her shoulders back, Theia straightened from her slouch, careful with her choice of words. "Can you think of a reason someone might have that symbol tattooed on their body? Their wrist, perhaps?"

A tattoo? Of a cross? Matthew frowned, giving a small chuckle. "Look, I'm no expert on tattoos per se, but hazarding a guess, I'd say a cross is the most common to have."

"Yes, but a *double* cross. Like that?" Theia eyed the page.

"Well, yeah." Matthew shrugged. "I mean, it's not as popular as, say, the Maltese Cross, but I wouldn't say it was unusual."

Theia shifted her gaze, another question forming. "Do you know of any specific groups or organizations using the double cross as a symbol *and* requiring their members to have it tattooed on their bodies?"

Again, acting as if the question was obvious, Matthew turned his palms upward. "Dozens of gangs and clubs in America have tattoo insignia, not to mention probably every native tribe on the planet. No doubt, many feature crosses in some form or another. But to pinpoint that exact design, I really couldn't say."

Theia huffed. It was clear she wasn't getting the answers she wanted. "Matthew. Professor." Her tone was sterner. "We need to narrow that list." Deep in thought, she hesitated, then shook her head.

Matthew could tell whatever she was about to ask, she was already regretting.

"This organization would have to be incredibly well structured, perhaps even on a global scale; all of its members brandishing that same tattoo insignia, and… having existed for a very, very long time." She squared her emerald eyes on his. "How many fit that bill?"

Matthew raised his brows, blowing out a long sigh. The specificity was more than he'd bargained for. "Um, probably not many. How many years are we talking here?"

"Hundreds… Millennia even."

Millenia? That shortens that list to about—zero.

Matthew thought hard. "Freemasons, possibly? Though technically only well documented since the seventeenth century, they originated in the time of King Solomon, which predates Christ by a thousand years or so."

"Do they require tattoos?"

Matthew stooped. "Um, no, I guess not." *Back to square one.*

Eyeing a collection of framed coins near the katana sword, Matthew stood, approaching them. They had no bearing on their conversation, but he couldn't help himself.

Admiring them, he stayed on topic.

"But, you know, there are dozens of organizations, perhaps hundreds, that have existed at one time or another, many secret, simply fading into history with little to no trace. Who knows if any required tattoos?"

With his back turned, Audree flailed her arms at Theia, whispering across the table, "Tell him! Tell him!"

Matthew spun his head, first at Audree, then Theia, his ears as sharp as his eyes. "Tell me what?"

Theia sprang to her feet, shooting Audree a frosty glare. Then she turned to Matthew with a courteous smile. "Thank you for sharing your time and information," she said. "Is there anything I owe you?"

Matthew's gaze flitted back and forth between the two women, torn between the allure of Theia's presence and the tantalizing mystery behind the double-cross tattoo. "If I had more to work with..." he began to explain.

Theia interrupted with a dismissive wave. "It's fine," she said. "You've been very helpful." Despite her cool composure, however, Matthew sensed a subtle hint of dissatisfaction in her voice.

"Listen, we have a database at the museum we use to cross-reference all kinds of symbols and artifacts. If you want, I can see if anything comes up."

"That would be great." Though Theia's tight smile sent the message that she was not expecting results. "But please, Matthew, don't put yourself in any trouble on my account. You've done enough as it is, for which I'm grateful."

"No trouble at all." He nodded his chin to his chest, mimicking dozing off. "It's literally what I do. All day, every day. Day in, day out!"

That at least gained him a chuckle.

She escorted him to the front door, where they bid their farewells. Just before the door closed behind him, Matthew turned back, doing his best impression of the famous detective Columbo. "Oh, ma'am, ma'am, just one more thing..." Theia pulled the door wider, her eyebrows lifting.

Matthew squinted. "Can I get your number, ma'am?" Mirroring the TV Columbo's actions, he patted down every pocket until he finally retrieved his phone. "Just in case I happen to find something."

Theia laughed. Even as she gave her number, she couldn't contain it. Matthew had Columbo down to a tee.

"Thank you, ma'am. Have a good night," Matthew replied, feeling a bit disappointed that the evening was ending so soon. But he hadn't come away empty-handed. Descending the marble staircase, he couldn't help but think, *who needs a Pulitzer when I have her number?*

When Theia returned to the living room, the telltale signs of Audree's hallmark disappointment were hard to miss; folded arms, pouted bottom lip, and a menacing frown.

"I don't want to hear it, Audree," Theia warned as she made her way to the couch.

"You should have told him," Audree persisted, referring to Theia's family history and the men who had been following her. "Don't you see it was an ideal opportunity?"

"Yeah right," Theia scoffed. "Because that doesn't make me sound crazy at all. Besides…" She caught herself, before accidentally revealing the real reason. Whenever people close to her got involved in her past, her real past, bad things tended to happen. To them.

"Besides what?"

"Never mind."

"You're doing it again!" Audree leaped to her feet. "How are you supposed to solve a puzzle when you're withholding all the pieces?" She sighed deeply. "Honestly, you're like a damn iceberg!"

Theia was just about to sit when she straightened sharply. "You're saying I'm cold-hearted?"

Audree's expression softened. "No sweetie. I'm saying, there's so much under the surface you haven't even shared with me yet. At some point, you have to take a chance and open up."

After a moment of pondering Audree's advice, Theia squared her eyes, inhaled a breath, and said, "I'm tired. I'm going to bed. I'll call you tomorrow."

She turned, leaving.

As she climbed the stairs to her bedroom, Audree shouted after her, "Okay! A conversation for another time then. Love you! But he was cute, right?"

Yes, that he was!

From the top of the stairs, Theia shouted back, "Night, Audree! I love you, too."

CHAPTER 16

Converging Parallels

Friday! Theia was fighting with New York City traffic again. And as usual, she was losing.

The traffic light changed from red to green, then again to red. Releasing the footbrake, she advanced a total of—ten feet. "Yip-a-dee-doo!" she droned sarcastically, each stretched syllable measuring her boredom.

Having left work much earlier than usual, she assumed she would have missed the Friday afternoon Lincoln Tunnel migration, avoiding the tourists who often flocked in early for the weekend shows. But no. Her fingers drummed impatiently on the steering wheel.

There better have been an accident or something.

Though she didn't actually mean that, she figured; if she was going to be stuck in traffic, an accident seemed an easier pill to swallow than hordes of tourists. Nevertheless, even clear sailing all the way home wouldn't have improved her mood.

All day, she had been playing devil's advocate with herself, mulling over the previous night's discussion, wondering if she should have divulged more to Matthew and Audree. *But how? How do you even begin to explain it?* It was her life, and she could hardly explain it to herself.

Not to mention the potential danger to which it would expose them, simply by knowing. It was a dilemma for sure, but safety always came first, even if it cost progress.

The traffic lights again danced their way through green and red. This time, she didn't move an inch. "Ugh!"

AT THE NORTH end of Theia's street on the opposite side of her apartment, a passenger door opened on a parked golden-brown car. From inside, a pair of pristine black brogue shoes stepped out onto the pavement. The pencil-thin man unfolded from the seat. At six feet four inches tall, he towered above the car's white leather roof. He ran a palm over his tightly gelled black hair as his squinted eyes canvassed the street for the all-clear.

Griffin leaned over from the driver's seat to the passenger side, waving a rolled-up magazine in his hand. He shouted through the open door, "DeRose! Don't forget this."

DeRose reached inside, snatching it, then tucking it safely inside his suit pocket.

"And remember," Griffin added, tapping his wristwatch. "She leaves work at four, so no messing around. In and out and back here. Got it?"

DeRose checked his own watch as he closed the door.

Piece of cake, he thought, then headed toward Theia's apartment. His suspicious eyes probed the street, occasionally checking behind him. Up ahead, he noticed a small boy playing with his ball on the pavement. To avoid being seen, he slipped in between the parked cars, crossing to the opposite side of the street, to Theia's side.

DeRose kept a watchful eye on the young boy. Drawing nearer to the townhouse, he recognized him; it was the same boy he had seen before, playing in the exact spot during his last visit.

He had even handed the kid his ball when it had rolled to his ankles. He remembered the lad taking great interest in his wrist tattoo. Not wanting to bring attention a second time, he bowed his head, scratching his temple to hide his face as he zipped inside the entrance.

Taking stock, he glanced around the vacant lobby. The floor indicators above the pair of stainless-steel elevators on his right remained steady on floors one and three. The U-shaped marble staircase ahead echoed with silence. Satisfied he would not be disturbed, he turned his attention to the row of galvanized steel mailboxes on his left.

From his trouser pocket, he produced a small keychain looped with various tools, keys, and lock picks. Remembering Theia's mailbox and its lock style, he chose the appropriate tool, picking the lock in under five seconds. Each time faster than the last. He reached in, pulled out the small bundle of mail, and sifted through it. Then, unrolling the magazine from his jacket pocket, he added it to the pile, returning them all inside.

After closing the mail door, he tried it, making sure it had locked.

Mission complete. *Easy!* Although it was a lot easier before—when they could mail it. Now she'd adopted a mail filtering service, and union mailmen were apparently immune to bribes, this was their only option.

Before returning to the car, he checked his watch again, casting a curious gaze at the empty staircase that ascended to Theia's apartment. *Hmm, maybe just a quick peek?*

He headed upstairs, his long, gangly legs clearing three steps at a time.

SOMEWHERE UNDER THE financial district, Theia's neighbor, Mr. Philips, was whooshing through the underground tunnels of the New York Subway system. He, too, had left work early that day, common for Wall Street on public holiday weekends. The yuppy financial execs would jet off to The Hamptons or The Catskills to their rural retreats. Mr. Philips, on the other hand, never ventured out. He probably would if asked, even though social settings unnerved him.

But no one ever invited him.

Instead, he would do what he always did; his routine.

He liked to read, take long walks, and as self-appointed chairperson of the neighborhood association, write complaints or petition for needless improvements.

The cramped train eased to a halt. When the doors slid open, only a handful of commuters filtered onto the platform, four to be precise, fewer than usual. Normally, he counted between eight and twelve at this stop, but only on Fridays. To his frustration, he was never able to accurately count the number boarding, though he guessed it had to be between twenty and thirty on average. Every night, his compulsion to stand and tally the heads was always superseded by his social affliction. Standing would move him closer to strangers and he much preferred his solitude at the edge of the bench. Guessing would have to do.

The automated P.A. chimed its tinny announcement. "This is Chamber Street Station. Please stand clear of the door. Next stop, Franklin Street." *Four more stops.* Then he would be at Christopher Street Station, in West Village. Home.

MRS. WILSON CONCLUDED her interview with Mr. Thompson. Even by her account, he was a short length of a man, only around five and a half feet and probably close to that around the waist. On the end of his nose perched small, round wire spectacles complementing his kind face that, although otherwise deathly pale, had blushed crimson cheeks.

His appearance and jolly demeanor reminded her of how a mall Santa must appear on the other three hundred and sixty-four days of the year, without his false beard.

Now, headed for the front entrance, he and Mrs. Wilson strolled along a busy aisle as they chatted about family. Mrs. Wilson could hardly contain herself.

At the door, they turned to face each other, shaking hands.

"It was a pleasure meeting you, Mrs. Wilson. We'll see you tomorrow. Ten sharp," Mr. Thompson said with a cheerful wink.

"Thank you, Mr. Thompson, thank you so much." Impulsively, she bestowed a tiny curtsy.

"Oh, oh, I almost forgot." Leaving her to ponder, Mr. Thompson ducked behind his counter. A moment later, he returned heaving a white grocery bag bulging at the sides. "We have the best fruit in the area. Better than those chain stores, you know. It's why people keep coming back."

As best he could, he hoisted the heavy bag with his stubby arms. "Go on, take it."

"Oh, I couldn't, Mr. Thompson, really. I mean there's so much."

"Now, now. You're not special, Mrs. Wilson. *Everyone* gets a bag of my famous fruit on their first day at Thompson's Groceries. And every Friday after."

Feeling like a child climbing off Santa's knee, and with a complimentary 'department store gift' no less, Mrs. Wilson skipped merrily from the store. Outside, she excitedly glanced inside the bag, the plastic straps already cutting into her fingers. Among the fruit was a smaller paper bag with its neck twisted closed. She untwisted it, spreading it apart.

To her delight, she found it filled with an assortment of chocolate and candies. She smiled. Only now did that answer the question as to why Mr. Thompson had been so inquisitive about the age of her son, his likes, his dislikes. Her heart warmed from his kindness. A kindness she was long overdue.

IN THE HALL, outside Theia's doorway, DeRose studied the lock—a Yale. He flicked through his picks for a suitable match. Then, with two hands, one for each pick, he jiggled the lock open. Before entering, he withdrew a device from his outer jacket pocket. About twice the size of a car remote, it resembled a small radio with a fixed antenna and single LED light.

After switching it on, he held it near the door and pressed the side button until the LED changed from flashing red to steady green. Only then did he enter Theia's apartment. As he closed the door behind him, he verified the status of the security keypad on the inside wall.

With the keypad still showing 'armed' and not beeping for a code, DeRose smiled proudly to himself. He then kissed the device before returning it to his pocket.

Never having been inside her apartment, he gathered his bearings. Directly in front, stretched a long hallway with a modern-styled wooden staircase floating on its left. Opposite, through a cased opening, appeared to be the living room. His eyes narrowed beyond the couch to the far side wall. It was hung with various artifacts and framed coins. He crept forward, paying no attention to the bookshelf on his right.

Entering the living room, he was captivated by an array of relics meticulously arranged on an adjacent wall table. Strolling alongside it, his fingers delicately traced the contours of each ancient object. Time slipped away.

AT LAST, A break! Theia thought. The flat-lined traffic on Ninth was finally showing signs of a pulse. As she inched past an intersection, she craned her neck toward two cars, each with their front ends smashed. One was being winched onto a truck bed. *Oh, no!* There *had* been an accident. A flutter of guilt hunched her head for her earlier impatience and cursing.

Reaching the next block, the cars accelerated freely. She breathed a sigh of relief. If the pace continued, she should soon be home.

CHAPTER 17

The Proverbial Carrot

When Matthew used the words 'timeless' and 'airy' to describe his tiny basement office at the Natural History Museum, he had never meant them as a compliment. Old and draughty just didn't seem to project the right image. His mother repeatedly advised, 'Always present the better part of yourself if you ever want to advance in life.' Advice, apparently, the whole world seemed to have adopted. Or at least, anyone with a social media account. Which was everybody.

But as Matthew sat at his double-pedestal desk staring into the abyss of his computer monitor, he wondered if those words were instead a curse. Now monogrammed into his mind, they were a constant reminder of the life he wanted but didn't have. And no matter how close he came to achieving it, the goal always seemed to advance *with* him. Like the proverbial carrot at the end of the stick—almost within arm's reach, yet never attainable.

A Chinese jade-green jar sat next to Matthew's monitor; it held his dozen pens and highlighters. Budding like headless flowers in a vase, they were the only source of color in his dreary office. Behind him, a bank of crooked wooden filing cabinets sagged, burdened by files collecting dust.

Apart from one or two pens, nothing in his office was close to new or updated, especially the furniture. So old, in fact, his squeaking chair and battered oak desk with misaligned drawers would stir more interest if exhibited upstairs on the museum floor. But old he could handle. After all, he was a history nerd. Depressing. Well, that was another matter.

For the umpteenth time, Matthew's forefinger bounced on his mouse wheel, which advanced yet another image of a double cross onto his screen.

The search field criterion was still highlighted: 'Patriarchal Cross.'

This was not his first search. He had also researched via his laptop on arriving home from Theia's the night before but accessing the museum's database remotely provided only restricted data. Plus, the digital archival records were completely off-bounds beyond the confines of the premises. And that was where Matthew wanted to focus his search. It cataloged every artifact the museum, or its sister museums, had ever owned or displayed, along with all the known history and expert findings. A lengthy inventory, but so far, nothing resonated.

The door to his office swung ajar, creaking on its rusted hinges. The curator leaned in. Nearing retirement years, the old man peeked over his half-rimmed glasses. "The shipping truck is here, Matthew. They're loading it now. How's the inventory report coming along?"

Matthew sat upright to attention, his eyes sparkling to life. A finger click minimized his screen to show a half-completed report, its flashing cursor still where he left it.

With a smile, he assured, "I'm just finishing it up now, Mr. Liebermann!"

CHAPTER 18

Golden-brown Lincoln

Nestled among the array of framed artifacts in Theia's apartment was a modern square clock void of any numerals or Roman symbols. Just simple, steel minute and second hands against a white background. At first, the time it displayed did not register but when it did, DeRose shoved out his fist to confirm with his wristwatch. He gasped.

Oh, crap!

Moving quickly, he carefully returned the carved wooden bowl to what he thought was its spot on the side table then made fine adjustments to its position, making sure it appeared undisturbed. He then spearheaded for the door. Remembering to use his special alarm jamming device before opening it, he snatched it from his pocket as he ran.

Clumsily, his spindly fingers lost grip. After a brief juggle between each hand, desperate in their attempt to catch it, it fell to the hardwood floor.

When it hit, the back flew off, spewing out both batteries.

DeRose dropped to his knees, scrambling to reassemble it, slotting each battery the correct way back into the spring-loaded chambers.

With the batteries reinstalled and the back cover clasped in place, he held a breath before testing it. Without it, he couldn't leave the apartment without triggering the alarm. When the LED lights lit up successfully, he exhaled a long breath of relief. Before climbing to his feet, a sliver of light caught his eye, leaking from beneath the bookshelf. He waved his hand, and the warming sunlight cast an orange glow on his fingers. Resting his weight on the bottom shelf of the bookcase, he placed his ear on the floor, straining to peer underneath.

Surprisingly, it rolled sideways under his hand. He froze, then cautiously jiggled the bookcase left and right, which rolled freely. "What the…" He scrambled to his feet, easing the bookcase open to reveal Theia's secret room. By now, the afternoon sun was angling its brilliance across the room, illuminating Theia's research like a hoard of golden treasure in a cave. The innumerable specks of suspended dust dancing in the light made the air almost opaque.

Wasting no time, he combed through the many documents and files strewn haphazardly over the center table. One file captured his attention immediately: *The Jorvik Files*. With his long arm, he reached to the middle to collect it. At first, he tugged at its tight magenta elastic band, then decided against removing it. There wasn't time. Instead, he flicked at the corners of the pages. *Maybe next time*, he thought. Placing the pile back to the center of the desk, he glimpsed the rear wall from the corner of his eye.

A pinboard on the leftmost wall.

He approached it, passing in front of the window. After randomly examining several handwritten notes and pages, his eyes focused on the lower corner to the page of symbols. The one with the double cross encircled in red. He unfurled the bottom of the page, leaning in to study it closely. At first, he frowned, but then after comparing it to his own tattoo partially hidden under his watch strap, he chuffed a half laugh.

His face straightened when he flipped over his wrist.

She had been due home five minutes ago; it was time to leave this place. As he darted by the window, he caught sight of the boy in the street just standing there, staring right at him. DeRose quickly sidestepped from the window, pressing his back against the pinboard. *Shit.* Perhaps he hadn't seen him? He wanted to wait before testing that theory, but time was pressing.

Carefully, he peeked an eye past the window frame. By now, the boy had collected his ball under his arm and was heading toward the building, still staring up.

Shit. Shit. Shit.

They were supposed to be invisible. In and out. Deliver the magazine as usual. That was the plan. That had *always* been the plan. Sure, breaking into her apartment had been discussed, but always deemed too risky, it had never been sanctioned.

DeRose watched as the boy slipped gracefully between parked cars, coming to a stop smack dead in the middle of the road, never once taking his eye off the window—or him.

From this angle, DeRose could also see their vehicle, the golden-brown Lincoln, farther up the street. Griffin's head poked from the open window. His focus too, was on the boy, probably wondering why he was so riveted on the window of Theia's apartment.

DeRose dialed his phone as he beelined for the door. "Hey, I'm on my way out. Listen, there's been a change of plan. Yeah, yeah, I know, that's why I'm calling. I need you to do something. And Griffin, you're not gonna like it."

MRS. WILSON WAS humming to herself when she cornered the pavement onto their street. Although she hadn't expected to find David playing outside, she stretched her neck to look for him.

In case he arrived home first, she had left him a note explaining about the impromptu interview with Mr. Thompson. Also, with the weather as beautiful as it was, she mandated that he should play with his ball outside and wait for her. At first, she assumed he had not taken her advice but then, exactly where he should not be, she spotted him—in the middle of the road.

I've told him a thousand times to stay on the pavement.

As she quickened her step, she saw David staring. Her eyes followed beyond the parked cars and streetlamps to the opposite pavement. Ominously looming, a tall man fixed on her son. Perhaps it was her motherly instinct, but even from this distance, she could sense David's fear.

"David?" she cried out as she hurried her step. "David? Get off the road!"

The angry growl of an engine revved loudly behind her, followed by screeching tires and the acrid stench of burning rubber. Before she could react, a flash of golden-brown hurtled past.

"David!" she screamed, her blood turning to ice.

She dropped her purse and groceries and ran. Apples and oranges bowled in every direction. A parked SUV with tinted windows blocked her view, sending her into sheer panic. The car screeched again, its tires skidding. *No!*

She darted between the parked cars and onto the road, catching a fleeting glimpse of the rear door slamming shut. The wheels spun furiously, kicking up a cloud of white smoke that hung in the air like a ghostly apparition.

In a desperate sprint, she chased after the car. But her David was gone, leaving only scorched tire marks in its wake. Amidst the eerie silence, David's soccer ball rolled to her feet, as if racing to its mother to recount a tragic tale.

Falling to her knees, she extended open hands; a futile effort to reach for the fading car. She sobbed uncontrollably.

A tall man in a dark suit dashed from the pavement. Reaching her side, he dropped to his knee, his face, a canvas of pure white. Though a stranger, she instinctively grabbed his hand. Locking hopeless eyes with his, she bawled. Her words hiccupped, sharp inhales interrupting each crying syllable.

"My Da-vid. My… Da-vid. They… took my Da-vid."

"I-I saw," Mr. Philips stuttered. "I was just coming home f-from work, and …"

Sheila wept into his shoulder as he offered a fragile embraced.

Thumbing his phone, he raised it to his ear. "Um, police. Get me the police. There's been a kidnapping."

At the end of the street, she watched as the golden-brown car turned a corner, vanishing along with her child.

CHAPTER 19

The Witness Report

Turning into her street, Theia's jaw dropped wide at the unfolding mayhem. Silencing the radio, she leaned over the steering wheel, pressing her face close behind the glass. "No, no, no, no!" Her volume increased with every word, an unease rearing in the depths of her stomach. Somehow, she knew the commotion ahead was related to her.

The stationary cars in front had brought hers to a standstill. Unable to make any further headway, she exited her car leaving the engine running. Without closing her door, she sprinted past the gridlocked vehicles toward the emergency lights flashing ahead.

Mid-way there, she was met head-on by a female police officer whose job it was to barricade her and everyone else from the scene. "Ma'am, ma'am," the officer warned as both hands thrust out, signaling Theia to stop. "Please, ma'am, it's a restricted area."

"I live here," Theia shrieked. She pointed over the officer's shoulder, trying to duck past. "That's my apartment. What's going on? What happened?"

Theia darted side to side, the insistent officer mirroring her every movement, blocking any attempt to pass. "Ma'am, I need you to calm down."

But Theia was determined. Light on her toes, she lunged forward, swiftly dodging past the officer, who, unable to grab her from behind, could only yell, "Ma'am stop, please."

Theia sprinted toward the ambulance.

Within seconds, Theia was at the center of the chaos, spinning in a circle, trying to unravel the scene. Police officers were everywhere. Over the crowd's collective murmuring, the squelches and beeps and indistinguishable scratchy chatter belched from the emergency personnel's radios.

On the sidewalk, she recognized a few of her neighbors, some being interviewed. One was Mr. Philips who appeared to be giving a statement. And then, at the foot of the ambulance, through a semi-circle wall of paramedics and police, she glimpsed Mrs. Wilson.

Red-faced and teary, she sat with her feet dangling from the rear of the ambulance. She huddled into a blue blanket as questions fired from all sides.

To Theia, she looked like a lost child fearful of the world around her.

Theia shoved through a paramedic. "Mrs. Wilson, what happened? Are you all right?"

Immediately, Mrs. Wilson threw off her blanket, flinging her arms around Theia, sobbing.

Having only met once, Theia assumed hers must be the first friendly face Mrs. Wilson had seen. Theia hugged her tightly, patting her shoulder.

"It's okay, Sheila. There, there now." Her hand now rubbed the back of Mrs. Wilson's head as it rested against Theia's shoulder. "What happened? What's this all about?"

Through the sniffles and crying, Sheila whimpered, "My boy. They took my boy."

Theia's voice caught, a gasp escaping her as she uttered, "David?" She pushed Sheila back by her shoulders. "*Who* took him, Sheila? What happened?"

But Sheila just shook her head. Tears came harder. Words barely distinguishable, she squeaked, "I don't know," then collapsed her head back onto Theia's shoulder.

Theia gazed ahead, adrift in a torrent of thoughts. Her gut told her who took him. It was *them*. Had to be.

This time, they had crossed the line. *They are going to pay for this.* But, after years of searching for their identity in vain, she couldn't help but wonder, how would she ever find them?

Nothing much had changed with the onset of the night except for the emergency lights which seemed to strobe brighter, flashing their frenetic kaleidoscope of reds and blues against the polished cars and darkened building façade. Prying spectators had also gathered, forming a long line along the yellow ribbon barrier. Detectives had been and gone. So too the FBI—standard protocol for child kidnappings, all asking the same questions phrased a dozen ways.

Theia sat alone on the third step to her townhome entrance. Weighted with worry, her head sank heavily into her hands.

Mr. Philips took a seat next to her, for a moment, just sitting. At one point, he even tried placing a comforting arm around her shoulder, but lacking social confidence, patted it with his fingertips instead. "Are you okay, Miss McDormand?"

Theia's hands stayed firmly planted on her forehead, eyes burning into the pavement between her feet. "I just don't understand," she whimpered. "He's just a little boy. Why would they take him? Why? What use is he to them?"

Theia had quizzed Sheila with similar questions but with the boy's mother too distraught to provide any detail, all she had managed to learn was that David had been snatched by a tall stranger in a car. With little to go on, she couldn't help recalling the haunting images of the thousands of 'missing child' posters attached to lampposts and trees around the city.

The six o'clock news, almost nightly, reported yet another child abduction, child missing, child lost. And how often were they ever found? Unfortunately, that answer she knew.

The statistics were not good.

"It's a terrible affair." Mr. Philips shook his head with revolt. "Shocking. There was nothing I could do, you understand. It all happened so fast. But don't worry." His shaking head switched to nodding. "I have a photographic memory. I gave the police a very clear description. They'll find him."

Theia's head jerked from her hands, her eyes leveling on his. "You saw them? Who were they? How many? What did they look like? What kind of car were they driving?"

Mr. Philips leaned away, the sudden pressure to recall quickly making him skittish. "Um, um, two, there were two, um and, and um, they had a... golden-brown, um, 1978 Lincoln Mark V... definitely a Mark V, with a white leather rear roof."

Theia gasped. The description matched the one she had seen with the ominous figure inside; the one she now knew had been watching her.

Mr. Philips paused. He seemed troubled. "I um, did find it odd though."

"What? What was odd?"

"The man who took him wouldn't be your everyday kidnapper. Well, I doubt it."

"How do you know?"

"The suit. Most odd. Made from fine cashmere, exquisitely styled, masterful bespoke tailoring. One of the finest I've seen, even for New York. Savile Row, probably. *Very* expensive. And then, to be driving a car like that, an old junker, and snatching children in broad daylight; most odd. Most odd indeed." Comfortingly, he patted the back of Theia's hand. "But like I said, try not to worry; the police will handle it. Besides..." The last part he boasted proudly. "I got the license plate too!"

Theia sprang to her feet, spinning on her heels, wearing a glare enough to freeze a furnace. "You need to tell me *every* detail... NOW!"

CHAPTER 20

The Decision

An hour or so later, Theia sat trembling on the edge of her couch. The front door burst open and then slammed shut. Audree charged into the room, wheezing from her run.

"Oh, my God, Theia! I came as fast as I could."

Without slowing, she rushed across the room, parking her purse and coat on the first table she passed. She plonked herself next to Theia who was adrift in a solemn gaze. She touched her friend's shoulder, her voice tender. "Are you okay, babe?"

Theia leaned her head, resting it on Audree's chest.

Audree wrapped her in her arms and rocked back and forth. She kissed the top of Theia's head. "It's gonna be all right, hun. Just you see."

The comfort brought Theia to a flood of tears. "My God, Audree," she sniveled, "this is all my fault."

"No. None of this is your fault. Kidnappings happen all the time. Don't put this on yourself. No, ma'am," They hugged silently for a moment. "I tell you what," Audree suggested. "I'll make us a nice cuppa, just the way you like it. Then you can fill me in on all the details. Okay, sugarplum?"

As Audree headed to the kitchen, she glanced back. "Four sugars, right?"

Theia's brows creased into a perplexed look.

Audree winked. "I'm just testing ya. Don't worry, missy. I've gotcha covered!"

Theia's face formed the beginning of a smile. Audree could always lighten the mood and lift Theia from her melancholy. For somber situations such as these, she was perfect company.

She really couldn't wish for a better friend.

In the kitchen, as the kettle warmed, hissing and gurgling like an idling locomotive, Audree opened cupboard after cupboard searching for the tea, sugar, and cups. She realized in all the years she had known Theia, she'd never once made her tea, the ritual was always her own.

Lying on top of the island counter were two stacks of mail beside Theia's car keys. The magazine cover on top of the first pile pictured a smiling Asian woman in a starched white coat. It was titled, 'Dentistry Today—The Patient Perspective.'

Judging from the adhered address label, it had been mailed to Theia's dentistry office.

Whether from boredom or curiosity, she picked it up. After a momentary scan of the unappealing cover, she swiftly returned it to its pile. The next pile was Theia's personal mail. It too had a stack of magazines; the uppermost one was turned around from her angle. She spun it the right way up and then picked it up. Unlike the other magazine, this one had no address label affixed and the corners were curled up as if it had been rolled.

On the front cover was a photograph of a debonair Englishman, nobly displayed in front of his rural English castle. The cover line asked, 'What's Next for Britain's Most Charismatic Englishman?' With equal loss of interest, and with the kettle now steaming a whistle, she flung it back to its pile.

A while later, Theia and Audree sat diagonally from one another on the U-shaped couch. Theia finished the last drop of her tea and placed her mug on the coffee table. Audree collapsed back into the plush couch, her puckered lips releasing a long, deflated breath. Her eyes stared into space.

"Okay, so you think the two men who grabbed David are the same men who've been following you... because they were wearing suits?" Audree's words aired an obvious tone of skepticism. "And that's all you've got?"

"There has to be a connection," Theia reiterated. "How many kidnappings occur from two men wearing expensive business suits?" Theia threw her hands in the air as if any such idea was absurd. "It just doesn't fit. Besides, I know..." She reworded her sentence. "I *feel* something is off."

Audree shook her head, appearing unconvinced. "I don't know, Theia. There are all manner of people who snatch kids, for any number of reasons." She reached across from the corner of the couch and placed her hand on Theia's, resting in her lap. "Honey, I think you're a mess right now. Ever since that run-in with the *tattoo guy,* you've been adding two plus two and coming up with five thousand. I get it, but you have to stop. It's taking over your life."

Theia's body straightened from her slouch, the edges of her eyebrows dropping, framing her pitiful eyes. "You have to believe me." Right now, she *needed* Audree to believe her.

Audree squeezed Theia's hand and leaned close. "Of course. I believe that *you* believe it. But listen, girl. How many times have you told me you felt your life was threatened—endangered—by these mysterious men in dark suits? And on any of those occasions, were you ever harmed in any way? Any way at all? No. Any other friend would simply think you were paranoid or..." She shook Theia's hand from side to side. "Or they'd think you were crazy! But I don't. And I get that your life is built around mystery, which," she said reassuringly, "we will get to the bottom of, one day. But this whole kidnapping thing? I mean... why a neighbor's child that you barely know? Why not you? Why now? I'm just not seeing the connection."

Tears built in Theia's eyes.

She had listened to every word, and they'd made perfect sense. Any other friend would have had her committed by now. But without Audree in her corner, without her support, she knew she would fail. If they were ever to find David again, she was going to need her help.

"Audree, you're right. And I'm grateful for you standing by me." She sniveled. "And I know I haven't told you everything; I *am* sorry for that. But I promise, I *will* tell you. Everything. But for now, just listen to me. I need to explain something, so you *don't* think I'm crazy."

Theia's head bowed, her mind forming the words. "I have this ability, a sixth sense if you will. Like a gut instinct, but it's much more than that. The best way to describe it is… I can read your thoughts but without any words; your emotions, intentions, your… I don't know. It's hard to explain." She squared her eyes on Audree. "But Audree, as hard as it is for me, please believe me when I say: this business with David, his kidnapping, *is* because of me." Stricken with guilt, Theia broke into another sob.

Audree quickly slid to her knees in front of Theia and pulled her face cheek to cheek. Theia whimpered in her ear, "Please believe me, Audree. Please."

"Hey! I believe you, hun. I believe you. I'm sorry." After a few moments of gentle swaying, Audree sat back on her heels. Influenced by her friend's encouraging plea, she spoke resolutely, "Okay, sugarplum, you're the brains. How do we get David back? What can I do to help?"

Theia reached to the lamp table for a Post-it Note with writing on it, handing it to Audree. "Can you please give this to Bill and have him look into it? It's the license plate number and description of the vehicle." Audree quietly examined it in her hand while Theia reached for her purse. "Of course, I'll pay him for his time," she said as she withdrew some cash.

Audree swiftly pushed Theia's hand back into her purse. "Don't be silly. What do you take me for? Anyway, he may not be New York's finest private dick, but he loves me, and he'll do anything for me.

Besides, Bill hates anyone who harms kids. He'll be all over this case. Trust me."

"Thank you, Audree. You're a good friend."

Audree chuckled. "What's this *good* crap. Girl, I'm your bestie." But Audree's face turned serious. "If this *is* all related, if these men who are stalking you *are* involved with David's kidnapping, then I think it's time we had another little chat with our friend, the professor. We need to figure out what the connection is and to do that, you'll need to tell him everything. And Theia, I mean *everything!*"

"Okay." Theia wiped the tears from her cheek. "I'm ready."

"All righty. I'll call him first thing in the morning, see if we can—"

"No!" Theia blurted. "Call him now. Tonight."

CHAPTER 21

Proof

The decision to not wait for the elevator may have saved time but the three-story climb had Matthew gasping for air. He rapped his knuckles against the enameled black door, nursing the stitch in his side. A moment later, the door swung open.

During the cab ride to Theia's apartment, he had replayed the conversation with Audree over and over in his head. The word 'emergency' and the inflection of urgency in her voice had sent him racing for his jacket and shoes. But with time to think, he wondered how serious this actually was.

Theia was wealthy, and from his experience, wealthy people's scale of urgency was drastically different from that of the humble layperson. For all he knew, she had lost her car keys. Or broken a fingernail. But now, standing in the hall across from Audree, he could see from her alarmingly grave expression it was indeed serious.

"Thank you for coming, Professor," Audree said in a low monotone voice. "I know it's late. Please, come in."

Matthew stepped in ahead of Audree and then trailed her to the living room. The overhead floodlights were off this time, only the four large corner lamps around the centered couch gelling their warm glow that lured him like a crackling campfire on a frosty night. The shadows in the room reminded him of the History Museum after hours. Free from the crowded public, the eerie dark halls, meagerly lit, produced ominous silhouettes from the figures and statues appearing to huddle in its corners. Tonight, he sensed that same eeriness.

"I came straight over. What happened?" Matthew said, removing his jacket and scarf.

Theia sat poised in the center of the couch, her back erect, hands resting on her knees. Directly in front of her, upon the coffee table, lay the unsheathed Japanese sword and its scabbard, resting parallel on a white cloth towel as if on display. Theia's eyes locked onto its polished steel. Not even Matthew's entrance or his question had broken her gaze from it.

Audree pointed to the couch opposite Theia. "Please Professor, take a seat."

As Matthew settled onto the couch, the cozy campfire atmosphere gave way to something more sinister, as if ghost stories were being shared.

Judging from Theia's glum appearance, he somehow knew hers would be next.

"Matthew," Theia said, her eyes remaining fixed on the blade. "If you were told a story, a story so incredible it defied everyday belief, would you simply dismiss it or try to understand?"

The question and the sad, almost disturbing, tone of delivery surprised him. If there *was* an emergency, she behaved unusually calm for one. "I'm not a man of faith," he said. "More a man of science. I guess for me, I would need some kind of proof. Evidence if you like."

"Yes," Theia said, sounding disappointed with his answer. "That's what I thought you'd say."

The prolonged silence that followed made Matthew uneasy. "Is someone going to tell me what's going on?" He glanced over to Audree and then back again to Theia.

Theia reached for the sword. One hand gripped the hilt, the other supporting the flat of the glistening blade, gently coddling its length in her open palm.

"Did you know, Matthew, that Japanese steel used to be inferior to the West? Earlier swords were notorious for breaking in battle or they would dull from their first cut. To compensate for the impurities, bladesmiths learned to fold the steel thousands of times to strengthen it. A dubious process and an art form unrivaled, even today. The result was this. The perfect blade, strong yet malleable, with a razor edge not even time could fade."

Her flattened fingers slowly folded around the blade.

"Careful," Matthew cautioned, inching to the edge of his seat.

Theia clenched her eyes and inhaled a deep breath through her nose. Then, to Matthew's astonishment, she jerked her hand along the blade, her whole body flinching from the pain.

Matthew's voice filled with alarm. "No, Theia! What are you doing?"

In an instant, he leaped from the couch, soon followed by Audree who screamed in panic. Eyeing the blood now dripping from Theia's fist, Matthew grabbed the edge of the white towel and yanked it so fast from the table that the scabbard on top barely moved. He pressed it into Theia's palm, then fashioned a tourniquet around her hand. Audree continued to rant as she paced behind him.

"I'll take that," Matthew said, prying the hilt from Theia's other grip and placing it carefully onto the coffee table. Blood dripped from the blade. Thinking fast, he asked Theia, who sat misty-eyed, "D'you have a first aid kit? A bandage? Anything? I need to stem the flow. Theia?"

Theia shook her head.

Matthew turned to Audree. "Do you have a car? We'll need to get her to a hospital."

"Yes, um, no. Not here. I cabbed over. We can use hers. Hun, where's your keys?"

"I don't need a hospital, Audree. I'm fine," Theia said calmly.

"Fine?" Audree screeched, her hand burnishing her forehead, the other propped on her hip. "Look at all that blood. Hun, you're gonna need stitches. A lot of 'em. What the hell were you thinking?" She nervously patted Matthew's shoulder. "How deep is it? Take a look."

Matthew was reluctant. The sight of blood turned his stomach. But egged on by a nod from Theia, he carefully unraveled the blood-soaked towel. As her fingers unfolded, he skewed his head away in anticipation, as if viewing the sliced flesh from an angle would be somehow less nauseating.

What he discovered, however, was not a gushing wound, but a dark red line spanning Theia's hand. "W-what? It can't be." Not believing his eyes, Matthew dabbed at the wound, clearing away the residual blood. In a matter of seconds, the wound healed completely. Other than the blood, no evidence of a cut remained. He rounded his eyes on Theia's, his mouth falling slack. Behind him, Audree flustered and babbled. Her noises ceased when she too looked on in awe.

"Will you believe my story now, Matthew?" Theia asked.

CHAPTER 22

The Reginleifs

The miracle Matthew and Audree had just witnessed fetched a reverent silence. Theia wiped down her blade, and Matthew and Audree returned to the opposite couch.

"What I am about to tell you," Theia said, as she gently slid the mirror-like blade into its scabbard, "may place you both in terrible danger."

They looked at one another. Audree nodded as if to say, *yes, I accept that*. Matthew simply said, "All right. We'll cross that bridge when we come to it. *If* we come to it."

Theia looked calmer now, a weight taken from her. Finally, someone was listening.

Matthew made himself comfortable. "How about you start from the beginning?"

"The beginning?" Theia murmured, then stood and wandered around the couch to the mannequin. She gazed upon her Samurai Warrior armor, caressing the shoulder with the back of her hand. "There have been so many beginnings, I've lost count. I suppose I will begin from where it first began for me. Although it was a very long time ago, I remember it like it was yesterday..."

"My name is Theia Damaris Cassia Reginleif. I was born in England in the year of our Lord 873, in the small hamlet of Ulleskelf, a peaceful parish on the River Wharfe, just north of the great city of Jorvik, now known as York."

Closing her eyes, Theia was instantly transported back to a time almost twelve hundred years ago, every detail real. Every sound of the clucking hens, of the wooden cartwheels trundling under saddling loads of hay and harvest, echoed in her ears. Even the stench of livestock and trodden horse manure, which masked the sweet aroma of fruit stalls and pots of honey mead, scented her nose.

As Theia narrated her story, her American accent became intertwined with the melodic Yorkshire accent—to that of old Northern England.

"My father was born in Norway, becoming a typical fisherman, like his father, and like his father before him, until his king made him a soldier in a great seafaring army for the Viking invasion of Britain in 865. Then, after five long, loyal years of his service to the crown, he was released from his duty and given land. Being only a fisherman or a warrior, my father knew nothing of farming land. Until he met a Jorvik maiden.

"A local girl, born a farmer's daughter, she taught him how to sow the land and harvest crops. It was a hard life, but they were happy." Theia smiled, her eyes still closed.

"He always insisted she was the most beautiful woman who had ever lived. And quite remarkable. More courageous than ten Viking drengrs and incredibly strong for her tiny frame." Theia's smile withered. "But as it seems, not strong enough to survive childbirth." She paused in thought then opened her eyes. Although the mannequin stood before her, she gazed right through it, her mind still forming the images of her past. Both Matthew and Audree sat engrossed.

"Men in those days would usually betroth another wife for companionship, and to cook and raise children. But my father never did."

She sauntered past the vaulted windows to the opposite wall table spanning the entire width of the room. "Being raised then wasn't anything like it is today. As soon as you could walk, you were put to work. That's just the way it was. But my father taught me many things: how to fight, farm, hunt. The keys to survival. By the time I was ten, I could speak four languages!" She chuckled.

"I can still remember my tenth birthday. It was more special than all the others. We didn't have birthday parties, cakes, or presents. No, nothing like that. A birthday then meant a trip to the village, and *oh* what a treat that was." As she continued to stroll along the walls of her room, Matthew and Audree twisted on their seats to follow her.

Not once did they glance at each other as if to question what they were hearing.

"Although it was a small village, it was hustling and bustling with crowds, cattle, and tradesmen. So much more to explore for a humble farm girl who had grown up in near solitude, knowing only her father."

Facing the wall, she came to a stop. With one hand, she reached and lifted from its nail a tiny box frame measuring only four inches square and roughly one inch deep. Inside was a dark wooden necklace engraved with a symbol. She ran her fingers down the glass, her eyes twinkling.

"It was the day I first saw him. Asma was his name."

Once again, she closed her eyes, her mind exploding with vivid memories so real her heart raced as if experiencing them for the first time.

A dark-haired boy mischievously dodged through the muddy streets engorged with a complex arrangement of traders' stalls and farmers. Narrowly, he avoided running into something or someone at every turn, only to stop dead in his tracks when he almost collided head-on with Theia.

The image was so real that Theia stepped back as if trying to avoid the boy.

"Asmodeus De Atta," she announced, his name rolling off her tongue with a long unspoken medieval dialect. A nostalgic smile spread across her face, her hand shifting over her heart. "I don't think I've ever spoken his name aloud, at least not in a thousand years. He was almost twelve, and I…" She paused. "I was quite taken by him. My father would forbid us to play together but we always found a way." She shrugged mischievously.

Behind her eyelids, her eyes flitted.

The following summer, Asma and Theia chased each other near the town's outskirts. There, they fell into a pile of loose hay, giggling, finally catching their breaths.

Asma brought Theia to her feet, then untied a necklace he wore. Although simple, she could see it had been delicately constructed, finished with care. Made from dark wood and leather string, it had a blue lightning bolt symbol engraved inside a circle in the middle of its face. Asma tied it around her neck. Flattered, she rolled it between her fingers.

Theia pulled the small frame with the tarnished necklace inside tight against her chest.

Asma gazed amorously into her eyes, and then quickly pecked a kiss on her cheek. He turned and ran away, leaving Theia standing, blushing and smiling.

"Asma was all I knew outside of the farm and soon, he became my entire world. All I could think about was him. We planned to marry on my fifteenth birthday, but alas, it was never to be."

Theia's memory was transported to four years later.

Her soft smile faded along with her color. Her body twitched as she relived the nightmare.

The thunderous clouds rumbled overhead as the stampede of horses trampled through the village, knocking fleeing people to the ground. Footmen soon followed, yielding swords and axes. They savaged the local villagers who were defenseless against them.

An innocent woman carrying a basket filled with fruit became surrounded by horsemen. They mocked her as she stood screaming. Another woman cradling her small child scurried for cover, helped by her protective yet powerless husband.

"Years of peace were finally broken, and religious uprisings began between the pagans and Christians. I was only fourteen when they came."

Theia's father placed her behind the wheel of a horse cart and moved his finger to his lips, signaling her to be quiet.

Reliving her past, Theia reached her hand into the empty space of her living room. She whispered, "Fader!" as a tear welled in her eye.

With a single blow from his foot, her father splintered a three-rung wooden step leaning against the back of the cart. From the fragmented pile, he salvaged the largest piece, dragging it behind him like a caveman yielding his club.

Theia watched as he fearlessly charged the oncoming wave of barbarians, flailing his stick. They were no match for his sheer size and strength as he took them down one by one. But the numbers were too many; soon, he became surrounded until Theia finally lost sight of him.

All she could see was the barbarians raising and lowering their swords as they stood encircling. She would never see her father again.

Too terrified to cry, her fearful gaze searched to the other end of the street for Asma. Before long, she spotted him hiding under a cart diagonally opposite, signaling her to remain low and out of sight. But Theia yearned to be with him, just as any young girl would yearn for the comforting embrace of her beloved.

She made a break for it. As she ran, a horseman charged behind her and pulled an axe from his back pouch, which he hurled, striking her directly between the shoulders and knocking her violently into the mud. However excruciating, she still managed to lift her head, her hand reaching for Asma in the distance.

Asma screamed her name like a battle cry and launched to his feet. As he plunged through the quagmire toward her, a bowman released his arrow. It pierced Asma's back, sending him crashing to the earth just meters from reaching her. Unwavering, he crawled to his feet. But as soon as he staggered one more step, another arrow struck his back, dropping him to his knees. The third arrow sealed his fate and silenced his cry for Theia.

His head slumped to the ground, splashing face-first into the trampled mud.
"They destroyed everything. Asma tried to save me but they—"

The painful memory, too harsh to bear, she turned her head sharply to the side and squinched her eyes tight. "I thought I'd die too, but sadly… no."

Despite her grave injuries, she miraculously crawled to Asma's side, where she sobbed over his lifeless body.

Several of the invaders had gathered as interest in Theia grew. She should be dead. Their leader trotted closer on his mottled black Destrier horse, holstering his long sword in a scabbard on the side of his saddle. He reached for Theia with his strong arm and strung her over his horse's neck, the axe still protruding from her back. Kicking and screaming, Theia watched her village burning to the ground and fading behind the billowing smoke.

"I never saw my people again. When my fatal wounds healed, they feared me as a sorceress or a witch. They discovered, as did I, that death would not come for me as it did others. Too afraid to let me go, and unable to kill me, or afraid to even try, they kept me chained and imprisoned—for the next two years."

Theia shivered in a cold, dark cell.

Her only comfort from the damp stone floors was a pallet of straw and a tattered gray coverlet, to which she clung. High on the wall, a narrow slit allowed in the only light which beamed a pitiful line slowly traveling the room as the sun made its passage.

"When I saw an opportunity for freedom, I took it. I'd waited and waited, planning my move carefully. Picking up on the routines until the time was right."

When a guard delivered food through an opening in the barred cell wall, Theia sneaked the cell keys from his belt. Using them to escape, she disappeared down the corridor toward the intense light of the outside. To freedom.

Now, halfway along the side table adorned with various antiques, she ambled onward, allowing her fingers to gently graze across the top of each of them.

"And then I traveled to the farthest of reaches, to lands and places I had never dreamed of. I learned cultures and languages—many of which don't even exist today. The first part of the Middle Ages I spent wandering England. But then I made my way through Western Europe until eventually heading east into Eural-Asia."

Theia's eyes, for the first time since her tale began, honed directly on Matthew and Audree. And for the first time, they glanced at one another.

"I was never able to stay in any place longer than about twenty years, otherwise people would notice I hadn't aged. It started with compliments, but soon brought questions. Then I knew it was time to move on. I suppose I stopped aging when I turned about twenty-one or—"

"Twenty-one!" Audree interrupted. "But you don't look twenty-one now." Immediately embarrassed for having told her best friend she looked older, she backpedaled. "You look amazing though. Doesn't she?" Audree turned to Matthew who just nodded.

"Yes, you are quite right, I *can* age," Theia said, smiling from the shrouded compliment. "Whenever my body heals from an injury, especially fatal injuries, my body ages slightly and when it does it causes great pain, often more pain than during the injury itself. The whole body suffers."

Now having completely circumnavigated the room, Theia returned to the couch and sat.

"As I traveled, I was always aware of being watched. Followed. Sometimes, they would try to catch me or even kill me. They have invented so many ways to try and have almost succeeded." Recollecting her time in Baden-Baden, Germany, she glanced over her shoulder to the adjacent wall. Among the framed relics, she focused on one in particular—another tiny box frame displaying an old spent bullet, slightly rusted but still showing sparkles of blue.

Knowing it had meaning, Audree and Matthew also glanced at the frame, though of course, they failed to understand its relevance.

"But on other occasions, I feel they…" Theia paused, trying to make sense of her words.

"What?" Audree asked as she leaned forward. "They what, hun?"

"That they are secretly trying to protect me."

"Protect you?" Audree stretched her neck higher. "Wait. I thought you said these people were trying to kill you? And now you're saying they're… protecting you?"

"It's… complicated, I know. Trust me Audree, I don't understand it myself." Theia glanced over to Matthew who appeared lost in thought. So far, he had not uttered a single word. Perhaps her story was too incredulous for him to grasp. She hoped not. "Matthew," Theia said softly.

To her relief, he didn't dart for the door. Instead, he framed a question. "I'm hung up on something you said. You mentioned *secretly.* That they were *secretly* trying to protect you."

Audree bounced in her seat next to him. "That's the part you're hung up on. Secretly? Seriously? She's a million damn years old. That don't *hang* you up a little?" She turned to Theia, shaking her finger. "Which reminds me. I've been buying you that expensive moisturizer every Christmas. For *years!* What in the hell do you need moisturizer for? You could have told me. Are you even using it? I could've bought myself a goddamn cruise with that sum of money!"

"I believe I told you I have good genes, or something like that," Theia admitted. In reality, she couldn't recall all the lies she'd told over the years just to survive. "I'm so sorry, Audree. I couldn't tell you the truth."

"Why not? I'm your best friend."

"*Because!*" Theia drew a deep breath. "People who know the truth get hurt or end up… dead." She regretted not sharing that crucial piece of information earlier, but she'd had no other choice.

Audree stood. For a moment, Theia wondered if she might leave.

But then Audree came over to her couch and sat next to her. Held her hand. "We're in this together. Don't worry about me, hun, I can handle myself. Besides…" She pulled out a silver necklace tucked between her bosom. "I'm wearing my knock-off Saint Christopher. I'm invincible!"

They both gave a faint chuckle.

Audree's in, Theia thought, *but what about Matthew?* She glanced over at him.

He sat back and crossed his legs. "So," he said. "You were going to tell me why you think they are secretly trying to protect you."

Theia sighed, then shared a grateful smile. "Yes. There have been occasions where people have been chasing me, I assume to kill me, and from out of nowhere, I'd receive a mysterious helping hand from a stranger. Often, without their help, I'd have been captured or killed. But as fast as they appeared, they were gone as if trying to hide their identities. I was beginning to wonder if these men in suits were the ones trying to protect me, even though they'd always made my skin crawl. But now they've taken David, obviously they have ill intentions. I'm so confused."

"Men in suits?" Matthew questioned. "And David? Who's David?"

"Yes, David. Well, he's the reason we called you. He's my neighbor's nine-year-old son from across the street. I arrived home today and learned he'd been taken by two men wearing dark suits." She picked up the Post-it from the table in front of her and read from it. "They were driving a 'golden-brown, 1978 Lincoln Mark V with a white leather rear roof.'"

"And you think these kidnappers…?"

"Are the same men who have been following me? Yes." Theia waived the Post-it. "This same car has been parked outside my apartment. They've been watching me."

Matthew stood and paced the floor, absorbing the information. Both hands rubbed his forehead as if a headache formed. "I see. But have you any idea why they would want your neighbor's son? And he's only nine years old, you say?"

"Yes, he's just a child. And there's no reason as to why. None. I hardly know him, really."

Matthew moved on to the vehicle. "And this car, this Lincoln 19…?"

"'78 Mark V," Theia reminded as she referred to the paper in her hand again.

"How do you know it was that same car the kidnappers used?"

"Mr. Philips from downstairs recognized it. His parents used to own one, apparently. He gave a detailed description, right down to the wheel hubs. He got the license plate too but—"

"My boss ran it," Audree interjected. "No match. They must have used false plates."

"Your boss?" Matthew asked.

"Yeah, he's a dick."

"Uh?"

"A private dick." Audree rolled her eyes at Matthew's befuddled expression. "A *private detective.*" She overpronounced each word. "He's looking into the vehicle description, too."

Theia could tell Matthew's head was spinning. "I know this is a lot to take in, Matthew. May I ask you to take another look at something?" She handed him the torn-out page with the encircled double cross. "Remember this?"

"The Patriarchal cross from the other night. What about it?"

"Just over a week ago, I saw it tattooed on a man's wrist. He was wearing a dark suit, and he approached me in the underground garage at work. I'd fumbled, dropped my car keys and he handed them to me. Impeccably dressed. Same M.O. as the kidnappers.

"Since then, it's been bothering me where I'd seen that tattoo before. Tonight, I remembered. Though it's been some time, I'm sure it was the same tattoo. Which means these people have been around for a *very* long time."

"How long?"

"Six hundred years. At least." Theia paused until the memory properly formed. "I'd just arrived in Calais off a British clinker ship in 1485."

"Holy shit!" Matthew couldn't help the words spill from his mouth. "I'm sorry, go on."

"After three decades of bloody warfare in England between the houses of York and Lancaster, I craved a fresh start. France seemed as good a place as any, despite its reputation for political instability. Little did I know, however, that a new horror awaited me there. Just one year before my arrival you see, Pope Innocent VIII had declared the papal bull *Summis Desiderantes,* which labeled witches as daughters of Satan and a menace to the Church. Soon after, the Church sanctioned the Malleus Maleficarum, an official guide to finding and prosecuting witches.

"The resulting hysteria spread like wildfire. Any philandering husband with a new mistress was proclaiming his wife a witch. So many burned." Even as she pressed her hands tightly against her ears, the haunting screams echoed in her head. She had fought for so long to repress the horrors of that time, but now, like a released dragon, they were free to plague her dreams once again. No wonder, she thought, it's been so difficult to recall the events.

"After their attempts to catch me failed, I believe I was named a witch to broaden the net. With the whole town in pursuit, I wasn't able to stay hidden long. Soon I was captured, enduring days of unspeakable torture. Memories of that time are hazy; I recall them starving and beating me, sending me to the brink of death. When my wounds miraculously healed, my jailors immediately condemned me as a witch, sentencing me to death. But the night before I'd burn, a mysterious stranger intervened, bribing a guard and leading me to freedom. I don't recall much about him, except for the mark on his chest, a double cross hidden beneath his tunic."

"Do you remember his face? What he looked like?" Matthew asked.

"No. Just a vague image is all I have."

Matthew appeared disappointed.

"Why?"

"I'm wondering if they too are immortal like you and have been tracking you this whole time. If they're not, then it can only mean information about you has been passed down from mortal to mortal in an organization managing to remain secret for generations. I don't know which is more incredible." Matthew's head shook as he thought intensely. "But I think we're asking the wrong questions. Instead of asking who these people are, we should be asking who *you* are. And what role *you* play."

I've spent a lifetime trying to answer those very questions, Theia thought.

"Finding out who I am will have to wait," she said, hardly believing those words would ever leave her lips. "Right now, we need to find the men who took David. He is my only priority now."

"I understand," Matthew insisted. "But right now, those men are missing pieces in this mysterious puzzle. To complete the picture, we need to start with the pieces we do have, and that means understanding your role in all this."

Audree chimed in, "And with Bill working with the police, we can attack this from two angles. Increase our chances. As I said, Bill will get his teeth into this."

"Precisamente!" Matthew exclaimed, his New Jersey accent destroying the Italian attempt. He reached into his backpack, swiftly pulling out his laptop and flipping it open. "I know just where to start."

CHAPTER 23

The Immortal Light

"Wakey-wakey, ladies," Matthew chirped.

Despite his sleepless night, Matthew emerged from the kitchen wide eyed and sprightly. He carefully balanced a large white tray of English delights: a ceramic blue teapot; a small jug of milk; a bowl of white granulated sugar cubes; three mugs; and an almost fresh pyramid of currant scones stacked on a small plate.

Dawn had finally broken, distorting the window frame shadows into long thin trapezoids across the shimmering white marble. On the far couch, Theia buried her head into a down pillow, a warm blanket scrunched to her ear. Audree lay sprawled across the opposite couch, arms wide, mouth agape, a gurgling sound emanating from the back of her throat. Matthew set the tray on the center table between his laptop and a scattered pile of open files and books from Theia's hidden room. The open laptop whirred its fan, the processor thirsty for air after hours of use.

Matthew's vociferous voice, together with the rising sun, did little to rouse Theia or Audree. "C'mon ladies, it's morning! Chop-chop!" He clanked the ceramic mugs together, then unforgivingly dropped a stainless-steel spoon into one, which clanged like a shopkeeper's bell.

Theia stirred first, releasing one last gargle. With one eye closed, she stretched her limbs and neck, then sat straight. Her bedraggled head of hair sprang wildly, the frizzy mess glowing like a halo from the golden rays behind. Audree was still out for the count. Matthew snagged a pillow from his center couch, hurling it at her.

"Hey!" she moaned, grudgingly bringing herself upright. She rubbed her eyes with the back of her knuckle, then strained her voice amidst a yawn. "What time is it, anyway?"

"I dunno. But we've got work to do," Matthew said, pouring steaming tea into the three white mugs. "I searched everywhere for coffee," he uttered in disbelief. "But it seems you don't have any. I made us tea." He glanced at Theia. "Sugar?"

Still with an eye closed, she silently extended a thumb and smiled.

"One lump or two?"

She switched her thumb into two fingers.

Assuming Audree was a sugar kinda gal, he prepared hers the same way. "I've been working through the night while you guys were snoring away." He looked directly at Audree. "And you do snore by the way, big time. Sounds like a motorbike revving up. Anyway, I've discovered some interesting facts." He slid his laptop to the edge, tapping the seat cushions on either side of him. "Come. Take a look."

"Are you always this lively in the morning?" Audree asked.

The two ladies joined him. Theia reached for her tea with both hands and clasped it to her chest. Audree quickly returned to retrieve her blanket and then made herself comfortable, curling her legs beneath her on the couch. All three stared at his screen.

"Before we start. Please understand, our historical records, while vast, only go back as far as the eleventh or twelfth century."

Theia huffed and nodded at the same time.

"Don't worry," Matthew reassured, "I've still made some remarkable discoveries." He touched the mousepad, livening the screen from hibernation. A Gantt chart reappeared. "I've created a kind of chronological tree representing the evolution of religious organizations from as far back as our database will allow."

"English, please!" Audree blurted, already confused.

He pointed at the numerous thin bars running horizontally across the screen. Each of varying lengths, the bars hovered above one another at various points along the X-axis.

"Each one of these bars represents a religious organization. The horizontal axis is 'time' starting from year zero—Christ." He circled a voided area with the cursor. "As you can see, the first thousand-year span is blank."

Matthew leaned to retrieve the single page and laid it in front of Theia. He tapped on the double cross image. "I think it's fair to assume whoever these people are, whether they're from some kind of cult or sect, they're religious. Probably fanatically so."

"Amen to that," Audree interjected, appearing to be the only one finding that amusing.

"I asked myself," he continued, "what single religious organization, so well structured, so well interconnected on a near-global scale, could track you—or whatever they're doing—for hundreds and hundreds of years. You know what I found?"

Audree and Theia held in breaths as they slowly shook their heads.

"Nothing!" Matthew said. "I found nothing. There is no *single* organization. But…" He zoomed in on his chart. "There are, however, several organizations that have…" Using his fingers, he counted, reciting a list. "…The means, international support, a common interest, *and* if you look closely enough, have common geographical ties."

"Sooo…" Theia dragged out the word in confusion. "Then you're saying… I'm sorry, what *are* you saying?"

Matthew poised his forefinger in front of his face as if it held the answers, then plunged it straight down to the keyboard, clacking on the spacebar. Many of the bars on his graph disappeared, the remaining few sliding together and enlarging to fill the screen. "I have filtered out all the organizations that are unrelated." Pointing to the lowest and farthest left horizontal bar, he explained, "This is the earliest I've found. The Knights Templar. As you can see, they existed during the medieval ages up to the fabled Black Friday in 1307 when King Philip IV of France ordered their arrests."

"Friday the 13th," Theia said, her eyes cornering. "We hadn't labeled the day back then, but I do remember the time, unfortunately. They all burned at the stake for heresy."

"Not all. Some escaped and continued to operate in secret until 1312 when they were finally disbanded." Again, counting on his fingers, Matthew furthered, "They were incredibly well organized, had developed a means to communicate over great distances and even formed the first known international banking system. They were more than capable of disseminating secret information within their network and tracking Theia during their two-hundred-year reign."

"And after that?" Theia asked.

Pointing to the next horizontal bar above the first, which just overlapped the first bar but further to the right on the timeline, he continued, "This is The Knights Hospitallers, which formed around the twelfth century and became one of the most feared military orders of its time, and of course, extremely religious."

A click on his mouse pad enlarged an image of an ancient document, centering on the screen over the graph. "The *Ad Providam*, a decree issued by Pope Clement V ordering the power and possessions of the Knights Templar over to the Hospitallers, empowering them beyond any rivalry." He pointed to the lower corner of the decree. "Notice the date of the decree—1312, the same year the Templars were finally disbanded." Matthew's inflection excitedly rose at the end of the sentence.

Audree and Theia's vacant stares and gaping mouths suggested he was not being fully understood. "Don't you see?" Matthew said, minimizing the image of the decree and showing his Gantt chart once again. "How can I put it? The information, the wealth, the artifacts, and even some of the surviving Templars did not die out with its dissolution in 1312. It was simply transferred."

"To the Hospitallers?" Though Theia guessed right, she sounded unsure.

"Yes! Exactly that, Theia."

Theia pointed to the remaining collection of bars sitting above the first two. "What are these organizations? These here?"

"All of those orders overlap each other at some point on the timeline. And all are connected in various ways."

"How?" Theia asked. "In what ways?"

"They have similar beliefs, ordinances, governance and sometimes similar financial support. They go by various names. The Order of St. John… Um." Not remembering the list of names, he clicked on the next bar to open their titles. His finger scanned the lines, as he read another. "The Most Venerable Order of the Hospital of Saint John of Jerusalem."

"Damn!" Audree exclaimed. "What a mouthful."

"There are… so many." Matthew stood and walked around the table. Akin to a trial lawyer, he paced the floor, delivering his closing argument. "These organizations existed and overlapped through time having similar religious ties, some even being operated out of the same priories. Secrets will inevitably have passed between them." Pointing to his laptop from across the table, he added, "Those last two organizations are currently in operation today, as are the Freemasons! That may explain why you could never find a *single* organization existing throughout your entire lifetime. Unless it was able to operate entirely under the radar, it doesn't exist, aside from as a string of separate organizations acting as one."

"But that doesn't answer why they would want to protect me. Or harm me for that matter. I don't present a threat to anyone. I am… nobody."

"You're *not* nobody. Obviously, you're somebody, which leads me to the why and the who. First, let's talk about the who—*you*."

Still pacing the floor, he continued his jury delivery. "Unlike today, family names and given names were indicative of who you were. Your family name represented the group or vocation to which you belonged, such as Hunter or Baker or Thatcher, while your given name would reflect something particular to your birthday, such as when or where you were born: Cliff, Glen, Dale, Brooke, and so on."

Thinking of two more, Theia included, "Dawn or Summer?"

As if it were becoming a game, Audree added with excitement, "Misty, Eve, um, Randy. Hmm, maybe scratch that last one!"

"Exactly," Matthew said. He stopped pacing and then looked directly at Theia. "Your name, Theia Damaris Cassia Reginleif; I did some research. Do you know their meanings?"

Theia cleared her throat. "Yes, my father told me. Theia means light. My mother chose the name."

"Goddess of Light, to be more specific. But it also means, *A Gift of God*." Matthew returned to his seat between Theia and Audree and folded his convertible laptop into two, the screen facing up. Using a digital pen, he wrote 'Reginleif' on the notepad displayed on the screen.

"You spelled it wrong," Audree said. "The 'g' and the 'i' need to be swapped."

"No, he has it correct, Audree."

"But that says Reg-in?"

"Yes, but the pronunciation is still Reign. Go on, Matthew"

Matthew pointed the pen at the name. "*Reginleif*. Your family name: a Nordic name from the time of the Vikings."

Theia wasn't sure if that was a question but answered, "Yes."

He then drew a diagonal line, dividing it into two: Regin/Leif.

"Leif translates to *heir* or, in your case, *daughter*. And 'Regin' means 'power' or 'mighty' but also means 'The gods.' Reginleif—'Daughter of the gods.'"

"And Damaris?"

"Just one second." Matthew minimized the notepad to reveal another page teeming with information. He scrolled to the definitions section "Means 'the dominant one.'"

"Ain't that the truth!" Audree chuckled in her sassy voice. "Don't know about a gift of God though."

"What about Cassia?" Theia asked, growing more intrigued. "That was my mother's name."

As this name didn't seem to fit with Matthew's enthusiastic trend, he was reluctant to share it. "Um… yeah, 'Cassia.' It means cinnamon."

Audree sniggered. "Cinnamon? Sounds like a stripper name."

Theia leaned into her lap, her scowl aimed like a weapon at Audree.

"Well, it does!" Audree said, trying not to laugh. "I'm just saying."

Turning to Matthew, Theia surmised, "So, you're taking the meaning of my name literally? Do you think I'm the daughter of a god or something? Or the daughter of God *Himself?*"

"Possibly. But there is another alternative. Though, this is where it gets a little crazy."

Theia laughed, finally. "Crazier than me being God's close relative?"

Theia's reaction had Matthew second-guessing himself.

True, it sounded incredulous when put into words. Laughable even. Especially from him. Despite his years of religious study, he'd never once believed in any of it. A man of fact, of science, he required proof, not miracles. And while the evidence he was providing was largely circumstantial, he was beginning to wonder if she wasn't both.

Matthew clicked on another tab to reveal his next findings. "Here we go. I looked up another variant of the name Theia, from the Greek, *Theotokos*," he explained further. "It translates to 'Mother of God' or 'God Bearer' and is often used to describe Mary, as in the Virgin Mary."

"Yeah, well," Audree chimed. "We can forget about the virgin part! Stripper yes, virgin no."

Theia tossed her hair over her shoulder. "Really?" she whispered behind Matthew. "And when exactly have you ever seen me in a relationship?"

"Girl," Audree whispered back. "If you're still a virgin after all those years, we gonna have to have a serious chat, you and I."

Ignoring their girlish bantering, Matthew prepared his final piece of the puzzle. "Ah, here it is. This was written by the Sibylline Oracles, who were theological prophets around the time of Christ. This passage is from 'The Oracle, Book III.'"

Matthew read from the article on his screen, word for word. "'*Be of good cheer, O maiden…*'" He emphasized the 'O maiden,' glancing directly at Theia. "*… and exult; for the Eternal, who made heaven and earth, has given thee joy, and he will dwell in thee, and for thee shall be an 'immortal light.'*"

"Immortal light?" Theia turned pale as she sat straight.

"Yes. Has that triggered something?"

"I've read those words before, in a poem, a message from *them* before they tried to…" Not wanting to relive the moment in Baden-Baden when she'd been ruthlessly gunned down, she simply concluded, "Anyway, that's obviously me."

Matthew pondered, "Maybe."

"Maybe? Who else would it be?"

"What if 'given thee joy' and 'dwell in thee' meant the immortal light was *not* you per se, but instead, lived within you in the form of a child?"

"A child?" Theia retracted her chin.

"I think we have to consider that a possibility." Matthew unfolded his laptop to show the Gantt chart once again. "Look at all of this, religious orders spanning millennia, the Patriarchal cross you keep seeing, the very definitions of your name, not to mention that tiny detail of you being over eleven hundred years old! As crazy as it sounds, the facts fit."

Theia still appeared in shock.

"To answer the why—why you are here," Matthew concluded, "I think you may be walking this earth until you birth the second coming of Christ."

Everything stopped. The room was pitched into silence, no one daring to breathe. This was far too important to ruin or to understand.

Theia spun in her seat. "What?"

"This is all just a guess until we find the missing pieces," Matthew said, trying to muddle his specificity. "Right now, I'm just providing options. Possibilities. That's all."

"Possibilities! I wish." Theia suddenly looked as though she could cry. Her voice softened. "But I'm afraid you're wrong about that last option, Matthew."

"Why?"

Audree agreed with Matthew. "Yeah, why not? His theory makes sense and…"

"Because!" Theia grimaced, now tearing up. "I can't have children. Okay? Is that good enough for you?" Her testy remark ended that line of questioning.

After that, the room fell to silence. Again.

"I'm sorry if I…" Matthew held his tongue, not knowing what words to choose.

"No, Matthew," Theia said, wiping a tear with her little finger and sniffling, "Please, don't apologize." She pointed at his computer. "What you've done in such a small amount of time is—amazing. Truly. It's remarkable what you've discovered." She squeezed his knee. "And thank you for believing me, sticking with me." She turned her head to Audree. "You, too."

"Of course, dumpling," Audree said, returning a smile, yet she couldn't resist adding some sass. "Just don't be letting this 'being a goddess thing' go to your head."

Theia gave a short laugh, one of those defeated, unfulfilled laughs where all other emotions were used up. "I'll try!"

"You better, Ms. High and Mighty!" Audree bobbed her head. "You might be twelve hundred years old but you're still just a little farm girl from Ukley-wuckley or whatever you call it."

"Ulleskelf," Theia corrected with a smirk. "In the district of York!"

"York!" Matthew's head suddenly perked. "Of course. It had to be."

Theia and Audree remained silent as he relished in his 'ah ha' moment. "To find the missing pieces," Matthew said excitedly, "we need to go back to the very beginning. Further than even our database will go. A place holding the largest collection of ancient artifacts and records dating back two thousand years, complete with the largest cathedral library anywhere in Europe."

"Where's that?" Theia asked.

"The Old Palace and Minster. In, none other than York, England." He turned to Theia, his thumb and finger scratching at his chin. "Is your passport current?"

Before Theia could answer, a Whitney Houston ringtone broke the silence.

And I will always love you,
I will always love you,
Darling, I love you…

Like an Olympic sprinter hearing the gunshot, Audree dashed across the room so fast the seven-yard sprint left her completely out of breath. She scrambled through her purse, finally retrieving her ringing phone. Taking a deep breath, she answered with a nonchalant tone, "Hello, this is Audree. Oh, hey, Bill." As if she didn't know who was calling. "What's up?"

With everyone staring and hanging on every word, she huddled around her phone, trying to whisper. "Uh-huh, yeah, uh-huh. Seriously?" Her voice amplified with excitement, "No way. Oh, my God…"

Theia stood and took a step closer. "What is it?"

Covering the mouthpiece, Audree said, "Bill thinks he found the car." She removed her hand. "Uh-huh. Right. When? Now? Not without me, you're not." She listened for a second then firmly applied, "No, come and get me. Bill. Bill! I swear to God, you get your ass over here right now." Obviously, having won the argument, Audree's voice now switched back to her sweet, loveable tone. "Okay, I'll see you soon. Oh, Bill, I almost forgot, I'm at Theia's house. Do you have the address? Never mind, I'll text it. Byee. Love ya."

Hardly able to withstand the growing anticipation, Theia pleaded with clasped, praying hands, "Please, tell me some good news!"

"He found it. The car. Said it was easy. Apparently, there aren't many vehicles fitting that description in the city. He's traced it to an apartment in West Bronx. It has a different plate number, but he's convinced it's the one. He already notified the police and they're checking into it, too. But Bill wants to head over there. Keep an eye on the place until the police arrive."

Theia's clasped hands flattened against her chest, her head falling back.

"Oh, thank God. Please let David be okay." Then without wasting time, she marched toward her bedroom. "Give me a few minutes to get ready."

"No. We've got this."

Almost out of the room, Theia stopped abruptly. "What? Audree, there is no way I'm not coming with you. Have you lost your mind? David is missing because of me."

"Hun, listen. Bill and I can handle this. Plus, the cops are on it. And trust me, we'll call in the National Guard if we have to. If David's there, we'll get him back, I promise."

Theia folded her arms and pushed out her hip, stealing an Audree pose. "And what am I supposed to do? Just sit here?"

"No. You have to go with him. To York." She pointed at Matthew still sitting on the couch. "He's right, Theia. Regardless of what's happening with David, you need to get to the bottom of this. To find out who you really are."

"No!" Theia yelled, her arms quickly unfolding, another Audree-ism. "I can't. Not now. I'll go *after* we get David back. There's just too much going on. I need to know David's okay first."

Audree approached her and embraced Theia's shoulders at arm's length. "Look, what if we get there and discover it's not them, that we have the wrong car? We'll have to start our search all over again, from scratch, right? And we'd just be wasting time. Doubling our efforts is the only way. You're the smart one; you know I'm right. Besides, I can't stand to see you so lost and alone all the time. You need this. Go. Find your answers. Now's your chance."

"But…"

"Please, please." The *begging for ice cream* tone kicked in. "Do it for me, baby. Go! Or you'll never be free. You'll regret it if you don't. We'll sort things this end."

Theia's glazed eyes, wide and wavering, drifted over to Matthew. At first, his head was down, organizing his thoughts, a plan. Finally, he stood, leveling his eyes on Theia, then asked, "Are you ready to go home?"

CHAPTER 24

Tickets

Audree was standing on the curbside with Theia and Matthew when Bill pulled to a stop in front of Theia's townhome. With the engine idling in park, Bill exited his non-discreet, slightly dented, silver Toyota sedan and moved to the passenger side to open the door for Audree. Playing her part, she knew not to open her door lest she offend him. Albeit that wasn't the only reason; an old-fashioned lady at heart, it well suited her to have doors opened by a gentleman.

Bill pecked a kiss on Audree's cheek. "Hey, babe." Then reaching for Matthew's hand, he almost shook it from its socket. "Bill. Pleasure."

"Thank you for doing this, Bill," Theia said, stepping forward. "I hope you find him."

"Don't worry, doll. I'll find him." Bill's voice was deep and raspy from years of having smoked. "And I'll make sure those sons of bitches pay. That I can promise you."

"Yes, well, just please be careful," Theia replied awkwardly.

Bill peeled open one side of his brown leather jacket, revealing a holstered .357 Magnum revolver clipped to his belt. "Oh, I'm careful, all right," he said. "I never go anywhere without Justin."

"Justin?" Theia frowned.

"Justin Case."

"Don't worry, hun," Audree said, seeing Theia's hand planted nervously on her cheek. "We're just keeping an eye on things until the cavalry arrives." She stepped in and gave her best friend a giant bear hug. Theia wrapped her arms around Audree, resting her head affectionately on her shoulder. After a tender moment, Audree slackened her arms, prompting Theia to cling tighter. "Hey, come on now, sugarplum, you don't want to miss your flight. You still have to pack yet."

Theia finally let go and checked her watch. "Oh, my God, you're right. I can't believe I'm doing this. This is so spontaneous."

"Spontaneous? Girl, you have been waiting a thousand years for this!"

Theia giggled. "I suppose."

Audree slid into the car seat; her attentive chauffeur closed the door and circled the car.

The passenger side window droned open, and Audree stuck her head out. "Hey, girl. When you get back, I'm going to ask you one question." She raised a forefinger for clarity.

"What's that?"

"After a thousand years of searching, did you finally find what you were looking for? And girl, the answer had better be yes!"

Theia pressed a tight-lipped smile and nodded.

"Matthew." Audree stretched her head out further. "We hardly know you and yet I feel very comfortable around you so I say this from the bottom of my heart; if you let anything happen to her, I will hunt you down and slaughter you with my own bare hands, you understand?"

A reassuring smile graced Matthew's face. "I understand. I won't let anything happen to her." He drew an 'X' on his chest. "I promise."

Turning to Bill, Audree slapped his thigh. "What're waiting for? C'mon. Let's go." As Bill eased away, she waved out the window. "Byeee, love ya!"

Theia yelled after her, a reminder to call her the second they heard something.

Audree watched them grow smaller in the side mirror until they made a turn. She didn't notice, however, the rainforest green Cadillac with smoked windows, parked at the north end of the street. Nor did they spot the figure sitting inside it.

THE DRIVER OF the Cadilac stared ahead, a phone wedged between shoulder and ear. Balanced on the center armrest between the two front seats, his laptop sat open angled toward him. A list of credit card purchases was displayed on the screen. The title read, 'Theia McDormand, Bank of America - Recent Transactions.'

"The friend is leaving," he said. "Want me to follow her, or stay here?"

"No. Stay with the Reginleif girl." The deep monotone voice had a slight scratch of middle age with a distinctive English accent.

The driver clicked on the last credit card transaction, which enlarged a detailed pop-up window. The vendor was British Airways. The amount: $12,600. "She purchased tickets to England an hour ago. Are you seeing this?"

"Yes, we know about that."

"Does *he* know?"

"He does. He is… most pleased. We are making preparations."

Slumping in his chair, the driver stuttered, "We… we finally succeeded?"

"Perhaps."

"Perhaps? This is everything we've worked for. All of us. This has to be it."

"This is fortuitous, yes. But remember, we cannot intervene. Kidnapping that child could have had catastrophic consequences. Fortunately for DeRose, it's turned out the way it has. But it's not over yet. So, we don't drop our guard."

"The prophecy, it remains intact?" Already suspecting the answer, the driver just wanted to hear it.

"It appears so. Despite DeRose's recklessness, his actions may have inadvertently brought us closer to the Third Article. Closer than we have ever achieved."

"The Third Article!" The driver gasped. "I thought I'd never see the day."

"The day would come. We're just a little caught off guard by this sudden turn of events. We must tread carefully. There can be no mistakes."

The driver watched as Theia and Matthew ascended the steps and returned inside. "Griffin and DeRose: what do you want me to do with them?"

"That depends. For now, your only job is to make sure she gets on that flight without incident. And don't forget to send photos. They're forecasting rain and mist for when they arrive. I don't want our man losing them in the crowd."

"Yes, sir. Of course, I'll do whatever is necessary." Speaking with a nervous humbleness, he added, "Please, let him know I can always be counted upon."

"That won't be necessary. You should know by now that there is little I can tell him he doesn't already know."

CHAPTER 25

The Stakeout: Part I

From the passenger seat of Bill's Toyota, Audree watched with growing concern as the final sliver of sun ducked below the concrete skyline. Being parked in a sleazy side street in a run-down area of West Bronx was not someplace she wanted to be. Especially at night.

Earlier, when it had been daylight, she had spied the graffitied walls and cold steel bars guarding every building's ground-floor window. Obviously, the bars were designed to keep people out, but in poor David's case, they would be his jail.

That terrible thought had kept her going, kept her strong. That and Bill. Next to her, his eyes glued to his side-view mirror, staring at the building entrance diagonally behind them.

Another lowrider approached from behind.

As it cruised past, thudding music from its lowered windows rattled Bill's car like a poor-quality speaker. Audree cowered, while Bill remained seated, apparently unfazed, as if he hadn't even noticed. Yet, she knew otherwise.

Bill noticed everything.

And if there was any cause for alarm, he would let her know.

Peering over her shoulder through the rear window, she resumed her surveillance. "We've been here for hours, Bill. Are you sure this is the place?"

"Yeah, it's right there." He twisted in his seat and pointed behind him toward the building's main entrance. However, someone would miss the indistinguishable gray door if they were looking right at it. "Apartment 156A. That's the only way in or out."

"But aren't we looking for the car? The orange one?"

"No darlin'. And it was golden brown. I wouldn't be hanging my hopes on seeing that anytime soon." Bill turned to Audree. "Kidnapping a boy in New York City, in broad daylight, in *that* car, with witnesses; I'm guessing they've ditched it by now."

"Oh, really?" Her tone was curt. "And when were you planning on telling me that? I've been peeling my eyes for that goddamn orange Lincoln for hours." She threw her hands up. "What the hell are we looking for then?"

"You said they were smartly dressed, in suits. Tall, right?" He twisted his neck to scan the dimly lit street lined with boarded-up storefronts. "Smartly dressed around here is gonna stand out like a son-of-a-bitch."

After a few moments of watching and waiting, Audree shook her head and sighed. "I still can't believe those damn cops didn't hang around. A kidnapped child, and all they did was knock to see if someone was home… then left."

Bill's eyes remained fixated on the side mirror. "You gotta understand how the system works, babe. The owner of the vehicle has a clean record. Right now, he is merely under suspicion. No judge in his right mind would issue a warrant without further evidence or motive. If the license plate had matched, on the other hand, then that would have been a whole different story. But it didn't, so here we are."

"We haven't heard from your cop friend yet either. I thought he was going to call you?"

"O'Malley? He will. As soon as there's something to tell me, he'll call."

Boredom kicking in, Audree poked around inside the glove compartment for no other reason than to look. She deflated a long slow sigh, her fingers drumming on her knees. "So, what's the plan?"

"The plan?" Bill let out a low, gruff snort. "We wait, darlin', we wait. As long as it takes."

CHAPTER 26

German Cadmium

Theia's return from the bathroom was perfectly timed. She took her seat next to Matthew at the airport lounge bar just as the barman served their drinks onto two napkin coasters, a well-garnished vodka tonic and a bourbon straight.

"Make sure you drink that," Theia joked as she mounted the stool. "The last time you ordered one of those, you ended up wearing it."

It took a moment for Matthew to recollect. "Ah, the gala night. Not my finest moment. When I'm nervous, I tend to be a bit of a klutz. Not a good trait when dealing with priceless relics, is it?"

"I hope you're not referring to me!" Theia said, pausing her reach for her drink.

Matthew laughed. "I can see it now. I'd be in my boss's office telling him I had discovered an ancient ninth-century relic in pristine condition, and, oh by the way, let me introduce you to her."

"Charming!" Theia said.

Matthew's eyes drifted. "For years, I have been searching for a paper to write, something to launch my career to the next level. To discover something truly amazing. And here I am, sitting on the most incredible story since Christ... and I can't even write about it. Typical."

"Is that why you're doing this, Matthew?"

With the whirlwind of drama and snappy decisions of late, she hadn't stopped to consider his reasons. "Until two weeks ago, you hadn't even met me, and now here you are, jetting off to England, putting your whole life on hold for a complete stranger; all for a story?"

"No!" Matthew hesitated. "I suppose, in the beginning, maybe. And, of course, Audree can be very persuasive! But then..." He trailed off, shrugging, aiming his dark brown eyes directly at hers. "I don't know. As I got to know you more, I just wanted to help, I guess."

The sincerity of his words brought a smile to Theia's face. "Whatever the reason, Matthew, you're a true gentleman and I'm glad you're here." She placed her hand over her heart and cocked her head sideways. "Thank you."

For a moment, their eyes held, and she watched as Matthew's gaze toured her face.

His eyes lingered on her freshly rouged lips, tracing along her jawline towards her cheek, which she was sure was now blushing. A ringlet of blonde had escaped her ponytail and she felt it spiraling across her skin. When Matthew's eyes honed on it, she quickly tucked it behind her ear and then adjusted herself in her seat.

Matthew cleared his throat and moved to another topic. "That was quite the story you shared." But Theia, having told many of late, puzzled over which. Matthew hinted, "Last night, in your apartment."

"Ah, that story. The original!"

"I can't imagine what that must have been like to have your life turned upside down, your father killed, and your fiancé too. I forget his name. Alex, was it?"

"Asma," she said, eyes dancing as she recalled his memory. "He was so handsome. Though terribly mischievous, which my father hated. Always getting into trouble." Theia chuckled. "My father never cared for him, probably because when I was with him, I'd also wind up in trouble. He would try all ways to prevent us from being together."

She shrugged.

"Maybe all fathers are like that, especially with their only daughters. But there was nothing he could do. I was in love."

Theia sat in silence.

Her mind wandering to a darker place.

Her warm smile shrank.

From behind the bar counter, the mahogany-paneled wall morphed into a scene of carnage.

Her beloved Asma charged toward her, arms reaching, the pain of the axe still fresh in her back. She watched as she replayed the first arrow, taking Asma to his knees.

Her ears rang from the cries of villagers. Again on his feet, Asma charged. The second arrow hit, bowing out his chest from the impact. Helpless, she could only watch as the final and fatal arrow took him down. Before his head hit the water-logged muddy road, she knew he was already dead. She reached her arm out for him, screaming, "No!"

"No what?" asked Matthew.

Theia noticed her arm extended, holding a glass over the bar counter. The puzzled barman ceased his glass polishing, staring confusedly at her.

"Oh, I'm sorry, I thought you asked if I wanted another drink—" was the first excuse she could think of. She returned her glass to the counter just as Matthew jiggled his.

"I'll take another," he said, then turned to Theia. "Sorry, did I lose you there for a moment? You drifted off."

Theia tilted her head, offering a small smile.

"Actually, do you mind if we talk about something else?"

"Of course." He continued with a new tone, an inquisitive one, "There is another question. It's kind of personal. If you don't mind?"

When Matthew twisted in his chair to face her, she sensed the question would be deep. Whatever he asked, she would no longer be a closed book. Courageously, she turned to Matthew, taking a deep breath. "Okay. Shoot."

Matthew thought hard before asking. Then… "Dentistry? Really?"

Theia's tension snapped like a twig, her rigid posture loosening. She flopped back in her chair. "Oh, my God, I know," she admitted, her voice tinged with self-consciousness. "What was I thinking? It's pretty disgusting, right? Peering into people's... cavities all day."

"How come you didn't choose a different profession?" Matthew asked, frowning. "A lawyer, a doctor, a surgeon even."

Theia puffed out her chest proudly. "Um, I did."

"Did what?"

"Choose those professions. I *have* been a lawyer, a doctor, and yes, even a surgeon. Though, you might not want me operating on you; the last time I performed surgery was..." She raised her eyes to the ceiling in thought. "It was France, 1916, in a putrid tent during the Battle of Verdun."

For a moment, Matthew was speechless. "If I had a penny for every time a girl told me that story," he joked, then raised his bourbon to Theia. "To the most interesting woman I have ever met or will ever meet."

Theia smiled shyly as she clinked his glass. "What about you, Matthew? What made you pick your profession?"

"I just love history, you know. Always have. To hold an ancient artifact in your hands..." The grip of both his hands formed around nothing but space. "To discover what it was, what it meant to someone."

Matthew shook his head, savoring that feeling.

He glanced at Theia. "Everything I do involves solving puzzles. Well, not everything. Unfortunately, it's far removed from the adventures of Indiana Jones, which admittedly is what got me thinking about this career in the first place. Instead, most of my days are spent hammering away at a computer terminal." He shrugged. "In that regard, it can be dull."

"*This* is not so dull, is it?" Theia asked. Though her question was innocent enough, the hint of flirtation embedded in that sentence sent a wave of embarrassment washing over her.

"Oh, I don't know," Matthew humored, glancing around the bar. "Looks like a typical day in the office to me. I talk to all the old relics, you know. Only difference is, they don't usually talk back!"

"Relic!" Theia flicked the back of her fingers against Matthew's thigh. "Makes me sound like an old hag!"

"Speaking of relics," Matthew said, his inquisitive tone becoming familiar, "I'm guessing the items in your extensive collection, many of which are weapons, were not inherited after all." He paused. "They're personal belongings, right?" His admiration was evident as he concluded without waiting for an answer. "Which means you've been in some serious battles. Which means, you're quite the badass."

Theia smiled bashfully.

But then, his arched brows drooped. "But since I've met you, you seem much more... withdrawn. Introverted. It doesn't quite..."

"Fit?" Theia already knew where he was going. "I *was* like you say, fearless, and strong. Being immortal gives you that edge. But after a thousand years of being invincible, I suddenly learned I was vulnerable to my enemies. My shield of immortality had become nothing more than a technicality to them."

"Technicality?"

"I mean, they discovered how to kill me. Just as easily as anyone." She sipped her drink. "Shortly after the war had ended in 1945, I crossed the border from France into Baden-Baden, Germany. Allied forces had reseized many of the historical treasures that the Nazis had stolen and attempted to hide in salt mines and hidden vaults. One item in particular was an ancient transcript written in an unknown language, though the newspapers at the time reported it was of Nordic origin."

"Your father's birthplace," Matthew added.

"That's what drew me. It had been discovered on an expedition mounted by Himmler while in search of an ancient connection between God and an advanced human race. The texts were older than any found to date. I traced it to a church where they were being translated and preserved."

"And you believed they held answers to all of this?"

"I don't know." She shook her head. "I hoped it would. But it was staged." Her jaw tightened as she felt the anger rage within her. "It was bait to lure me into a trap. Set by those who have tried to kill me my entire life."

"Bait?" Matthew repeated. "So, the transcripts weren't real? The newspaper article was…"

"Faked. Yes. Instead of answers, it was given a message, handwritten in red ink from a quill pen. I will never forget the words I read that night; they haunt me still."

O Eternal Flame, O Immortal Light,
Blessed be Thy Sacrificial Rite,
Forsaken Ye of Man and Beast,
T' Niht O Light Will Darkness Keep.

"Immortal Light! The same phrase is quoted in the Oracle, Book III." Matthew appeared excited at the connection. Quickly, he withdrew a pen from his jacket pocket, making use of a napkin while the poem was still fresh. "Does it mean something to you?"

"No. I was expecting to find links to my past. Answers. Not mystery and poetry, nothing like that. Though it was no mystery they knew my name meant light, and that I was immortal. But it was that last line that sent ice coursing through my veins: tonight, I was going to die. At least, that's how I read it." She stared down at her hands. "And for the first time in my life, they almost succeeded."

"How? What happened?"

"They shot me. Many, many times. Only this time was different."

"Different? How so?"

"You've seen how fast my injuries heal."

Though it was not a question, Matthew nodded.

"And they all did, bar one," she said, spinning on her chair to face Matthew, she tugged her V-neck wide, exposing a faded round spot of darkened red skin on her left shoulder. Matthew had to move in the light to see it.

"The other bullets passed through except for this one. Rather than heal, it began eating me from the inside. Festering. They had devised a special bullet for me. To learn that someone would go to all that trouble to remove me from the face of the Earth was terrifying. For the first time in my life, I was vulnerable." Remembering the intensity of the pain, Theia touched her shoulder delicately. "I removed the bullet myself. Had it been two inches lower, I suspect I would have been killed." She eyed Matthew directly. "Permanently, that is."

"What made the bullet so special?"

"All I knew back in 1945 was that it appeared different from other bullets. It was blue and sparkly. I kept it. Still have it at home. Years later, when technology became more advanced, I had it analyzed. They found it was heavily laced with the rare element, cadmium."

"Cadmium?" Matthew cornered his eyes in thought. "That's a poisonous metal, highly toxic. But so is arsenic or mercury. Why cadmium?"

"I don't know why or how they knew it would work against me. But the point is, they know, and it certainly worked. After that day, I realized I could be killed almost as easily as anyone. Knowing *they* were out there armed with this knowledge was the reason I became, as you said, withdrawn. Reclusive, even. That very week, I hopped on a merchant ship bound for the U.S. under a new name, McDormand."

Matthew sat back in his chair, her story sinking in.

"I remember the ship, one of hundreds, all overcrowded with returning servicemen, literally numbering in the hundreds of thousands in an operation the US president coined, 'Home Alive By 45.' Many were wounded, all showing signs of battle fatigue, footsore and weary. It was only then, after centuries of warfare, that I finally knew what bravery meant, understanding a painful truth, that I'd never possessed any courage, not a single ounce."

Matthew placed a caring hand on her shoulder. "Oh, that's not true. Theia, I think you've been incredibly courageous."

"No." She sniffed hard, rigorously shaking her head in denial. "Not like those soldiers. I was a hypocrite. To have courage, you have to be willing to sacrifice everything—*everything* for what you believe in. To risk life itself. I was immortal. What the hell did I ever risk?"

CHAPTER 27

The Honeymooners

The seats on the Dreamliner were not called seats. They were called pods!

Although a comfortable night's sleep sounded perfect, Matthew decided he would stay awake to relish every moment of first-class comforts.

Plus, he had so many questions to ask, hotels to book, and a plan of action to discuss. More pressing, however, was the mystery of the four-lined poem that Theia recited in the bar. The detective in him was itching at a crack at solving it.

The configuration of the pods was 2-2-2. Matthew's seat was 2A, a window seat. After loading his hand luggage into the overhead, he turned to help Theia with hers only to find her gone. He perched on his toes, searching over the crowd of heads down the aisle. *Where the hell is she?*

When they boarded, she was right behind him. He shouldered his way back to the entrance against the flow of boarding passengers. Toward the rear of the first-class section, he finally spotted her on the adjacent aisle, loading her hand luggage into the overhead.

"Theia!" he hollered, conjuring a glance. "Are we not sitting together?"

"I guess not." She pulled a screwed-up face. "When I booked it, she said they were the last two seats."

"Oh." In an instant, the allure of first class and the thrill of the trip evaporated.

Halfway back, Matthew waited in the aisle, a passenger loading her bags.

Taking the opportunity, and as if his eyes couldn't survive eight hours without one last fix, he glanced across to Theia's pod. By now, she was sitting quietly, browsing a magazine with page-flicking disinterest. At first, he just gazed, satisfying his eyes with her beauty, her perfection. But then a thought occurred to him, one that was deeply saddening.

In the cab ride to the airport, Theia had endearingly mentioned she'd be lost without Audree. But, in truth, she was already lost. Alone. And she had been for a very long time.

Matthew was getting a taste of that. Knowing for the next few hours he would be without her company was depressing. He couldn't imagine eleven hundred years of living with that emptiness. Right then and there, he promised himself he would do everything within his power to help her—even if it turned out to be the last thing he would ever do.

Soon after he sat in his pod, his neighboring passenger arrived. With a mobile phone pressed to his ear, the fellow plonked his leather brief-case on seat 2B, removing his sports jacket.

Without making eye contact, he handed it to the flight attendant as a master would hand something to their servant. Not once had he paused for a breath, obnoxiously talking non-stop, or rather *lecturing* non-stop to the poor fellow on the line, obviously under his employ.

The next eight hours now seemed like an eternity.

After two minutes of listening to Mr. Know-it-all drone on, Matthew eagerly located the partition button on the control panel of his pod and pressed it. A slate-gray screen silently rose, separating his pod from his neighbor's. Sadly, it did nothing to drown out his babbling, but at least it sent the message he did not want to be disturbed.

From his jacket pocket, Matthew withdrew the small white napkin from the airport lounge bar. On it, he had written the four lines of Theia's mysterious poem.

Theia had corrected its spelling.

He puzzled over it. *So odd!*

Theia had mentioned it was a trap and after studying the final line, he became convinced of it. They had lured Theia to the chapel using the ancient texts as bait. Which meant they knew her ancestry was Nordic and that she would risk capture to seize them.

Curious, Matthew whipped out his phone, Googling a quick search: *Nordic Texts, Himmler Expedition*

He was expecting the search to come up blank, reeling when it didn't. The event was factual. That meant the newspaper article was also real.

So, if it wasn't faked, that could only mean that her enemies acted on opportunity.

The moment the newspaper hit the stands, they set the trap on the off-chance Theia might read the same article, choosing then to commit the theft.

An organized bunch indeed, Matthew thought.

Plus, for them to be able to switch the real transcripts with their poem, they would have had to convince the church their documents were at risk of being stolen.

Other than the police, who has that kind of power?

Intriguing as all that was, it still didn't explain the cryptic-style wording of the message or why they left it for her to find. If the plan was to kill her, why leave any documents at all? It wouldn't matter because she would already be inside the church surrounded, entrapped. That said, if they wanted her to discover a message, why not write something less obscure—'You are caught. We're outside. You're surrounded. Come out quietly.'

As they taxied, the captain made his announcement: *Seven hours and forty-five minutes of flight time at a cruising altitude of thirty-seven thousand feet.* Matthew sighed then pulled out his side tray, clicking his ballpoint pen with his thumb. Beginning with the first line of the cryptic poem, he began to decipher its meaning:

'O Eternal Flame, O Immortal Light.' This was obviously referring to Theia.

'Blessed be Thy Sacrificial Rite.' *Blessed? Sacrificial Rite?* Matthew thought hard. Rite meant ceremony, but religious in nature. He made a note next to this line—'A religious ceremony of sacrifice, that is sacred, blessed? Blessed by whom?'

He moved on to the next line.

Forsaken Ye of Man and Beast. For clarity, Matthew whispered 'man and beast' over and over before jotting his notes: 'Man=mankind, humanity. Beast=the devil. Evil.' Then underneath, he wrote, 'Humanity and the devil had both forsaken her. Why???' He underlined 'and' and double underlined 'why.'

T' Niht O Light Will Darkness Keep. This, too, seemed obvious. 'T' Niht', an old spelling meaning tonight. Matthew hadn't known that but assumed it. Again, under his breath, Matthew muttered a translation, "Tonight, the light—Theia—will turn to darkness and remain in the dark. Death." After the last line of the poem, he wrote a final note, 'Tonight, Theia will die.'

He summarized his translated notes into one sentence, which he whispered aloud. "Theia, in a religious ceremony, and because the human race and the devil..." He paused, trying to find the right words. "...abandoned you, you will die tonight."

Matthew's chin rose, his eyes staring through the twelve-inch monitor now displaying varying flight crew members showing how to inflate a vest.

The low rumble of the engines whirred into a deafening whine.

Matthew felt his weight sink into his seatback as the plane accelerated for takeoff. The cabin shuddered, the overhead bins squeaking and rattling as though coming apart. He clenched his eyes, his fingers whitening around the armrests. As if practicing meditation, he began taking deep inhales and long slow exhales. Only now did he remember he absolutely hated flying.

Once the wheels left the ground, the shuddering eased to a gentle vibration.

His closed eyes somehow granted his hearing a superpower, magnifying every sound tenfold. The high-pitch scream from the engine mounted gearbox, the glasses and bottles clanking in the first glass galley, a crying baby in coach. Then… thud, thud, thud!

That's new, Matthew thought. And a little disconcerting.

Then, over the loud growl of the engines, he heard it again.

Matthew's eyes sprang open. The next triple thud shook his partition door. *Oh, crap!* he thought. No way would he allow himself to be stuck listening to Mr. Know-it-all for the entire flight. *Go away! I'm not home.* The idea of pretending to be asleep crossed his mind.

Louder… *knock, knock, knock!*

Damn, he's persistent.

Reluctantly, he pressed the 'open' button, which silently lowered the partition door.

"Hello, Professor!" Theia poked her head in, wearing a huge grin.

Matthew livened, inching from his seatback. "Theia? How? I thought…"

"It's not just Audree who has the power of persuasion," she boasted. Leaning closer, she tucked the edge of her hand into her cheek as if telling a secret. "I told him we were on our honeymoon." She chuckled mischievously, reminiscent of a schoolgirl, before settling back into her comfortable pod for the long flight ahead.

Honeymoon? Matthew's smile beamed from ear to ear, as he imagined… if only that were true.

CHAPTER 28

The Stakeout: Part II

Breaking his own rules, Bill cranked the ignition, bringing the engine to life. Despite spending most of the day shaded from the autumn sun while parked across the street from apartment 156A, the onset of the evening had stilled the breeze to a stagnant mugginess that not even a cracked open window could dispel.

Audree's whining for cool air over the last hour was as much as Bill could handle.

Within minutes, fresh chilled air blasted the dampness from Audree's neck as she panned her body close to the air vent.

She tugged her neckline lower with both hands, exposing more of her cleavage. "Ahh," she sighed, rolling her head, gulping in the air. "I can finally breathe."

Bill's eyes remained glued to his side mirror, watching for the 'tall men in suits' to arrive—or the golden-brown Lincoln, should the kidnappers be foolish enough to still be driving it.

"Sup it up, doll," Bill said, out the side of his mouth. "I can only run it for a few minutes. We can't risk running it for much longer. Don't wanna draw attention to ourselves, do we?"

From years of stakeouts, Bill had developed a set of simple rules. And unless you followed them, the days and nights would be long and uncomfortable. The first rule—be patient and prepared for a long wait. The second—bring coffee, snacks, and something to pee in. And finally—wear layered clothing to maintain a comfortable temperature. One big no-no was running the car engine to keep you cool or warm. A car sitting parked with exhaust fumes billowing out hour after hour may as well have a sign on top saying 'stakeout in progress.'

"Is there any coffee left?" Audree asked as she searched for the flask.

"No. We drank the last of it an hour ago."

"Oh, okay." The poignancy in her voice drew Bill's eyes from the side mirror to check on her. Both of her hands were now fanning her dress at the knees.

Seeing her in constant discomfort was hard to bear. But he did warn her this was no day trip. It was hard work requiring more than a modicum of patience. Actually, endless patience.

"Are you okay, doll?" Bill asked. "We can leave."

"No," she snapped. "We're staying. I'll be fine once I cool down."

Bill cupped his hand on her knee, grinning. "You're one tough broad."

Relishing the compliment with a wiggle, Audree seized the moment to open a new dialogue—marriage! Endearingly, her head tilted, her hand gently caressing the back of Bill's hand in her lap. "Hey, did you hear that Zac and Cloe are getting married?"

Bill's attention had already shifted back to the side mirror. "Uh uh."

"Yeah, who'd have thought, Zac and Cloe? At least we'll have a wedding to attend. It'll be lovely."

Bill remained tight-lipped.

"Cloe's going to look beautiful in a wedding dress," Audree's rambling continued, her one-track mind as relentless as her tongue. "Of course, she has the perfect figure for it. Hmm, I wonder if she'll let me lend a hand with the planning. That'll be fun, don't you think?"

Bill's silence wasn't a deliberate evasion of the question but rather a consequence of his diverted attention. Three dubious figures, having migrated from a nearby street corner, now stood directly across the street, their demeanor betraying a suspicious interest in Bill's car.

"Bill! Bill! Are you listening?"

Damn it! Bill cursed to himself. *I knew it. This goddamn idling engine's drawn their curiosity.*

Two of the three appeared to be Latino. One paced roguishly at the edge of the curb, sizing Bill up. The third, a Caucasian, leaned into an aggressive pose, elevating his chin.

With eyes locked on Bill, he talked into his mobile phone.

Who's he calling? Bill wondered.

Reinforcements?

Without breaking his stare, Bill carefully unholstered his .357 Magnum, placing it on the seat between his thighs.

"I think it's time we left," Bill blurted over Audree, silencing her list of wedding ideas. Engaging the car in drive and pulling out, he threw her a glance. "We'll pick this up again tomorrow. All right, darlin'?"

Only now, did she glimpse the reason they were now leaving. With a restrained smile, she nodded quickly.

It took more than a few punk gang members to intimidate Bill. Although he had left for Audree's safety, and because their cover was now blown, he knew that the three hoodlums, now sneering confidently, thought otherwise. And that offended Bill's ego. Intently, Bill pressed his nose to the glass, leering at the Latino as he drove past with a *fuck you* stare showing that he was not afraid.

At the end of the street, Bill's car turned, vanishing onto the Grand Concourse.

Just then, a tall, slender man casually approached the building entrance, carrying Chinese takeout in a white paper bag with white string handles. He sported a sharp black suit and polished leather brogue shoes. Retrieving a set of keys from his trouser pocket, he sifted through them until he found the one with '156A' stamped on its brass head.

After casting a final eye around the street, he entered the apartment building.

CHAPTER 29

Lumley Castle

The wheels of British Airways Flight BA1326 screeched onto the southwest runway of Newcastle airport, spraying standing water into a torrent of trailing clouds.

It was a typical northeast day—gray and misty with constant showers from the depressing overcast clouds rolling in from the western Pennines.

Now armed with their rental car contract and toting their luggage behind them, Matthew and Theia shouldered through the sliding doors into the dismal downpour awaiting them outside. Sheltered under the entrance's overhang, the heavy, musky raindrops drummed on its aluminum roof like a giant snare drum. "Over there," Matthew howled, pointing toward zone F. "Ready?"

Theia stacked her purse on top of her Tumi luggage then unfolded the collar on her jacket, clasping it across her chin. After pulling it tight against the back of her neck, she nodded. With Matthew leading the way, they dashed across the zebra crossing toward the rental car parking area.

Opposite arrivals, parked in the short-term parking area, was a metallic black BMW with two smartly dressed figures inside. They sat in near silence except for the gentle purr of the powerful V8 engine and intermittent screech from the rubber wipers.

For the last hour, both gentlemen had struggled with the worsening visibility to identify the faces of each arriving passenger. Making it worse, many of them had their faces buried behind scarves or hidden by hoods or umbrellas. "This is getting impossible," the driver said nervously.

His passenger, with shoulders spanning the width of the seat, reopened the manila folder in his lap, examining the dossier inside. The front page had two passport-style photographs paper-clipped to the corner, one of Matthew, the other of Theia. He flicked over the page, revealing candid photos taken at Newark airport the day earlier. They showed Matthew and Theia walking into the departure terminal entrance, dragging their luggage.

Below the picture was a zoomed-in photo of Theia's unmistakable red Tumi case.

Studying it, the broad fellow returned his scan to the faceless travelers outside.

Not far ahead, a man and a woman ran with their heads ducked low, their clothing and luggage a perfect match.

"There," the man said as his eyes followed them to their car. "It's them!"

"About time," the driver remarked. His gloved finger anxiously pressed the dial button on his phone, mounted on the dash.

It barely rang once before an aristocratic Englishman with flawless elocution answered. "Alistair, my dear boy, you have news?"

"Yes, sir. They're here."

"Excellent. Excellent. Now, be a splendid chap and try not to lose them."

If he did, Allister knew, it would be more than just a slap on his wrists. "Of course, sir," Alistair confirmed, then hung up.

When Matthew and Theia arrived at their silver Mercedes rental, the boot lid sprang open, awaiting their luggage. Matthew had been pounding on the remote as they approached, speeding their escape from the rain. While Theia slid straight into the passenger seat, Matthew wrestled their luggage into the boot. A moment later, he hurriedly settled into the right side of the car. Once seated, he leaned back in surprise, hovering both palms over the steering wheel. "Whoa!" It only dawned on him now that the British drove on the left, and the driver's side was on the right.

"That's the steering wheel, Professor!" Theia stated sarcastically. "You know, the thing that aids us to our destination." She pulled her seatbelt across her chest. "I'm presuming you have seen one before?"

"Yes, I can see that. Thank you. So, I guess I'm driving, am I?" Matthew's voice was hesitant.

Theia giggled. "Would you like me to?"

"No, no, it's fine. I got it. Driving on the left is probably the same as driving on the right—except—totally opposite!"

He pressed the 'start' button, lighting up the car's interior panels, then adjusted his seating position and mirrors. His hand loitered over the gear shift while he familiarized himself, then engaging gear, he mumbled, "I just figured with you being from England and all, you'd wanna drive." But what he meant was, he *hoped* she would.

"You forget, Matthew, when I was last here, cars didn't exist."

"Oh, right," he said, still finding the timeline incredible to grasp.

As Matthew pulled away, he had to crane his chin over the steering wheel to see through the rain. "Well, I don't want to be rude or anything, but I can see why you left. I thought England was supposed to be green, not gray."

Theia too sat forward, her hand on the dash. "You've never been to England before?"

"Yeah, once, when I was writing my thesis. But that feels like ancient history now."

Theia chuckled.

"Where's the exit?" he asked.

Theia pointed. "It's over there, beneath the large blue sign with exit written on it."

"Right. I just couldn't see it with this rain."

"Two minutes in and you're already lost."

After a short, slow quarter mile, the road intersected with a three-lane roundabout. Matthew's anxiety welled as he approached. He'd seen roundabouts before but had never understood which lane he was supposed to be in. Taking a gamble, he crept into the outer one and then circled the roundabout as other cars whizzed by much faster.

Almost free and clear, he exited south. An angry driver slowed along-side him and leaned on his horn, then gestured something obscene wildly through the side window before speeding on. Matthew reacted by jerking the car into the shoulder.

Theia shrieked. Instinctively, she reached for the steering wheel to steady it. "Careful."

"I'll be all right once we get on the main road," he affirmed, catching his breath.

"This *is* the main road, Professor!" she snapped.

Theia then examined the map on Matthew's phone. "Where are we staying, anyway?"

Matthew hadn't told her, wanting it to be a surprise. On the flight to London, he had spent an hour searching for the perfect location. And when he'd found it and booked it, he could hardly contain his excitement. While their mission here was a serious one, it didn't mean it couldn't be nostalgic and fun, and—Matthew hoped—romantic.

Just outside the City of Sunderland, by the small market town of Chester-le-Street, stood Lumley Castle. Now owned by the Earl of Scarborough, it had a few decades since been converted to a lavish period hotel, appointed with seventy-three bedrooms, a dungeon, and its very own resident ghost—*The Lady of Lumley*. When he booked the rooms, he couldn't help but wonder if Theia had known the orig-inal owners while they were alive, especially the wife, Lady Lily. To hear Theia's account firsthand would be a historian's dream and an enchanting start to their trip. Besides, he was also eager to discover if the legend of Lady Lumley's death was, in fact, true.

As it went, two priests had reportedly murdered her because she refused to convert to Catholicism, hurling her lifeless body into a well on the castle grounds.

Concealing their crime, the priests had informed their master that his wife had left him to become a nun! Even more suspicious, her name was stricken from official records as if she had never existed, making finding any documentation nearly impossible.

"We are staying at a castle not too far from your birthplace," Matthew shared. "Built by Sir Ralph Lumley, it's been around since the fourteenth century. A time when you were still here."

He paused, waiting for a reaction.

None came.

When Matthew peeked over, she appeared to be in thought.

"Do you remember him, at all?" he asked curiously. "Or his wife?"

After a moment, Theia stiffened. Both hands slapped on her cheeks as she gasped, "Lumley? Sir Ralph Lumley and his beautiful wife?"

Matthew's eyes bulged as they darted back and forth between her and the foggy road.

Theia took a deep breath, then said, "Nope, never met them, or heard of them." A cheeky smile swept across her face.

Matthew shook his head, snickering at his own naïveté.

Very funny!

FOR THE NEXT twenty minutes, the car ride was quietly peaceful, uninterrupted by conversation. The long-forgotten beauty of the English countryside had captivated Theia. By now, the rain had subsided to an occasional spit. Streaks of golden light angled from the heavens to the mystical meadows below. It had been hundreds of years since she had witnessed the beauty of this place, and to her amazement, it appeared untouched by evolution, industry, or a thriving civilization.

Matthew slowed, crossing a two-lane bridge serving as a natural moat around the castle grounds. Directing the way to the entrance was a towering maroon sign with an artist's rendering of the old castle and the words, 'Welcome to Lumley Castle.'

Matthew's eager toes danced on the pedals. "You're going to feel right at home here."

CHAPTER 30

Room 156A

DeRose paced the floor as if trying to wear a straight line into the carpet. Judging from the cheap, nylon low pile carpet, the sort that made your hair stand on end from the static, it wouldn't take him long. Across the room, Griffin sat at a square wooden table by the window.

He flipped his cards in some version of Solitaire.

The apartment was almost bare. When the former tenants had moved out, they'd abandoned the items too worthless to transport, such as the brown polyester three-seater couch centered in the room, fit for the dump. The blank wall opposite the couch had a single coaxial cable poking through the plaster, dangling to the floor in a loose coil. No TV, just a less dirty rectangular spot on the carpet where its cabinet had once stood. The only remaining furniture was the hardwood table and a pair of unmatching chairs parked by the window where Griffin dealt his deck.

DeRose checked his wristwatch again, pacing. "What time did he say he'd call?"

"He didn't," Griffin replied with a smirk. "Why not grab a seat?"

The paper-thin curtains, half torn and tattered, did little to block the stifling late afternoon sun painting streaks across the floor.

Fortunately for them, the window air-conditioning unit still worked, though it did nothing to filter the musty stench of age that rose from the carpet the warmer it got.

While the squalid conditions were bearable, the anticipation of the potentially life-changing phone call was not. After all, he rarely ever spoke to his boss.

Not his regular boss, nor the one his boss reported to.

No. This boss was *the* boss. All bucks stopped with him.

And it was not as if he could just quit if the phone call went south. This job required commitment, dedication, and a lifetime of service. Harsh though it may seem, the potential for reward was substantial. A job many would kill for.

But as the carpet wore thin beneath his feet, he worried he may have to.

"Relax!" Griffin repeated for the umpteenth time, then kicked out the vacant chair with his foot. "Take a load off."

DeRose plonked himself at the table, slamming his hands flat on top. His cheek twitched while his fingers tapped incessantly as if playing an invisible keyboard. When he spoke, there was no hiding the nervousness in his trembling voice.

"We had no choice. We had to grab the kid. Right?"

"Uh-uh. *You* grabbed the kid," Griffin snapped. "Let's not confuse *we* with *you*. If you'd done what you were supposed to, we wouldn't be in this mess. What was it I told you before you went? Quick in and out and get back to the car. But no..."

For a moment, DeRose ceased all movement and then—his fingers began again, accompanied by his tapping feet. "What do you think he's gonna say?"

Griffin sniggered, flipping over another card. "I don't know, but I'd make sure your affairs were in order if I were you!" Then he laughed louder at his joke.

Not amused, DeRose sat motionless except for his bottom lip, which he chewed. Then, slapping both hands on the table, he launched to his feet. "Shit, shit, shit," he recited over and over, continuing his back-and-forth pacing.

"Okay, now you're annoying me," Griffin mumbled. "Why don't you go check on the kid? See if he… you know, wants something."

DeRose knew fine well Griffin didn't care two hoots about the boy. Nor about anyone but himself for that matter. But it would serve as a welcomed distraction.

He slid open the double bolt on the paint-chipped bedroom door, then with a turn of the handle's latch, unlocked it. The handles were reversed, positioning the locks on the outside of the bedroom. DeRose creaked the door ajar and leaned his head in.

The dimly lit room smelled earthy, like a still pond on a sweltering day. A fly buzzed near, and DeRose swatted at it. A trickle of light spilled through a hole in the boarded windows, barely lighting the far corner where a makeshift bed of musty blankets layered to form some semblance of a mattress. David huddled on top; his legs folded beneath him. His trembling hands held an old doll with blonde hair. More befitting for a girl, but it was all DeRose could salvage at such short notice.

"Get you anything, kid?" DeRose offered in his kindest voice.

David slowly shook his head, his chin barely lifting off his chest. His puppy eyes, glazed with fear, only dared to rise as far as DeRose's feet.

DeRose instantly calmed. The sight of someone more anxious, more terrified, than himself regained some perspective. With genuine sincerity, he pledged, "Hey kid. Don't worry, this'll be over soon. You'll be back home with your mommy before you know it, okay? I promise."

David nodded.

As he closed the door, DeRose's mobile rang. He raced to answer it. "Yeah."

The caller's voice spoke with an eloquent English accent, a vernacular of a gentleman. "How's our young David doing?"

DeRose took the question as accusatory. "Look, I screwed up. What was I gonna do? I couldn't leave him there after he saw me roaming around in her place, could I? Damn it, what a mess..." The pacing was now at twice the speed. "Please, I know I messed up. Give me another chance?"

"Yes, it was rather incompetent of you, my dear man," the voice said, oozing a calmness that surprised him. Given the circumstances, he'd expected a wrath like no other. "As it happens," the voice continued, "your imbecility has quite unexpectedly given rise to an uncanny chain of events. Fate, perhaps? I'd even conjecture that *you* have played a key role. A prophetic catalyst if you will."

DeRose's panic de-escalated. His pacing ceased. Instead of anguish, it was curiosity now eating at him. "Why? What's happened?"

"Let's just say, your head is no longer in the noose." The Englishman's tone became grimmer, deeper. "But I need you to do something for me."

HALFWAY THROUGH A fresh deal, Griffin hovered his card hand while his eyes sharpened on DeRose. By now, he'd expected him to be begging for his life. DeRose's sudden calm and halted pacing meant something had happened—something big.

Shifting in his chair, Griffin strained his ears, but DeRose turned his back and moved to the opposite corner. Head down, he faced the wall like a scorned child. Despite DeRose's attempt to lower his voice, Griffin could still make out his fragmented words, though they provided little insight into the ongoing conversation.

"I understand, sir. But what if..." DeRose straightened abruptly, his voice humbled. "Yes, yes. Of course. Right away." Nervously, his hand clawed at the back of his neck, then slid around to his face.

By the motion of his weaving head, Griffin deduced that DeRose's massaging of his temples was intense. "Okay. No, no, no, I can handle it. Yes, sir. I will."

Finally, moving in slow motion, DeRose lowered the phone to his side.

"Sounded like it went well?" Griffin mocked, resuming his deal.

"Yeah, what do you know?" DeRose hadn't turned to face him yet.

"So, what's the plan? What're we doing with this damn kid?"

DeRose didn't answer. Instead, he profiled his face on the bedroom door. And for a while, just stared at it. Then, in a somber tone, he whispered under his breath, "I'm sorry, kid. I'm gonna have to break that promise."

CHAPTER 31

Afternoon Tea

The skeleton key twisted in the lock of the oak-paneled door to the King James Suite. Ahead of Theia, the bellboy, dressed in an authentic copy of fifteenth-century period attire, wheeled in her luggage and placed it carefully on a stool against the wainscoted wall.

Adjacent to it, a fire dwindled in the grand marble Adams-style fireplace. The bellboy made a small courtesy adjustment, roaring the flames to life.

"To madam's liking?" he asked.

"Yes, thank you." Theia pulled a tip from her purse and extended it to him.

Humbly accepting, head bowed, he reminded her, "Afternoon tea is served in the library until five; evening dinner in the Knights Restaurant begins at five-thirty. Will there be anything else, madam?"

"No, thank you."

After the bellboy left, Theia surveyed her grand room. It was warm and inviting, with vibrant reds and terracotta. Red was the color of royalty, stature, opulence, and splendor.

And such was this room. Teasing the air, her nose caught a familiar scent: roses and lilies with a perfect hint of jasmine. Had her eyes been closed, she could easily have imagined herself amidst a budding English country garden in springtime. Around her, the church-like walls curved toward the ceiling which in turn vaulted into a cathedral arch.

Exploring further, she made her way to the bedroom through the Gothic arched door.

Showcased against the wall, the magnificent twenty-foot tall, four-poster bed ornately hung its gorgeous brocade fabrics tied at each post; the fairytale mattress was so high that steps were provided to climb its height.

Theia's phone chimed.

Recognizing it as a message from Audree, she quickly plucked the phone from her coat's outer pocket.

Hey girly, just checking in. Hope the flight was smooth?
Nothing to report yet :(Bill and I waited around all day but
no sign of the bad guys or David yet.
Bill said cops will call again Monday.
Hopefully with search warrant. Stakeout duty again this afternoon.
We'll find him, hun. Don't worry.
Luv ya xxx
Bestie

Theia's expectant shoulders gave way to disappointment. Before she could ponder the message further, the room phone rang on the bedside table.

Placing the receiver to her ear, she couldn't utter a single word before Matthew asked in an overly English accent, "Afternoon tea, madam?"

"Sounds perfect!" She eased a smile. "Give me five…" But upon sighting her weary reflection in the gilded framed mirror, she revised that to, "*Fifteen* minutes to freshen up." Returning the phone to its cradle, she anxiously reviewed Audree's text. *Be careful, Audree,* she thought. For two days, her stomach had been in knots over David; now, she had three to worry about.

A tad more than fifteen minutes later, Theia entered the grand library room. She spotted Matthew in the far corner, standing next to one of several floor-to-ceiling mahogany bookcases separating the seating areas into square enclaves.

Inches from his face, an open leather-bound book saddled wearily over his palm while his other hand caressed the page. When he saw Theia, he slammed the book closed with one hand.

He moved to greet her.

Again, with an English pompous accent reminiscent of a parlor servant, he bowed. "Good afternoon, madam."

Theia, laughing, reciprocated. "Good evening, fine sir. Pray, how goeth thine day?"

She curtsied demurely. Matthew grinned so wide, it appeared his mouth might travel around to the back of his head. To speak in even a semblance of the language of bygone days...

Offering his arm, he escorted her to an easy chair in the corner and adjusted her chair, taking a seat. The history professor in Matthew brimmed with excitement to share his historic findings. "My room has an original William & Mary wingback Victorian chair. Can you believe it! A nineteenth-century antique chair in a hotel bedroom! Amazing! These Brits don't know what they've got."

Theia giggled. "When we pulled up to the hotel, you told me I'd feel right at home here." She prodded Matthew's knee with her fingertips. "I think it is *you* who feels right at home."

Matthew smiled.

The female server approached their corner, wearing mock, full medieval attire, her accent muddled between Scots and English. "Hello. Welcome to Lumley Castle. Are you wishing to take afternoon tea?"

"Absolutely!" Matthew answered, carrying on the guise of a refined gentleman. "I believe we *do* wish that!" He dipped his chin at Theia, begging her agreement.

"Oh, most certainly. That would be divine!" she gushed.

The server handed each a menu, now looking amused as if believing their affected air was something put on for her specifically.

"We have several options to choose from depending on your mood and appetites."

"I don't know about you," Matthew blurted, "but I'm famished."

"Me too," Theia agreed.

Matthew turned to the server, his refined accent already lost in the hunger of the moment. "We'll take whichever has the biggest portion, I guess."

"Certainly, sir. If you will allow me, I recommend the grand afternoon tea?"

"Grand it is!" Matthew said as he and Theia handed back their menus. When the waitress left, Matthew slumped back in his chair and released a long breath.

"Are you tired, Matthew? We can call it a night?"

Matthew rubbed his eyes. "What, and miss all the fun? Besides, I'm not really that tired." The talk of tiredness, however, brought an unstoppable yawn. "Well, maybe a little! I'm just excited to be here. I don't want something as boring as sleep to ruin it! Perhaps it was the added concentration during the drive that took it out of me."

"We almost didn't make it here!" Theia laughed. "Maybe tomorrow, I should drive."

Matthew smiled embarrassedly. Defending his ego, he shook his head. "Why are British roads so damn narrow and winding, anyway? And why do they insist on driving on the left?"

"Tradition," Theia stated. "You mean the great and powerful professor hasn't heard this one?"

"No, pray tell."

Theia adjusted her seat. "In ancient times, when travelers would pass by each other on their horses, not knowing if the passerby was friend or foe, they would grasp their swords, ready for battle. Most people being right-handed in the use of their weaponry, they would pass each other on the left, exposing their fighting side."

"So why did Americans switch to the right? Were we just clueless about swordsmanship?"

"Ha! No. Well, as carts increased in size, so did the number of horses. Soon, horses pulled carts in tandem, and the driver would sit on the left to allow his right hand to whip. But sitting on the left made it harder to gauge clearance as they passed travelers on the left, so they switched to the right. But those larger carts and entourage of tandem-driven horses were more typical on the Western frontier. Here in England, small carts persisted, as did the left-hand rule."

Beguiled by her firsthand account, Matthew looked amazed for a minute or two. "Everything I know is from a book," he said. "It's astonishing to learn history from someone who lived it."

Theia leaned forward with a flirtatious giggle. "I actually read that one time on Wikipedia. Sorry! But it sounded convincing enough."

Matthew gave a hearty laugh. "Ah, I see the British humor resurfacing with your return."

The server returned shortly with their afternoon tea, placing the silver tray on the round table between them. They noted the usual assortment of teapot, sugar, and milk, and a three-tiered plate decoratively covered with delightful finger sandwiches, cakes, and scones.

She poured the tea to their liking.

As they delved into the afternoon treats, Matthew explored another topic. "Speaking of old stories, in the last couple of days you have shared some amazing ones. Truly incredible. But there have been moments where you appear adrift. Like in some kind of a trance. I've had to call your name several times before you finally snap out of it." It wasn't presented as a question, but Matthew waited for an explanation.

The statement threw Theia off guard. About to sip her tea, she instead placed the china cup in its matching saucer and put the saucer back on the table. "Sometimes, I have these visions," she explained. "Memories really. But I experience them as if they are happening in real-time. The images, sounds, smells, even sensations like pain, all come flooding back as real as you are now."

She lowered her chin, her voice sad. "It makes it difficult to let go of the past, to forget."

"Do they usually occur so frequently?"

"No. Hardly ever actually. I suppose all the digging into my past must have triggered it. However, my psychic radar is always on. Without that, I'd probably be dead."

"Psychic radar?"

"Yes. It's more like… a gut feeling. I tried explaining it to Audree earlier, but it's difficult to put into words." Theia's eyes combed the ceiling. "Do you understand what auras are, Matthew?"

"Uh, yeah. The life force, or energy of something living, right? Or are you talking about the actual visible glow around something, like during an eclipse?"

"I guess it's a little of both for me," Theia said, trying to frame the words. "Try to imagine if I could *see* a person's aura, and if it were yellow, or green, or red, for example. I'd experience it as innocence, deceit, or love. Sometimes, a person's aura is dark. Their intentions and their inner thoughts are more insidious. Sometimes… I see the intensity of a person's light, which…"

The room darkened so fast, it startled Theia.

It was Japan, 1868, during the battle of Aisu.

Theia stumbled across the bloody battlefield, the battle now over, only the inglorious smell of death rising from the mesh of bodies interwoven in a fabric of corpses.

Their blood and feces spilled into the waterlogged clay, pooling on the surface. Her shogun and best friend, Nakano Takeko, lay wounded among the dead, or those soon to be. Theia rushed to her side and clasped her hand, then wept. As soon as she held it, she knew Nakano's time had come.

"Theia!" Matthew called out, breaking her from her vision.

"I'm sorry," Theia said as she refocused on her story. "Sometimes, the diminishing light of someone's aura tells me that the person will soon die."

After thinking about that, Matthew gazed around the room. "So, you can simply look at all these people and know if they're good, bad, or if they are going to die soon?"

Theia's eyes followed Matthew's. "No. It doesn't work like that. I have to physically interact with them. The more intense the interaction, the more I see." Her posture stiffened. "Remember the man in the underground parking, the one I told you had the double cross tattoo on his wrist?"

Matthew nodded.

"He had no aura."

"None? Does that happen often?"

With a look filled with dread, Theia shook her head slowly.

"Maybe that makes perfect sense," Matthew said, a spark coming to his eye. "The men tracking you undoubtedly know everything about you, right? They would know you could sense their ill intentions *if* that's indeed what they have. Wouldn't it make sense they would've learned to control or subdue their feelings, their auras, like a stone-faced poker player?"

"Maybe," Theia uttered, sounding doubtful.

Matthew upped his beat. "Hey, tomorrow, we're getting answers. Okay? Hang in there."

Theia nodded. "So, what *is* the plan tomorrow?"

"First, we meet my university friend, Aiden, at St. Peter's Church. He's the pastor there. I'm hoping he can get us access to the archivist department at the Old Palace at York Minster." He swiped his phone, hoping to find an email response. "I've been trying. But so far, no success. If that doesn't work... well, we'll figure it out."

Theia smiled.

"But tonight," Matthew continued, "I thought we could start by researching one of the most ancient, most ritualistic cultures for which this area is most famous—"

"What's that?" Theia's interest perked.

"A pint at the local pub! What say ye, young lass? Fancy a visit to yonder fine hostelry?"

Theia instantly agreed. It had been a stressful few days, to say the least, and Matthew's was the first company she had enjoyed, outside of Audree's, in many years.

"I'll need to freshen my makeup and put on my dancing clothes!" Matthew jested. "How about we meet in the lobby at..." He checked his watch. "Seven o'clock?"

"Well, if you're freshening your fine self," Theia said as she hoisted an eyebrow, "that'll give me time for a hot bath. Seven it is."

As they stood, Matthew stared intently at her.

"What?" Theia asked.

He began fidgeting with embarrassment, like an awkward young boy telling the girl on the playground he fancied her. "About what you said earlier, I was just wondering, you know, what *my* aura says to you?"

Theia laughed. Since she'd first laid eyes on Matthew, she had known instantly that his aura was warm and friendly, dependable, and loyal. All the pleasant colors. He was a good person—probably. Having been fooled before, she was never one hundred percent sure. Plus, she always tried to keep people at a distance. Including Matthew. Erring on the side of caution, she protected herself behind her wall of seclusion. However, that wall had been dismantling brick by brick with every minute she spent with Matthew.

Never before had she analyzed an aura on request, but in fair spirit, she stood back to examine his. Matthew flung both arms to the side and twisted a half-turn left and right as if modeling an outfit. Studying him intently, she folded her arm across her torso and perched her other elbow on top as her thumb and forefinger massaged her chin. Without physical contact, it was difficult to clearly distinguish. Nonetheless, she concentrated her stare.

At first, his aura began shimmering with his characteristic colors but then, studying deeper into his soul, a rich sunset red radiated so vividly that it masked all other colors.

Its warm, phosphorus glow touched her heart. Red was the color of love. Wasn't it?

In any case, it matched the color of his abashed cheeks and neck.

Her heart fluttered, cheeks blushing pink too. She turned away, clearing her throat. "Um, yes. All very nice. You have an… agreeable aura, Matthew." She noticed their lunch bill had not been signed; a welcomed distraction for her. She grabbed the leather folder and pen and began scribbling on the receipt. "Twenty percent for a tip okay?"

"Agreeable?" Matthew said, chortling. "I'm… agreeable? That's it?"

"Yes, well, like I said, it doesn't always work." Closing the folder on the receipt, she glanced up at Matthew attempting a straight face. Poker was not her game.

Matthew held out his hand, his confidence beaming. "Shall we?"

Accepting it, she hauled herself to her feet. They stood close, eyes locked, the room's conversation muted to silence. All she could see was the glowing red of Matthew's aura, glistening like a California sunrise.

But then it changed to something unexpected. To something terrible. Its luminance faded.

Stricken, she snapped her hand from Matthew's. Flushed cheeks cooled as she gasped for air, her heart pounding.

"Is everything okay?" Matthew asked.

"I'm fine," Theia fired back before he had time to finish his question.

Turning for the door, she spluttered, "Seven, right? Fine." Not even when Matthew called her name did she stop to look back. "I'll see you in the lobby, Matthew," she cried as she scurried from the room.

Theia burst into her suite, slamming the heavy door behind her.

She threw her trembling back against it, one hand pressed to her breaking heart. Tears broke through her resistance and spilled down her cheeks as she slid down the door. She could not control the heart-rending sob, the sorrowful plea escaping through her fingers.

"No, God, please. Not Matthew."

CHAPTER 32

The Lambton Worm

Matthew sighed at his poor timing when he and Theia stepped into The Lambton Worm amid the melee of rush hour. Three deep, the punters stood shoulder to shoulder, wrangling for a front-row audience with the over-tasked bar staff, each jostling and shoving, casting dirty looks at each other. Shouting their orders above one another, their words were indistinguishable. Yelling in a New York bar would get you thrown out in a New York minute. Here, it seemed customary. Or at least necessary.

By now, Matthew was regretting having ignored the advice from the hotel's hip concierge lady. Advice she apparently gave to all international guests:

Avoid 'The Worm' on Sunday evenings. Karaoke night draws a crazy crowd.

Admittedly, Matthew had felt cool informing her they were New Yorkers, that crazy crowds were their jam. Truth be known, it was the first time he'd used the word jam in any sentence not involving bread.

"I'll get us a drink," Matthew shouted, prompting Theia to wander off in search of a table. Impersonating the famous detective Columbo, he called after her, "Just one more thing, ma'am." She turned her head, and he asked, "You wanna beer?"

Missing her usual smile, she gently nodded.

Matthew braced himself.

Okay, here we go. When in Rome. Then he stormed the bar, feeling more like an angry rugby player charging into a scrummage than a patron simply seeking a beer.

A few bruises later, frothy ales held high and spilling down his arms, he shoved his way back through the mob. To his relief, Theia had found a quiet table by a fireplace roaring a warm romantic glow.

"Wow, that was an experience. Sorry it took so long." He slid her beer across to her.

Theia was pleasant but distant. Matthew knew something was troubling her. She hadn't uttered a single word during their fifteen-minute hike to the pub. His best guess was he had embarrassed her by asking about his aura.

No regrets. Though, with her coolness now, he tried to regret it. But learning from her expression that she held a hidden kindling for him was hard to regret.

Showing his emotional card came easily, but he knew that was not so for Theia. She was a closed book. While winning her emotion and catching a glimpse inside this mysterious woman was nearly all he could think about, he now feared he may have moved too quickly.

Finally, Theia turned her solemn gaze towards Matthew. She opened her mouth to speak but paused, as if grappling with the words. Whatever she would say, Matthew sensed it was difficult for her. Like that awkward breakup conversation, only he was the one being dumped.

"Tomorrow…" she said, then stalled as if Matthew's eyes had stifled her courage.

Matthew interjected, trying to be positive, "Yes, tomorrow. I have a meeting set up with Aiden, but we have to arrive after morning ma—"

Theia cut him off, "We are going home tomorrow, Matthew."

Her statement silenced him for a moment while he struggled to understand. "You mean, *your* home, right? You mean York?"

"No, I mean *New* York."

"What? Why? We just arrived a few hours ago! What's changed? Has something happened?"

Theia maintained her stone-like posture. Rigid. Unreadable.

He leaned back in his chair. "Look, I'm sorry if I embarrassed you earlier…"

"It's not that, Matthew," she said almost in tears. "Please, just trust me on this." The sigh he released seemed never-ending. To say he was disappointed would be a gross understatement.

"Is it David? Have they found out something about the kidnapping?" Whatever it was, it must be dramatic and terrible to warrant this degree of upset.

Theia shook her head.

Despite her sudden eagerness to leave, he wasn't convinced she wanted to. Answers meant everything to her and maybe held the key to saving a small boy's life. No, something had scared her; it showed in her eyes. "I have an idea," he said. "Tomorrow, why don't we—"

"I've seen something, okay?" Theia blurted. "I… It's not safe here. We need to leave, first flight."

"Hey, hey, it's okay," Matthew said, trying to calm her. "You don't have to be afraid anymore. I won't let anything happen to you."

"You don't understand, Matthew." She looked him in the eyes this time. "I mean, it's not safe here… *for you.*" A single tear escaped onto her cheek that she quickly wiped away.

Matthew furrowed his brow, shaking his head. "What? What do you…" He stopped himself. It was pointless. She had already locked up.

Palms up, he slid his hands across the table, his fingers beckoning hers. Initially, she went to hold his hands but then withdrew hers to the table's edge as if afraid to touch him.

"It's okay," Matthew assured. "Please."

With some reluctance, she slipped her hands into his while closing her eyes, turning away her face. But as Matthew's thumbs burnished the backs of her hands, she yielded. She opened her eyes, peering at him.

He laughed. "See, that wasn't so bad, was it?" He shook her hands. "Now, why are you acting so tense? Please, talk to me. I can't help if I don't know what is going on."

She inhaled a breath. "Earlier I... I saw..."

Matthew chuckled again at the suspense. "Saw what?"

"Doesn't matter what I saw." Theia squeezed his hands. "It's gone now. I can't explain why or how. But we should go, just in case."

Matthew's voice firmed, resolute.

"Listen. I don't know what you saw, and don't even care. We're seeing this through to the end. You and me. We're a team. Okay? No more running, no hiding. Fuck 'em. Fuck all of 'em. Whoever this organization is that wants you dead, we'll find out. We'll get you your answers. And Theia," he said as he ducked his head close, "we *can* do this."

Theia remained silent but her expression betrayed a deep wish to believe him.

"Tell you what," Matthew compromised as Theia was still unconvinced. "Let's meet with Aiden at St. Peter's Church tomorrow. If he can't get us into the Old Palace records, it's game over anyway, and we go home. I promise. We'll take the very next flight. *But*, if he can, I say we pay a visit and get some answers, finally. And *then* we go home. All I'm asking is you give us one more day. We'll be in a church and a cathedral, the safest places on Earth. Right? What do you say?"

His pep talk worked. The sparkle returned to her eyes, her passion for discovery, for answers.

Theia tugged at his hands. "One more day," she said, her voice cracking but her confidence was building, allowing her a small chuckle.

"Let's drink to it," Matthew said, raising his pint. "Cheers!"

"Skål!" Theia returned in her deepest Norwegian accent, clinking his glass.

"Skål!" Matthew aped. They each chugged a large gulp of beer, wiping froth from their upper lips with the backs of their hands. The 'skål' had made Matthew wonder. "You mentioned you knew four languages by the time you were ten. So how many do you know now?"

"Not really sure. Many were dialects that aren't around today. I probably wouldn't remember most of them, not having spoken them in so long."

"Which ones *do* you remember? Say something in another language."

"Like what?"

"Anything."

Her eyes rose in thought, scouring the coffered ceiling for phrases. Finding one, she spoke it fluently, "Je mourrai pour ceux que j'aime."

"French. What does it mean?"

"It's my family motto." Her emerald eyes stared deeply into his as she translated, "I would die for those I love."

Matthew's breath caught in his throat. For a fleeting moment, he wondered if those words, those magical promises, were meant for him… and him alone.

CHAPTER 33

Give it up for Theia

When the hand mic first switched on, it sent a piercing squeal through the giant loudspeakers. Matthew flinched, clenching an eye shut, tugging at his earlobe.

Then, the voice boomed, "Who's ready for some karaoke?" In the far corner of the room, the bald host donning outlandish Elton John-styled glasses stepped onto a triangular portable stage. "How's everyone doing tonight?" The crowd cheered. "Before we bring up the usual weekend warriors, let's invite the newbies! Any newbies in tonight?" He squinted over the spotlight, shielding his eyes with a hand. "C'mon, don't be shy."

Theia's eyebrows arched; she clapped with excitement. "I love karaoke!"

"Really?" Matthew found it hard to believe. "I'm sorry, but you don't seem the karaoke type."

"My best friend is Audree! Like I have any choice in the matter." Grinding wood on wood, she slid back her chair. "You want to give it a go? It's fun."

"Hell no! But you, m'lady. Go right ahead."

This, I've gotta see, he thought. Before she could change her mind, Matthew sprang to his feet and yelled toward the stage, "We've got your first performer right here!" Both his index fingers pointed down to Theia.

"Let's hear it for our first, brave pop star!" the host announced, enlivening the audience. Then, as Theia approached the crowd, like the Red Sea for Moses, they parted to allow her through.

In the days Matthew had known her, Theia had breached the realms of credibility, made the impossible possible, and broken the very laws of nature itself.

She was twelve centuries old. Immortal. All of this, he somehow accepted without any question. And yet, watching her climb the stage in the spotlit corner of this rowdy English pub, he had never been more surprised than he was at this precise moment.

The song was selected, the mic stand adjusted, and her performance began.

A second round of applause erupted at the start of the music, then quickly withered. Drums burst in rapid beats like the snare percussion of a military march. A bagpipe followed, accompanied by a soft violin. The unfamiliar tune, likened to old Celtic, sent shivers across Matthew's shoulders and neck. Gaining volume, the loudspeakers reverbed the peaceful sound as if echoing from the hallowed halls of a grand cathedral.

And then came her mystical voice. So beautiful. So angelic and soothingly eerie yet hinting at sadness—everything in that described Theia. Her soft hypnotic voice swooned the entire bar into a synchronous spellbinding sway. Even the bar staff paused their polishing and pouring.

It was a sad song. Though Matthew understood few of the words, it didn't matter. The song's sorrowful soprano was enough to break hearts and summon tears. For Matthew, it almost did.

At the end of her performance, the music faded, leaving only her voice resonating with a delicate vibrato as it too fell to silence. For the first time since they'd arrived, the room was quiet. Dead quiet. No clanking glasses, no punters yelling orders, not a single natter. And then, like a home team goal scored at a football final, the roar from the crowd almost blew out the windows.

The host clapped his mic. "Wow! What a performance. Give it up for Theia, all the way from New York, everybody." As she stepped from the stage and headed to her seat, the host challenged the Sinatra wannabees. "Who's the next brave soul?" Without a response, he added, "We may be having an early night after that!"

The crowd parted for her once again, Theia beaming a seductive smile while leveling her eyes on Matthew. In that moment, he felt the whole world around him disappear, time slowing.

She was his rockstar, and he was unconditionally thunderstruck.

As the night went on, neither Matthew nor Theia wanted it to end, but the jetlag and the long day ahead demanded their beds. They strolled the intimately lit tree-lined drive back to the castle.

"I really needed that. Thank you, Matthew. Maybe not that last beer, though. Phew!"

Theia's magical performance had pushed Matthew over the edge; he was totally smitten. He studied her, taking in every mannerism: her cute, girlish walk, each graceful tiptoed step, the swaying arms—a body showing happiness. The image made him smile.

"Miss God of Light," Matthew uttered, "you were amazing tonight. You never cease to amaze me, Theia."

"You can thank Audree. She's dragged me to more karaoke bars than I care to remember. *Her* voice puts everyone to shame."

"Okay." With cupped hands around his mouth, Matthew screamed to the starry sky, "Thank you, Audree!" A few startled crows launched from the branches.

Theia's uncoordinated finger fumbled across her lips. "Shh."

But Matthew didn't care if he woke the whole of England. "I've never had so much fun on a date before."

Theia halted her step, focusing her effort on sober speech. "Is that what this is? A date?"

"No, I-I didn't mean that. I meant…"

Theia giggled mischievously, then walked onward.

Matthew smirked at her teasing. "Yeah, well, you know what, m'lady," he said, catching up to her, "I think you may be a little too old for me, anyway. I draw the line at a thousand years."

Theia gasped and whimsically punched his arm. "I'll have you know that older women are beautiful lovers,'" she said, quoting the famous country song.

Soon, they reached the castle entrance. Even his elf-sized steps and amble hadn't slowed time enough to prolong their moonlit walk. On the contrary, it seemed twice as fast as their walk to the pub. Ahead, the giant arched oak door studded with black rivets hung ajar on its giant band and gudgeon hinges, marking the official end of their night. They stopped ten yards in front, facing each other.

"I had a great time tonight," Matthew whispered. "Let's um, get some rest; we have an early start."

With a drunken salute and a snap of her heel, Theia slurred in a deeply silly voice, "Yes, sir, Professor. Will report in the courtyard at oh-six-hundred, ready for duty, sir." The 'sir,' she shouted.

Unable to resist, he whisked his hand around the small of her back and squeezed her to his chest, landing an impulsive kiss.

Reacting, Theia gripped his lapels with both hands and shoved him back. Though he'd wished for that precious kiss, it wasn't planned. Now, he regretted it.

"I'm…" was all he managed before she snatched him close. Then, raising herself on her tiptoes, she reached her lips to his.

Her warm hand cradled his right cheek, her other fingering through the back of his curly hair, gripping a fistful and pushing his lips tighter to hers.

As Matthew's arms enveloped her frame, the warmth of her bosom, pressing softly against him, sent his heart racing and blood pulsing. Savoring her, his hands explored every inch of her back. The long passionate kiss dissolved into a series of shorter ones until, finally, the occasional peck. She opened her eyes and gazed into his. Matthew's had remained open, selfishly clinging to her beauty.

Dropping back on her heels, Theia's hands gently brushed Matthew's scraggly hair from his eyes. She smiled. "I'm so tired. I need to go to my *King James* Suite." As she backed away, her arm straightened, prolonging the touch of his face. After a few steps, she turned toward the heavy oak door. "I wouldn't want to keep the King waiting!" she said, giggling at her silly joke, followed by a more sincere, "Night, Matthew."

When he heard his name from those lips, his heart skipped. Dazed, he stuttered, "N-night," then watched her until she disappeared behind the door. Before she did, she stole a last glance over her shoulder. *Yes!* Matthew thought.

In her room, wearing her white silken tank top and shorts, Theia climbed onto her four-poster bed and collapsed backward into the plush mattress. Arms and legs sprawled like a star, she gazed up into the fabric-hung canopy. Her memory rushed to recall the night, longing to relive it.

She giggled at his goofy jokes and hilarious Columbo impressions. Every gesture, every word was replayed. It was evident by now that her emotional wall had been completely defenseless against him. Like a wrecking ball, Matthew had demolished it.

Having stood for centuries, that wall was her only protection. Now laid in ruin, she felt a vulnerability the likes of which she had long forgotten. But the flutters in her chest, the tightness in her stomach, the constant obsessing about Matthew, were sensations she had not forgotten. True, she hadn't experienced this sensation in over a millennium. Not since her precious Asma.

Unmistakably, this sensation was love. She dared to voice the words in her head lest she not believe it. *I love him.* She smiled tenderly.

Soon, that smile faded, a dark thought invading her reverie. Her immortality forbade her to love. Of course, it would never work with Matthew. How could it?

The wall had served to protect her, but it also served to protect others. If Matthew loved as deeply as she did, it would only bring him pain and suffering. Moreso if she allowed it to continue.

Again, she remembered that torturous image from earlier, the vision of Matthew's diminishing aura that could only mean his death. Yet in the bar, she had experienced a different one, brighter, full of life. Although she was relieved, it still concerned her.

Puzzled her.

If it was some kind of a message or a warning, she hadn't understood it. But she'd witnessed it. There was no doubting that.

It was her job to protect Matthew, emotionally and physically, both of which she jeopardized the closer they became. She sighed heavily. These dark reflections were dampening her mood. Yet, as much as she hated it, she vowed to distance herself. To try, at least. It was best for everyone.

Except me!

Searching for answers had been a lifelong journey, but without someone to share them, what was the point?

Reaching under the tasseled shade, she switched off the bedside lamp, tucked herself between the crisp, cool cotton sheets, and rolled to her side. Sadness faded, and it wasn't long before a loving smile returned to her lips. Tonight, she conceded, she would allow herself to dream of love. Tomorrow… well, that was another day.

CHAPTER 34

The Chase

The Next Day.

Since the crack of dawn, Bill's Toyota had been parked diagonally across the street from apartment 156A. Audree sat next to him idly swiping through the latest social media posts on her iPhone.

Bill reached behind his seat to retrieve a red flask.

"That's the soup," Audree said as he unscrewed the lid.

"Huh?"

"That's soup. The tartan one has the coffee in it."

"Hmm. What kind of soup?"

"Tomato," she said, still swiping at her phone. "I made it myself."

With a guttural grunt, he returned the flask to the back seat and retrieved the tartan one instead. He unscrewed the lid and poured his coffee into it.

The cool, crisp morning air produced a cloud of steam that quickly rose and warmed his frigid face.

Audree pointed to the opposite side of the street where a golden ray of sun broke across the pavement. "We should have parked over there. At least there, we'd be warm."

"My vantage point's better from here," Bill said, regarding his side mirror. "Sorry, babe."

Just then, Bill's phone rang.

He answered, holding it to his ear. "Ya." He listened for a beat then passed Audree a promising glance. And a thumbs up! "Great, nice work, Chief. We're here now, holding down the fort." Bill listened to the Chief's instructions. "Okay. Got it. Oh, and Chief, don't be sending any rookies. I've got a bad feeling about this one."

Audree stared in anticipation as Bill hung up.

"Well, good news, love. That was O'Malley. I don't know how he pulled it off, but he's managed to get Judge Perez to sign off on the warrant. Attaboy."

"Oh my God, that's great." Audree's knees bounced. "So, when do they get here?"

"Dunno darlin'." He returned to his reconnaissance. "An hour, maybe less. Here's hopin'."

Audree let out a long sigh as her head sank into her shoulders. "I wonder if I should text Theia. Or wait. I'd hate to fill her with false hope. Do you still reckon we got the right guys?"

Bill spoke from the side of his mouth, his eyes glued to the side mirror, "We'll know soon enough, babe. Soon enough. Maybe hold off calling until the backup crew gets here and we know for sure."

"It's just," she went on, "we've watched for two days straight. I'm beginning to wonder—maybe we got it wrong. Maybe they don't even live here. Or maybe they've snuck out in the middle of the night."

Bill nodded slowly. "It's easy to lose hope." He patted Audree's knee without looking. "God knows I have. But two days ain't nothin'. I've been on stakeouts that were staffed twenty-four hours a day. For weeks. But sometimes, simple patience and luck pay off more than…"

Bill stopped mid-sentence, drawing Audree's attention away from her nails. She glanced over her shoulder out of the back window. "What's up?"

Bill threw his hand up, his finger pointing. "Shh. Hang on a sec, doll."

Twenty yards behind Bill's car, a dark green Cadillac pulled to a stop in the middle of the street. It waited, fumes bellowing from the exhaust.

What's this guy doing? Bill thought.

A moment later, two men in suits, one tall and slender matching the description, exited the building.

"It's them!" Bill growled, spurring Audree to crane her neck for a better view. The shorter man circled the rear of the Cadillac and then climbed into the back seat. The taller man opened the nearside rear door and pushed a small boy inside, immediately following.

Audree gasped. "That has to be David. Oh, my God, it *is* them!"

The vehicle crawled down the street, cruising past Bill's car, the smoked windows making it impossible to see inside. Bill fired up the ignition and pulled out to follow. When the Cadillac reached the end of the street, it made an immediate sharp left, following the one-way traffic.

Whereas, when Bill arrived a second behind, he was met with a line of cars arriving from his right—a funeral procession, no less.

"Damn it!" he yelled, inching forward, trying to break in. He turned to Audree, "Call O'Malley. Hurry!"

Audree grabbed her phone. "I don't have his number. What's his number?"

"It's in my phone, goddammit!" Bill watched as the kidnapper's Cadillac disappeared amongst the throng of vehicles. He leaned on his horn, jerking ahead. As he muscled his way in, the last half of the funeral procession was forced to a sudden halt.

Audree switched phones but was having no luck unlocking it. Either Bill had changed his code, or her frantic pressing with inch-long nails kept hitting the wrong number. Frustrated, she dropped his in the cup holder and grabbed her own again. She hit the emergency call button and pressed it to her ear. "Get me the police. Hurry... Yes, hello, my name is Audree Shaw, and we're following a…" she covered the mouthpiece. "Bill, what car is it?"

Bill skirted through a tight gap into the next lane. "Caddy," he yelled. "Dark green. Older. A ninety-eight, I think."

She screamed the description into the phone. "A child has been kidnapped. Can you relay this to Captain O'Malley, please?" She listened briefly. "I dunno, somewhere in the Bronx." Leaning over the dash, she noted the street signs. "We're south on Monroe, passing Mount Hope Plaza. Please hurry!"

Bill swerved a hard right, ducking into a gap in the third lane that was too small to fit a scooter. The car behind screeched its brakes, horns honking in a cacophony of tuning trombones.

Angry drivers waved their fists through open windows, hurling vile abuse as they drove alongside. *A typical New York day.* Unfazed, Bill maintained his attention eight cars ahead. This was their only chance of getting David back safely and he was not about to lose them, not under any circumstance.

The car in front of Bill's pulled into another lane, allowing Bill to speed up. The rapid acceleration thrust Audree back in her seat. Bill eyed yet another gap opening on his left, the lane he'd just occupied a second ago. He slammed his foot to the floor to squeeze in.

Too focused on his left, he hadn't noticed the taillights of the car ahead glowing red.

Audree's eyes bulged. "Left, left, left. Watch it!"

Bill skidded left, swerving into the second lane, but his car's rear bumper whiplashed, clipping the vehicle in his rear quarter.

"Ahh. Oh, my God, we're gonna die!" Audree shrilled, her free hand now pressed against the ceiling of the car, bracing her in her seat.

For a moment, Bill wished she weren't with him. Then, he could really gun it, not worrying she might get hurt. Sure, he might get hurt himself. But that didn't matter. The only thing that mattered was the boy. Only the boy.

Approaching an intersection, the traffic lights switched from amber to red. Bill screeched to an abrupt stop. Beyond the crossroads, about four cars ahead, the Cadillac cruised away amongst the other traffic. *No! I won't lose him,* Bill vowed, his fingers squeezing on the steering wheel. He locked his arms straight and floored it. The engine whined in protest as it revved, the rear wheels spinning, spewing a thick cloud of black smoke and the acrid scent of burning rubber.

Audree screamed, "Red light, red light, red light." Instinctively, her feet stomped into the footwell, onto imaginary brake pedals. Bill's Toyota launched like a dragster as the intersection traffic advanced on either side.

The spinning wheels hydroplaned, sending Bill's car snaking and skidding. He grappled with the steering wheel, fighting to maintain direction.

"We're gonna die," Audree squealed. "Please, Lord, I'll go to church."

Almost unscathed, he traversed the final lane of the intersection. But then, an old Chevy truck pummeled into the rear wing of his Toyota, spinning his car as if it was on ice.

Bill quickly regained control and steered toward the Cadillac ahead, which now began weaving aggressively between the lanes. "Goddammit, he's onto us," Bill said. "Where are the damn cops?"

Audree was still recovering from her near-death experience. "I don't know, Bill," she yelled, "probably at that hundred-car pileup back there. What the hell? Are you trying to get us killed?" She returned her phone to her ear, hollering at the police operator. "How far off are you? They're getting away." She relayed the information to Bill. "There's a patrol car behind us, two at an intersection ahead."

Seizing a break in the traffic, Bill pressed on the pedal and weaved around the car in front, tossing them both hard to their side.

"Bill!" Audree cried. "Slow down. Someone's going to get hurt. The cops have them now."

"Don't have 'em yet, darlin'." Bill accelerated through an impossibly tight gap. "Hold on!"

CHAPTER 35

St. Peter's Church

High up on the northern banks of the River Wear, where the mouth opened to the trepid North Sea, a humble church basked its eastern front in the abstinent sun. An unassuming structure, it was unlike most other stone churches. To begin with, it was on the smaller side and featured a distinctive twin nave design—two rectangular buildings that ran adjoining with a connecting roof, forming the building into an M shape. Surrounding its grassed five-acre plot, a modern society had sprouted: towering flats, neighborhood housing, and the Sunderland University's technology building boasting its post-modern-style architecture. And of course, the iconic National Glass Centre, opened by royalty, and which celebrated the city's claim to fame.

The brand-new tires of Matthew's rental scuffed along the curb of St. Peter's Way, sending juddering feedback to the steering wheel, his driving showing little improvement. Once they'd parked, he and Theia exited, bracing, heads down against the wind's blustery bite.

Overhead, fat-bellied seagulls cried and complained, planning their next assault on the quayside's returning fisherman. Matthew sniffed a long breath, taking in the salty seaside air. Like a splash of cold water, it awakened his senses. Shoving his hands deep into his pockets, and hunkering into his jacket collar, he led the way along the path toward the church entrance.

"Finally, a place even older than you!" Matthew hollered over the wind. "This is one of England's oldest churches *and* the first to commission stained-glass windows."

"Oh, wow," Theia said, lacking enthusiasm.

Matthew laughed. "Okay, I get it. You're not as impressed with the history as I am."

She shrugged.

"You want impressive?" He pointed to the church now only yards in front. "This was built in AD 674." He repeated the date for clarity. "Know what's impressive about that?"

"That it's old? And far more ancient than me?"

"No. Well, yes, that's pretty amazing! But more remarkable than the year is the AD."

Becoming intrigued, Theia brushed away her hair, which now whipped at her face. She frowned at Matthew, who stood at the entrance, holding the small arched wooden door open.

Sheltered from the howling wind, he explained, "AD—Anno Domini and BC—*Before Christ* sets the foundation for our Gregorian calendar, right? Our dates are measured against the birth of Christ. In the Middle Ages, there was no standard and each country referenced different historical events as a basis for their calendars.

"Nothing was unified. But today, virtually every country recognizes the Gregorian calendar. Saint Bede, who founded this church, was the first to suggest it. Without him, we'd all be on different dates. And here we are."

As she brushed by Matthew's arm and entered, Theia paused her step. "Oh… wow!" she exclaimed, this time sounding genuinely impressed.

"No shit, oh wow," Matthew mumbled, following her in. "History's awesome!"

As they stepped inside the southwest corner of the nave, the spacious interior took Matthew by surprise. From the humble exterior, he'd been expecting two cramped rooms.

Yet, spanning the length of the nave, a row of beautiful stone columns and arcades soared to the ceiling, opening the twin naves into one. They supported heavy black oak rafters that arched the peaked roof like an upturned boat hull.

Fighting the urge to explore, Matthew searched for his old friend.

Father Jacobs had his back facing them, replacing the altar's votive candles with new ones. Matthew recognized him instantly, chuckling to himself and shaking his head. He paced the faded wool runner toward the chancel, taking in the scent of sweet orange from the fresh polish. Theia followed a step behind.

"Father, forgive me for I have sinned," Matthew announced, drawing close.

Father Jacobs spun his head, his curious expression quickly dissolving into a mischievous grin when he spotted Matthew. "If you're here to confess," he quipped, "then ah'd better clear me schedule."

With firm grips, they shook hands and hugged, slapping each other's backs. "Matthew, Matthew, how long's it been, my old mate?"

"Too long." Matthew stepped aside, inviting Theia forward. "This is Theia, the um… collector I was telling you about."

Theia offered her hand. "Hello, nice to meet you."

"And you, ma dear. You're American too, unless ma ears deceive me."

"Um, yes, I live in New York now, like Matthew, but my family heritage stems from *old* York, actually. Just near here!"

"Oh, very nice. Will you be visitin' family while you're in town too?"

"Um. I don't think so." Theia embarrassedly shook her head. "We only have a few days."

Matthew jumped in to save her. "Which is why we need to be brief, unfortunately. Is there someplace we can talk?"

"Of course." Father Jacobs waved welcomingly. "This way." He directed them toward his office through a small museum and gift shop, while Theia made conversation.

"So how is it you two know each other? University, was it?"

"Aye," Father Jacobs answered. "Though, Matthew and I started on the wrong foot. *I*, the devout Catholic and *he* the rebellious agnostic."

"Rebellious? Really?" Theia looked stunned.

"Oh yes. And quite the ladies' man. All the women swooned over his American accent and long wavy black hair."

Theia glared at Matthew, showing a glint of jealousy. In response, he frowned, vehemently shaking his head in silent disagreement.

"We both studied theology at Oxford," Father Jacobs went on, "though for very different reasons. I took the faithful route, while Matthew's reasons were more..." He offered to Matthew to provide his own adjective.

"Scientific."

"Scientific. Aye, exactly." Taking issue, Father Jacobs dallied outside his office door, then turned to Theia. "Tell me, who studies theology but doesn't believe in God? That's just—"

"No, I didn't *not* believe!" Matthew remonstrated. They squeezed into the tiny office. "I was open to the idea of it. Still am. I just thought I'd tackle it from a scientific perspective, is all."

"But there's something you failed to understand, Matthew." Father Jacobs waved a finger, following them in. "And that's the point; there *is* no science in religion. Just faith. It's like understanding the nature of consciousness. What *is* consciousness? We can't pin it down. Surgeons disagree about where it resides and what it is. They used to say it was in the brain, that it lived there! Well, many a 'brain dead' person remembers what happened while they were 'dead!' So, where consciousness resides, nobody knows.

"But none of us deny it's there. We know it. In *here.*" He patted his heart. "And God too. He lives in here; we simply know he is in us."

Addressing Theia, he concluded, "As you can see, m'dear, nothing much has changed. Except now, we're…" His arms opened in a wide circle. "Civil. No more bloody noses or black eyes."

Theia gasped. "You guys *fought* over this?"

Behind her burning glare, Matthew sensed the real question. *You hit a priest?* "Don't look at me!" he protested. "I was the one bloodied nose and black-eyed!" He thumbed at his old rival. "Father Jacobs over here has quite the right hook. Looks do deceive."

"Yes, well," Father Jacobs said, appearing embarrassed. "Not our finest moment, eh, Matthew?" He pointed to the chairs. "Please, sit, sit."

As they did, Matthew explored the tight space. Except for a few tiny picture frames and one gigantic one, the room was bleak, and uninviting. Similar to his own office.

"As I recall," Matthew inquired, "you ranked top of our Oxford theology class. Wouldn't that have granted major credit when choosing your first assignment?"

Father Jacobs gave a proud smile. "Aye. It did."

"So why here?" Matthew swiveled his head again. "Why St. Peter's of all places?"

Father Jacobs delivered his political answer, the one he undoubtedly used to impress the clergy to gain the assignment. "I've always loved this building, its history, its fundamentals in teaching. Plus, it's a small, simple parish and no shortage of sinners."

The detective in Matthew wasn't buying it.

"Yeah? So, nothing to do with the football club?" He pointed to the adjacent wall at the gigantic picture he'd eyed when he came in—a five-by-three-foot framed and autographed soccer jersey taking prized place in the center of the wall. The red and white stripes were distinctively those of the local Sunderland AFC Football Club. Irreverently, the smaller-framed religious prints and Catholic crosses had found relegated posts in darker recesses.

Father Jacobs snorted, trying to keep a smirk from bubbling to the surface.

"I'd forgotten how astute you were, Matthew. Always observing things. Analyzing." He looked at Theia. "He's a modern-day Poirot." His recliner creaked as he sat back. "Okay, ya got me. I do love the club." He flailed his arms again. "They're ma team. Around here, football's its own religion. I sometimes wonder what they need me for! But to my original point, this building's no less extraordinary. It's always amazed me. You know, it was built in the seventh century." He shook his head in wonder. "Incredible. Though, most of it was destroyed by wretched Vikings a couple hundred years later." He mumbled, "Those accursed pagans."

Matthew cast a glance at Theia, who had dipped her chin as if bearing the brunt of blame.

"Aye," Father Jacobs continued, admiring the historical walls around him. "It still gives me shivers knowing the father of English history wrote his manuscripts within these very walls."

Matthew perked. "Don't suppose any are still here?"

"No, very little, I'm afraid. Everything we have is on display in our little museum outside. The rest were relocated, some to Switzerland, some to Harvard, but most to the Old Palace in York… which is why yer here, right?"

"Yes, as I mentioned on the phone, we're searching for documents relating to certain family archives of people who lived locally, dating back as far as… the eighth or ninth century. I know they're held under lock and key, only accessible by the curator, so I was wondering…"

"If I could get you access?" Father Jacobs grinned, then opened his desk drawer and pulled out a cardinal red Sunderland AFC rosette, two ribbons hanging from it. He extended it to Matthew. "Here you go."

Confused, he took it from him. "Um, what's this?"

"On the back!" Father Jacobs directed.

Matthew flipped it, finding a handwritten name and number on the back.

"Morgan Holloway," Father Jacobs trumpeted. "Curator at the Old Palace and a close mate o' mine. She's expecting your call and should be able to provide everything ya need."

Matthew stared at the rosette in disbelief. Deep down, he'd half expected a dead end. Access to the private records meant an opportunity to solve the question of Theia; more than that, it prolonged this intriguing adventure another day.

"That's what you needed, right, Matthew?" The unexpected silence provoked the question.

"Yes, yes, absolutely. This is… I-I'm so grateful," Matthew stuttered. He reexamined the rosette's frontside, then huffed from his nose. "But you know, Aiden, you could've just as easily written the number on a piece of paper instead!"

"Well, you know as I do, Matthew, we're all about spreading the good word!"

Matthew chuckled. "Thank you." He waved the rosette. "I owe you."

"A pint," Father Jacobs suggested, brows arching. "Except this time, no fights!"

They all stood.

"What would be the fun in that?" Matthew goaded, reaching to shake his hand. "Hey, perhaps when we're finished in York, we can stop in before returning to the States. Catch up." He glanced at Theia. "What do you think?"

Before she could answer, Father Jacobs bellowed a laugh. "Out of the question, I'm afraid. I'm leaving for London tomorrow. A historic event, not to be missed."

"Oh?" An expert in religious studies, Matthew puzzled over what it could be. "A clergy thing?"

"No, nothing like that. Sunderland are playin' in the F.A. Cup Final at Wembley Stadium against those…" He screwed up his face as if he'd just sucked on a lemon. "…those Geordies."

Matthew scratched his head. "But *you* are a Geordie. Are you not?"

Father Jacobs gasped at such blasphemy.

"I didn't mean to offend." Matthew stepped back, not wanting to rekindle their fighting years. "But isn't that what they call people from the Northeast of England?"

"Forgive me, Matthew." His stunned friend leaned on his desk, his other hand flat on his chest. "I've been called many things but... just because Newcastle sits next to Sunderland on the northeast coast, it doesn't mean we're one and the same. We are not. *We* are Mackems. *They* are... Geordies."

"Okay, okay. Got it!" Matthew said dourly. "I won't be making that mistake again."

"Nor should ya," Father Jacobs warned. "Be careful sayin' things like that around here, Matthew. Lest you want a fight on ya hands. Geordies are not just the opposing team around here; to Mackems, they're the enemy."

Showing his support, Matthew pinned the rosette to his lapel. "Well, best of luck. Go, Sunderland!" he chanted, raising a fist. "Or Mackems, or whatever."

Father Jacobs turned to Theia, shaking her hand. "I hope ya find what you're lookin' for, dear."

"Me too," Theia said. "Enjoy the game."

Nearing their car at the end of the long path, Matthew unclipped the rosette and tucked it into his inside pocket, Theia looking on.

"Just in case Miss Holloway supports the other team!" Matthew explained, eyes glaring. "After that debacle, I'm not taking any chances!" He eyed his watch. "Any word from Audree?"

"No. Not since last night. But it's early there, five hours behind."

"Yeah, knowing Audree, she's probably still in bed!"

CHAPTER 36

Bedlam in the Bronx

The dark green Cadillac whizzed through the traffic, arousing a trail of angry drivers in its wake. DeRose eyed Bill's Toyota, now only three cars behind, maintaining pace.

He shifted nervously in the backseat. "We need to get over to the left. The turn's coming up."

"I'm trying," the driver barked, fixated on his side mirror.

Gathering closer, the insistent Toyota weaved around yet another car. DeRose gasped. "Shit. He's almost on us. He's gonna follow us straight there. Move it!"

"If you think you can do any better," the driver growled, "*you* drive."

DeRose didn't argue. Instead, his eyes remained glued on the Toyota which snaked in and out of its lane with unrelenting determination. "Who *is* this guy?"

Griffin shook his head next to him, David sandwiched between them. "I don't know, but let's not find out."

UNTIL NOW, BILL'S plan had been working. Ducking into any lane that moved faster had gotten him closer to the kidnappers. However, it had also drifted him to the far-right lane, opposite theirs.

Now, at a complete standstill, he could only watch as the Caddy moved in its lane, swallowed into a sea of red taillights. *No!* Growing anxious, he spun the steering wheel left, attempting to cut into the stationary traffic. Going heavy on the accelerator and brake in rapid succession caused his car to rock aggressively though not gaining an inch. Even his constant horn blasting went unnoticed, diluted by the dozens of other drivers honking on theirs.

Gridlocked by cars on all three sides and a busy sidewalk on his right, Bill's frustration boiled. "You motherfuckers!" he roared, rattling the steering wheel with both hands as if trying to pry it from the dash. Bill rarely lost control.

It sent a clear message to Audree they were losing them. "Where the hell are the damn cops, lady?" Audree yelled into the phone. "You said they'd be at an intersection. What intersection?"

Bill shifted into Park and cracked open the car door. Using the door as leverage, he secured a foot on the door sill and boosted his five-foot-nine frame high on his toes. He found them, six cars ahead, slowly creeping into the left turn lane.

Audree leaped from the car, her voice ringing with excitement. "Bill, the cops are just two lights ahead." But as Bill watched the Cadillac cornering at the lights, he knew that was one intersection too far. "They're gone, babe," he uttered, hardly able to believe his own words. "They've turned. They're gone."

"What? No! Bill, do something!" Audree paced in a tight circle, hand flat on her cheek. She cried into her phone, "Oh, my God, we've lost them. We've lost David."

Bill's insides churned. Hearing Audree's cries for him to 'do something' stung pretty hard. Powerless, he could *do* nothing.

He *was* nothing.

It was their only chance of saving David, and he'd blown it. Big time.

He clenched his fists imagining the kidnappers rejoicing at their escape, with poor David losing all hope. He thumped his car's roof. *I gotta do something.*

Studying the congested street, an idea came to him, the kind of idea that only a desperate person would think of. One thing for sure: Audree wasn't going to like it. Not one little bit.

"Audree, get in!" Bill yelled, ushering himself back into the car. Bill snapped himself in and scanned a three-sixty. "Buckle up, babe."

Audree scanned with him. "We're hemmed in, Bill. Where are we—"

"Hold on!" Bill steered the car right, mounting the pavement. Pedestrians darted from his path, their faces a mix of anger and surprise.

Some kicked and thumped at Audree's door.

Audree screamed, cowering away, "Bill, what the hell are you doing?" *Something—just like you wanted me to.*

He plowed through a gray recycling bin, sending it flying into the stationary traffic. Audree scrunched her knees to her chest, twisting on her hip. "We're gonna die, we're gonna die," she chanted in a high-pitched tone. "Oh, my God, we're gonna die."

Despite the carnage in his wake, not to mention the lawsuits mounting against him, Bill couldn't help grinning like a madman. Back in pursuit, he mused miserly, *you ain't outta the woods yet, you sons of bitches*, then stomped on his horn, sending pedestrians running for cover.

The sidewalk, barely wide enough to accommodate his vehicle, was coming to an end at the approaching intersection.

Just before it, a blue mailbox and a newsstand, piled with bound newspapers, blocked his way.

Oh shit! He saw it only at the last second. "Hang on, babe," he yelled, locking his elbows straight and stepping on the gas. "Keep your head…"

Smash!

His left two wheels bounced airborne as he plowed through the mailbox and mounted the pile of newspapers, scattering pages into a rain of confetti.

Audree kept her head buried in her lap.

At the intersection, Bill joined the slow-moving traffic in the direction of the kidnappers. *Yes! Got you now!*

Cast by shadow and neglect, the narrow one-way street descended a hill deeper into the ghetto. The steep angle afforded Bill a view over the cars ahead.

None appeared to be a dark green Cadillac.

Finally, Audree relaxed her legs into the footwell as she peeked through the cracked windshield. Now smeared with mailbox blue, Bill's silver hood rippled in waves to a crumpled front grille.

"You okay, darlin'?" Bill said, checking on her. "Slight detour. Quite the ride, huh?"

Slowly, she unfolded her head like a blossoming flower. The expression on her pale face told Bill she was still in shock, but uninjured. "Sorry, babe. I didn't have a choice. I think they turned down this street, but I'm not seeing 'em." His eyes examined every vehicle, every parked car. "You see anything?"

It took a while for Audree to respond. She was still taking stock of her limbs. "I swear to God, Bill," she said in a coldly calm voice. "If you ever pull that shit again…"

Bill just glanced a sheepish eye at her.

Straightening herself in her seat, she joined Bill in his search, returning the phone to her ear. "Are you still there? Thank God. They're now heading east, but we've lost them." After a moment, she asked Bill for the street name but with him not knowing it either, she peered out the side window, looking for a sign. "We don't know what street, but it was just before the police roadblock." Suddenly, she screamed at Bill. "Stop! Back up, back up."

Bill slammed on his brakes. "What? What did you see?"

"Back up. I think I saw them down that side street." She pointed behind, over her right shoulder. Bill checked his mirror. A line of cars had stopped directly behind them.

Again, Bill eyed the sidewalk.

"Sorry, babe," he announced as he spun right, mounting yet another curb. It took several passes of forward and reverse before his vehicle clumsily completed a tight one-eighty. Fortunately, this time, there were no pedestrians. Not on this deserted street.

As Bill cautiously crept along the cracked pavement, the tires rumbling against the neglected asphalt, he rounded the corner onto an eerie stretch. Audree pointed ahead and yelled, "There, there, there. See them?"

"I see him." Sure enough, it was the same Cadillac, parked mid-street.

A hint of white suggested it was idling.

Barely straight on the road, Bill floored it, sending his car into a swirly skid. Almost at the same time, the Cadillac also spun its tires, racing away. Although Bill was gaining on him, he suddenly slammed on his brakes, skidding to a complete stop.

Audree was stunned. "What are you doing? They're getting away," she yelled, pointing a finger at the Cadillac, now disappearing at the end of the street. Bill engaged reverse and then hooked his arm over his seatback and peered over his shoulder. Flooring it again, he backed up the street to where the Caddy had been idling.

He gazed up at the derelict building on his left.

"Why were they stopped here?" he muttered to himself.

"We can figure that out later, Bill. Right now," she said as she bounced in her seat. "We need to go. We're losing them."

Bill sat calm, analyzing.

The building's entrance had three steps, laden with trash; its steel door, layered with years of graffiti, was ajar. He studied the floors above. "This place is empty. Been empty for years."

"Who cares! Let's go!"

Bill turned to Audree. "The perfect place to commit a murder, don't you think? No witnesses."

The question stifled her ranting. Then she spoke. Her voice was almost a whisper and filled with doubt. "But what if they're in the car? Getting away. How do you know if..."

"The driver left 'em." Glancing back up to the building, he mumbled, "They're in there. I know it." Suddenly moving with a sense of urgency, he unfastened his seatbelt and opened the door to leave. "You stay here. I'm going in."

"No!" Audree's bark was shrill. "We wait here for the police."

Bill stopped halfway from the car. "We don't have time, babe. I've gotta go now." He gave her his look. The determined one. The one pointless to argue with. "You stay put."

"If you're going, I'm going." She pressed the release on her seatbelt which raced up her chest, snagging on her Saint Christopher necklace.

The chain snapped.

Before she realized it, Bill leaned in, placing his hand on her cheek. "No darlin'," he said softly. "You stay." Thinking of a valid reason, he added, "Besides, I need you to tell the cops where we're at. I'll see ya soon." He kissed his fingers and then touched her head.

Audree was motionless, quiet for once. The operator's voice bleeped from the phone on Audree's lap. "Ma'am, ma'am, ma'am…"

Bill headed up the steps. At the top, he withdrew his .357 Magnum, aiming it forward with locked arms. Pacing carefully, he inched through the open doorway into the dark, desolate corridor.

CHAPTER 37

York Minster

Theia felt a terrible unease as the imposing walls of the great city came into view. Originally built by the Romans in AD 71, York's fortifying walls had undergone many enhancements during the Middle Ages when war was rife, and repairs and improvements were frequent. Today, encircling the medieval city two-and-a-half miles, it stood as the most impressive and complete city wall in all of England.

Access to the inner city was provided through four barbican gateways known as 'bars.'

Theia leaned in her seat, staring up at the city's southwest entrance, the Micklegate Bar. Its ominous crenelated battlements towering fifty feet high sent shivers down her spine. "Oh, my God. I remember this." She voiced the Nordic words by which it was named. "Mykla Gata."

The focus in her eyes drifted. Her world darkened.

She felt the ropes in her hands, her gray Shire tugging her shuddering cart over the damp cobbled road. Creaking like an old ship in a storm, the wooden wheels fought for grip in the patches of pooled water and mud. Around her, York's modern high street dissolved into darkness, replaced by crooked logged structures with makeshift thatched roofs, temporary housing for those forbidden entry to the walled city. Malnourished and disease-riddled, they huddled from the cold and gazed with sorrowful faces at the passing travelers.

Closer to the bar, her nostrils flared at the scent of decaying flesh.

Following her nose, her gaze aimed upward above the arched city entrance; there, pierced on long wooden spikes were three putrefied heads, their hair matted, eyes sunken, the blood now turned an almost tolerable brown.

This was a stark warning to those who entered, saying 'traitors are not welcome here.'

This was Jorvik, the great city. Or so it had once been. In AD 306, Constantine the Great had been crowned Caesar here, heralding the city the governing center of the mighty Roman army.

It had been coveted by many an empire and defended and conquered by countless armies and kingdoms. Now, impoverished and plagued by disease, its weary citizens waned from decades of war, famine, and hardship. Despair spread to all.

But she wasn't here to stay. In her cart was everything she owned.

Aside from her treasured possessions, all was for sale. Soon, she would find herself rid of this place and on the next ship to France, swearing never to return.

Eight monks patrolled the narrow entrance. Ahead of the guards, they were the first line of defense in the city. They swung their thuribles on chains, wafting clouds of burning frankincense to cleanse the souls of those who entered. As she approached closer, one monk thrust his thurible towards her face, swinging it like a pendulum.

"Would you care to donate for 'Cancer Research?'" a middle-aged woman asked as she swung a pink bucket in front of Theia's car window. Theia blinked. The eight monks were now gone, replaced by eight ladies all wearing pink t-shirts with 'Race for Life' printed in bold white across the chest.

Theia lowered her window while rummaging through her purse. "Oh, I'm sorry. I was miles away." Before dropping a handful of cash into the donation bucket, she added, "I've only got American dollars. Is that okay?"

"Honey, as long as it's not Monopoly, we're fine!" the lady replied with a chuckle.

Matthew drove on through the archway inside the walled city but then slowed to a crawl. "Jeez. Could these streets get any narrower?"

Theia laughed. "This is nothing. Wait until you see *The Shambles*. You'll have to duck to enter the buildings."

"Duck?"

"Because when they were built centuries ago, people were shorter!"

"Oh, from malnutrition."

"Exactly." Theia was surprised, though she should have learned by now that stumping Matthew on historical references was not so easy.

As they rounded a corner, the soaring limestone structure spired into view like a mountain backdrop dominating the horizon. Standing twenty-three stories high, Italy's Tower of Pisa could fit inside. And more than twice the size of an American football field, it was the largest Gothic cathedral in all of Northern Europe.

The cathedral entrance was no less grand, its double iron doors set deep into intricately carved Romanesque arches. Today, as on most days, they were wedged fully open, inviting visitors inside. After parking, Matthew and Theia entered the cathedral and proceeded to the information desk. "Hi, my name's Matthew Colombo. We have an appointment with Morgan Holloway."

"Certainly. I'll need a copy of your ID," the volunteer said as she slid an open book across the desk. "If you could sign in, I'll let her know you're here."

Matthew snagged a pen from a jar, leaning in to sign the visitors' book.

Theia turned her ear to the angelic sound of a harmonic organ echoing from the cathedral's choir. It was familiar, as was the cavernous interior. From the west entrance of the nave, she moved as if entranced, down the center aisle, marveling at the grandeur above. Several rows from the awe-inspiring Central Tower, she gazed upon the Fifteen Kings carved choir screen. *Wow.* It was just as she remembered it.

AFTER HIS NOON prayer, a Benedictine monk rose from the front pew and crossed himself. Dressed in his traditional black robe, he headed down the aisle toward the main entrance to make his leave. A few feet past Theia, he came to an abrupt stop.

What! It can't be!

His head whipped around.

I must be mistaken.

Carefully, he slid himself into a neighboring pew chair midway down the aisle. Hands clasped, with his head slightly bowed, he sat as if in prayer, his eyes studying Theia over the tops of his fingers.

The blonde hair had almost fooled him, but those eyes, those eyes he would never forget. Even if green instead of blue.

A few moments later, a dark-haired gentleman charged to a halt in the aisle next to him. Trying not to be loud, the young man shouted a whisper, "Theia! Theia!"

Theia! It is her!

The monk felt his heart pulsing through his ears.

Theia threw a glance over her shoulder. The man behind beckoned with a wave. "We've got to go."

As Theia approached him, she cast a glance directly at the monk. Quickly, he snapped his eyes to the floor and stooped his head.

Despite their whispering, the monk could hear everything.

"Miss Holloway is on her way," the man said, his accent indistinguishably American. "We're getting complete access. All the archives. Ain't that great?"

Theia beamed a smile, pulling her jacket collar tight under her chin.

"Are you cold?" the American asked.

"It's nothing. I just got a chill, that's all. These places are draughty!"

"C'mon." He placed his arm around her shoulder. "Let's go find your answers."

The second they moved toward the Minster's west entrance, the monk scrambled from his chair and scurried after them.

THEY HAD ONLY been waiting a few minutes when Matthew heard the curator's voice.

"Professor Colombo?" Morgan Holloway held out her hand as she sauntered toward him.

"Yes, but please call me Matthew." He shook her hand, then introduced Theia. "This is Theia, my… assistant." As Theia took Miss Holloway's hand, she cocked Matthew with a scornful, yet impish expression, obviously not impressed by her new label.

"Father Jacobs said you needed access to the archives. The ninth century, yes?"

"And eighth, if possible," Matthew added. "That's if it's not too much trouble?"

"Yes, of course." She pointed to the entrance. "The archive building is just across from Dean's Park. If you'd like to follow me?" They left the way they'd come in.

Miss Holloway was not the image Matthew had expected. For the curator of the country's largest archive, a position surely coveted by most everyone in her field, he had imagined instead some stuffy-nosed, middle-aged aristocrat. Or a dusty old librarian with an outdated dress code and wearing half-framed reading glasses on the tip of her nose, attached to a lanyard and looped around her neck. Yet, on the contrary, she was stunning, her face straight off the cover of Vogue.

"We appreciate your allowing us access," Matthew said. "We heard you had this place locked down like Fort Knox. We can't thank you enough."

Leading ahead, Miss Holloway cast an appreciative smile behind her.

"Anything for Father Jacobs."

"Lucky for us, you guys are close," Matthew noted.

"Yes, Father Jacobs is quite the character," Miss Holloway agreed affably. "But that's not the only reason for extending this courtesy.

I would do this for any of our pastors. The Diocese is a tight-knit family where everyone looks out for one another. Connected." She grinned playfully. "Not unlike your New York Mafia. The only differences, of course, are the corruption and murders."

"From whom?" Matthew joked, passing her a wry smirk.

Both the curator and Theia laughed, though Theia's laughter seemed forced. Having been pursued her entire life by religious fanatics, the joke had hit a little too close to home.

Crossing the grassy grounds of Dean's Park, Matthew glanced ahead.

The Old Palace was aptly named. Unlike any other records building he had ever seen, cut from the same magnesium limestone as the Minster and with its tall arched stained-glass windows, it could easily have passed as a cathedral itself.

"Our cathedral archives at the Old Palace are the most complete anywhere in England," Miss Holloway boasted. "Some of our collections date back to the first century."

"The first century? Now that's impressive," Matthew said, nodding. "Sounds like we're at the right place."

"Well, we'll see. It depends very much on the type of record. The eighth century is somewhat limited. What in particular are you looking for?"

Theia answered, "We would like to start with a name search. For *Reginleif.*"

"Hmm. Pagan, yes?"

Amazed by her accuracy, Matthew eyed Theia.

Though she was right, Theia nonetheless added, "Nordic, actually," her corrective tone carrying an element of jealousy.

"Of course," Miss Holloway agreed. "A Valkyrie name if I'm not mistaken?"

Indeed, she was right again. Although Matthew had known that, it had taken him hours of research to learn it. She outshone even the smartest of his Oxford scholars, including himself; he no longer wondered how she'd achieved her prestigious position at such a young age. He felt a metaphorical boot on his hind, a reminder of the need to advance his own career.

"Here we are."

The arched wooden doors of the Old Palace had appeared as one from a distance, but now up close, Matthew could see they were split down the center into two.

Miss Holloway opened the right side and then entered.

Pinned on the leftmost door, in full view, was a large poster, a glossy print of a debonair Englishman standing in front of the newly renovated building. The gentleman's face stretched into a cheesy Cheshire Cat grin, locking in a handshake with Miss Holloway. While Theia hadn't paid it any attention, Matthew read the wording: 'Renovations Provided by Mr. Goodwin.'

A twinge of frustration pricked at his ego, remembering his modest, run-down office in New York and their persistent lack of funding.

Must be nice to have such a generous benefactor!

They entered the Old Palace.

CHAPTER 38

The Old Palace

The familiar aroma of musty chocolate enveloped Matthew. He had encountered the scent before, during his days unpacking ancient wooden artifacts at the Natural History Museum. While his colleagues found the smell sickly, Matthew grew to crave it—the scent of old, old wood. But the signature perfume he now experienced at the Old Palace was something else entirely.

It didn't emanate from the thousands of square feet of aged mahogany shelves or the varnished oak floors or wainscot paneled walls. No, the source was the millions of pages of priceless, leather-bound books filling the shelves.

Miss Holloway led them diagonally across the room, passing a clear acrylic case housing several open books for display. She pointed at it without slowing. "We have some newly renovated books on display. I'd give you the grand tour, but I'm sure you have busy schedules."

This seemed to be a polite way of saying *she* had a busy schedule. Matthew paused to study the display, nonetheless. Inside was the prayer book of Catherine of Aragon, Henry VIII's first wife. Next to it was the first book ever printed in York, some five hundred years ago. Prior to that, all books had to be handwritten by scribes.

Wow! Fascinating!

Miss Holloway swiped her card at a discrete doorway then disappeared down a stark, dimly lit corridor. Theia hung back, holding the door open.

"Matthew!" she whispered, her motherly tone sounding mildly reproachful. Though softly spoken, it echoed off the cavernous plaster walls.

Matthew pulled himself from the display and hurried to catch up.

They rushed after Miss Holloway, finding her standing before a brushed stainless steel vault door, her fingers deftly punching in a code. Despite the centuries-old building, in keeping with its original features and non-modernized look, Matthew was surprised at its state-of-the-art technology.

"What, no retina scanner?" he joked.

The keypad beeped in acceptance, the door's electronic bolts retracting with a clunk that echoed through the chamber. Miss Holloway turned to Matthew as she tugged the heavy door open. "Unfortunately, that was outside our budget. Perhaps next year."

Although Matthew had been joking, Miss Holloway's response was serious.

As they stepped inside, Matthew and Theia were immediately hit by a sudden change in temperature. Theia rubbed her arms.

"We keep this room at a constant temperature and fifty percent humidity," Miss Holloway explained. "It can feel quite cool after a while." She closed the door behind them. As it sealed shut, Matthew wiggled his jaw from the sudden pressure bump. Miss Holloway walked on. "I'll give you a quick tour, then leave you to yourselves."

Beyond the entrance room lay the conservation area, strikingly modernized compared to the rest of the building. Its center table looked as though it belonged in an operating room, only much larger. A specialized canopy hung overhead, equipped with an array of lighting options including UV and high-intensity bulbs, and black and red lights, all for specific examination purposes.

Miss Holloway swung open a polished steel door set into the white-washed wall, flicking on the light switch. As hundreds of strip lights shimmered to life, they illuminated a seemingly endless expanse of steel shelves stretching from floor to ceiling, arranged in narrow aisles.

Every square centimeter was occupied by labeled boxes, meticulously ordered in chronological sequence. "This is the main archive storage room. We have over three hundred thousand archives, logged and labeled." She pointed to a computer station outside the room. "Everything in here you can access through that terminal."

Next, she led them past two techs dressed like doctors in white coats, wearing surgical face masks and gloves. They were operating a camera suspended from the ceiling.

On the counter beneath was an ancient book, its browned pages spread apart. Miss Holloway provided a cursory introduction as they passed by. "Veronica and Jess. They're digitizing records this week." Neither peeled their eyes from their task.

Finally, they came to a long table with a row of computer terminals. "This is where you can gain access to our digital records. For security reasons, none are directly connected to the web, only the Minster's intranet and archival database." She paused for questions. "Okay, I think that's everything." With a resigned smile, she thumbed over her shoulder to a glass-walled room behind. "If you need me, Matthew, my office is over there."

"We're so grateful. Thank you, Morgan."

As Miss Holloway took her leave, Theia smirked at Matthew, repeating her sentence in an overly exaggerated, sexy voice, "Matthew, my office is over there!"

"What can I say?" Matthew snickered. "It's the hair!"

Theia rolled her eyes.

Matthew borrowed a stool from one of the other terminals, wheeling it next to another. He offered it to Theia, and they sat. Wasting no time, Theia typed into the archival search field—R-E-G-I-N-L-E-I-F, hitting enter. The computer's loading icon spun endlessly.

Everything about the conservation room was cutting-edge, impressive. But it apparently didn't apply to the processing power of their mainframes. Growing impatient, Matthew wheeled himself back to the next terminal.

"I'm gonna check on that passage from the Oracle Book III," he said. "The one referring to you being the 'immortal light'."

"Okay." Theia reached inside her pocket. "I'm giving Audree a quick call. She should be up by now."

Matthew turned his gaze on Theia, watching as she swept her hair aside, bringing the phone to her ear. After a moment, she glanced down at the screen, furrowing her brows. "Everything, okay?" Matthew inquired.

"It's busy."

"It might be this building?" Matthew suggested.

Theia's face showed concern. She dialed again.

CHAPTER 39

Wanna Play a Game?

The reek from the derelict building in Bronx's east side had Griffin holding his breath, retching. With a mix of rot and ammonia, it reminded him of a public bathroom long forgotten.

"Shh!" he whispered, grabbing David's shoulder, stopping them both dead.

"What?" DeRose asked, almost walking into the back of him.

"I think I heard something."

Their eyes now adjusted to the poor light and their hearing was sharp. They listened.

"I don't hear anything," DeRose whispered. "It was probably just a rat. I told you, this place has been deserted for years. Not even the homeless come here. Not anymore."

Less convinced, Griffin shoved little David deeper into the building. At the end of the corridor where the pale light dimmed to near dark, Griffin turned the handle on the last door. He crept inside, DeRose and David close behind. Unlike in the corridor, light flooded this spacious office from a tall sash window. The bright room had a connecting doorway leading to a slightly smaller area, both appearing empty.

Griffin quietly closed the door to the corridor behind him, rotating its deadbolt, locking them in.

He unholstered his .38 Special revolver and pressed his head to the door, listening intently.

All seemed still.

He glared over his shoulder at DeRose, standing in the middle of the room with David trembling at his side. "C'mon," he urged. "Get on with it, so we can get the hell outta here."

This place gives me the creeps.

DeRose looked surprised. "I… right now? Here?"

"Yes, here," Griffin snapped. "Where else?"

DeRose stared down at the perplexed puppy-dog eyes staring back. Eyes that couldn't comprehend the evils about to take place.

"Damn it, DeRose," Griffin whispered through his teeth. "I knew you were going to fuck this up." He tapped the gun's nozzle against his own temple. "Don't think. Just *do* it."

Yet DeRose remained stupefied. He had killed before… but never a child.

Griffin changed his tone. "Fine. Fine," he said matter-of-factly. "Don't. No problem." Then from inside his pocket, he retrieved his phone and proceeded to type. "I'll just call him right now. Let him know you couldn't handle it. Then I'll hand the phone to you to explain why."

"No!" DeRose barked, pushing out his hand. "Stop. I've got this. Just give me a sec."

"We don't have a sec." Griffin continued typing.

"Okay, okay," DeRose yelled. "Just put it away."

Griffin lowered his phone.

With remorseful eyes on David, DeRose reached for the holster inside his jacket. "Hey kid, wanna play a game? First, you need to close your eyes."

A distant clatter in the hall turned Griffin's head sharply. "Wait!" Again, he listened at the door. *That didn't sound like no rat to me.* He raced to the window to check the street below. Their dark green Cadillac was gone, replaced by a Silver Toyota.

It was the one that had been following them. The crumpled rear end from the traffic collision confirmed it. Pacing the sidewalk next to it, an irate black woman blasted into her phone, her arms wildly gesticulating.

The rotting windowsill shook when Griffin whacked it with his fist. "Damn it!"

"What is it?" DeRose asked, pausing the withdrawal of his gun.

"We've lost our ride, *and* it looks like our tail found us."

DeRose stepped back. "What? What do we do?"

Griffin thought hard. Moving in quick bursts, he scanned the street again and raced into the adjacent room. It had *another* door. He opened it. Another dark corridor. Total darkness consumed the left, but to the right at the far end, he made out a sign jutting from the wall. *An emergency exit!* He returned to the room. "There's a rear stairwell. Take care of your business—*quietly*—then we'll head out the back door. Hurry, we don't have much time."

"Quietly?" DeRose gasped, knowing exactly what that meant.

"Yes. It's now or never!" Griffin raced back to the window.

Nervously, DeRose released the grip on the gun behind his lapel, then reached to the small of his back. Unsheathing the blade from under his jacket, he sighed. "I'm sorry, kid." He raised the knife above his head, daylight mirroring off its angled steel edge.

David screamed at the top of his lungs, darting for the hall door. Frantically, he tugged and twisted the handle with both hands.

"Help!" he screamed again, hand pounding. "Help!" He continued pounding.

Before the boy could make another sound, DeRose slapped his gangly hand firmly across the lad's mouth, his knifed hand wrapping tight around David's chest, hoisting him into the air. Arms flailing, legs kicking, David fought for his life.

Even from behind DeRose's clasped hand, his high-pitched cries screeched like a boiling kettle.

"Goddammit!" Griffin wailed. "Don't you understand quietly? Shut him up." He pointed his gun to the smaller room. "Do it in there."

Barely able to control the squirming boy, DeRose clamped his hand tighter over David's mouth and backed through the open door.

"LISTEN, MISS SUNSHINE," Audree said, blasting the police operator as she paced outside the derelict building, "I don't know where we are. I already told you; we turned down some deserted…" Audree spun, facing the building. At first, she questioned her ears. But the second scream she clearly heard. A child's scream.

Halting her pace, she spun on her heels, glaring up at the bleak six-story building behind.

"David!" she gasped, covering her mouth. "No!" Leaning into her phone, her voice quivered, "Where the hell are you? This is all gonna be over by the time…" Then her heart suddenly sank, a terrible realization dawning.

She had spent this whole time worrying about David, but now that worry had just doubled. Again, she turned to the building, her eyes welling. *Bill!*

Her nostrils flared. She gritted her teeth. Despite Bill's clear instructions to stay put, she would not stand by helplessly while they were both in danger. Full of rage, she slated the operator, "Lady, just trace this *goddamn* phone."

Leaving it face up on the defaced brick wall, she marched up the steps, peering into the darkness. "Hello?" Emptiness swallowed her voice.

Beside her, a three-foot splintered doorframe leaned against the wall. She gathered it with two hands, cradling it close to her bosom as if it were a bridal bouquet, then stepped inside.

Moments later, her phone vibrated silently on the outside wall. On the screen: '911 Emergency' displayed in red, and a timer ticked forward, counting the call time—24:17, 24:18, 24:19.

A pop-up window flashed the message: 'Incoming call' with a photo of Theia holding a cocktail and the name 'Bestie' below.

Yards away, Bill's Toyota idled in the lowly street, its front doors wide open. In the footwell on the passenger side lay a silver Saint Christopher's necklace with a broken clasp.

CHAPTER 40

Audree's Loss

Bill poked his head around the corner, staring down a long dark corridor.

His eyes watering from the stinging stench, he pulled his jacket lapel over the bridge of his nose. At the far end, he glimpsed movement in the sliver of light beneath a closed door. *Gotcha!* Aiming his gun higher, he edged closer.

By the door, he listened in silence. At first, it was quiet, but then came a faint shuffle. Testing the handle with a jiggle, he heard a muffled high-pitched squeal, accompanied by a man's angry voice. "Argh! You little shit."

Bill stepped back, ready to kick in the door.

Before he had a chance, David cried out from within. "Nooo!" The sound was followed by a painful groan and the hideous noise of a body collapsing to the floor. After that, silence.

With a well-aimed boot, Bill smashed the lock, splintering the door wide. He locked his arms out straight, double gripped on his gun. Across the room, through a second open doorway, the tall man stood, breathing heavily. He glared back at Bill with cold eyes, wiping blood from his hand. In his other hand, he firmly gripped a large knife.

Young David lay crumpled on the floor at his feet, his superhero t-shirt torn from his tiny shoulder. Motionless, his face was pale, blood trickling from his mouth.

Bill gasped. "What have you done?" Gripping tighter, he cocked the hammer with his trembling thumb and stepped forward, his arms now reaching through the doorway.

Spitting, he yelled again, "What did you do?"

"Nothing," the tall man said smugly, glancing at the boy, then again at Bill. "Listen." He positioned his hands defensively. "There's a lot at stake here. More than you could possibly fathom." He stepped closer to Bill. "You're a man with skills. We could use someone like that. There's always room for…"

Bill squeezed the trigger.

The bullet struck DeRose's shoulder, spinning him a quarter turn. Bill didn't hesitate to fire the second, this one sending DeRose slamming back against the wall. A smeared red stripe followed him down the faded yellow plaster as he slid to the floor.

In a seated position, his head slumped forward.

The gunshots had startled young David, who instantly sat up. Seeing Bill pointing the gun, he shuffled backwards, cowering.

What? I don't understand. "David?" Bill said in disbelief. "I… I thought…"

Bill's eyes focused on the man he just shot. Behind the smeared blood on his hand, he could see two opposing crescent-shaped marks. He recognized that mark immediately, having seen similar on dozens of other bodies. Here, it was the size and shape of a small boy's bite. The blood on DeRose's hand was not David's. It was his own.

Bill lowered his gun. "David!" He spoke softly, pacing toward him, one slow step at a time. "It's okay, David. I'm Theia's friend."

Untrusting, David shuffled farther back, nursing a bruise on his forehead from DeRose's strike. Bill stepped into the room through the smashed doorway. He raised his open palm. "David, your mom, Sheila, is waiting for…"

Bang!

Bill felt the impact of the floor on his back first, closely followed by his head, cracking hard against the concrete. An explosion of white flashes consumed his vision, a concussion forming. His senses returned, and the all too familiar stinging pain of a gunshot wound radiated from his shoulder. *Where the hell did that come from?*

But in drafting the question, he'd forgotten to clear the damn room. If he could locate his dropped gun, he would shoot himself for this, a rookie mistake.

He rummaged the floor around him, his head rearing and rolling. He found it. Above him, out of reach. Using his legs, he inched his dead weight across the floor. Arm extended, fingers wide, his gun was almost reachable.

Click!

The distinctive sound of a hammer being cocked.

A .38, just like his old service gun. Bill held still.

Shit. This is it. I'm done.

Careful not to make a sudden move, he slowly lowered his chin, lifting his head from the cold surface, wanting to see where the next bullet was coming from. At first, all he could make out was a dark figure standing at his feet, silhouetted against the bright window. He could only assume the gun was honed on him. He blinked, trying to focus.

And then the mysterious figure spoke, his voice deep.

"Damn, you're persistent. Who the hell are you? The kid's father?"

Distant streets blared with sirens. The overlapping emergency vehicles' sirens inferred not one but a fleet. Blaring louder with each passing second, they were closing in. Fast.

Griffin turned his ear to the window. "Guess I'll never know." Griffin raised his gun, pointing it directly at Bill's head. "This one's for my friend."

By now, Bill's eyes had adjusted. At least he could see it coming, which was how he preferred things. He clenched his teeth, bracing for the end.

"Hey!" Audree shouted, stepping into the room.

Griffin spun his head faster than he could his gun.

In high-heeled shoes and a multi-colored floral dress, she wielded the fragmented door frame like a baseball bat. It struck square on Griffin's temple, as precise as a home run hit. Knees buckling, he crumpled where he stood, a breached dam of blood spilling from his head.

Audree dropped the stick and sank to her knees at Bill's side. Shifting his jacket lapel to the side, she revealed a sky-blue shirt now glistening burgundy. "Oh, my God, Bill. You're shot." She pressed on the wound, halting as Bill flinched and let out a groan. "I don't know what to do," she cried, clumsily fidgeting over him. "Tell me what to do."

"Audree," Bill griped in his gruff voice.

She leaned in. "I'm here, I'm here. Tell me!"

"Stop. Fussing. Woman. I'm gonna be fine. It's just a scratch."

Audree had forgotten what a tough bastard he was. "You better," she warned, "or you'll be in so much trouble."

"The kid." Bill pointed to the adjacent room. "Check on the kid. He's pretty shaken up."

After pecking a kiss on his forehead, she struggled to her feet and stepped into the middle of the room. Peering through the open doorway, a red smear of blood was visible running down the wall, more of it on the floor where DeRose had been a moment earlier.

Both he and young David were gone.

She gasped. "He's gone!" Then she rushed into the room.

"No, Audree," Bill yelled. "Wait!"

But as usual, she didn't listen.

Audree spied a half-opened door leading to another dark hallway. Without stopping, she charged through, instinctively turning right to run point-blank into the sharp point of DeRose's knife. The cold steel sent a searing pain surging through her gut, stealing her breath.

Both of her hands fell against DeRose's chest, her jaw falling slack, yet unable to utter a sound. She stared in disbelief.

DeRose released his grip, leaving the seven-inch blade firmly lodged deep inside. As her knees folded, she went down. Her hands desperately clutched at his lapels, his shirt, his belt, until—finally losing the strength—she collapsed to her knees.

She watched helplessly as DeRose limped down the corridor, a hand pressing against his own gut wound, dragging poor David with him by his shoulder.

Her world went dark, and she slumped to her side.

CHAPTER 41

S.W.A.T.

Smoke billowed from the barrel of Bill's gun, unleashing a shockwave that tore through the corridor.

At the far end, DeRose keeled forward like an axed timber.

His face hit first, his lifeless eyes fixed open. Next to him, David covered his ears from the deafening gunfire and dropped to the floor, huddling against the wall.

With the assurance that DeRose was finally down and David safe, Bill knelt by Audree's side. Only then did he notice the knife protruding from her gut. "Goddammit, Audree," he yelled angrily. Gently, he rolled her onto her back, his caring hand stroking her cheek.

Her eyes hung with heavy lids. She managed a whisper, "David?"

Bill moved closer. "He's fine, darlin'. We got him. You and me, babe. We're a team. We did it. Now, just hang in there. Help will be here soon; they're almost here."

Sirens wailed outside. Bill could see through the small office window across the street where flashing strobes reflected off the opposite building windows. As loud as he could, he screamed for help. Though he paused to listen, he knew his cries went unheard. He leaned over

Audree. "I'm gonna get you some help, doll," he said, then moved as if he was going to leave.

"No, baby. Stay with me." She feebly reached up with her bloodied hand. Not finding his face, Bill guided it to his cheek. "Don't leave me."

"We need to get you some help, darlin'."

"No. Don't leave me. Don't leave me." The last few words lacked the breath to form sounds. Audree's eyes slowly closed, her hand sliding down Bill's cheek.

"Audree? Audree?" Bill shook her shoulders, seeing her eyes lift slightly. "Stay with me, doll. Do you hear? Goddammit, don't you dare give up on me." He yelled for help again. But it was hopeless. Even if they could hear him, the extensive building with its many floors and a maze of offices and corridors—it would be like finding a needle in a haystack.

They'll never find us in time.

Bill's mind raced. He picked up his revolver, aiming it through the office to the outside window. Covering Audree's ear with his other hand, he fired, shattering the glass.

THE STREET BELOW was crowded. A dozen police cars arrived, an ambulance, an armored S.W.A.T. vehicle, and a small army of uniformed officers. Every police radio unsilenced with a squelch and then...

"All units, shots fired, shots fired. Second floor, south wing. Proceed with caution."

A team of eight cops dressed in military green utilities and black bullet-proof vests gathered at the entrance, the other team entering through the rear. In single file, with their M4 carbines raised to eye level, knees slightly bent, they stormed the building.

"They're coming, babe, hang in there," Bill said, fighting back tears. Then he did something out of character. He talked. "Hey, when's this wedding? Zac and Cloe. April, was it? And we're invited?"

Audree's eyes struggled to open. The wedding was all she had talked about of late.

Admittedly, Bill had usually tuned her out but now, it was all he wanted to hear. "Yeah, I think you said April. I'll need to get a suit. *You'll* have to pick it. You've seen my taste. Not worth a damn." Bill held her hand to his lips, affectionately kissing the back, tears streaming.

He sniffled, summoning more courage. "And you'll need a new dress, too. I know how you love to get new dresses."

Her eyes had closed now, her mouth hanging ajar.

The rest of his words were for his own comfort. Stroking her face, he smiled through the tears. "How about a double wedding? Yeah, let's do that. Where shall we honeymoon? You'll want a beach." He laughed. "Big surprise there. Yeah, we can do that. A nice warm beach. How about Jamaica? We always talked about going. I'll finally meet your family. What do you say?"

Reaching behind her neck, he lifted her limp body from the cold floor. Her head fell back as he cradled her to his shoulder, his frame shuddering with the release of silent tears.

After what seemed like an eternity, flashlights illuminated the corridor in front of Bill, casting his shadow onto the cracked plaster wall. He peered over his shoulder, squinting into the blinding light. Only a few feet behind him, in the small office, stood three military-styled officers each aiming their M4's directly at Bill. Their ghost-like stealth had surprised him.

The lead spoke authoritatively, "Sir, don't move."

Bill complied.

"Who fired the shot?"

"Me. I'm a cop. I mean ex-cop. Please, we need help."

"It's coming. First, I need to know it's safe. Who else is up here?"

"Two perps. Both dead. They kidnapped a child. David Wilson. He's…" Bill nodded to the end of the hall, expecting to find him still sitting there. To his horror, David was gone. An officer from the rear team stood over DeRose's lifeless body. He hadn't heard him approach either.

Bill panicked. "David! The kid. He was right there!"

"We've got him, sir. Our agent's taking him down now. He's safe."

The lead officer touched his earpiece to hear an incoming message from his team. Pinching the talk button on his chest radio, he commanded, "Roger that, building cleared. Send in the paramedics, second floor, end of south corridor. Two dead, one critical." The officer released his talk button. "Sir, are you injured?"

But Bill didn't answer. With his cheek pressed against Audree's, he rocked her gently as if soothing a crying baby.

CHAPTER 42

Emergency Room

Strapped to the gurney, Bill was loaded into the ambulance, a female paramedic holding a saline bag high above the I.V. in his arm. The hemostatic gauze taped across his shoulder had already stabilized the bleeding. The paramedic pressed an oxygen mask over Bill's face and tried to pull the elastic over his head. Bill grabbed the mask, pulling it from his mouth to speak.

"Audree. Where's Audree?"

"Sir, relax. Let us do our job." She tried again.

This time, Bill grabbed her wrist, raising his head. "Where—is— Audree?"

The other paramedic climbed aboard, closing the ambulance doors behind him. "Who is Audree? Is she your wife?" he asked. "Was she the lady with you?"

Bill nodded. "Is she alive?"

"On her way to Lincoln Hospital as we speak."

"That's not what I asked," Bill growled. "It's a simple yes or no."

Both paramedics exchanged solemn glances. The one holding the mask spoke delicately as if breaking bad news. "Sir, she's in critical condition, but she's in the best hands now. They'll do everything they can."

He found little comfort in those words. His head dropped back to the gurney. Seizing the opportunity, the paramedic slapped the oxygen mask onto Bill's face and began connecting a bundle of electrodes to his chest.

As he lay there, regret consumed him.

Why did I bring her? This was all my fault.

The million other ways this could have played out raced through his mind, none ending with Audree fighting for her life. The more he thought, the more he hated himself. Despite warning her not to enter the building, he knew her too well. *Of course, she would.* She shouldn't have been on the stakeout to begin with. And yet, had she not, he would be dead right now. But how could he live knowing she'd died saving him? In fact, how could he live without her at all?

They made the twenty-minute drive to the hospital in under twelve. Before he knew it, he was being wheeled along a hospital corridor, his speed gauged by the passing overhead strip lights whizzing by too fast to count. Among the dozen or so scrubs surrounding him, one was the female paramedic. She passed her report as they charged toward the surgery pre-op unit.

"William Kowalski. Sixty-one. Gunshot to the left shoulder, one inch below the clavicle. No exit wound. BP steady, one thirty over sixty, heart rate between eighty-four and ninety, O2 holding at ninety-seven."

"Very good," the physician replied. Then he instructed his charge nurse, opposite, "Prep room two. And let's get some imaging." He leaned over Bill. "We have to remove the bullet, Mr. Kowalski, but first we're going to take a few X-rays. See what's going on in there." He examined Bill's chest and abdomen, noticing the three older bullet wounds. "I see you're no stranger to being shot, Mr. Kowalski. Bit of a bullet magnet, are you? Who did you upset this time?"

The female paramedic answered, "There was a kidnapping on the south side."

"Ahh. The nine-year-old boy?" the physician recalled.

Bill's head lifted. "He's here? Why is he here? Is he okay?"

"Yes, he's fine. Not to worry, Mr. Kowalski. I just checked him over. Just a slight concussion. His mother's en route."

"And Audree?" Bill was afraid to ask but did anyway. "How's she doing?"

Again, the paramedic filled in the blanks. "I think she's his wife. The knife victim."

"Your wife is in surgery, Mr. Kowalski. It's too early to tell." He paused. "She's in very good hands."

Bill sighed. *She's in very good hands.* Those damn words again, almost as if a med school class had been dedicated to the construction of sentences conveying no information, just meaningless reassurance.

Arriving in pre-op, a nurse closed the curtain around Bill's gurney. "We're going to get you prepped for surgery, Mr. Kowalski. I have some forms for you to sign." She began stripping his clothes. "Any allergies to anesthesia, or iodine?"

"Where's my jacket?" Bill griped, his head searching.

"We have it. Don't worry. Your things will be safe."

"I need my phone."

"If there's someone you need to contact, we can do that for you, but—"

"Woman," Bill barked. His sharpness froze her tongue as well as her actions. "Get—me—my—phone."

"Sir, you have a bullet wound. You're heading for surgery in just a few—"

"Look, I'm not heading anywhere until you get me my *goddamn* phone."

Taking a moment of consideration, the two nurses exchanged reluctant nods. "Okay, Mr. Kowalski, you win. Two minutes."

The other nurse reached into a clear plastic bag, pulling out his bloodstained jacket. After a brief search through his pockets, she retrieved his phone, handing it to him.

Bill scrolled through his contacts, then stared at the name on his screen, his thumb hovered over the call button.

He swallowed hard.

There was little he was afraid of, but this next call scared him to death.

THE JOURNEY TO Lincoln Hospital did little to ease Sheila Wilson's nerves. When the uniformed officer turned up at her apartment and delivered the news she had been waiting for, it hit like a double espresso straight to the veins. Her eyes sprang wide, though it was not enough to dispel the shadows that had formed around them.

"Mrs. Wilson, we found your son. He has been taken to Lincoln Hospital and—" was all the female officer had managed to say before Sheila interrupted, yelling, "Take me to him, now!" Still draped in three-day-old clothes and with disheveled hair, Sheila hastily grabbed her apartment keys and raced ahead of the officer.

Despite Sheila's persistent inquiries during the seemingly endless drive, the officer could not offer more than what she was told: David Wilson was alive and receiving treatment in the hospital.

The police cruiser finally arrived at the E.R., slowing in front. Before coming to a stop, Sheila had already opened the door and leaped from the moving car. For someone who hadn't eaten or slept in days, she moved like an athlete in a 100-meter dash.

The automatic doors guarding the entrance to the E.R.'s reception opened painfully slow. Sheila pried them open, squeezing between then charging inside. The officer trailed behind, pleading, "Mrs. Wilson, wait!" Her stout legs and extra few pounds were no match against a mother's hope.

Wheezing, the officer paused at the reception desk inquiring about David Wilson's location. By the time she caught up with Sheila, she found her wandering down random corridors, desperately calling her son's name.

"Mrs. Wilson, please slow down. It's this way."

Directions only seemed to fuel Sheila's determination. She sprinted ahead, the officer groaning and yelling directions from behind.

Shelia's voice echoed through the corridors, "David! David Wilson! David, where are you! It's your mommy. David!"

The alarming cries drew nurses, doctors, and patients from their private examination rooms, among them Sheila's nine-year-old son.

Reaching the corridor's end, she spun around to see him, his narrow shoulders heaving from the run. Two nurses with panicked faces were just catching up behind him, their outreached arms evidently too slow to stop him.

Tension released in her shoulders for the first time in days. She held out both arms, fingers spread wide, her eyes a cascading river of emotion. David ran toward her. Sheila dropped to her knees to catch him, hugging him so tight she almost crushed him.

"Oh David, I'm so sorry. So, so sorry!" She pushed him at arm's length, looking him over.

Her motherly fingers brushed the hair from his eyes and stroked his blotchy cheek. She examined the blue Band-Aid taped across his forehead, the bruise around his eye and the torn shoulder of his favorite Captain Universe shirt, now held together by three safety pins.

It broke her heart to witness the trauma he had suffered.

He's been through enough.

She pulled his forehead to her lips and gently kissed him. Her voice quivering, she asked, "Are you okay, sweetheart?"

David didn't answer. Instead, he threw his skinny arms around his mother's neck, hugging as though he would never let go.

CHAPTER 43

The Call

Matthew pointed at his screen with Theia now peering over his shoulder. "Book III was first written by the Greeks and then later translated. The original printing dates back well beyond the birth of Christ. Much older than I thought." He sat back. "But that's not the oddest part."

"Oh, then what?" Theia asked.

"Book III appears to be a kind of apocalyptic account of the end of the world. Judgment day."

"Sooo. What's odd about that?"

"Why would Sibylline Oracles, theological prophets who discuss 'good cheer,' 'immortal light,' 'eternal joy,' and 'Jesus' prophesize the end of days? Odd, don't you think?"

Before she could answer, her phone rang six feet away by her terminal.

Pulling on the table edge, she wheeled her chair across to her computer station, grabbing it. Her eyebrows knitted together when she noted the caller ID.

"It's Bill!" she exclaimed, passing Matthew a confused glance.

She placed the phone to her ear, half smiling, half frowning. "So, what, Audree doesn't want to talk to—"

The abrupt pause in her voice caught Matthew's attention, steering his gaze toward her.

Slowly, her mouth opened, her eyes glaring and widening with each word she heard. Her cheeks paled a ghostly white. She gasped, bringing her hand to her lips.

At this point, Matthew had rotated his chair to face her, breath held.

Whatever news Bill was sharing, it was bad. Worse than bad.

Suddenly, Theia launched to her feet, sending her chair wheeling across the room. "No!"

Matthew stood quickly, gingerly approaching her.

"No, no, *NO*…" Theia's crying words blurred into sobs, sobs into screams. Her phone slipped from her trembling grasp and clattered to the floor just as her legs gave way.

Matthew bolted the last few steps, managing to catch her before she hit the ground. Heaped on the floor, Theia thrashed her arms and legs, trying to break free from Matthew's embrace. But Matthew held tight. After a moment, she fell limp in his arms.

And bawled.

Before long, Miss Holloway and her two staff members had gathered around them, staring down, speechless, faces aghast. By now, Theia was coiled in a ball, trembling in Matthew's arms. Though he had yet to learn the tragic news, he sieved his fingers through her beautiful blonde hair, whispering repeatedly, "It's okay, it's okay, it's all gonna be okay."

CHAPTER 44

Guy Fawkes Inn

Theia's restless fingers swirled a half-drunk glass of French Cognac. A candle, flickering inches away, consumed its wick at the center of the table. Captivated by its yellow light, Theia's mind wrestled with endless what-ifs, her knee bouncing rhythmically beneath the table. Across from her, a bourbon sat untouched, awaiting its first sip.

A stone's throw from the Minster and the Old Palace, the Guy Fawkes Inn had been the original birthplace of Guido Fawkes, the notorious conspirator who had unsuccessfully planned to blow up Westminster Palace in 1605 during the infamous 'Gunpowder Plot.'

Today, his ancestral home offered bed & breakfast accommodations, serving local beers and spirits in dark candle-lit rooms in keeping with seventeenth-century style. The only hint of electricity and modernization was the fluorescent lighting gracing the bar, and a muted TV hinged next to it. A man in a crisp white shirt and tie sat at the bar sipping a beer. He jabbed repeatedly at the remote control, surfing the channels with apparent boredom.

Matthew returned to the table across from Theia. He tugged on his heavy hardwood chair, screeching it across the roughhewed floorboards.

"Okay, we're all sorted. I got the last two rooms." He placed her room key by her almost empty glass as he sat. "You're on the top floor facing the Minster."

Theia sat in stunned silence, entranced by the dancing flame.

"You should have a marvelous view of the cathedral from your room," Matthew said. "She says it's their best. Guy Fawkes was apparently born in it. Pretty cool, huh?"

Matthew's attempt to engage her in small talk failed.

Theia's mind was elsewhere, conjuring horrific images of Audree being stabbed. Absentmindedly, she swirled the golden remnant of Cognac, barely sufficient to drink.

"Do you want another one?" Matthew asked. No response coming, he stated, "I'll get you another." He motioned to stand, hesitating when Theia showed interest in speaking. He sat back down.

"I can't believe it. Poor Audree."

The back of her wrist wiped a welling tear from the corner of her eye. "It's all my fault. All I ever do is hurt people. Pain. Suffering. Death. They follow me."

Veins pulsed in her neck. Her head shook as she spoke through locked teeth. "I'm sick of it. I should have never involved her. Thirty years, thirty fucking years I have known Audree and have kept her safe, isolated from all this… this fucked-up, whatever this shit is." She slammed the table as if swatting a fly. "And now look. Within days of involving her, she gets stabbed." Her tears streamed. "And poor Bill…" She gulped.

So concerned with Audree's welfare, she'd almost forgotten about Bill. The trickle of tears transformed into a torrent, her voice rising, almost squeaking.

"Oh, my God, Bill. I'm so sorry. I am so, so sorry."

Matthew reached across the table, gently gripping her hand. "I know how you must feel, but this isn't your fault."

Theia's back straightened, and her neck appeared to grow an inch. She ripped her hand from Matthew's.

"How is this 'not my fault'? People die because of me. *Me*. You *don't* know how I feel. How could you? You've seen this for five minutes; I have lived this… *lived* this for twelve hundred fucking years. Never moving forward, never able to love, to have a family. All the shit *you* and everyone else take for granted." She waved her hand around the room. "It's like I'm cursed. Well, I'm done. So fucking done."

With one swig, she downed the last drop of Cognac then reached for Matthew's glass to gulp half of his. She scrunched her face, the unrefined Tennessee liquor scorching her throat.

The man at the bar had finally settled on a channel—a talk show. Though still muted, closed captions flashed at the bottom of the screen.

Matthew stretched out his arms and clasped both her hands as if preparing to pray. "You're right. I'm sorry. That was insensitive of me. I've *no* idea how you feel." He shook her hands gently, confessing. "But… but I know… I know how *I* feel…" Eyes down, he took a deep breath. "Even though I've only known you a short while, and arguably this might not be the best time…"

While Matthew struggled to verbalize his emotions, Theia found herself drawn to the TV talk show playing over his shoulder.

The interviewer sat across a small round coffee-style table from a very suave Englishman. Theia squinted at the smart, well-groomed guest.

Even muted, the guest carried himself with powerful confidence. His thick, wavy black hair and deep-set eyes reminded her of someone. By now, Matthew's voice had faded. She leaned over the table, reading the captions:

Michael: "So, I hear you're running for office, Mr. Goodwin?"

Mr. Goodwin: "What a coincidence. I've been hearing the same!"

[laughter]

Mr. Goodwin: "But seriously, as much as the sordid state of this government concerns me and while nothing would give me greater pleasure than stirring up new politics and bringing much-needed radical change, that's not why I'm here."

Michael: "No, of course not. But, if you do decide to run, Mr. Goodwin, you've got one voter, right here."

Mr. Goodwin: "Thank you, Michael. I appreciate that. Maybe one day?"

[applause]

Michael: "So, why don't you tell us about your latest project…"

Mr. Goodwin: "Well, thank you for asking, Michael." He turned to face the camera, which slowly zoomed on his face.

Where do I know him from?

"I'm sponsoring the creation of the new youth center to improve the lives of the less fortunate. The center will also provide programs tailored toward education, my goal being to reduce youth crime, and get them early, so to speak. Turn adversity into opportunity, hopelessness into encouragement, unemployment into enterprise. Let's help the children. After all, our future's in their hands, and we need to do everything to support that."

Despite his speech connoting a not-so-hidden political pitch rather than a purely philanthropic one, the TV audience and host appeared enamored by it—and him.

More applause ensued.

As the Englishman nodded humbly to the camera and the audience, his name appeared on the screen: 'Amodeus Goodwin - Britain's Favourite Philanthropist.'

Theia's lips mimed the name, her mind narrowing on a memory. "Amodeus? *Asmo*deus. *Asma!*" She leaped from her chair and raced to the bar, leaving Matthew alone and confused. Pointing to the TV, she screamed at the gentleman holding the remote. "Turn it up, turn it up."

On the TV, Mr. Goodwin stood to his feet, buttoned his suit jacket, and gave a friendly wave to the audience.

"Thank you, thank you," Mr. Goodwin yelled over the crowd's cheers. He flashed a bright smile. *That beautiful smile.* "I'll see you all at the grand opening!"

Reacting as though she'd just seen a ghost, she pulled both hands to her mouth, gasping. "Oh, my God. It's him." She felt the blood drain from her face.

Even as her chest swelled for air, none would enter her lungs. The shadowy room tunneled, its peripheral darkness encroaching on the bright screen of the TV, shrinking it to a white dot. Her world spiraled into chaos and she fumbled for the counter.

Next to her, the crisp-shirted gentleman jumped from his stool to steady her. "Are you okay, missus?" He guided her by her shoulders into an adjacent barstool.

Matthew rushed to help.

Half unconscious, Theia leaned over the counter, her head resting in her arms.

"Can we get some water, mate?" the gentleman asked the barman, who was already one step ahead, handing one over. "Here you go, miss. Take a sip. You'll feel better."

Theia raised her head. Like a boxer struggling against the ref's count, her eyes fought to come around. The gentleman placed the glass to her lips, and she sipped it.

Matthew held her from behind. "What happened?"

"I dunno, mate," the gentleman replied. "One minute she was fine; the next, she turned white."

As if trying to keep her warm, Matthew rubbed her shoulders. "Theia? Are you okay? What happened?"

Blackness gave way to light, and she refocused on the screen. "It's Asma," she whispered, her voice trembling.

"It's who? Theia, you're not making any sense."

Speaking louder, over the show's band and earsplitting applause, she pointed to the TV. "Asma. My Asma. It's him."

Matthew peered at the screen. "Who? What?"

"Don't you see?" Theia's face lit up, a child on Christmas morning. "My Asma, he's alive!"

A disbelieving giggle escaped her, the corners of her mouth forming gentle creases against the rounding of her cheeks. For a millisecond, Matthew smiled with her—at her joy, the rekindling in her eyes. But it faded along with his hopes and dreams.

THE GENTLEMAN RETRIEVED his pinstriped jacket from his chairback and put it on. After buttoning it, he discreetly tugged on his shirt cuff, concealing the partial tattoo on his wrist. He glanced at Theia, grinning proudly, then headed for the door.

Mission accomplished!

CHAPTER 45

Ampleforth Abbey

Brother Dominic slammed the car door outside his quarters at Ampleforth Abbey. The gravel crunched underfoot as his brown leather sandals pounded with hastened steps. The chapel was far. But it was forbidden for him to park any closer; chapel parking remained exclusively reserved for visitors. Those were the rules, and they were never broken.

Not here.

Yet, as his lungs protested and phlegm gathered at the back of his throat, the monk thought: *today, rules don't apply.* Not with the news he was about to break.

A fiery dawn had begun its morning feast of stars and a navy sky. But still shrouded by night, the chapel's formidable structure remained abundantly floodlit; angelic sodium beams rising its face in cones but not quite meeting the lofty eaves.

Bellowing fog, he climbed the time-trodden steps, tugged open the oak doors, racing down the echoey corridor. Running was also forbidden here, but this rule he would break.

Ahead, a double line of monks was silently marching toward him. They halted when the renegade shamefully plowed through them.

Even as his shoulder accidentally brushed against a fellow brother, he maintained his course without a hint of acknowledgment or apology. Outraged, the twelve monks' silence erupted into tearoom gossip and natter.

A narrower corridor split off at a right angle. Almost passing it, the monk slid on his leather soles, the polished wax floors adding distance before they stopped. From here, he could see the double-arched doors to the private chapel. Closed.

Of course. At this hour they would be. Reverend Thomas would be immersed in private prayer, a moment of sacred solitude. The realization of breaking yet another rule weighed on him, for he had never dared to disrupt the reverend's sanctified time before.

The double doors burst open with a deafening crash.

Kneeling at the altar, head bowed, the startled reverend cowered forward as if the doors behind had exploded. He sheepishly glanced over his shoulder, his arms lowering from shielding his balding head. Though Pope VI had banned the customary monks' shaved tonsure decades since, Reverend Thomas' tonsure haircut, bald encircled with silver, was natural.

"Dominic?" the reverend yelled, recognizing him. "What on Earth? Have you lost your mind? I'm in prayer." The reverend took a minute to climb to his feet, osteoarthritis plaguing his knees from fifty years of kneeling on thin pads and cold stone floors. "Explain yourself."

Dominic needed a minute. The run had him doubled over trying to catch his breath. Using a pew for support, he nursed a stitch in his left side.

"Dominic!" Reverend Thomas yelled again. "Speak man. What is it?"

"Reverend Thomas—I apologize for the intrusion—but—but I have found her."

"Her? Who are you talking—"

"*Her!*" he shouted brazenly. "The Reginleif girl."

Stunned, the reverend's face bleached to the color of his hair. Unable to assimilate the information, he simply stared into space, agog.

"Reverend?" Dominic pressed.

"But... but that's not possible." The reverend's vacant stare focused on his younger monk. "You must be mistaken, Dominic. That... That cannot be."

"*No*, Reverend. There is no mistake. It was her. She's here, with an American."

Reverend Thomas trembled. His knees gave way and he stepped forward grabbing a rail. Dominic moved to help him but stopped when the reverend threw up a halting palm. After gathering his thoughts, he let out a deep sigh. "Very well. Assemble the order." He eyed Dominic directly. "Do it now. This morning."

"But, Reverend, that will take hours."

"We don't *have* hours. Get as many as you can."

Dominic poised, awaiting instructions. Details perhaps? Or to be properly dismissed? But the reverend roared in urgency, flicking fingers at the open door. "Now, Dominic! Go!"

Wincing, Dominic clutched his side and shuffled away.

The reverend turned to the altar. He approached, dropping to his knees. This time, the searing arthritic pain went unnoticed. His neck creased as his humble gaze climbed the eight-foot cross standing tall upon the altar. Hanging from it was a beautiful, molded carving of Jesus, lacquered to a sheen. Jesus' head drooped forward; the sleepy, half-open eyes in glossy enamel blue burned into the reverend's very soul. He crossed himself and then kissed the silver crucifix hanging from his neck.

"Oh, Lord, please forgive me."

A FEW HOURS later, in front of the Guy Fawkes Inn, Matthew hurled Theia's Tumi suitcase into their Mercedes rental car, bringing the trunk lid to a gentle close. "Okay. All done. Ready?"

Theia stood on the pavement, chewing her lower lip. An arm folded across her torso; her other elbow rested on it. With a cocked head, her hand nervously tugged on her earlobe.

The bell of Great Peter's tolled once from the northwest tower of the minster, prompting Matthew to check his watch. "Eleven o'clock. Better get going. You don't want to be late."

Theia nodded yet didn't move.

Matthew walked over, touching her shoulder. "Are you okay?"

Theia hesitated. "Yes, no… I don't know, Matthew. Maybe we should…"

"I know you're nervous," Matthew said. "But this all makes sense now. I couldn't figure it out before. There was this missing piece to the puzzle that I couldn't solve, but now it all fits."

He grasped Theia's shoulders, affectionately aligning his eyes with hers, his voice sweet and gentle. "I don't know why you're here, but I'm guessing you're about to find out. That's what you've always wanted, right? Answers."

Theia managed a tight smile and a nod.

"Now we know Asma's alive and immortal like you, there's clearly a connection between you two. He must be the reason you're here, and maybe…"

Matthew hesitated.

He couldn't believe he was saying it, but deep down knew it was true. "Maybe you're meant to be together. I mean, last night's TV show… What are the chances? Don't you agree? To me, and it's only my take on it, but it's all too, how can I say… planned out."

Again, she nodded, then asked, "Are we sure it's him? I thought I was sure, but what if I'm wrong? What if I'm…"

"Theia, I've spent two hours this morning trying to get through to somebody, anybody at Goodwin Castle who could arrange a meeting— and nothing. But as soon as I mentioned it was regarding, 'Theia Reginleif, an old friend,' the man himself called me back within five minutes with a personal invitation. So, yes, I think it's him." He opened the car door for her. "Shall we?"

As Theia's door closed and she wrestled with her seatbelt, Matthew sucked in courage from the fresh morning air, then joined her.

Before pressing start, he confirmed, "So, you're good?"

She smiled. "Yes, I'm good, Matthew. Just… nervous, I guess."

She looked lost.

"Well, that's normal. I mean, it's been, what, twelve hundred years?"

"Eleven hundred and thirty-four."

Her correction, sharp off her tongue as if she had meticulously counted every passing day, was like an arrow to his heart. "Wow, so yeah, that's a long time." Matthew hesitated on a thought, a question he'd promised himself he wouldn't ask. One that had kept him from sleeping. "Do you think you still, um, still love him after all this time?" He felt the tension build, like a bowstring drawn, ready to release the arrow.

Theia's eyes gazed vacantly through her side window. "You know, not a day goes by without my thinking of him. Even after all this time. I guess, maybe, I never stopped."

And there it was. The fatal arrow released with precision.

"Right. Great. Yeah, this is… this is gonna be great," Matthew chirped, cranking the ignition. A quick check in all three mirrors and a glance over his shoulder, he steered onto the quiet one-way street, still mumbling, "Gonna be great! Yup!"

Farther down the same street, two men in dark suits sat inside a parked metallic-black BMW with tinted windows. As the rented silver Mercedes passed them by, the BMW pulled into the street to follow. The passenger was the channel-surfing, remote-hogging gentleman who'd helped Theia in the bar the evening before. He pressed a phone to his ear. "They're leaving now, sir."

CHAPTER 46

Father Andrews and Father Timmons

Reverend Thomas basked in the warm light radiating through one of the chapter room's four tall windows. To address to the order, he wore his formal ankle-length black tunic with a magenta cummerbund. His silver pectoral cross was looped around his neck and glistened in the sun.

Immortal Light, he thought. He bowed his head in shame. A miracle child. Blessed. The Pope himself dulled against her.

Around him, the soaring oak-paneled walls of the chapter room infused a cozy ambiance into such an expansive space. The rectangular room surrounded a sturdy conference table stretching half its length, nine of its thirty seats already occupied. Five occupants were formally dressed, the other four in their daily robed garb. Dominic stood in wait by the solid arched entrance door, directing members. Finally, the last two arrived.

Slowed by age and infirmity, they shuffled at a leisurely pace.

Dominic, on the other hand, at only forty-five, was by far the youngest member in the room. Although the order had new, younger blood, none were present.

Nowadays, the order had little need for recruitment, their reformative roles being more clerical and ceremonial, managed easily on a skeleton staff. Besides, being a secret order, recruitment was a delicate and grueling process. Joining was by invitation only, after a strict vetting period of which the applicant was unaware. Should a new member make it to novice, it would take an easy three years before ordination to monk. The teachings alone consumed most of that time.

As expected from the younger element, Dominic respectfully helped the elders to their seats, and joined them at the table. Heads swiveled, each member inquiring as to the nature of the emergency meeting. Slowly, the purr of chatter settled to silence as they patiently stared at Reverend Thomas, still gazing across the manicured garden grounds.

"Brothers," he said, "thank you for coming at such short notice." Pausing, he sighed deeply. Before delivering his news, he turned to eye each member, their anxious expressions returning his gaze. A time flashed in his memory when the table had been crowded, decades ago. Many then were young. Today, almost all the scalps were either balding or silver.

Honored as their leader, he pressed tight lips, though not quite smiling, and strolled to the head of the table.

"For centuries, our order has existed in secret, fearful of reprisal and persecution, even from those within the Church. Knowledge passed down through time, generation to generation, father to son, priest to priest…" Reverend Thomas squeezed a fellow brother proudly on his shoulders. "We have persevered against all odds. How, you may ask? Because, my brothers, there is nothing more important than our success. Few would understand the gravity of our cause, the weight of our burden. But we understand. Our predecessors understood, certainly those who gave their lives for the cause understood."

In respect, he took a moment of silence.

Then, speaking with a deep sincerity, he posed an obvious question to his captivated members, "But I ask you, what *is* our cause?"

The brothers glanced at one another, confused.

At first, none dared to speak. Though the answer was fundamentally obvious to everyone in the room, it was clear the Reverend Thomas was probing for something else. Finally, one brother, the next in age to Dominic, gave the generic answer. "The perseverance of Christ and his word?"

The remaining brothers nodded in agreement, relieved someone had offered an answer.

"Is that it? Is that all? Nothing more?"

Reverend Thomas shook his head and then continued encircling the table. "No. That, my brothers, is simply the doctrine of all Christians, from the laity to the Pope. Our purpose is more than that. Let us not forget, gentlemen, we are still at war. And we are the soldiers of that war—the protectors of humankind. Regardless of faith." Resting both hands on the table, the reverend leaned forward. "And sometimes, as soldiers, we are tasked with the unthinkable."

EARLIER THAT MORNING, in a narrow side street not far from the Guy Fawkes Inn, two monks sat in wait. Father Timmons was in the driver's seat, while in the passenger seat Father Andrews' eyes burned into his iPad. Neither wore their robes today. This mission was especially delicate—off the books, you might say.

Father Timmons danced his spindly knees under the steering wheel. "I'm gonna need to pee before long!" he said, scanning the high street shop fronts in search of a public bathroom.

"I thought you went before we left?"

"That was hours ago." He eyed his Casio. "It's almost eleven already."

"You'll just have to hold it."

"I can't." He fidgeted in his seat. "I-I really need to go. I'll burst soon. Or, you know…"

"Ugh!" Father Andrews pulled his water bottle from the cup holder, unscrewed the cap, then after lowering his window, poured the remaining few mouthfuls onto the pavement. "Here, use that and be careful."

"What? No way. I can't pee with you sitting there."

"Seriously? Fine." Father Andrews exited.

Outside, he placed his iPad on the roof, not daring to peel his eyes from it. He zoomed in on the screen with his thumb and forefinger, the map narrowing on a stationary small red dot flashing on High Petergate Road, just outside the Guy Fawkes Inn.

The sound of urine swirling inside a plastic bottle followed by a long, relieved sigh resonated from the open window. "Better?" Father Andrews asked.

"Ah, much. I don't think it's going to stop. Think I'll have to do it in two sittings. Hey, let me ask you something. Why would Reverend Thomas send us, with no experience, on such a critical mission? I mean… we're not exactly James Bond material. And this," he added in relevance to the Citroen, "isn't exactly an Aston Martin."

"Speak for yourself," Father Andrews jested. "I'd whip 007's butt any day… provided we were playing chess." He poked his head through the window to find his friend still peeing into the bottle and abated his eyes. "I guess we were the nearest on such short notice. Why? Are you nervous?"

"Of course. Are you not?"

Father Andrews stared into the footwell at the shoe box that Reverend Thomas had handed him that morning, along with his instructions. "I'm terrified," he said. "But I have faith that…"

Blip, blip, blip…

Snapping his back straight, Father Andrews grabbed his iPad from the roof with both hands. He gasped. "Heavens, they're moving!" He scrambled into the car just as Father Timmons was zipping his fly, the almost full bottle of urine still frothing in the cup holder. "Hurry. Let's go!" He slapped the dash.

Father Timmons twisted the key, bringing their scarlet Citroen to life.

Carefully, he eased from the side street, the one-way lane so narrow that the tires of their compact vehicle barely squeezed between its tapered curbs.

"Wait!" Father Andrews commanded, staring at his iPad. "They've stopped."

"Are you sure?" Father Timmons slowed to a stop and looked over his shoulder to the empty street behind. "If someone comes, I'm going to have to move. Shall we circle? It's not too far and we'll still be close enough to follow if they start moving."

"Let's just wait. See what they do." A thought occurred while he eyed the stationary blip flashing on his screen. "You did put the tracker on the correct vehicle, right?"

"Of course," Father Timmons scoffed as if obvious. "The gray Mercedes."

"Silver Mercedes. Metallic silver."

"Gray, silver, whatever. Don't worry, Dominic told me the reg plate too. Trust me, it's the right vehicle."

Father Andrews returned his eyes to the iPad. "I wonder why they stopped?"

"Maybe they forgot something."

"Maybe, but Petergate's a one-way street. They'd have to circle to go back. I don't understand it. Unless… the tracker fell off!" A look of horror fell across each of their faces as they exchanged bulbous stares. That mistake would be a catastrophic one.

The mission would have failed before it even began.

Suddenly, the iPad blipped again.

The flashing dot had moved a quarter mile in an instant. "Oh no. They're already at Low Petergate." He gulped, looking back at Father Timmons. "Maybe the narrow streets were blocking the signal."

"The tracker's range is less than a mile. If we lose them—"

"We won't. Go, go."

He ground the vehicle into first gear, pressing the gas pedal so hard it raised them both in their seats and spun the wheels. For having only three cylinders and a one-liter engine sized to fit on a motorcycle, it accelerated faster than either of them had anticipated. The car teetered on the edge of losing control as the rear wheel bounced on a tight curb, wagging the car like a dog's tail. The bottle of pee ejected from the cup holder spilling into Father Andrew's lap. Half of it emptied before his fumbling hands could return it to the holder. Frantically, he wiped his cuff against the iPad screen. "Oh, come on!"

"Sorry," Father Timmons announced. "It looks like it's still intact."

"More than I can say for my dignity!" He shook drips of urine from his hand. "Yuk. Disgusting."

As they approached Low Petergate T-junction, the silver Mercedes with Matthew and Theia inside sailed past. Father Timmons braked hard screeching and skidding their tires as they neared the stop sign.

"Don't stop. That's them. Go, go, go," Father Andrews rallied. "Can't afford to lose them."

Without yielding, their compact car cornered behind Matthew's, causing the black BMW, which was closely trailing, to brake hard. "My fault," Timmons shouted, raising a hand in apology. The passenger of the BMW brandished an angry fist as they cut in front.

Once outside the cramped city, Matthew's silver Mercedes accelerated on the two-lane country road. Behind it, the red Citroen and the black BMW followed in a single procession.

"Okay, brother, we're on his tail. Now what?"

Father Andrews said nothing. Instead, he leaned forward and removed the lid from the shoe box between his feet, peering inside.

AROUND THAT SAME time, Reverend Thomas concluded his address to the handful of order members gathered inside the chapter room. Lifting the heavy Bible from the table, the Reverend thrust it into the air. The several aged brown pages with frayed edges in his other hand felt much lighter.

He shook the Bible above his head. "Revelation 19 proclaims good will prevail over evil in an almighty bloody battle. The beast and his false prophet will burn in a lake of fire and sulfur."

Next, he shook the pages, the Bible thudding to the table, lifting everyone in their seats. "Yet, 'The Five Articles of the Ancient Prophecy' describe the coming of the beast and his reign on Earth. For centuries, we have pondered the contradictions…"

An elderly member interrupted, "Why are we discussing the Articles? Their prophecy failed back in 1945. We have celebrated Karl Hoffmann Day ever since."

The reverend's mouth held open from the interruption. A sigh closed it. He had been avoiding the point, knowing how it would be received. "I'm afraid Karl failed, bother." Those members who had been staring at the table joined the others as they whipped their heads toward the reverend.

As if all speaking in unrehearsed choir, they chanted, 'What?'

"It has been brought to my attention earlier today that the Reginleif girl is alive and has found her way home. She is here, in York, as we speak."

The room erupted as the men chattered incessantly among themselves. "Gentlemen, please," the reverend bellowed, trying to calm the panic.

"Do we know it is her?" shouted a member. "Perhaps there's been a mistake."

The reverend looked at Dominic, who responded for him, "Um, no mistake, I'm sure. Her face matches our records, and she still goes by her first name. I followed her all afternoon. Trust me, it is Reginleif."

The room erupted a second time.

"Gentlemen, please."

The fearful members randomly spouted off questions exploding into argument.

"So, what now? What can we try?"

"It's over. There's nothing left *to* try."

"We need to proceed quickly. Do something. Form a plan?"

"We have a plan," Reverend Thomas supplied confidently. "Earlier this morning, I dispatched two of my men, Father Andrews and Father Timmons, with specific instructions. They will succeed where others have failed."

One senior monk stood to his feet, slapping frail hands on the table. "You, arrogant fool," he spat, his blanched cheeks turning red. "How can you be so sure? Our order has tried for centuries and has failed. And you think sending out two men—"

"Agreed," one monk cried out.

"And, what if they do fail?" cried another. "Then what?"

All good questions, the reverend thought. But even if he had the answers, it would not bring the peace they so desired. Instead, he stood proud, chin high, his pigeon chest shielding him from the bombardment of questions. Yet beneath his positive exterior, he felt as though he had failed them all. For thirty years, he had led this order, never once suspecting this day would come.

Because of him, the order's numbers had diminished to a fraction of former years. A mistake that may now cost them dearly.

The fate of humanity now rested in the hands of Father Andrews and Father Timmons— the order's chess club president and the organizer of the Ampleforth Annual Fundraiser.

"These men of yours, Reverend," an elder asked, "what *are* their instructions exactly?"

The room quieted.

"To kill the Reginleif girl. No matter the cost."

CHAPTER 47

Tell God You Failed

Following the reverend's instructions to a tee, Father Andrews stretched the surgical glove over his right hand, snapping it on his wrist. He had already retrieved the semi-automatic pistol from the shoe box. It was balanced on his left knee, the empty magazine clip balanced on his right. He reached into the footwell, into the opened shoebox, retrieving what appeared to be a small wooden domino box with a sliding lid. Pushing with his thumb, he slid it halfway open. Inside, stacked end to end, rows of blue bullets glistened like gemstones in the sunlight.

One at a time, his shaking gloved hand loaded them into the magazine clip.

Next to him, Father Timmons fidgeted on the steering wheel, weaving their little red Citroen in and out of the narrow country lane, trying to see ahead. "Hurry, brother," he urged. "As soon as you get it loaded, I'm going to pull alongside."

"I'm trying," Father Andrews growled. "It's not as easy as it looks."

Again, Father Timmons steered the Citroen into the oncoming lane, his head almost pressed into the lower corner of the windshield. "I can't see if the road ahead is clear on this bend. We're going to need a straight run before I can… whoa!" He jerked their car left back into his lane, narrowly avoiding a head-on collision with an oncoming motorcycle.

The violent shift threw Father Andrews' pistol into the footwell along with the box of bullets, which emptied over the carpet. "Take it easy, brother. You're going to get us both killed," he griped, then leaned between his legs, reaching for another bullet. "Just drop back a bit. You'll get a better view ahead if you do."

"I don't want to drop back too far; we'll never catch back up in this thing! How many you got loaded?"

Father Andrews thumbed another bullet into the clip, each easier than the last. "Uh, I don't know. Four, maybe?"

"There's a straight section coming up. It's our only shot. Four will have to do."

Father Andrews whacked the clip into the gun's grip then held it with two hands in his lap, and stared aimlessly out the window.

"You have to rack it to load the bullet," Father Timmons reminded. "Like Reverend Thomas showed us. And keep the dangerous end away from me."

Using his puny fingers, Father Andrews tugged on the slide with his left hand. His fingers instantly slipped off, the sweat acting like an oily lubricant.

The curve of the road straightened.

"We have to do it now," Father Timmons prompted. "Hurry. This is our only chance."

Swapping his grip, he used his gloved right hand to yank back the slide. After several failed attempts the bullet finally chambered. "Got it." He lowered his window. "Okay, brother. Let's get this over with."

Father Timmons pulled into the oncoming lane, pressing the pedal to the floor.

The tiny motor had accelerated well from a stopped position, but at highway speed, it was barely perceptible.

The engine squealed at maximum revs, slowly creeping alongside Matthew's car.

FOR THE LAST fifteen minutes, Matthew had been eyeing the mirror at the car behind.

"Look at this idiot," he grumbled to Theia. "I can't believe he's trying to overtake us on *this* road."

Theia twisted in her seat to look behind them. "They might have an emergency. We're not in any hurry. You want to slow down, let them pass?"

"Screw that," Matthew snapped. "They've been weaving and swerving since we left the city. They're gonna cause a pile-up. Nah, they can stay behind. See how they like that." He slammed his toe aggressively on the accelerator and sped up.

"Are you okay, Matthew?"

"Yup. Dandy."

Yet, that was a lie. He was still simmering over the current turn of events. Yes, answers were what they'd come for. But, never once had he considered that finding them would lead Theia into the arms of another man. A man with a castle, no less. A do-gooder fucking philanthropist. Her first, and apparently, only true love. How could he compete with that? Truth was, his race was lost before the starter pistol had even fired.

Theia's phone rang.

She scrambled through her purse. "That'll be the nurse calling me back." Finding it, she answered, "This is Theia." She listened patiently and then, sagging her shoulders, deflated a long sigh. "Oh, thank God. Thank you so much for letting me know. And what about Bill, Bill Kowalski, how is he?"

The answer summoned a chuckle. "Sounds like him! Well, that's great. Thanks again! Please pass on my thoughts to them both." Hanging up, she returned her phone to her purse.

"Well?" Matthew asked. "How is she?"

Theia stared into her lap, absorbing the wonderful news. Savoring it. "She's going to be okay. The operation went well. They're moving her from ICU today." Clasping her hands, she closed her eyes and prayed aloud, "Thank you, thank you, thank you."

"And Bill?"

"Oh, they discharged him yesterday, but he's refusing to leave. Can you imagine? He created quite a ruckus when they told him he wasn't family and couldn't stay with Audree in the ICU." She chuckled again, then collapsed back in her chair. "Oh, I can finally breathe. For once, I think everything might just work out."

"Yup!"

FATHER ANDREWS FRETTED at the sight of Matthew's Mercedes inching away.

"Faster," he complained, "you're losing them."

"But I can't. My foot's on the floor," Father Timmons screamed, rocking back and forth in his seat as if that might help urge the small Citroen forward. "Can you get her from here, brother? I doubt we'll get another chance."

Father Andrews leaned his head outside into the icy airstream, his mousy fine hair whipping in the wind. Spotting the BMW in the side mirror, he promptly withdrew his head back inside.

Reverend Thomas had emphasized the importance of avoiding recognition. The Citroen, however, posed no issue. Following the sordid deed, their instructions were explicit: incinerate it. The reverend was keenly aware that the police were more likely to believe the Abbey's vehicle had been stolen and used in a horrific shooting than entertain the notion of two monks committing a random murder in broad daylight on their day off.

Father Andrews brought the gun to eye level. Through the driver's side rear window of Matthew's car, he had a clear shot of Theia's head. Though shooting from this angle was going to require excellent aim and a lot of luck. Crossing himself, he poked the gun through the open window.

"Steady! Steady!" he repeated. He squeezed the trigger slowly.

Suddenly, a thunderous air horn blasted.

The earsplitting decibels ripped him from his aim. Growing larger in their windshield, an articulated lorry hurtled toward them, headlights flashing. "Watch it!" he screamed.

Father Timmons stomped his brakes. Yanking the wheel, he skidded into the left-hand lane, not a moment too soon. With the force of an intercity train, the lorry thundered past, shuddering their car in its wake.

Father Andrews' head fell against the headrest, his arms collapsing between his knees while he gathered his nerves. "Holy Mary! That's the third time today you've nearly killed us, brother!"

Father Timmons' face was drained of color. Matthew's car was now disappearing around a bend a quarter mile ahead. "Look. Now what?"

"Keep going. Maybe we'll catch up. Give it everything it's got."

Once again, Father Timmons pressed his foot to the floor. Except this time, they heard the growl of a powerful engine, reminiscent of a performance race car. Only, it didn't come from their modest little Citroen; it came from behind.

Before they could turn to look, a black BMW had already sped alongside them. Matching their speed, it didn't overtake. The smoked passenger-side window lowered.

"What's this guy want?" Father Andrews asked, leaning across.

His blood ran cold, finding himself staring down the barrel of a muzzle suppressor. Behind it, a slick-haired gentleman in a dark suit and black leather gloves squinted over the sights.

Father Andrews gasped.

Clap, clap!

The driver's window of the red Citroen exploded into tiny fragments.

Father Timmons' head threw to the side then flopped forward onto his chest. Leaning against the seatbelt, he slumped, collapsing over the steering wheel. The car veered off-road and into a ditch. From the passenger side, Father Andrews grappled helplessly with the steering wheel. Despite his efforts, the car bounced, slewed, then rolled twice, before crunching onto its roof. The three remaining windows exploded in a shattering pop.

Dangling upside down from his seatbelt, Father Andrews slowly came to, feeling a warm trickle above his ear then streaming across his cheek. It dripped from his nose, splashing onto the clear beads of glass sprinkled over the tan headliner. The whine of the engine lowered, sputtering and shaking him fully awake.

He surveyed his surroundings.

Father Timmons hung motionless beside him, the back of his hands pulled to the headliner above as if commanded by some vile puppeteer. Though his eyes were half-open, they held no spark of life.

Regardless, Father Andrews reached for his shoulder and shook it. "Timmons? Timmons!"

He gulped, only now remembering the gunman, the two shots, the failed mission.

I need to inform the reverend!

Put Plan B into effect—if there is one.

He searched for his phone. He spotted the gun, the iPad next to it, its screen shattered. No phone.

With trembling hands, he struggled to unfasten the seatbelt, which now felt like a tourniquet on his thighs. After several attempts, he succeeded. His body slumped against the ceiling, and he groaned as the back of his neck and then his knees made contact, framing either side of his face.

A searing pain radiated from his shoulder. Having dislocated it twice from his boisterous tree-climbing years, he suspected today marked the third. Daring not to move in this doubled-over, pathetic position, he sobbed, shedding tears for the pain and, more profoundly, for the loss of his friend and the overwhelming emptiness that failure brought.

If I could only get to the road.

Get help.

Call the reverend.

Determined, he carefully unfolded himself flat, bearing the pain.

With only the use of one elbow, he crawled over the shattered glass, face down from the wreck, pausing only to grab the gun. *Just in case.*

The grassy embankment was shallow but for Father Andrews, it was Everest. His goal: a patch of sunlit grass unshaded by copper-leafed oaks. There, he would be warm until help arrived.

Looking back at the red Citroen and the road, he observed the dislodged divots where the car had dug in and rolled. Hanging from the front wheel arch was a completely misaligned wheel and suspension assembly. Thankfully, the engine had now died. Less risk of a fire at least.

Reaching the golden spot, he maneuvered onto his back and, for the first time, allowed himself to savor the serenity of nature—the morning dew's fresh, floral scent, so potent it could deceive the season into feeling like spring. Overhead, a round of robins danced. Beyond them, high above, surreal whispers of white smeared a pale blue sky.

Father Andrews soaked in the warmth of the sun. Squinting, the golden rays desiccated his eyeballs.

Just then, a shadow cooled his face.

It took a moment for his pupils to adjust. It wasn't a cloud; it was a figure standing over him. A tall man smartly dressed in a dark suit with a crisp white shirt and tie.

Salvation!

"Please," he whispered, raising his left hand, "I need help, a phone."

His eyes adjusted further, capturing the man's wry expression, the unsympathetic grin, unfriendly.

Father Andrews' spine ran cold.

He's the gunman, come to finish the job!

Despite the searing pain in his shoulder, he clenched his quivering grip on the gun, attempting to raise it. The looming figure stomped his hard leather sole onto his wrist before it was barely off the ground, then shook his head. As if relishing in the suspense, the dark figure slowly aimed his gun at Father Andrews' chest.

Father Andrews panted heavily.

Although a man of faith, he was not a man of courage. Not daring to stare down the muzzle now pointing at him, he returned his eyes to the peaceful sky, to the sun blazing high above. This time, he did not squint, instead choosing to welcome the blinding light.

He wept. His voice trembled as he chanted the Lord's Prayer.

"Our Father, who art in heaven, Hallowed be thy name, thy…"

The gunman's abhorrent words rumbled deep, drowning out Father Andrews. "When you meet your God, tell him you failed."

CHAPTER 48

The Goodwin Castle

You've arrived at your destination, chirped the female voice on Matthew's phone. Yet, that last bit of guidance proved unnecessary; he had already spotted the colossal wrought-iron gates from a quarter mile away. Approaching with caution, the twelve-foot walls, supporting massive gates, gracefully curved toward the entrance on both sides. The remnants of English damp weather had left their mark, staining the once-red brick and tanned coping with a subtle lime green hue. Atop the towering columns that supported the gates, two winged gargoyles perched, frozen halfway in flight, as if victims of Medusa's gaze.

Matthew lowered his window, nearing a keypad and speaker erected on a three-foot black steel pole, his finger hovering in search of the talk button.

Before he located it, the ominously silent gates opened, inviting them in.

Matthew ducked his head, scanning the perimeter wall for a camera. As expected, angled down on either side of the gate, he found them: two metallic gray units, zooming and panning on their vehicle. He turned to Theia. "Okay. This doesn't feel creepy, at all."

A short distance inside the rural property, Matthew watched through his rearview mirror as the gates closed behind them. After about four hundred yards of winding roads, the heavily treed drive finally straightened, giving way to a lush green pasture scattered with an occasional elm.

"Wow," Matthew said when the magnificent castle came into view a half mile ahead. "I knew this guy had money, but jeez."

Theia remained silent and still except for her hands, which fidgeted constantly, sliding back and forth on her thighs. Matthew felt a terrible sense of remorse. Throughout the entire drive, he had pitied himself, never once considering how Theia must feel. Her anguish had to be eleven hundred and thirty-four times worse than his. He gently squeezed her knee. "It's gonna be okay."

The sheer enormity of the building only became apparent when they finally neared the foot of it, although it was not the menacing castle Matthew had envisioned. With its numerous fleche spires and decorative finials, it appeared more stately, lordlier, though no less intimidating.

The road split into a circle guiding them under a grand *porte-cochere* entrance where the welcoming committee stood in wait: six tall men, all well-groomed yet somehow weathered, their rugged complexions seeming at odds with their suave Armani suits.

Another older, suited gentleman paced to a stop in front of the six. With gray hair, shorter and stouter, Matthew assumed he was in charge—a butler perhaps. Which would make the men behind… servants? Matthew parked and then glanced at Theia as he killed the engine. From her stony expression, he could sense her unease. He felt it, too.

The stout fellow encircled the car and opened Theia's door. "Good morning, madam, and welcome. My name is George, George Henry." His elocution was delivered perfectly.

He reached for Theia's hand to help her from the car and also in greeting.

Theia politely smiled as she introduced herself. "Theia. Theia Mc...
Reginleif." To anyone else, freely speaking her name might have seemed
like a trivial freedom, but it was evident to Matthew that, for Theia,
the moment was nothing short of liberation.

She's already beginning to feel at home.

No formal introduction came Matthew's way.

"If you would follow me," George humbly beckoned. "Mr. Goodwin
is anxiously awaiting your arrival." The six men parted, allowing them
to pass between.

They entered the castle up two small steps, following behind George.

Inside, Matthew looked around in amazement. Before them,
across the entrance hall was a giant, stone, bifurcated staircase with
a central, rolled, rich magenta carpet. His eyes climbed the carpet to
the half-landing then to an enormous, framed oil painting, spanning
twenty feet.

It portrayed a bloody battle scene, a life-sized horseman yielding a
sword raised high, about to strike. The rider's face looked uncannily
similar to Mr. Goodwin's.

George made his way toward it up the first flight.

As they followed, Matthew spotted dozens of men loitering in the
great rooms abutting either side of the entrance hall. Some wore their
suit jackets, others wore shirts and ties. Some sat, others stood, creating
an atmosphere akin to a silent cocktail party where no one seemed to
be having much fun.

Or drinking cocktails for that matter.

All were focused on Matthew and Theia as they passed along the
hall. Turning to Theia, Matthew whispered, "How many staff does
this guy have?"

The half-landing branched off and continued its ascent to the floor
above. There, they crossed an open foyer toward two giant oak doors
carved in intricate detail. Matthew studied them as he approached.
Though the carving was somewhat abstract, he could make out the
tree's swirling branches and hanging fruit— perhaps oranges or apples.

The unusual style was challenging to date. Certainly, it was not something he had ever come across before or found in any book.

Two men stood guard on either side, arms pressed straight, eyes forward.

Who has guards inside their home?

George rested a hand on the giant brass knob, but before opening the door, he thrust a hand toward Matthew, who was already queuing for entry behind Theia. "If you don't mind, sir?"

"What?" Matthew said. "There's no way I'm letting her in there without me."

Theia turned to Matthew and placed her hand on his cheek. "It's okay, Matthew. Please, just give me a minute. This I must do alone."

Reluctantly, he took two steps back.

George rapped his knuckles twice on the rightmost door then opened it just enough for Theia to slide in, alone. He promptly closed it behind her, turning his back to it.

Matthew plunged his hands deep into his trouser pockets, then yanked them out. He paced back and forth, folding and unfolding his arms. The silence of the three men standing guard amplified his impatience.

"So, you're his… assistant?" Matthew asked George, who only smiled in return. "Butler?" Same response. "You deliver his mail? Serve tea? Escort guests? Things like that?"

George didn't seem up for conversation.

Matthew squinted over George's shoulder at the carving. Stepping closer, he ran his hand over the varnished wood. "Is that… is that an apple?"

George stepped in front, his shoulder knocking Matthew's hand away. "If the gentleman would prefer?" George said, pointing to a chair in the foyer's opposite corner.

Matthew glanced at it. "No, thank you. The gentleman prefers to stand." He paced a couple of steps and then asked, "Look, what exactly…" He would not get an answer. "Never mind."

Inside, Theia stood with her back pressed against the door, her eyes sweeping the generous room. The grand fireplace took center stage on the east wall, tall enough that she could walk inside without ducking. Even from this distance, she could feel the warmth of its roaring flames tingling her left cheek.

A man stood with his back to her, facing them. Wearing a dark blue pinstriped suit, he appeared average in height and build. As she laid eyes on him, her stomach fluttered, her heart racing. She wanted to run toward him but was as afraid as she was excited.

Asma spoke, his back still turned. "Come on in, my dear. Don't be shy."

CHAPTER 49

Redemption So Soon

The chapter room was a buzz of coffee shop conversation as the monks brainstormed in groups. Reverend Thomas, however, chose the peaceful solitude of the tall corner window, resigning himself to quiet thought and prayer.

The heavy door flung wide as if angry, followed by earnest sandals pattering on the hardwood floors. Though the reverend had anxiously expected news from Dominic, the urgency of these steps approaching from behind was not a good sign.

To bear the news, he held his head high, pushing back his shoulders.

A good four inches shorter than the reverend, Dominic had to perch on his toes to whisper in his ear. The news was worse than Reverend Thomas had imagined.

Shaken to his core, his knees buckled. A nearby chair back steadied him.

The background chatter was silenced.

Straightening himself, the reverend solemnly walked to the end of the table to address his members. "Gentlemen." The tension was palpable. "The police have just discovered a car off the road outside of

Kirk Hammerton. The car is one of our registered vehicles. Both men at the scene are dead. Shot. They have been… they have been executed."

The room exploded into disarray.

"Kirk Hammerton?" one monk cried out. "That means… we are too late. By now, he has her."

Another gasped in disbelief. "Father Andrews and Father Timmons are dead?" He plonked himself into his chair, eyes welling.

Taking a moment for the distressing news to sink in, the monks consoled themselves and their thoughts —deflated, beaten. Several members crossed themselves and began to pray.

The remainder gazed silently.

"I told you this would happen, Thomas," blurted Father Macintyre, the feisty elder. His pale hand struck the table again. "How could you be so naive?"

The reverend did not answer. Instead, his somber eyes, weighted with failure, sank to the table. "I hope you have another plan, Thomas. What will we do now?"

"There is nothing we *can* do now," answered another monk.

A younger member suggested timidly, "What about the American? Maybe he will…"

"The American?" the elder blasted. "A historian from the Natural History Museum. What use is he against an army of mercenaries hired by the dark lord himself?"

The junior member cowered after bringing it up.

"What we need is a miracle."

"No. What we need is an army," added the elder.

"Gentlemen. Brothers. Have you all forgotten?" Reverend Thomas silenced everyone. "Have you all lost your faith? The scripture states good will prevail over evil. *The Antichrist will finally be defeated by the armies of God under the leadership of Christ.*"

The feisty elder erupted, standing and spraying spit across the table. "And who will defeat him, Thomas? You?" He pointed randomly at his brothers. "You? You, brother?" Glancing back at the reverend, his voice was low, but his scornful tone was clearly evident. "Or will you send more men? More lambs to the slaughter. Boys doing God's work?"

As a matter of fact, the reverend thought, that was precisely his next plan. Though sharing it after such an outburst seemed like poor timing.

The elder shook his crooked finger, eyeing all around the table. "Lest you all forget, *if* the scriptures are wrong and the Dark Prince succeeds in spawning a child from the womb of the daughter of God, then his child, as written in the Third Article, will mark the beginning of the end—Armageddon. Suffering and death to all humankind."

While all knew perfectly well the scriptures and the Five Articles of the Prophecy, hearing their possible near future sent an icy chill across the room.

The elder directed his point to the reverend. "Our order now numbers the fewest members of its seven-hundred-year history. Many of us are too old, too frail, no match against his army of trained killers."

"We don't need an army," the reverend calmly explained as if possessing all the answers. "An army is how *he* would fight. It is not how our Lord would fight."

"Our Lord, He has told you his plan?" the elder asked sarcastically.

Before answering, he gave the question deep thought. "I believe He has."

Several monks let loose long sighs as their hope wilted. One elder, silent as yet, referred to Father Thomas with a kind sincerity, "I commend you on your faith, Thomas, but Father Macintyre is right—we need actionable bodies on the ground. We must act." The aged monk pushed from his chair and struggled to his feet; a neighboring monk helped him. "I, for one, am ready."

Reverend Thomas smiled, tearing up. "You honor me, Father, but that will not be necessary. There are... two others."

"Two others? Who?"

Father Thomas felt every eye draw to him for an answer. An answer he knew they would hate. But as head of the order, he alone was burdened with the tough decisions. And that included ordering ill-prepared innocent men into the lion's den. Yes, Father Andrews and Father Timmons were dead, their blood on his hands. And because of that, he knew his fellow monks would believe he was making the same mistake twice. Perhaps he was.

But it was the only hand he had left to play.

Trying to instill confidence, Reverend Thomas stiffened, announcing their names as if they were entering the room at a formal gathering. "Father Chandler and Father Huckabay."

"*Chandler?* Douglas Chandler, the Durham soldier? He's only a juniorate. Not yet ordained," an elder asked, glancing around the table as if someone knew something he didn't.

"Nor is Huckabay ordained," declared another, equally confused. "He only just completed his postulancy."

"I… ordained them this morning after they made their sacred vows," the reverend provided. "They have also been thoroughly briefed and understand the stakes."

"You did what?" Father Macintyre gasped in horror. "You've crossed the line this time, Thomas. You can't fast-track years of training into… into one meeting and a splash of holy water. It makes a mockery of all we've been through."

"Well, I ordained them via conference call. It is done." The confidence in his voice tapered along with the tempo. He imagined himself sitting at the other end of the table listening to his own sacrilegious words. He too, would have the same shocked expression as his brothers. Defensively, he hoisted his hands. "I understand your reluctance, brothers. But as you all know, time is of the essence; I must do what is necessary."

None could offer alternative solutions.

"Who is this Huckabay fellow, anyway?" asked an elder, his voice rickety. "I don't remember him. Anyone like to *enlighten* me?"

Dominic answered as if talking to a senile grandparent. "He was the convict who wrote to us from prison in Edinburgh, remember?

The addict. We all met with him about nine months ago when he was released. The order voted on him. I believe you were there, brother."

"Yes, yes, of course." He nodded. "I remember now." His face said otherwise.

Dominic added, "And we all know Doug Chan..." He corrected himself, forgetting he had been ordained that morning, "*Father* Chandler. He's been with us for two years now, perhaps a little more. An excellent study. He knows the prophecy well."

Father Macintyre frowned. "But he's a broken man, as I recall, seeking atonement for his sins on the battlefield."

"Not sins," Reverend Thomas spat and squared his shoulders. "Orders. He was a sniper and killed one time during his first and, as it turned out, last tour in Afghanistan."

"He killed a child."

"The enemy," the reverend retorted. "He did what he had to do. It was war. And yes, he killed a child. But let's not forget, gentlemen, *we* are trying to kill the purest soul to walk this Earth in two thousand years. All to save humankind. Are we any different?" He paused for an answer.

None came.

Finally, an elder slumped forward, his arms collapsing on the table in disappointment. He sighed. "So, that's it? They're our only option? A convict and a discharged soldier. Both broken, both seeking redemption."

Though the elder's words were not meant to be encouraging, Reverend Thomas rather embraced them. He nodded slowly, a smile forming. "They're perfect!"

CHAPTER 50

Matthew's Return

Theia crept toward the welcoming stone fireplace. Asma, like many of his tin armor suits, stood motionless.

"Theia Reginleif." The words played in his mouth as he gazed into the flames. "I have thought of that name every day of my life, and now… and now, you are here." He turned to face her.

First his head, then his body.

As their eyes locked for the first time in eleven centuries, Theia's doubt was erased in an instant—it *was* him.

Asma smiled. "Ahh, Theia. What a woman you have become." He went to her.

Dreaming of this day so many times, she never thought it would happen. Could happen. In her dreams, their love for each other was boundless, a magical fairytale. Yet, as she very well knew, dreams and reality were rarely the same. Now, after so long apart, did they have a hope of simply picking up where they'd left off?

Theia trembled as he approached, so close she caught his scent: a whiff of musk and soap, clean and sharp.

With both hands, he cradled her face. Theia's bottom lip quivered. "Oh, Asma, is it really…"

Asma pulled her to his lips, gently together, then slowly apart. Noses almost touching, they gazed into each other's eyes. She no longer wondered.

It was as if the years in between had never happened.

His eyes hadn't changed. Still dark and deep set. Mysterious.

Theia wrapped her arms around his neck, pulling herself to her tiptoes, her cheek pressed against his. "How can this be, Asma? I don't understand why… how? I thought you were dead. I watched you die, saw the arrows with my own eyes."

Asma pulled away. He brought her hand to his face, kissing the back, then stroking it. "Come." By the hand, he escorted her to the two giant Chesterfield sofas by the fire, taking a seat by her. "You have many questions, I know. That is for later. For now, let's be together, just you and me. Let me look upon you."

Theia's melancholy sobered. *You have many questions.* Those words forged a new reality, a one she had not conceived. After she learned of Asma's existence, only the night before—from a television show, no less—she thought she had stumbled on something neither of them knew. That each was alive. She imagined how Asma would react when he saw her, the questions he would have like the ones now racing through her head.

That maybe they could join forces.

Discover their purpose—together.

Who they both were?

Why they were both here?

Yet, sitting across from him now, she could not help sensing he already held all the answers.

"So, you know? You know why we are here? Why we've walked this Earth for over eleven hundred years?"

Theia's unremitting eyes required answers. *Later*, wasn't going to cut it.

"Very well." Asma sighed. "There is a prophecy."

Oh my God! I'm about to discover the truth. Finally.

Theia panicked. After so many years of searching, the moment had finally come. But now, for some reason, she felt rushed; she *still* wasn't prepared!

"Wait!" she loudly interrupted, closing her eyes and shaking her finger. "I need a drink."

"Of course." Asma stood, approaching his open drink cabinet, and grabbing a crystal tumbler. Holding the empty glass, he chuckled, eyeing Theia over his shoulder.

"I have only ever loved you, my darling. Waited for you my entire life, and…" He shrugged. "I don't even know your drink!"

Theia laughed. "Bourbon! No—vodka! Vodka-tonic!" she called out louder, correcting her first choice. Why had she suddenly thought of Matthew's drink first?

Asma returned to their seat, a drink in each hand. His was deep golden, Scotch probably.

He looks like a Scotch drinker. Theia took a large gulp, downing half in one go. Asma chortled, drawing back his head. Already, he was impressed.

As the alcohol singed her throat, she waved an inviting hand, rasping, "Okay. Go on."

He recapped, though, for someone with impeccable English, his delivery was hesitant and difficult, like someone trying to explain in a foreign language with a poor translation. "There is a prophecy. It is said that… two eternal… beings shall… unite and their… offspring shall be… um…"

Theia gasped. "The second coming of Christ?"

"Um." Asma thought for a beat, then chuckled. "Something like that." He sipped his Scotch.

"So, he *was* right?"

"Who was right, my dear?"

"Matthew. My friend. That's what he predicted, too." But then her eyebrows furrowed, her jaw pushing forward in confusion.

"What's wrong, my dear?"

"There's just one problem," she said, slumping. "Like I told Matthew and Audree. I can't have children."

Asma chuckled again. "I know, my dear. But you are wrong. According to the prophecy, you can only bear *my* child. It is your purpose, Theia. Our purpose."

Her eyes welled at the thought of becoming a mother. "But if that's the case, then why now? Why wait all these years? Surely, we should have rediscovered each other sooner?"

"Because, my dear, you had to seek me out. Fate, and fate alone, had to bring us together. As it did when we were children."

"This whole time, I thought you were dead." Theia's eyes teared. "I've never even tried to look for you. Had I known, I would have."

"Of course. And I you. It was only until later I learned my true reason for being here, and that led me to a lifelong search for you. I even found you, but that is not enough. *You* had to find *me,* in your own way." Asma smirked. "I might have tried on the odd occasion to push fate my way, trying to get you to find me. But it never happened. Not until now."

She gasped. Of course, he was referring to the constant spam emails and magazines he sent her, trying to rouse her memory.

She frowned. "But why?" Her hand reached for his knee. "Why do I need to find you if you already knew where I was? Why couldn't you just come to see me all those years ago?"

"Because, my dear, our task is too important, and that would have broken an article of the prophecy."

"Article? What article? I don't understand. How do you even know about this? Where did…"

Asma deflected, grabbing her hand which was still warming his knee. "Come now. I can't possibly share a lifetime of information in one night. The important thing is, we have found each other. Now, we have all the time in the world. And more. Besides, your friend…"

He glanced over his shoulder to the door.

"Matthew. His name is Matthew."

"Matthew," he repeated, a tight-lipped smile ensuing, "is waiting. Let's not keep him. And you both must be exhausted from the journey. I'll have George prepare the rooms. We can talk later, yes?"

Theia nodded.

"*George!*" Asma yelled.

Before he and Theia had time to stand, the giant door swung ajar just enough for George to squeeze in and bow a humbled nod. Surprisingly, Matthew snuck in a second later, closely followed by the two guards, one discreetly tugging on Matthew's arm. Matthew thrust a punch forward, freeing it from the guard's grip. Even from across the room, Theia tuned into the torrent of thoughts and emotions behind his eyes.

"Matthew, I presume? Nice to meet you, old chap," Asma said as he cheerfully walked, arm outstretched, to shake his hand. "Sorry to have kept you, old boy. Also, I understand I owe you a debt of gratitude for bringing my dear Theia to me. How can I ever repay you?"

He shook Matthew's hand while casting a scornful eye to his guards over Matthew's shoulder. The guards bowed their chins and left.

Theia joined Asma, standing at his side.

Matthew locked eyes with her, his voice tinged with sadness. "All I want is for her to be happy."

"Of course, as do I," Asma said, wrapping a bold arm around Theia, squeezing so hard, he lifted her onto one foot. "That is all I want too. Now, you are both my honored guests. George will prepare rooms for each of you, and tonight, you will join me for dinner."

"That's very kind, but you two obviously have a lot to discuss." Matthew looked at his watch. "I really should be going."

"Going?" Theia screeched, half surprised, half angry. "Where would you go? We just got here!"

From Matthew's blank expression and lack of an immediate response, it seemed he had blurted that on the fly. "Um, back to New York." His words flowed a little smoother. "I have a job waiting for me and… well, anyway, I really should be getting back."

She hadn't imagined him leaving, and the thought of it now turned her insides.

"Will you be okay?" Matthew asked.

Reluctantly, she nodded, trying to mask her inner turmoil.

But Matthew knew her too well, sensing her unease and hesitation. "You sure?"

"Yes, yes, it's fine. You have your work, of course. Go ahead. Go. I'm good." A lot of words for one unbothered… in fact, a fluster of words.

"Okay, um…" Matthew awkwardly stepped forward to hug her. At first, they patted each other's backs as if old acquaintances uncomfortable with intimacy. But then Matthew squeezed her close. Theia inhaled his neck. One last scent to remember him by.

Asma cleared his throat, interrupting their embrace. "Matthew, my man George can drive you to the airport if that is where you need to go?"

Matthew pulled back, his big brown eyes staring into Theia's. He glanced at Asma. "Oh, very kind, but no thank you, I have the rental car to return." His eyes returned to hers. "Well, this is it then. Take care of yourself, Theia."

Theia blinked quickly to prevent a tear.

George made himself known and then escorted Matthew from the room. At the door, Matthew turned for one last look.

Theia forced a chuckle, expecting one of his famous lines as always when leaving a room. "Another Columbo one-liner?" she asked before he could speak.

Matthew's smile was shallow, his voice sullen. "Maybe another time."

"This way, sir," George prompted from the hall.

As soon as the door closed, tears streamed down Theia's face—too many tears for her *friend*.

Asma pulled her close to his chest. "Now, now, my dear, now, now."

Mounted above the main doorway of the Goodwin Castle hung the family coat of arms, a black shield with a profiled golden dragon in its center. Surrounding it were six blue lightning bolts all encircled in blue rings. *Lightning bolts. In a circle. Where have I seen those before?*

The family name underneath read, 'De Atta.' Matthew paused to examine it on his way out. Something about it vexed him.

"If you please, sir." George beckoned.

Matthew followed.

Inside the rental car, Matthew glanced at the second-floor window unable to shake the image of Theia's saddened face. *Did she want me to stay?* Although he had wanted to, more than anything, he wondered what part of this mysterious equation he played. Perhaps his only role was to bring them together, and that he had done. *Nice job.*

His heart breaking, he pressed the ignition and drove away.

THE CHAPTER ROOM was quiet and as solemn as a funeral wake. The reverend sat staring at the table with his elbows resting on it, fingertips bouncing together inches from his face. The house phone rang; he snatched it on its first ring. "Yes." He listened intently. After a few seconds, he hung up without saying a word.

Inhaling a deep breath, he announced, "The American has left Goodwin Castle. He appears to be heading back to the airport."

"And the girl?" A voice filled with hopeful timbre spoke from the corner of the room.

"The girl…" He hesitated. "The girl is not with him."

Heads lowered.

CHAPTER 51

The Moment of Death

Inside their black BMW M5, the suited pair of men sat quietly eyeing hundreds of travelers hauling suitcases to and from Newcastle Airport's terminal building. The driver was the channel-surfing gentleman from Guy Fawkes Inn.

Alongside their car, a double-yellow line stretched the length of the curb, with 'DROP-OFF ONLY' painted sideways in bold white on the gray asphalt.

For the last five minutes, the driver had been spying through his side mirror at the middle-aged, heavy-set woman wearing a luminous yellow jacket with 'AIRPORT STAFF' written in bold on the back. Occasionally offering directions to lost travelers, her primary job appeared to be herding parked cars that had outstayed their welcome in the drop-off zone. Once again, she leaned sideways, looking beyond the line of cars toward theirs. That was the second time she'd looked. Checking her watch, she began a slow saunter toward them.

The driver mumbled, "We're going to have to move in a sec."

"No," his partner snapped. "We don't move until we have confirmation."

As the stout woman filled the frame of his mirror, he squared his head. Staring forward, he pretended not to see her waving there.

Tap, tap. Her woolen knuckles sounded soft against the glass. Appearing surprised, he peered through his driver-side window. She gestured for them to move on. Instead, he lowered the window.

"Hello. How are you, today?"

"I'm fine, sir. You can't park here. It's for drop-offs only, and you've been here some time already. I'm going to have to ask you to move along."

"Yes, of course. We just dropped a friend off and now…" He fished for words, trying to buy time, then recalled her helpfulness with directions. "We aren't sure where we're going. Could you possibly help? We don't want to pull off without knowing which direction to head at the roundabout. You know what it's like when you come to an unfamiliar area."

She huffed and stooped lower. "Where are you trying to get to?"

"Um, I'm not quite sure, it's something like… let me check…" He picked up his phone, tapping and swiping the screen with his finger. "Ah ha. Oh, no, that's not it…"

Her patience thinned and her foot tapped. Other cars behind needed attending. "Sir!"

"Almost there…"

"Sir!"

"Just about…"

Suddenly, his passenger snapped his fingers twice and pointed ahead. Through the windshield, there was Matthew, dragging his suitcase from the rental return toward the terminal entrance.

He disappeared inside.

"Found it!" he shouted enthusiastically.

The lady pursed her lips, her impatient eyes glaring.

"Thank you, miss. I think we're good. It's been a pleasure. Cheerio, and keep up the good work."

Selecting drive, he eased from the curb, the V8 engine purring as they headed off.

His passenger, wasting no time, made the call his boss was waiting for. "Sir, he stopped once for fuel then came straight to the airport. He's in the terminal now. We're heading back."

Following signs for the airport exit, they neared the roundabout—the same one that confused Matthew on the day he arrived.

As they approached, he tapped the driver's thigh and pointed behind them, signaling to turn back. "Yes, sir, of course, sir," he said, into his phone. "What exactly would you like me to do?"

At the roundabout, the driver continued full circle back toward the terminal.

"Yes, sir, I understand. I'll take care of it."

When he hung up, the driver asked, "What are we going back for? The lady at the drop-off sure as hell won't let us park there again."

"We're not parking. You're dropping me off. I'm getting on that plane. With the American."

"What? You're going to New York? Why?"

With a cold monotone voice, he replied, "To kill him."

THEIA UNZIPPED HER suitcase on the bed, unfolding its top. She began unpacking, her motivation dwindling rapidly. She should be happy. After centuries of searching, she had finally discovered her true purpose, and more answers were coming—everything she had wanted. But without Matthew, it seemed to matter less. It had only been two hours since he'd left, though it had felt much longer.

Having Matthew around gave her a sense of safety.

She had tried to sleep, but that didn't work, her mind just racing. Earlier, she had distracted her one-track mind for about fifteen minutes, surveying the room's ancient memorabilia reminding her of centuries of old. But more than that, it reminded her of him. Matthew.

If he were here, he'd be examining every piece, sharing every detail, seeing and touching things he would only see in a book or on a screen. The most interesting of which, and eerily coincidental, was an armless mannequin facing in from the room's corner as if on guard duty.

It was attired in beautiful body armor made for a woman, the intricate stitching, expensive stamped leather and untarnished metal plating suggesting this was a ceremonial suit worn by someone of wealth, never intended, or used, on a battlefield.

As she continued unpacking, a sudden surge of panic struck her.

Gasping for breath, she clawed at her throat, her lungs ablaze, desperate for air that would not come. Darkness spilled in, enveloping her world. Initially, her heartbeat thundered, racing faster and louder, but soon it dwindled, its rhythm slowing and becoming irregular, until finally, it ceased altogether.

All senses diminished.

She recognized the signs and had experienced them before. It was the moment of death.

Suddenly, from the darkness, Matthew's face flashed into view, a god-awful sight, his eyes open, yet lifeless. With pale skin, he lay staring up, mouth ajar.

In an instant, the image was gone. Sight, sound, touch, smell, all returned. Air flooded her lungs as she inhaled a giant breath.

Matthew!

Rummaging through her purse with reckless speed, she hunted for her phone.

Unable to locate it, she emptied the contents onto her bed. She snatched her phone, quickly dialing his number.

"Come on, come on!" Pacing the floor, she willed the ringing tone to be answered. Nothing. She tried again, except this time...

"Hello."

"Matthew? Are you okay?"

"Theia? Is everything okay?"

Theia's shoulders slumped as she breathed a sigh of relief. "Yes, yes, I'm fine. I just wanted to see, to check... where are you?"

"I'm at the airport. All checked in, just waiting on—"

"Hello? Matthew? Matthew!"

"Departure... three... tomorrow—"

"Matthew, you're breaking up. Hello?" Theia's anxiety returned.

After a long pause, Matthew's voice came through scratchy. "Can you hear me?"

"Yes, yes. So, everything's okay?"

"Oh yeah! Everything's great. Looking forward… my… class pod!"

"You're breaking up again."

"It's a bad sig… here… call you tomorrow."

A knock sounded at the bedroom door.

Theia yelled into the phone as if that might increase the signal's strength. "Okay. I've got to go. Bye, Matthew. Have a safe…" But the line was already dead.

Knock, knock!

Theia checked her watch before opening up. Had she lost track of time for dinner?

"Sorry to disturb you, madam." George stood, one arm folded behind his back, the other holding a black garment bag. "Sir wondered if you would prefer to wear something more… uh, stylish for this evening."

"Oh, um, thank you." Theia took the bag and smiled at the kind gesture, then questioned her current wardrobe.

Oh. Do I not dress stylishly?

"I'll collect you at five o'clock and escort you to dinner if that pleases you." His head bowed.

Again, she scanned her wristwatch: s*hower, nails, hair, make-up, in forty-five minutes! There was no way!* "Sure, that'll be fine," she said, her smile straining as she closed the door.

The image of Matthew's face returned, haunting her thoughts.

That had never happened before, not so clearly, so vividly. Plus, she wasn't even touching him. Perhaps it was something else—a panic attack?

Great, she thought. *Now I'm neurotic. At least Matthew is at the airport and safely on his way home. I'll call him tomorrow.*

She unzipped the newly delivered garment bag, carrying the dress to the window to view it in the daylight. It was a black leather one-piece: strapless, form-fitting, and short! The bosom cups were edged in black lace and a large silver zipper ran the full length in front.

Sexy, she thought. *Stylish? Hmm, don't think so.*

At the window, she gazed upon the expansive manicured grounds and the beautiful English countryside beyond. Above, an airliner etched a con trail across a midnight blue sky.

She sighed heavily, then hurled the dress like a frisbee onto her bed and marched to the bathroom, undressing as she went.

CHAPTER 52

The Church of Satan

"Bourbon, double," Matthew demanded, plonking himself onto the barstool at the Newcastle Airport departure lounge bar. Flipping open his backpack, he removed his laptop and unfolded it on the bar counter. While it booted, a loud cheer roared from behind, raising him off his seat.

Jeez! Matthew's heart skipped a beat.

At least half the bar was brimming with football supporters, red and white jerseys dangerously intermingling with black and white from the opposing team. Not being a fan of English football, Matthew only recognized the Sunderland colors, from the fabled red and white jersey taking pride of place in Father Jacob's office back at St. Peter's Church.

What was it he'd called them again, 'Mackems?'

The barman delivered his bourbon, which Matthew grabbed before he could set it down. First a quick sip, then his eager fingers drummed the words, 'De Atta' into the search field. He waited. The open-source connection was painfully slow, the page taking an age to load.

The supporters began singing their game songs. Sounding more like Zulu war chants, they waved their half-drunk beers above their heads.

Nestling into the stool two seats down on Matthew's left, a businessman ordered a drink. He exchanged a friendly smile.

Matthew's screen finally listed the results:

– De Atta, Family Name Meaning: Serpent of God

He tapped his mouse pad, delving further. Another list of feasible options populated:

– Old English (Medieval) meaning: Death
– Dark Angel
– Mohamed Atta: Hijacker ringleader on AA Flight 11, September 11 attacks
– Pythagorean Numerology, Atta has a value of 6.

Below the list, an artist's rendering of the devil rising from fire sent a chill over his skin. Clearing the search field, Matthew frowned. He typed another criterion: 'Asmodeus Name Meaning.'

Asmodeus, Hebrew, is a prince of demons, or in Judeo-Islamic lore, king of the earthly spirits. Asmodeus' name means, 'the destroyer, the exterminator.'

There was yet another image of the devil.

Matthew chewed his top lip, shifting to the edge of his stool and moving closer to the screen.

A brawl suddenly erupted in the corner of the room, amplifying the already boisterous ranting and roaring. The supporters quickly formed a circle, jeering as if amid a chaotic cockfight scene. Security swarmed to break it up. Anticipating trouble, they had gathered at the entrance. The disapproving barman shook his head in disdain while meticulously polishing a glass.

"What's going on?" Matthew asked.

"Not from around here are ya, mate?" He pointed his chin at the crowd. "Two rival teams: Sunderland and Newcastle. They hate each other—with a passion." He leaned in nearer to Matthew, speaking from the side of his mouth. "There's going to be hell on earth, I can tell you!"

"Right!" Matthew said, remembering Father Jacob's advice. *How could I forget?*

"You American?" asked the businessman.

"Um, yes I am."

"I'm heading there myself." When he sipped his drink, Matthew eyed his watch. He wasn't an expert, but it looked expensive. As did his suit and shoes. The man continued his idle chatter. "I've traveled a bunch in Europe, but never the States. Always wanted to go, mind you." He turned to Matthew. "You recommend any tourist attractions while I'm there?"

Drawn to his laptop, Matthew had no interest in idle conversation. "Um, no, not really. I don't get out much." While the latter was true, Matthew would make an excellent guide, having been brought up there and knowing every historical fact.

Returning to his keyboard, he typed: 'Blue Lightning Symbol.'

The results brought further discomfort.

The lightning bolt often is found in many ancient mythologies including Pagan, Norse, Celtic, Finnish, Slavic, and Huracan. Symbolizes power from the skies, a demi-god or an angered god, also weapons and war.

Matthew sat back in his chair, rubbing his cheeks. Why hadn't he checked this before now, his name, the symbol? At first, he considered calling Theia, telling her what he'd found. But how might that look? She knew he had affection for her. It would come across as childish jealousy, nothing more. Especially with such trivial evidence: internet searches.

Plus, this Asma fellow seemed like a nice guy.

The businessman finished his drink and thrust his empty glass forward. "Hey, mate, can I get another one here?" He jiggled the ice in his glass, luring Matthew's eye again. Tattooed on the inside of the man's wrist was a double cross poking from behind his sleeve—just as Theia had described. Trying to grab the barman's attention, the businessman extended his hand further.

It tugged his shirt cuff back, revealing the tattoo in its entirety. Matthew's eyebrows rose, his jaw falling slack. The tattoo was not just a double cross; it had an infinity symbol turned sideways at the base. *That is not the Patriarchal cross!*

He spun on his stool, angling his laptop screen away from the businessman. He changed the category on his archive software to 'Symbology' and in the search field typed: 'Double Cross with Infinity.'

An image of the symbol appeared, identical to the man's wrist. Underneath, it read: 'The Church of Satan.'

Matthew gulped, slamming his laptop closed. The blood drained from his face as the realization hit him—they had been searching for the wrong symbol. It wasn't a symbol of Christ but of the devil. *Theia!* He needed to warn her. He picked up his phone, only to find no signal.

"Crap!"

"Are you all right, mate?" the businessman asked. "Your stock prices taking a nosedive or something?"

"Um, no, I just… don't like flying." Matthew didn't dare look him in the eye.

He swiftly packed his laptop, left a twenty on the counter, and snatched his jacket from the back of the chair.

"You're leaving?" the man asked, half turning toward him.

Matthew didn't reply. Didn't look. Instead, he beelined for the exit, deftly maneuvering between the man's chair and a crowd gathered near the bar.

The businessman pivoted on his stool. "Come on, stay. Have another drink. It'll settle your nerves. Trust me."

Already on edge, Matthew jerked away colliding with a soccer supporter, spilling his drink. Curses erupted from the supporter, who forcefully shoved Matthew back toward the bar, bringing him within whisper distance of the businessman's face. Any attempt to conceal his rising panic crumbled the moment their eyes locked.

Trembling, Matthew backed away. He turned and pushed through the supporters, darting for the exit, knocking over a chair as he ran.

Once in the concourse, he checked his phone.

One bar of signal strength!

He tried calling. It rang.

Pick up, pick up, pick up.

The phone went quiet. He looked at the screen. No bars!

While walking, he hadn't paid attention to where he was heading.

I need an exit.

The sign overhead indicated it was back the way he'd come.

Shit!

Securing his backpack tighter, he turned around and began a speedier walk, apologizing as he brushed by unhurried travelers. Back to his phone. Still—one bar. Again, he hit the call button.

Dialing... *Come on, Theia, please.* It rang once, then... quiet. No bars!

Argh! Outside. I need to get outside. Where's the damn exit?

The tension churned his stomach.

Nausea bubbled from his gut up to his throat, like an erupting volcano.

I'm going to be sick. Need the bathroom. Quick!

Farther ahead, a 'Men's Room' sign jutted from the wall. He picked up his pace.

To his horror, a yellow plastic cone blocked the entrance: closed for maintenance. With acid burning his throat, he kicked it away and sped to the nearest sink, just in time for his gut to wrench. Three heaves before he was done. He patted cool water on his face. Now refreshed and ready to leave, he collected his phone from the counter.

Three bars!

He gasped and tried to call again. The ring echoed louder this time, less crackly. Rooted to the floor, his body frozen, he dared not make a move, fearing the loss of the precious signal.

Finally, her voicemail.

"Hi, you've reached Theia McDormand. Um, leave me a message. Bye!"

"Theia!" he yelled frantically. "You're in grave danger…"

INSIDE THE GOODWIN Castle, Theia was slowly beginning to relax. Cozied by Asma's roaring fireplace, their romantic dinner was in full swing. At his master's request, George had set up a small round table for two with candles, much more intimate than eating in the enormous dining room, Asma had commented.

Asma's phone rang.

Eyeing the caller ID, he frowned. "Hm, mind if I get this, my dear? Business!"

"No, no, by all means."

"Yes, my dear man, I wasn't expecting a call from you until tomorrow. I trust there isn't a problem?"

He listened, he and Theia ogling one another. "Hmm, so, you're saying we need to pull the trigger on the deal now rather than later?" Asma rolled his eyes and shook his head as if the conversation was dull. Theia chuckled. Up until now, everything had been so serious, including Asma. She was glad to see he'd not lost his mischievous nature.

"Yes, my dear man," Asma continued. "But obviously, I preferred that to be done overseas, as we discussed."

He listened further, frowning deeper. "Hmm, I see the dilemma. Quite the pickle. Hold on would you, old chap?" Asma covered the mouthpiece and leaned across the table. "What do you think I should do, my dear?"

Confused, Theia pulled her head away. "Do about what?"

"This deal I've got. Shall I pull the trigger now or wait?"

Finding the question absurd, she laughed. "What deal? I don't know…"

"Oh, come now. Remember, you're now running my company alongside me. *Me et te!* So, what's it going to be, partner? Decision time. Now, or later?" He moved his head left and right.

Theia thought for a moment. "Um, well, I always think sooner is better than later." With a single nod, she affirmed, "Now. Do it now! Final answer."

A smirk pressed across Asma's face. "My thoughts exactly, my dear!" Theia beamed a smile, proud of her decision.

Asma removed his hand from the mouthpiece. "Sorry to keep you, old boy. I was just conferring with the lady of the house, and we both agree that you should go ahead and take a stab at it now." Asma held his hand up over the table and Theia high-fived it!

OUTSIDE OF THE airport's men's room, Asma's man returned his phone to his outer jacket pocket. After a swift scan of the concourse, he confidently marched inside. As he entered, Matthew stood facing the mirrors between the row of sinks and toilet cubicles, his side to him, phone against his ear.

Wasting no time, the six-two, herculean-sized man lunged at Matthew, shouldering him off his feet. Matthew bellowed from the impact as he slid across the glazed tiled floor, slamming into the wall. Dazed, Matthew still clung to his phone.

With alarming speed, the huge man closed the distance before Matthew could react. Effortlessly, he hurled him into the air by his throat, pinning him against the wall, feet dangling. Kicking.

Matthew croaked, "No! No! Please!" But his efforts were quenched to near silence, giant hands tightening around his throat. At first, Matthew clung to the man's wrists but then in a futile effort, he punched at the man's rugged face.

Having little effect, he switched hands.

Brandishing the phone like a dagger, he plunged it downward. The corner struck just above the man's eye, gashing it wide.

The man dropped Matthew. Stepping back, he drew his hand to his brow. A warm stream trickled down his cheek. His palm wiped it. Finding it soaked in blood, he clenched his fists and growled through gritted teeth. Matthew's expression twisted in a silent scream as the giant man reasserted a double grip on his lapel, yanking him up, their faces inches apart.

His unforgiving eyes bore into Matthew's. Then with one forceful shove, he sent Matthew hurtling into an adjacent cubicle, the door crashing inward. Matthew crumpled, his neck scrunching at the foot of the toilet.

The man stepped inside. Killing Matthew was a job, something he'd been ordered to do. But staring down with blood seeping into his eye, he knew this one, he was going to enjoy. His enraged scowl twisted into an unsettling grin.

While Matthew's efforts to protect himself were gallant, his brawling arms did nothing to stop the force coming at him. In an instant, the heavyweight knees were crushing Matthew's chest.

Again, the man reaffirmed his grip on Matthew's throat.

Before long, Matthew's flailing arms turned from defensive punches to paltry slaps, until finally, they collapsed motionless by his side. Unsatisfied, the man squeezed harder, savoring the face staring back as it bleached from pink to pale gray, and the pupils dilated to a comatose black. Staring. Mouth slack, without breath.

CHAPTER 53

The Rosette Effect

Slap! "Breathe!" *Slap!* "Come on. Breathe!" yelled the skinhead.

"Fuckin' hell, Stevie, I think you did it," another skinhead said, leaning over him.

The thick accent sounded familiar, similar to Matthew's good friend from St. Peter's, Father Aiden Jacobs, though notably less refined.

"He's coming 'round!" the same voice yelled again.

This time, Matthew recognized it for sure.

Yes, undeniably Sunderland—*Mackem.*

Matthew wheezed air through his bruised windpipe, then coughed. Though hazy, his vision returned.

My throat hurts! Where the hell am I?

With the hard, cold tile pressing on his back, he quickly determined he was lying down. Something else cold and white, like glass, pressed against his cheek. His hand reached for his throbbing throat, blinking quickly, trying to refine the blur.

From the haze, a figure emerged straddling him, so close that Matthew had to cross his eyes to focus. As the face sharpened into view, it startled him, jerking his body tense.

He had pronounced cheekbones, hair shaved to the nub with green tattoos crawling up his neck like vines. Smaller ones—self-made—dotted his face. The intimidating figure sat back on his heels, with two others standing behind him, both inquisitively staring. All donned the distinctive red and white striped jerseys, red scarves wrapped around their necks.

Sunderland supporters!

The tallest one they referred to as Patty. Another skinhead, but with more attractive features—a kind of Hollywood ruggedness with pale blue eyes. Though his words were soft and concerning, he sounded as tough as he looked. "You all right, bonny lad? We thought you were a gonna."

A gonna?

Matthew's eyes zigged as the fog began to clear. He inspected his surroundings. Gray partition walls on either side, narrow—a cubicle of some kind! Still puzzled by the cold glass against his cheek, he turned his head to examine.

A toilet! I'm on the frigging floor of a public bathroom?

Patty spoke again, "That fucker was trying to kill you, mate!"

Suddenly, he became lucid, panicking, feet kicking, arms thrashing, instinctively fighting against the memory of the large man squeezing the life from him.

"Easy, easy now," Patty said as he stepped forward, pushing his kneeling pal to the side. He extended a friendly arm. "Let's get you to your feet, mate."

With a tug, Matthew was standing, though still dizzy and confused.

The upright position made him want to cough more. Patty and Stevie held his elbows, keeping him steady.

Matthew tried to speak but the words caused him pain, coming out raspy, like a whisper, "What…" A cough interrupted his sentence. His hand massaged his throat. It was sore to touch. "What… happened?"

"We were wondering the same thing." Patty pointed to the floor behind him. "Who is this twat, anyway?"

Matthew inhaled sharply and threw himself deeper into the cubicle. Stevie grabbed hold of him.

"He's... still... here?" Matthew gasped.

"Aye, man," Patty said. "We yanked him off you. Just in the nick of time, too."

Inching from the cubicle, Matthew peeked around the corner at the floor. Sure enough, the suited man lay on his back squirming. Four Sunderland supporters surrounded him, each with one foot stomping on a limb. The man's head tilted off the floor tiles, eyes wide, angry yet scared. Blood trickled from his brow.

Matthew remembered; he'd bludgeoned him with his phone.

My phone? Theia!

He dropped to the floor, hands frantically scouring for his phone.

"Are you looking for this?" Stevie asked, holding out Matthew's phone, covered in blood. "I think it's buggered, mate."

Matthew snatched it and pressed his thumb on the broken screen. Failing to get a response, he pressed the power button. Still nothing. *Shit!* Matthew's shoulders slumped. He needed to warn Theia. "I need a phone." In a second, he'd eyed them all. "Now!"

Patty unlocked his phone, handing it to him. "Here you go, mate."

Matthew stared at the screen, and then it dawned on him; he didn't know her number. *Who the fuck remembers numbers these days, anyway?* He could barely remember his own.

The man on the floor writhed, prompting the four to apply more weight to his wrists and ankles. Patty repeated, "So, who is this guy? Shall we let him go, like?"

"*No!*" Matthew's attempt to yell sounded more like the half-broken voice of a teenage boy. With a look of terror, he pointed at the restrained man, finger shaking. "He's... a servant of Satan!"

The room lapsed into silence. Then, the supporters exchanged bemused glances before erupting into deep, boisterous laughter. "Satan?" Patty exclaimed, his laughter-filled voice resonating as he gripped Matthew's shoulder and gave it a playful shake. "Have yer been dropped on yer head, mate?"

You idiot, Matthew thought, imagining how that must have sounded.

Having neither the breath nor the time to explain, he limped toward the bathroom exit, continuing to massage his throat.

Before escaping into the airport concourse, he remembered the Sunderland AFC rosette. The one on which Father Jacobs from St. Peter's wrote the curator's number. He pulled it from his inside jacket pocket, pinning it proudly to his lapel in full view. Now, pointing back at the downed man, he cackled, "He's… a Newcastle supporter! A Geordie!"

In an instant, the room's laughter ceased. Every Mackem head honed in on their wriggling captive, eyes narrowing and nostrils flaring. They closed in like a Venus Fly Trap enveloping its meal, some pulling back clenched fists, others reaching for his throat.

The man made another futile effort to free himself. Failing that, he fearfully yelled, "No, wait, wait, *wait!* Ahh!"

As Matthew stood outside the men's room regaining his bearings, the screams behind him went silent.

CHAPTER 54

Father Chandler and Father Huckabay

Parked in front of the terminal, the newly appointed fathers—Father Chandler and Father Huckabay, sat in their white Citroen C1 drinking coffee from plastic cups.

While dissimilar in virtually every way possible, they'd developed a unique kinship from months of working together at a small parish outside of York. Father Chandler was the younger, in his late twenties, sporting a military haircut with chiseled looks.

Having been raised in a military family, he was highly disciplined and respectful, especially concerning rank. Eager to advance in the order, he was keen on his studies.

Father Huckabay, on the other hand, was less refined. Much less. Despite surpassing Father Chandler by only a few years, his weathered skin and long straggly black hair with streaks of gray aged him into his early forties. Both, however, were from strict orthodox Catholic families, and both were equally estranged as failures and embarrassments.

Sprinkling baccy into a crisp Rizla roll, Father Huckabay spoke in his east Scottish accent, "You ken we're parked in a handicapped spot, right?"

He pointed with his elbow to the middle-aged woman in the luminous yellow jacket patrolling the cars. "She's gonna gee us a ticket if she sees us."

From the driver's seat, Father Chandler reached across and retrieved a disabled parking placard from inside the glovebox then hung it on his rearview mirror. It even had his photo on.

Father Huckabay chuckled, licking and rolling his freshly made cigarette. "Our first day on the job and we're already deceiving the public!"

"We're not deceiving anyone," Father Chandler protested. "I got that when I was medically discharged from the Royal Marines. Comes in handy in times of need."

Father Huckabay's chuckle developed into full-on laughter. "You're fucked in the head, pal. That's why you got discharged. I'm pretty sure your legs work fine."

Father Chandler remained silent, conceding the point. But then added, "Well, it benefits us today. Besides, we're doing God's work. We're allowed, like that saying, 'All's fair in love and war.' All's fair in the pursuit of God's own business."

Father Huckabay just sniggered.

"Anyway, *Father*," said Father Chandler, irked, "I'm pretty sure monks don't go around saying, 'You're fucked in the head.' I'm sure that's in the rulebook somewhere."

"They haven't given me a rulebook yet, so until they dee… fuck it!" Father Huckabay flicked open a lighter, bringing it to the cigarette nipped between his lips.

Chandler twisted around, deepening a frown. "Um, you're not planning on smoking that in here, are you?"

Father Huckabay huffed. Snapping the lighter shut with a wrist flick, he tucked the cigarette behind his ear.

Chandler studied his unseasoned friend.

"What?"

"You sure you're suited to this line of work? I'm trying very hard to visualize you in confession."

"Fuck yeah." Huck nodded.

Chandler cringed as if the words from his Scottish brother had inflicted a stabbing pain.

"How can ye forgive those poor bastards if ye hav'nae sinned yersel'? Trust me, ah ken whit I'm talkin' aboot."

Chandler shook his head and sighed. He glanced at his wristwatch. "What time was his flight leaving, again?"

Huck tightened his brows, unscrewing the coffee flask lid. "You ken, I dinnae think he told us flight details. Just to folla him, and report when he's left."

Chandler opened his door to exit the car.

"Where ye going?" Huck asked, pausing his coffee pour.

"Inside to find out. Unless you want to sit here all day for nothing!"

As he exited the car, he welcomed the stretch on his legs, also relieving the arch of his back and the strain on his arms. Before closing the door, he glanced across to the terminal.

What the…?

Amid the travelers streaming out of the terminal, there stood Matthew. He paused on the pavement beneath the exit's overhang, scanning the surroundings from left to right. Chandler sank back into his seat while keeping his eyes glued on Matthew. He waved his hand absentmindedly to capture Huck's attention. In the process, he unintentionally swatted Huck's arm.

"Oh man!" Father Huckabay yelled, hot coffee spilling into his lap. "What are ya deein', ya roaster? I thought you were—"

"Huck!" Father Chandler interrupted. "Look who decided to stay."

Without peeling his eyes from Matthew, fearing he'd lose him, Chandler began fumbling for his phone in the center console. Finding it, he elevated it to eye level, hitting redial.

It rang twice, the voice answering sounding flat. "Yes."

"Reverend, something's happened. The American didn't leave."

After a long pause, the reverend asked, "What's he doing now?"

"I don't know. Looks like he's just waiting on a taxi."

Another long pause, and then the reverend chanted a line as if venting his inner thoughts, "The Lord is good to those whose hope is in Him…"

"Reverend?"

This time, the reverend's voice rumbled with unwavering confidence and newly found faith. "I have a new mission. Listen to me very carefully…"

CHAPTER 55

A Friendly Ride

The wintry twilight released its grip, ushering in a crystal-clear night that appeared to siphon away Earth's last vestiges of warmth. Matthew nestled deeper into his jacket. Pulling the collar snugly around his neck, he watched as another fortunate soul slammed the taxi door against the biting cold. The seemingly endless line inched forward by one.

One! Why couldn't it have been three, or four?

Who travels alone anyway?

He reluctantly acknowledged that he was one of those people. Though, it hadn't started out that way.

His patience was wearing thin. The pressing need to reach Theia, coupled with the repetitive watch-checking, only served to stretch the taxi line even longer.

A moment later, a white Citroen pulled to the taxi rank's curb.

The window lowered, drawing Matthew's eye to the corner. A head leaned out with greasy black hair, straggly with the occasional silver streak, and center-parted. Assuming he'd ask for directions, Matthew was already preparing his *I don't live here, I've just landed* response.

The car passenger spoke with an almost incomprehensible Scottish accent. "Can I offer ye a ride, pal?"

Is he talking to someone else? Has to be, surely.

But as he turned his head, he saw the man unmistakably glaring back. "Um, no thank you." His memory conjured the words of his primary school teacher, Mrs. Longbottom, as she reinforced to the class never to accept lifts from strangers (especially when Satan's cronies are on your heels). Matthew added that last part. A new amendment.

"Oh, come on, Matthew. You'll be waitin' all neet in that line."

Matthew ceased his rocking side to side which was helping circulate his thickening blood. He examined the man's face again. "I'm sorry, do I know you?"

"No, but we ken who ye are. Look pal, we're all on the same side here. We just wanna help."

Having narrowly escaped strangulation just twenty minutes earlier at the hands of someone resembling a well-groomed banker, he was done trusting people. "Yeah… well go help someone else, *pal.*"

When Father Huckabay climbed out, Matthew stepped back, squaring his shoulders.

Casually, the man reached for the rear door handle and pulled the door wide. "We work for the Church. I'm Father Huckabay and this," he pointed inside the car, "this is Father Chandler." His friendly tone became serious. "Look, Matthew, the Reginleif girl's in danger. We have a plan, and we think we can help each other."

"H-how do I know you're not working for Goodwin?"

"For one, Matthew, our boss disnae provide us wi' snazzy suits an' fancy shoes!"

"Who's your boss?"

Huckabay pointed to the sky.

Matthew wanted to believe them. Certainly, *he* didn't have a plan yet. He'd been wondering that himself as he waited in line. He ducked to look at the driver who had his arm resting on the steering wheel, his body twisted, head stooped, staring back. Indeed, neither wore suits, as he said. That was a plus.

In a commanding manner, much like a cop frisking a suspect, Matthew demanded, "Show me your wrists. Both of you."

"Nae bother." Father Huckabay raised his hands as if submitting to an arrest. Inside the car, Father Chandler extended both arms, wrists up. No tattoos. Another plus.

The scraggly Scot lowered his arms. "We are the good guys, Matthew. Gee us a chance. C'mon man. Strength in numbers, you know." His welcoming arm directed Matthew to the back seat. As Matthew finally accepted, Huckabay asked, "Nae suitcase?"

Matthew shrugged. "It's on its way to New York, I guess!"

The backseat felt cramped climbing in. Affording his knees more room, he moved to the middle, sprawling his legs into each footwell. The car pulled away, soon speeding south on the A1 country highway.

Without a forthcoming explanation, Matthew's frustration was mounting. "Okay, guys. Is someone going to tell me what the hell is going on?"

Father Huckabay leaned around the front passenger seat, facing him. Matthew's face drained, a frisson of fear shivering down his spine. Gripped in Father Huckabay's hand was a semi-automatic pistol, and it was pointing directly his way.

"What's this?" Matthew shrieked, his brain whirring fast.

You idiot. Why didn't you listen to Mrs. Longbottom?

With a flick of his wrist, Father Huckabay spun the gun on his trigger finger as they did in the Westerns. Holding the black steel of the barrel and offering the inverted wooden grip toward Matthew, he asserted, "This is fer you."

Matthew stared, brows knitting. *It's a ruse. No way is he giving me the gun.*

"Go ahead, take it," Father Huckabay insisted, wiggling it. "Yer gonna need it, pal."

Maybe there was no threat in this after all.

Matthew could breathe again—for a moment, just until he considered Father Huckabay's words. *I'm in deep shit.*

THEIA GAZED AT her full plate. While the food was excellent—beef Wellington with roasted balsamic Brussels sprouts and candied roast carrots in a shallot and white wine sauce—she had hardly touched it. Somehow, her usually hearty appetite seemed to have left along with Matthew.

"Have I mentioned how stunning you look, my dear?" Asma complimented. "But I notice you're not wearing the outfit I sent. Not to your liking?"

"No. I mean, yes. It was… gorgeous. Just a little tight."

Yet, in truth, it had fit perfectly, as if tailor-made. *Probably is,* she thought. *I wouldn't be surprised if he has a live-in tailor working tirelessly, producing suits, fine shirts, and all sorts of garments for his many TV appearances and photo shoots.*

And not forgetting his band of Merry Men.

Tonight, she wasn't in the mood to dress sexily; it seemed somehow inappropriate, despite how the full-length mirror in her room flattered her when she posed like a model in front of it.

Theia's fork rolled a Brussels sprout back and forth on her plate.

"Is the food satisfactory?" Asma further inquired. "You haven't eaten much at all."

"Oh, it's delicious, I'm just…"

She paused, not having realized until now how depressingly forlorn she must appear, melancholy excuses rolling off her tongue as from an unsatisfied child.

In contrast, Asma was making a gallant effort, the perfect gentleman, garnishing her with compliments and pleasant conversation.

Notwithstanding, she had a lifetime of questions, and the man with the answers sat directly opposite. By all accounts, she should be grilling him like an interrogator. Instead, she only felt—empty, her mind wandering to another place, wondering at which point over the Atlantic Matthew would be by now. She peeked across the table at Asma's concerned face, guilt surging inside of her.

She rested her fork, then reached across the table for his hand, sighing. "I'm so sorry, Asma. I'm just tired. But I couldn't be happier." Even Asma's acute ability to recognize a lie seemed deceived by Theia's convincing smile.

He gripped her hand tight. "It's a lot. All this. It will take time, my dear. But time is what we have. The important thing is we have finally found each other."

A short while later, the door creaked open, and George meekly stepped inside. He cleared his throat, standing with fingers interlocked in front, head slightly bowed.

Asma scowled. "Forgive me, Theia. We weren't to be disturbed. Allow me a moment."

He walked over to George, who whispered, "Matthew didn't make it onto the plane, sir."

"Yes, I'm aware. I was just speaking with our contact at the airport, and we had to… expedite things."

"About that, sir. I've been unable to reach our contact. According to his phone tracker, he just arrived at The Royal Victoria Infirmary."

Asma recoiled, his blood boiling. "Imbecile. I'll deal with him later. What of Matthew? Is he still alive?"

"We're working on that, sir. But I think it's fair to assume so."

Asma's eyes shifted, pondering his next step. "Notify the men. Be ready. If Matthew is foolish enough to return here, detain him for me. I would like to … speak with him."

"Yes, sir. Of course, sir." George gave a single nod and dismissed himself without looking up.

Lost in thought, Asma stared at the spot George had occupied. After adjusting his tie, he turned to Theia. "I'm so sorry, my dear." He forced out a cheesy grin. "I'm a busy man, and sometimes, items require my attention. Where were we?"

CHAPTER 56

The Five Articles

Father Chandler exited the highway, following signs for A168 South, Marton Cum Grafton.

"Okay, so let me get this straight," Matthew said, piecing together the story in the back seat. "You guys are Benedictine monks and for almost twelve hundred years—"

"Technically, seven hundred," Father Chandler corrected. "Before that, it was another Catholic order."

"Whatever. But in all that time, because of some *prophecy*, you have been trying to kill Theia and... and you're supposed to be the *good* guys?"

Father Chandler addressed Matthew through the rearview mirror. "Actually, in the beginning, our priority was protecting her by keeping her from De Atta. For a while, the order even considered forcing them together to break the prophecy."

Matthew rigorously shook his head as if trying to shake the information off. "Force them together?" He threw up his hands. "That doesn't make any sense. You told me it would bring Armageddon if they ever got together."

"Forcing them together could be perceived as an intervention and a violation of the Second Article. And any single violation is enough to break the prophecy. But they also feared in doing so, it may be considered fate. So, it was decided that option was too risky."

"So, killing Theia seemed less risky? I can't believe the Church would ever allow—"

"The Church would never sanction this," Father Chandler interjected. "Even we struggle with it, but it has to be done."

Matthew stirred in his seat, eyes darting between the two men. "But you *are* the Church. You're monks. You're Catholic."

No response.

"You mentioned the Second Article. What *is* that? Is that this prophecy you're referring to?"

Father Huckabay, who had been facing Matthew, turned to face forward. Father Chandler cast frequent glances through the reaview mirror.

Still no response from either.

"Why would bringing Theia and Asma together violate this prophecy? And what does fate have to do with anything? What does that even mean?" He paused. "Guys? Guys, give me something here. As you said earlier, strength in numbers and all that."

Finally, Father Chandler spoke, "Matthew, please appreciate there are things we cannot discuss. You just have to trust us."

Matthew's eyebrows reached his scalp. "Well, I *don't* trust you." He motioned for the car door. "You know what? I'm not buying any of this. Let me out." A loud rush of air gushed through the gap as Matthew cracked open the rear door.

"No, Matthew!" Father Chandler stomped on the brakes, swerving the car off the country road. "Okay. Okay." He shifted to face Matthew and waited for him to close the door. "What I'm about to tell you is highly confidential. We *are* Benedictine monks, Catholics, but we are also members of a secret organization inside the Church. Our order has protected the secrecy of the Articles and their content for centuries, ensuring the information is securely passed on to other generations."

"You protect the prophecy? Keep it secret? Why? If it contains valid predictions as you say, then why not break it all open? Involve the full power of the Church? You could—"

"Because it would serve no purpose!" blurted Father Chandler. "They wouldn't believe it. Even members of our own order question its validity."

"They question it? But it *is* real, right? You just told me…"

"Of course," Father Chandler cried. "Theia and Asma are proof of that. But over the years, our order has become divided. Some believe that the remaining Articles are not prophecy but mere propaganda to strike fear into our hearts to weaken us."

"Remaining Articles?" Matthew's mind swirled. "How about you tell me exactly what this prophecy is? From the beginning."

Father Chandler inhaled deeply. "The prophecy is like a 'how to guide,' a rule book for Armageddon. Do you study the Bible, Matthew?"

"Yes, I mean I did. I read some theology during my time at Oxford."

"Okay. So, as you know, the Bible maintains that good will prevail over evil. Always. Especially in the final battle of man against beast."

"You're talking about Revelation?" Matthew remembered his studies.

"Not just Revelation. It is affirmed many times throughout the Gospels. And in every case, good always prevails. But the prophecy states that evil *will* triumph in direct contradiction of the Bible, one reason the Church would never accept it."

Matthew nodded, clearly understanding the institution of the Church and its inherent stubborn principles. Indeed, his many dealings with them regarding artifacts were often the most challenging and frustrating aspect of his job. Father Chandler was right.

A document claiming such contradictions would never be accepted.

"The prophecy is ancient," Father Chandler continued. "Its actual age is unknown, but it dates back at least a thousand years before the birth of Christ. It consists of the 'Five Articles'. The First describes the events surrounding the birth of two immortals, one from the City of Dan, born of darkness—"

"The City of Dan?"

"An ancient region in northern Israel. North of Galilee at the foot of Mount Hermon."

"Galilee? But that's where Jesus spent his formative years."

"Holy shit, he's right!" Father Huckabay jumped in, laughing. "You ken, I never put that together before. Sheesh."

"Is he with you?" Matthew asked, finding Father Huckabay's response rather un-monk-like. "Or did you pick him up along the way as well?"

Father Chandler didn't miss a beat. "The other immortal, from a northern city in a far land, would be born of light, blessed and holy."

"Theia."

"Yes. The Second Article describes how fate will bring them together, most likely in the region of her birthplace, York. Probably why De Atta has remained in the area, awaiting her return."

"Which she has, with my help," Matthew added glumly.

"But staying in one place isn't easy when you never age. Draws a lot of unwanted attention, which is one reason Theia has always moved around."

"How did *he* manage, then?"

Father Chandler shrugged, providing best guesses. "From a lifetime of practice? By necessity of needing to stay here? By forging birth documents, creating new identities, willing his wealth, estate, companies, everything, to… nephews or grandsons who suddenly spring from nowhere and then assuming their identity? And he's always private, always operating under the radar to avoid exposure."

That statement seemed to contradict everything Matthew had seen so far. "He doesn't appear to be operating under the radar. Far from it. He is on TV, in magazines, everybody knows him."

"True. This is a new strategy. We've never seen this before. For the last few years, he's suddenly favored the limelight, becoming this public figure."

Matthew's penny dropped. "To lure her in. Of course. How else would she find him? If he's famous, then she's bound to notice him, recognize him."

Father Chandler nodded. "It's clear now that was his intention. There is nothing he does without a plan behind it. He's shrewd, you see, always one step ahead, never to be underestimated. Fame, of course, brings its own risks, opening him up to inquisitive eyes. Only recently, there was an investigation by a female reporter at the *Huntington Herald* that caught quite a bit of local attention with its claims of a conspiracy in the Goodwin heritage. 'Philanthropist or Foolanthropist?' What an article that was!

"She reported that Mr. Goodwin had fabricated his rights to his inherited fortune, also that his birth certificate was forged, and there was a fake signature of the executor responsible for managing the probate of his estate. The article lacked answers, but certainly raised lots of unwanted questions. Bless her soul… well, she had no clue what she stumbled upon."

The long pause surrounding 'bless her' seemed to refer to the woman in the past tense. "What happened?" Matthew asked. "You make it sound as if she…"

Father Chandler closed his eyes, shaking his head. Father Huckabay answered. This answer, he knew. "Aye, she's dead, only yesterday in an explosion. *Boom.*"

"An apartment gas leak," Chandler added drawing out each word in disbelief. "No doubt her research burned along with her. She was only twenty-four."

"He's a monster!" Matthew gasped, both hands rubbing at his cheeks.

"No, Matthew. Not a monster. He is quite literally the devil incarnate, and his child will rain fire unless we stop him, or Theia."

Matthew reeled back. *Stop Theia?*

He knew exactly what it meant. "Isn't there a way to end this without bloodshed? You mentioned forcing them together would break the prophecy. Why is that?"

"Because it has to be fate alone that brings them together. While much of the prophecy's translation is unclear, one point is indisputable: the Reginleif girl must seek out the dark one of her own accord, without deliberate *outside* intervention. This is why De Atta has remained on the sidelines, unable to reveal himself to her. No doubt for centuries, he has protected her from us until such time as she discovers him, and they can reunite."

Matthew gasped. "Up until yesterday, she didn't even know he was alive." He covered his eyes with a palm, realizing a painful truth. "Wait. Did I… Am I responsible? I encouraged her to come here. This my fault? If I hadn't forced the subject, then…"

"This is not your fault, Matthew. Fate was at play; fate brought them together. There is nothing you could have done about that."

Matthew clenched his jaw, uneasy at the notion of being a pawn in some grand design. "So, if I hadn't brought her here, if they'd never met… what then? Would this never have happened?"

"We can't know for sure, Matthew. Besides, they still had sixty-three more years to complete the bond."

Matthew frowned at that specific number.

"They only have twelve hundred years to bear a child. That too is written in the Second Article. No doubt why De Atta has changed tactics. He knew time was running out."

"And if they don't complete the bond?"

"We believe the prophecy would simply time out. They become mortal. Or so we suspect."

Matthew's head fell back on the seat. "So, this *is* all my fault. Without me, she could have waited it out, then she'd be free."

"For her," Father Chandler said. "After twelve hundred years, the prophecy recycles, choosing another two. We believe it has been doing that for… well, for a long time. But it has always failed."

"How do you know that?"

"Because Matthew, we are all still here."

The overload of information had Matthew's head in a spin. Right now, all he could focus on was a solution. To save Theia. "So how do *we* stop it? You mentioned it can be broken, right? Intervention. Timing out. That's two. What else can we do?"

Father Chandler shook his head. "You *know* what has to be done, Matthew."

"We have to kill her, right? Is that what you're saying?"

"Or him. To prevent the Third Article from happening."

"Which is?"

"The birth of their child—the Antichrist."

Matthew gasped heavily. "Gotta be kidding me!" The burden of guilt now weighing heavier, he closed his eyes. "And the fourth, the fifth? What are those?"

"The Fourth Article is mainly about rituals and upbringing. A guide for his guardians, to prepare him for adulthood. It is during this time, during his adolescence, that he will grow more powerful and become all-knowing. It describes his coming of age."

"And the fifth? Armageddon, I assume?"

"Aye," Father Huckabay chimed in once more. "Some really bad shite happens then."

Twice now, the ill-timed humor from Father Huckabay seemed way inappropriate. Matthew thumbed at Chandler's cursing sidekick. "Are you sure he's a monk?"

"He is… an acquired taste," Chandler offered politely. "He grows on you."

Like barnacles on a boat hull! Matthew thought.

Refusing to accept the only two remaining options—to kill Theia or Asma—Matthew brainstormed aloud. "There has to be another way that doesn't involve someone dying. Has to be."

"There isn't." Chandler's tone was sharp, frustrated. "Fate *has* brought them together, with or without your help. Trust me, they're our only options."

"Aye, that's right, pal. Nae other options."

Suddenly, Matthew sat straight, his eyes darting side to side. After a frenzied search through several pockets, he retrieved a small napkin with the poem on it. He handed it to Chandler.

"Does this mean anything to you?"

Father Chandler read it, Matthew explaining, "Theia came by it back in 1945. She believed it was a message proclaiming she'd die that night. I'm guessing it was your lot who gave it to her."

Father Chandler snorted as he finished reading it.

"What?" Matthew asked, surprised at his reaction.

"I've studied all the reports from that night. We all have. It's *the* most important night of the order's history. Karl Hoffmann was a hero. He broke the prophecy." He shrugged. "Or so we thought. But nowhere in our records does it mention leaving this message. I can see why. Sharing it is a serious violation of our code. And before you ask, Matthew, yes, it's from the prophecy and yes, we believed the translation meant she'd die."

"But she didn't!" Matthew shifted with excitement. "If it was wrong about her dying then, why couldn't it be wrong now? That's the thing with prophecies: history has proven they're inaccurate."

Father Chandler had the look of someone about to break bad news. "It may not have been wrong, Matthew. At least, not yet. You see, that passage is an extract from the Third Article—referring to the period *after* the birth of their child. A time yet to come."

"I don't understand," Matthew contested. "Why leave her that message, then?"

Chandler shrugged again. "Maybe after centuries of trying and failing, Brother Karl wanted her to know that finally, she was going to die."

"So, she's going to die, anyway? No matter what?"

"The order believes so, but I believe there's another possibility. One where she doesn't die." Father Chandler looked at his watch. "We don't have time for this."

"Make—time," Matthew bellowed.

Father Chandler sighed. Leaning on the handbrake, he shuffled around almost facing rearward. "Before the prophecy was translated to other languages, it was written in Arabic."

He pulled a pen from his shirt pocket, flipped Matthew's napkin, and scribbled two symbols.

$$\text{ل}\quad\text{و}$$

"The first symbol is Arabic for 'to', the second means 'and.' They appear similar. While the official translation reads 'Man *and* Beast,' I believe it could read 'Man *to* Beast.' A small error in translation but a significant change to its meaning." He recited the last two lines. "'Forsaken ye of Man to Beast, T' Niht O Light Will Darkness Keep.'"

"Man *to* Beast." Matthew gasped. "You mean she will turn *to* darkness? Like Asma?"

"It makes sense," Father Chandler added. "She can be powerful and useful to him. Why kill her when he can rule with her at his side?"

"She would never turn," Matthew defended. "I know her. She wouldn't harm a soul. She's kind, she's…" But he had only known her for the briefest time, hadn't he? Perhaps he didn't know her at all. "What do you believe, Father?" Matthew asked.

"It doesn't matter what I believe, Matthew, or any of us. The facts remain as do our options."

Matthew massaged his temples, his mind working overtime.

"I know it's hard to understand. Our major focus *has* been on De Atta, but we've never been able to get close. He surrounds himself with a small army."

Father Chandler reached a hand to Matthew's knee, interrupting his thoughts. "But tonight, our plan *will* work, Matthew. I have faith."

"Faith?" Matthew's agnostic tone was well apparent. "Is God going to lend a hand? Pitch in?"

"I have faith in you, Matthew. *You* are our in. They won't be expecting you. Not like this. And we have never had someone on the inside before. That is why this will work."

Matthew nodded, slowly at first, his confidence building. "Okay."

Father Huckabay eyed his watch. "We best get going."

Father Chandler agreed. He pulled onto the road, heading south. Less than two minutes later, he announced, "We're almost there." He spied Matthew in the mirror. "You're clear on the plan?"

Matthew's sweaty palm squeezed the gun's grip in his lap. "Which part? The part where I take this gun filled with little blue bullets and kill the devil, or the part where, if I fail, you'll shoot him with a sniper rifle through the window? That sounds pretty straightforward—yeah, I think I got it."

"Hit center mass," Chandler reminded. "As I showed you. That's important. Only the vital organs. And you won't get much recoil on that thing. Those are low-velocity, hollow-point bullets. We don't want them passing through. Once inside, the cadmium will finish the job."

"Center mass. Got it." Matthew couldn't believe he was saying those words aloud. A week ago, he'd been stressing over an overdue inventory report; now, he was about to infiltrate Satan's own house and kill him. "Hey," Matthew said, realizing a flaw in their plan. "What if they search me?"

Now with the headlights off to prevent being seen, Father Chandler was leaning over the steering wheel, driving at a snail's pace. "Did they search you the first time?" he asked.

"No."

"Then I think we're good. Remember, you just came from the airport. They have no reason to suspect you're armed. Just tell them you missed your flight or lost your passport or something." Passing the Goodwin Castle's gated entrance, Father Chandler pulled off the road where the perimeter stone wall turned to hedges. "We're here."

From the trunk of the car, Father Chandler retrieved a canvas camo case spanning the width of the boot. Unzipping it halfway, he slid out a tan-colored L115A3 long rifle with a suppressor. He checked the bolt action by exercising it twice, then snapped a magazine to the breech. After removing the dust cap from the scope, he held it to his eye, panning it, testing the focus.

"Is that standard issue for all Benedictine monks?" Matthew asked.

Huck sniggered, mumbling something about his being delayed along with his rule book.

Father Chandler, on the other hand, remained stone-faced, his focus on the mission sparing little room for humor now. A glutton for detail, he summed the plan for a third time.

"And remember, Matthew, he's very careful never to stand by the window. Do whatever it takes to get him there. We'll be ready."

Matthew nodded, clumsily tucking his gun between the waistline and the small of his back. The cold steel was uncomfortable and sharp against his skin and required constant readjustment.

From the dark, he felt a hand grip his shoulder. He turned his head.

"Matthew," Father Chandler whispered, his voice softer now. "If we get a clear shot at Theia first, I'm sorry, but we're going to have to take it. There's too much at stake."

Matthew shuddered, the words delivering like a thousand volts. "No!" he begged, louder than he should. "Please, don't do that. I won't let you down. Promise me you won't."

Ignoring Matthew's plea, Father Chandler brushed past him, squeezing himself through the perimeter English yew hedges.

"Let's go!" he whispered from the other side.

CHAPTER 57

Mr. Goodwin, I Presume

Asma and Theia retreated from the romantic candlelit table to the comfort of the inviting fireside Chesterfield. Absorbing the warmth of the crackling fire, Theia curled her bare feet beneath her and sipped her Sauvignon Blanc. Asma's knees gently met hers as they locked in a gaze.

"When I was carried away from our village," Theia began, "it was burning to the ground with you lying face down, three arrows in your back." Recounting the vivid memory summoned a tear. She touched Asma's hand. "So, what happened to you?"

"Well, I died. At least, for the first time. The darkness and silence were like nothing I had ever experienced."

Theia nodded, recalling the same experience many times before.

"When I awoke, hours had passed. The houses were smoldering, and everyone was dead, except for one man—a fur trader. He helped me, and brought me to his village where, as you can imagine, they were somewhat bewildered to discover me in such good health after receiving three arrows to the back!" Asma laughed, as did Theia. "But eventually, I ended up with my real family. I don't mean parents, but the people who understood the prophecy, who knew who I really was. They raised me and have protected me ever since."

"Are those the same ones who have been protecting me?" Theia asked excitedly.

"Yes, you are very important, Theia." Then after a pause, he added, "To me."

"What about those who have tried to kill me my entire life? Who are they?"

The resentment in Asma's voice was evident. "Those, my dear, are a pitiful bunch. They will never accept the prophecy's inevitability, though they are powerless to stop it."

"And this prophecy…" Theia furthered. "You said it was about our child?" She warmed Asma's hand between hers. "Tell me more about our child."

LIKE A GHOST, Father Chandler seemed to float through the dense, dark woods surrounding the Goodwin Castle. Eyes peeled and scanning, he held his scoped rifle close to his chest, pointed down, finger at the ready. His toes, slithering silently between the dried foliage and twigs, found soft soil on every step, unlike Matthew and Father Huckabay who clumsily followed behind.

Their twig-snapping feet subjected them to his frequent glances, a look that even in the thick of night screamed *be quiet!* Before long, the woods gradually gave way, revealing a grassy clearing. Beyond the moonlit fields, Asma's castle emerged. Illuminated on all sides by sodium lights, it appeared even more beautiful at night. Father Chandler aimed his rifle to scope the building while Huck focused his binoculars next to him.

"Men in the ground floor room," Chandler recounted quietly. "Adjacent the entrance. Four, maybe five."

"Yes," Matthew whispered. "Saw them earlier. From what *I* saw, there were fifteen or twenty, easy."

Chandler's scope moved to the next floor, to the great room where Theia and Asma were immersed in their fireside soiree. From this angle, he could only observe the ceiling and its several chandeliers.

At the same time, Huck scanned the grounds near to the castle with his binoculars.

He almost called the 'all clear' when he saw a man patrolling outside.

"One guard. Lower east corner," he reported.

Chandler's scope quickly found him, wearing a military-style camouflage jacket and an olive-green beanie. Recognizing the strapped weapon over his shoulder, he gasped. "Fuck! SA80."

"What's that?" Matthew whispered, hovering in his wake.

"Assault rifle, fully automatic." He glanced over his shoulder at Matthew. "Military issue."

Matthew pulled a nervous face and then turned his eye to the distant driveway running to the castle. "Okay, well, here goes nothing. Wish me luck!"

"Oh, Matthew," Father Chandler said, suddenly remembering a critical detail. One that might save his life. "Try to keep your mind clear of our plan. We think he can sense your thoughts."

"Great! Thanks."

As Matthew disappeared into the thicket, Father Huckabay asked, "Why did ye lie tae him?"

Chandler just stared back.

"Back in the car," Huck continued. "Ye told him no one had tried this before. That we had the element o' surprise. But we *have* tried, even had someone on the inside. But they all failed. Everyone died."

Chandler relaxed his shoulders, sighing. "But, brother, all the others understood the gravity of the risks going in. Knowing the insurmountable odds couldn't have been easy. De Atta would have smelled their fear and sensed their plan in a second. Besides," he said as he rummaged his outer pocket for his phone, "Matthew's terrified enough." He dialed his phone. No introduction.

"We're in position," he said, then hung up.

After another quick scan through his scope, he threw his rifle over his shoulder, crouching to the ground. "Come on," he said. "Let's get closer."

BACK AT AMPLEFORTH Abbey, the reverend placed the house phone on its receiver. "So, it's begun, brothers. Tonight, the fate of humankind rests in the hands of our dear Matthew and our two brave brothers. Let us all pray." In unified reverence, the monks lowered their heads, clasping their hands while Reverend Thomas recited Psalm 35, the prayer of miracles—for soldiers before battle.

"Plead Thou my cause, O Lord, with them that strive with me, and fight Thou against them that fight against me. Lay hand upon the shield and buckler and stand up to help me. I will say unto the Lord…"

"… THOU ART my hope and my stronghold, my God; in Him will I trust," Matthew completed the prayer, delivering it into the cold night in a cloud of white smoke. He was surprised he had remembered it, having only read Psalm 35 maybe once before.

Science was always the lens through which he viewed the world, though tonight, he made an exception. Marching the frontline of the holiest of wars, he hoped, he prayed, he had more than just a gun and a plan on his side.

Approaching the castle's entrance, a half dozen armed men in suits spilled out, encircling him. Matthew did not have to try hard to appear shocked.

"Hey, what's this? I'm with Theia. I was here earlier, remember? The funniest thing—I lost my passport and…" A leathery hand gripped his shoulder, forcefully shoving him inside where George, the butler, stood waiting.

"George!" Matthew was relieved to see him. "Can you tell these goons to relax? Jeez!"

George maintained his boarding-school stance, rigid, chin held high.

Immediately, two guards honed their pistols close to Matthew's head, another searching him. The guard's hands yanked, tugging and delving, far less respectful and more thorough than any airport security search.

"Hey, easy," Matthew complained.

But when he tried to resist, the armed duo pressed their weapons closer, demanding a statue-like obedience.

It wasn't long before the guard found Matthew's gun, which he briefly examined and then handed to George. Matthew's heart pounded watching George withdraw the magazine and inspect the clip. George's already suspicious eyes narrowed on Matthew the instant he discovered the blue bullets stacked inside. Only then did Matthew tell himself:

I knew this was a crap plan!

George tutted three times, raising the magazine clip. "And what were you expecting to do with this? Well, well, Matthew. What a foolish thing to do."

Without uttering a word, Matthew stared, the color draining from his face.

"Cuff him," George demanded.

Matthew winced when the sharp plastic cable ties tightened on his wrists in front of him. Then, led by George, the guards shoved him through the adjoining room on the right, toward the east wing.

OUTSIDE, THE MONKS had found a closer spot in the shadow of a centuries-old elm, taking pride of place in the moonlit field. They lay flat. Chandler perched his rifle on its unfolded tripod, his open eye staring down the sights. Through the window, Matthew was led, his hands tied, across the ground floor room, disappearing from view.

"Shit! This isn't good," Huck whispered, focusing his binoculars. "I've lost him. We need to reposition so we can see into that room."

"No, we stay put. De Atta is the priority."

"Aye. And which room is *he* in?" Huck asked. The lack of reply proved his point. "Exactly. I dinnae ken either. But I can tell ye what room he's *gonna* be in… Matthew's. That's our best bet right now."

It made sense. "Okay. Let's go."

INSIDE THE EAST wing room, two guards slung Matthew into a hard wooden chair.

"Hey!" Matthew complained again.

The elegant room showcased a parlor-like ambiance, adorned with plush rugs and fine furniture. Beside him, at the center of the room, stood a pair of maroon floral couches facing each other, flanked by oversized lamps at either end. His eyes drifted to the stone-framed windows consuming half the exterior wall.

It's up to you now, brothers.

Before leaving, George instructed his men, "Watch him. I'll be right back."

GEORGE'S TAP ON the great room door was a little heavier this time, three fast taps instead of his usual slow two. He entered. Asma and Theia sat amorously close on the couch.

Asma rolled his eyes, huffing at the intrusion, though, in truth, he had been eagerly expecting it.

"Excuse me, my dear," he said.

At the door, George whispered, "Sir, we have him. In the east wing."

"Good. Hold him there. I'll tend to him in a couple of—"

"Sir," George interrupted, raising his voice. "Forgive me, but he was armed with this." He pulled the semi-automatic pistol from his jacket, away from Theia's eyeshot, and released the magazine clip, showing it to Asma. Asma's eyes glared when he saw the blue bullets.

"The monks!" His expression stiffened, his eyes listing in thought. "Have the men search the grounds. I'll be there, directly." He then returned to Theia, his face pale.

"Is everything okay?" Theia asked, moving to the edge of her seat.

"Yes, my darling." He smiled sympathetically. "But I have to take care of this pressing matter if we are to have any peace this evening. It shouldn't take too long. I promise you, this will be the last interruption."

Theia stood, stepping toward him. "No, no that's fine." She stretched her neck to one side. "I'm actually exhausted. Still jet-lagged! Maybe I'll just call it a night."

"Of course, my dear. We have all the time in the world," Asma said, embracing her and pecking her cheek. "You remember the way to your quarters?"

Theia nodded.

"Very well." Asma walked her to the stairs, watching until she ascended from sight.

When the east wing door opened, Matthew sat straight. George entered first, followed by Asma.

"Matthew, Matthew, Matthew. Who *have* you been talking to?"

Asma casually strolled by Matthew's chair, waving the magazine clip in one hand, the gun in the other. "Expecting trouble, are we?"

"*Mr. Goodwin*, I presume?" was the coolest line Matthew could conjure.

"Ooh, is that sarcasm I hear? I thought you Americans were incapable of such humor."

Tight-lipped, Matthew maintained his stare, having found his courage through hate.

Asma paced. "Only our monk friends know how to make these." He shook the magazine. "What else did they tell you?"

Matthew remained silent.

Asma stopped in front of Matthew. "Did they bore you with tales of prophecies and articles?"

Although Matthew held his best poker face, Asma saw straight through it. "So, they did! My, they *have* been rather chatty, haven't they? It matters not; I merely want to know what ludicrous plan they've concocted this time. Was it simply to saunter in here and shoot me? Was that it?" Asma laughed at the absurdity, as did the five guards under their breaths. "Really, Matthew. Whatever do you take me for?"

A psychopathic megalomaniac. However, Matthew decided to keep that thought to himself. Instead, he simmered in anticipation of watching Asma die.

All I need to do is entice him to the window. The monks will...

But then he remembered Father Chandler's last words of advice. Quickly, he diverted his eyes to the floor, trying desperately to clear his mind of their plan.

Asma's laughter faded, filling the room with an uneasy silence.

After a moment, Matthew curiously glanced up; Asma was studying him like an intriguing lab specimen, his eyes penetrating Matthew's mind, searching. His thinned eyes drifted to the window, then back to Matthew. "They're out there. Waiting. I know it."

You idiot! Matthew cursed at himself. *I suck at this!*

Asma's voice firmed, enunciating each word. "How many are with you?"

But Matthew remained steadfast in his silence. He smiled.

"Not talking? Oh, my dear boy, you will." Asma nodded to his nearest guard, who stepped forward, striking Matthew with a well-seasoned fist. Matthew grimaced as his lower lip gushed, bloodying his teeth. He'd been punched before but, *damn, that hurt!*

OUTSIDE THE CASTLE, the monks skidded to one knee in their new position, nearer to the east wing window. Huck swiftly scanned with his binoculars, Father Chandler resting his elbow on his bent knee, settling behind his scope. The new vantage point was an improvement, yet it still only afforded them a partial view inside.

"I count four guards. No Matthew though."

"Any sign of Asma or Theia?" Father Chandler asked, catching up with his scope.

"Um, nope. Nae gonna work. We have tae shift farther right. Get more of an angle."

After a brief scan of the room, Father Chandler agreed. About to move, noises from their left froze them. Instinctively, they collapsed to their chests, ears to the ground. Wide-eyed, they glared at each other.

Slowly, they each poked their heads above the grass. In the distance, men advanced from the castle entrance, their shadowy figures outlined by the ethereal blue moonlight. Flashlights, mounted atop their assault rifles, panned amber arcs across the verdant blades.

The monks bowed their heads, their new position providing scant cover; moving now would expose them.

"Now—the fuck—what?" whispered Huck.

CHAPTER 58

Hell Hath No Fury

Theia undressed down to her underwear, flinging her clothes onto the ottoman at the foot of her bed. The suitcase on her mattress was still half unpacked. She flipped it open, retrieving her pj's, laying them next to the black leather dress still sprawled across the bed from earlier.

Before heading to the bathroom, she glanced at her phone.

It had been sitting on her bedside table while she ate dinner.

Maybe Matthew left a message before his flight.

Avoiding the temptation to check, she went to brush her teeth.

HALF-CONSCIOUS, MATTHEW SLUMPED in his seat, chin hanging to his chest, blood oozing from his lip. A guard gripped his curly hair, yanking his head back, causing his jaw to sag open. Once more, he pounded Matthew's cheek with calloused knuckles.

Matthew groaned as his head rolled to his shoulder, resting a moment like that.

"My dear boy, why put yourself through all this? Tell me what I need to know, and you have my word, no further harm will come to you. How many are out there?" He paused. "What's their plan?" Asma checked his watch, then grinned at Matthew. "I can do this all night. You? I don't think so. Now, what's it going to be?"

Matthew whimpered something indistinguishable.

"What's that, my dear boy?" Asma moved closer, stooping lower. "Do speak up."

As a guard yanked Matthew's head up, Matthew spat, spraying a mouthful of bloodied saliva. Though Asma was untouched, he reacted as if he had been, feverishly scrubbing at his jacket, checking his unblemished shoes for spray.

For his insolence, Matthew felt the back of the guard's fist.

Asma inserted the magazine into the gun's grip, racking the slide. Stepping closer, he extended it, inches from Matthew's forehead.

This is it.

Matthew stared down the barrel. If these were his final few seconds, he wanted Asma to know he wasn't afraid, though in reality, he was petrified.

"Before you die, I want you to know something," Asma said through gritted teeth. "After your darling Theia has provided me with a child, I will have no further use for her. She will be disposed of." Asma turned the gun sideways, examining it. "I may even use those little blue bullets. I can't thank you enough for gifting me them."

Pointing the firearm back, he pressed it against Matthew's forehead. Matthew snorted in deep, rapid breaths through his nose, defiantly leaning into the gun.

Right then, the east wing door swung open as one of Asma's guards entered to report on their search. Despite Matthew having no idea of Theia's location in this enormous castle, he seized an opportunity to warn her through the open doorway, hoping his voice would carry. At the top of his lungs, he screamed, "Theia! Run!" It was a pitiful effort.

Using a backhand swing, Asma whacked the pistol's barrel against Matthew's head, opening a gash. In the process, blood sprayed onto Asma's cuff. Repulsed, he immediately stomped to the end table by the window, slamming the gun beneath a lamp. He pulled a crisp handkerchief from his jacket breast pocket and wiped furiously at his wrist as if his only shirt had been ruined.

UNABLE TO MOVE, the monks continued their surveillance of the east wing room, keeping a close eye on the armed guards fast approaching. Father Chandler had already drawn his sidearm from his belt clip and laid it on the ground near his rifle, ready for a firefight. It was only a matter of minutes before they would be discovered.

"That's him. That's De Atta," Huck whispered urgently, Asma coming into the frame through his binoculars. "Shoot!"

Father Chandler had taken that moment to assess the men searching the grounds nearby. Quickly, he returned his eye to the scope. Asma had his back turned to the window. From months of studying him, he could recognize his build, his hair, his stance. It was him.

He squeezed the trigger slowly, the way he'd been taught, but before it fired, Asma slipped from his field of view. He was gone. "Damn it! I had him!"

The rustling of Asma's men grew closer. Father Chandler poked his head up for another peek. One guard was heading in their direction. He ducked down, turning to Huck who lay as flat as he could, eyes like a deer's. "We're running out of time." He slid the sidearm across the damp grass. "You know how to use this?"

Father Huckabay's angst expression answered for him.

"It's loaded," Father Chandler whispered. "Just point and squeeze the trigger. Don't yank. You have fifteen rounds. Got it?" Huck nodded nervously, his trembling hand fumbling for the gun.

THEIA EXITED THE bathroom, brushing a stubborn tangle from her hair. She placed the hairbrush on the nightstand next to her phone. After stuffing the black leather dress inside her suitcase—it *was* cute after all—she flapped the lid closed, then heaved the case from the bed to the ottoman. She slid under the heavy quilt, fluffed the pillows, and sank into a feathery slumber.

Curiosity tugged on her eyes, drawing them to the phone. As if telepathic, she stared at it, trying to guess if it held messages from Matthew. She knew there wouldn't be any news from the hospital. Before dinner, she had called the shift nurse; both Audree and Bill were comfortable and asleep.

I need to forget about Matthew, she reminded herself.

Letting Matthew go had been the smart move. The best for everyone. Wasn't it? Besides, her future was with Asma, and from what she understood, it was an important one. Lest she not forget, one day soon, she'd become a mother, a role she had only ever dreamed of having.

Without further thought, she twisted the lamp switch, bringing the room to darkness.

She shuffled to her side, facing away from the phone. *I'll check tomorrow, just to make sure he made it home safely.*

Three and a half seconds later, she turned the lamp back on.

Okay, just a quick look.

Her thumb moved quickly, entering in the code. The pop-up message read:

3 - Missed Calls

1 - Voice Message.

She clicked the 'listen to your voicemail' link, and Matthew's name appeared. She eagerly pressed the phone to her ear, heart racing. But this was not the sweet message she had hoped to listen to.

Matthew's voice screamed from the earpiece, "Theia, you're in grave danger. Get out of there! Now! He's not who we thought he was; I was wrong about everything! The... the men with the tattoos, they're Asma's men! They're following me. I think I gave them the slip, and I'm heading back to... no! No, please! Aaagh!"

Theia's eyes welled, listening to some kind of an almighty struggle taking place. The sound of choking, that could only be Matthew, and then... *scuffle, smash, thump!* The message ended with the robotic female voice. "End of messages. To return the call, please press one. To save the message, press..."

She gasped, her trembling thumb hitting number one.

Pick up, pick up. Please, Matthew. Please, please.

Without ringing, it went straight to voicemail. She immediately hung up, trying again. No ring—just voicemail. Already halfway off the bed, she slid onto the plush carpet, collapsing onto her knees. Her shoulders quivered, and tears streamed down her face.

The phone slipped from her grasp, landing with a muffled thud. A guttural cry escaped her as she bawled. Only yesterday she'd collapsed in tears, learning about Audree and Bill. But Matthew had been there to catch her, to comfort her. And now he was…?

What had happened?

Her mind pulled in every direction.

Something had been off with Asma. Why didn't she listen to her gut? Trust it as she always had. *My poor Matthew.* He was hurt or even dead—and Asma and his thugs were responsible.

Her whimpering cry intensified into a wrathful roar. Anger boiled within, the likes of which she had never experienced. A millennium of pain and loss was finally enough. The inner warrior she once had been—fearless, adept—seeped to the surface as she slowly climbed to her feet. Head tilted down, fists clenched white, her piercing cold eyes reached across the room, settling on the armored mannequin.

I'm coming, Matthew, and God help anyone standing in my way!

CHAPTER 59

Two Swords for Sister Theia

Asma's senior guards engaged in conversation on the third-floor landing at the mouth of the stairs. Both understood the rules, especially the one they were breaking. Idle chatter was prohibited on duty, creating a distraction their employer could not afford. He had made that clear during his frequent inspections. Like a platoon leader, he would line them up and inspect their dress, adjust their ties, dust their lapels, and comment on the scuff on their shoes, while recanting his rules and reminders of rewards. Most of Asma's men being ex-military, the formality was familiar and their attention to perfection usually warranted few reprimands.

But for others, it was a constant effort, though the reward for service—the promise of power and immortality—outweighed the strict rules and tedious dress code scrutiny.

In unison, their heads spun upon hearing a door slam at the end of the west-wing corridor. Theia's door. With long strides and military-style pendulous arms, Theia marched toward them.

The curved body armor hugged her shapely figure, flaring from the waist into a pteruge skirt of leather and steel tassels.

Other than the battle dress, her expression and determined pace signaled to the guards she wasn't out for a leisurely moonlit stroll.

The first guard motioned toward her, but Theia made no effort to slow. The guard thrust out a halting palm. "Madam, please return to your room. We have a situation…"

"You're right about that," she said as she snatched his wrist, swiftly twisting it upwards. He winced, succumbing to his knees from the pain. A forceful chop broke his arm at the elbow, then a swept leg sent him plunging to the floor. The conflict, over in a second, barely interrupted her stride.

The other guard fumbled in his jacket, first for the radio, then opting for the gun. Bullets flew, though he knew they wouldn't kill her; perhaps they'd slow her down enough.

He hoped.

His aim was sharp, yet Theia swiftly dodged, vaulting off a table and racing up the wall with agile grace. He fired again as she descended, cartwheeling through the air.

The next shot barely missed as Theia's feet slammed into his chest, sending him tumbling backward. His gun, thrown from his grip, slid into the shadows under a nearby dresser.

Winded, and probably with a broken rib or two, he clambered to his feet. Despite the pain, he bared his teeth and raised his fists, then stepped forward to meet her.

THE GUARDS' GUNFIRE had echoed throughout the castle grounds. Matthew had heard it. As too did Asma who shot a concerned eye to George. He flicked his head toward the door. "Go!"

George summoned three guards to follow him, leaving two behind.

As he left the room, Asma yelled after him. "Notify the men. Get them all in here. Now!" He roared the last word with such rage, his face crimsoned and shook.

Although Matthew's throbbing concussion had his head dangling, he still managed to give Asma a glance from the corner of his swelling eye.

While it pained his jaw, he relished the moment with a satisfying grin. Like Asma, Matthew assumed the gunfire had originated from the monks.

Perhaps they couldn't position for a window shot and decided instead to storm the castle—literally.

But Matthew's grin was not for their brave attack or for his potential rescue. It was from the sheer delight of watching Asma squirm.

That was priceless.

FATHER CHANDLER STRENGTHENED his grip on his rifle as he lay pinned to the ground. Eyes shut, he mimed a final prayer. Very soon, they would be discovered, and he knew his long rifle was no match against the SA80, especially in the hands of a trained soldier poised and ready to shoot.

He rehearsed their limited options.

If he waited until the guards were closer, it would be game over before he could swing his heavy rifle to shoot. Attacking now was their only hope, however slim that was.

"Huck!" he whispered. "Get ready. We go on three. Okay?"

His nervous friend gulped, sheepishly pulling the gun closer to his face.

Chandler held up a fist and unfolded his first finger.

One.

Then his middle, *two.*

Then… a nearby guard's radio squelched, followed by mumbled chatter. Both monks froze, eyes locked. The guard uttered an indistinguishable response. After a moment of silence, Father Chandler lifted his head. To his surprise and relief, the guard was returning to the castle entrance along with the others.

Huck shuffled closer. "Did ye hear gunshots?"

Father Chandler's mind churned. "Matthew!" he exclaimed. "He did it!"

"Or maybe that wisnae him shooting," Huck suggested, his face paling. "What if…?"

As if reading his mind, Father Chandler's jaw dropped. The image of Matthew being caught and executed was forged inside his head. *Just like the others.* Growing more anxious by the second, he leaned into his rifle, staring down the lens into the east wing room.

THE MING VASE shattered into a mosaic of worthless shards as Theia's body smashed into it. Only three remained intact from the set of six lining the hall. She rolled off the table and slumped to the floor, face down.

What's up with this guy?

Does he have a vendetta against priceless vases?

Plus, she didn't appreciate being used as a sledgehammer. He fought dirty. She desperately wanted to kick his ass, but first, she needed air in her lungs.

Trying to crawl free, her fingers clawed at the carpet. The guard was over her in a second, hoisting her upright by her hair. Her squeal morphed into a growl of anger as she fought, attempting to pry his fingers loose. She almost succeeded, forcing his finger back beyond its natural limit. However, he countered by coiling his other arm around her throat, tightening it in a serpent's death grip.

Squirming only intensified his chokehold. Her windpipe flattened, extinguishing her screams. A vignette spilled over her peripheral vision, darkening with each stolen breath.

On the stairs below, the thunder of footsteps pounded against the wooden tiles.

Others are coming.

It seemed hopeless.

The guard arched his back, heaving his elbow high, lifting her airborne. The added gravity yanked on her neck. As she fought for air, her legs thrashed wildly at the empty space. The sudden imbalance prompted him to twist a half-turn toward the hall table. Her feet leaped from it and ran up the adjacent wall, somersaulting over his head.

Now freed from his grasp, she landed directly behind him. An instinctive, sharp but driven kick to the back of his knee dropped his height. Before he could react, she followed with a firm grip on the square of his jaw and the base of his neck.

A sharp jerk, and he was dead.

As his lifeless body keeled face-first to the floor, she massaged her throat, struggling to breathe.

Footsteps climbed the final flight, gaining volume—at least two or three men, she estimated, with more in the distance. On the wall next to her hung a shield with two swords mounted crisscross. She clasped the hilts in each hand, wrenching them free.

She moved quickly to the top of the stairs, huddling out of sight on one knee, head ducked and ready. The first guard approached the landing, the other two just a stair behind. Theia exploded from her crouched position, blades swinging. With a series of kicks and spins, she deftly sliced through the first, then the second.

The third managed a double shot from his Glock 17 before her blade found his throat. Neither of his bullets hit their mark.

A glance over the banister revealed more guards gathering on the ground floor. Four others on the flight directly beneath hurdled the stairs two at a time, guns drawn.

She curled her lip and raced to meet them.

By the time she reached the half-landing, Theia was in a full sprint. Bullets erupted, exploding into the plaster wall beside her. She dodged and rolled, quickly getting to her feet. The guard summiting the final step aimed.

His bullet threw her back, stealing her breath. Despite her armor, it penetrated easily, stopping inches from her heart.

Fueled by adrenaline and a warrior's cry, she swung her swords, hacking down the shooter. Another bullet struck, recoiling her shoulder. Using its momentum, she continued in a full circle, slashing a backhand swipe, spilling open the next in line. The third bullet felt like a baseball bat to the gut. She doubled over, her elbows digging into her sides. Summoning all remaining effort, she thrust both swords forward, piercing center mass on the final two assailants. As they tumbled backward down the staircase, she collapsed on the top stair.

She took the moment to address her wounds. Immortal she may be, but her wounds needed time to heal.

Time she did not have.

"WHIT ON EARTH is gaun on in there?" Father Huckabay roared, no longer having to whisper. "Soonds like a battleground."

Father Chandler furrowed his brow. Surely Matthew—the historian—with his one clip of ammo isn't causing all that commotion against a troop of trained mercenaries.

"Shall we go in? Help 'im?"

Father Chandler weighed that option in an instant. "No. We don't know what we'd be walking into. Let's stick with the plan."

Both returned to their rifle scopes and binoculars.

LET'S GET THIS over with.

Using the swords as a pair of canes, Theia hauled herself to her feet. Pain shuddered through her body. She repositioned her grip on the swords' hilts, then swung the blades to loosen her shoulders and prove to herself she still could. The swing was loose. Weak. It would have to do.

Before heading back into battle, she stretched her neck, cracking it to one side. She stepped down from the landing, but then paused. The silence below seemed odd. She angled over the banister, peeking to the ground floor.

No movement.

No sound.

No men.

Minutes earlier, orders echoed, feet shuffled—a small army approaching. By now, they should be swarming her. For a moment, she welcomed the peace, a well-deserved reprieve. But then she had a sobering thought. They weren't running. They weren't advancing. They were preparing. Planning.

An ambush.

Although she knew it, Matthew was in danger. Hurt. Perhaps dying.

That horrific vision mustered all the extra strength she needed. She sighed, then limped down the stairs toward the daunting quiet.

Cornering the final half-landing, she descended the last flight. Now she learned the reason for the silence. Asma's guards stood shoulder to shoulder the hall's width, blocking the grand entrance. Numbering twenty or more, they aimed down the barrels of their semi-automatic weapons.

In front of them, Asma proudly clapped, beaming a Cheshire Cat smile. "Bravo! Bravo! Well done, my darling Theia. What a warrior you are. Such vigor." His words carried like those of a creepy S.S. officer, speaking sweetly but with a menacing undertone. "Though, I'd rather hoped our courting had gotten off to a better start. But then again, no relationship is perfect, is it?"

Now at the foot of the stairs, Theia stiffened her posture, her shoulders squeezing together displaying her strength; she hid her pain well.

"You and I were put on this earth for one reason and one reason only," Asma pontificated, pacing. "Who are we to question what is written? It is prophesied." He paused his step, observing her. "Maybe, you just need some time to adjust to the idea?"

When he massaged his chin in thought, she whitened her knuckles around the hilts of her swords. Every pompous word that spilled from his mendacious lips sent her skin crawling.

"How about we just sit down and talk about this?" Asma offered. "You, me, and Matthew."

Matthew? Theia's head motioned mistrustingly to the side.

"Oh yes, he is here, in this castle." He pointed to the east wing. "In that very room." Theia peered through the east parlor to the closed door. "We were actually just discussing the future… his future, if I'm to be completely honest." Asma began a slow walk toward the room maintaining a vigilant eye on Theia. "Come, let us sit. I promise, no harm will come to you."

Theia motioned to follow, though cautiously.

"Um, let's lose the swords, shall we, darling?"

Theia paused. Her leery mind stirred as she eyed his small army, still posed ready to fire.

Asma waved a hand dismissively. Without uttering a single word, his men lowered their weapons in a single motion. A cheesy Cheshire Cat grin returned to his face.

Theia dropped her swords, which clattered loudly on the parquet tile.

"There now, see. All friends again." Like a gentleman, he waved her in front. "After you, my dear."

CHAPTER 60

The Fatal Shot

"Matthew!" Theia screamed as she charged into the east wing room.

Matthew sat crooked, chin resting on his chest. His zip-tied wrists hung between his thighs. She knelt in front, hands loitering around his cheeks as if finding him too delicate to touch.

She leaned under his chin. Looking up, she gasped. "Oh my God!" One eye, a painful shade of purple, was swollen half closed. Bruised blotches patterned his pallid face, his upper lip and chin stained red from the gush of blood now oozing at a glacial drip.

Matthew!

Theia whipped her head to Asma, sending daggers across the room. "What have you done?" she yelled hysterically. "He has done nothing to you. Look at him. Why? Why, Asma?"

"Nothing, you say?" Asma marched to the side table to retrieve the loaded weapon. Shaking it, he protested, "My dear, he came here armed with this—to kill me! By all accounts, I have every right to protect myself. He is lucky I'm so forgiving."

Forgiving! The word boiled her blood.

She launched to her feet, charging at him, stopping just ahead of him by the main window. Arms flailing, she ranted and cussed. "I don't believe you. I don't believe anything from you." Theia snatched the gun from Asma, leaving him with an owl-like expression.

The two guards stationed like century posts near Matthew motioned forward but stopped when Asma gave a look.

Theia continued her rant, "He didn't have a gun. Where would he get a gun? He was just heading home. You lie." Like a flag she waved the gun, having no idea it held the only munition powerful enough to destroy him. "You expect me to believe that *he*," she pointed behind at Matthew, "came here to kill you!" Her head shook. "He isn't capable of that. What I believe is that he discovered who you really are, whatever the hell that is. *That* is why he is bound and beaten." Her wagging finger now pointed at Asma. "So don't you dare…"

Asma stepped forward, his hand reaching for hers.

"Stay away from me!" Theia warned as she stepped back. "Don't you *ever* touch me."

A HUNDRED YARDS away, lying in the frosty grass, Father Huckabay puffed warm air into his cupped hands. "Ah cannae feel mah fuckin' fingers. It's Baltic out here." He flipped over his hands, staring at the back. "Bugger me, they're turning blue!"

"It's just the moonlight," Father Chandler said. "You'll live. Just keep wiggling them, and your toes. Keep the blood flowing."

"Easy fer you, mister military man. I'm nae used tae the cauld."

"For God's sake, you're from Scotland. It's always cold up there. What's happened to the hardy Scotsman? You lot even wear skirts. So don't give me *it's cold.*"

"Enough of ya pish. It's a kilt. And aye, ah ken it's cold up there, but ah don't go laying ootdoors in the middle o' the neet like some great eejit." Mumbling further complaints, he regained his focus through the binoculars. As soon as his eyes peered through the lens, his entire body jolted. "Holy fuck, it's her! It's the Reginleif lassie!"

Father Chandler quickly leaned into his scope. Through the east wing window, Theia stood erratically waving her arms, yelling at someone just out of view.

"Take the shot!" Huck commanded.

Father Chandler's heart raced, hands trembling.

"Now! Hurry! Shoot for fuck's sake."

Drawing on his training, Father Chandler shallowed his breath that had suddenly developed into a nervous pant. The crosshairs weaved and spiraled before finally centering on Theia's head.

He threw off a quiver developing on his hand, then regained his grip. *Breathe. Breathe. Steady…*

Just then, the haunting image of an Afghan child consumed his rifle scope.

The same child plaguing his dreams for the last three years.

A young boy, no older than twelve, with an innocent face and wide, gaping eyes, stepped from the pavement into the dusty urban street. His white pakul cap and white peshawari garb shimmered in the blazing midday sun. Even from a thousand meters away, the child's confusion was painfully evident. Egged on by those in the shadows of the doorway behind him, the little boy shuffled nervously farther into the street, stealing frequent glances behind.

Only forty yards away, the American convoy rumbled closer.

"Damn it, kid, don't do it."

The boy's hand twitched, raising slightly.

Glimpsing the detonator clenched in his grip, his tiny thumb hovering, Lance Corporal Douglas Chandler made a choice that would forever shape the course of his life.

He squeezed his trigger.

Flash!

Father Chandler shook away the vision, stretching and blinking his eyes. A cold sweat had formed across his forehead and the tremble in his hand had returned.

"Shoot! What are ye waiting fer?"

His heart pounded harder. *Breathe.* He returned to the scope.

"Hurry, brother! We can end this now. T'neet."

With a deep inhale and a long, slow exhale, he slowly squeezed the trigger. The firing mechanism coiled, ready, the crosshairs now stable on Theia's profiled face just behind her ear. In a split second, a twelve-hundred-year war would be over, the prophecy broken. No child. No Antichrist to rule humankind. So many lives would be saved with just one bullet. The cost—just one innocent girl.

Suddenly, his shoulders slouched, head stooping at the side of his weapon. The rest of his breath abruptly exhaled as his finger released on the trigger.

"Whit are ye daein', ye damn eejit? Pull the fuckin' trigger."

Father Chandler turned his head to his Scottish friend. "I... I... couldn't do it." Before Huck followed with another verbal assault, he added, "Look, why don't we give Matthew a chance? We owe him that."

"How dae we ken he's nae a'reedy dead?"

INSIDE THE EAST wing room, Matthew's unswollen eye glared nervously at Theia as she stood in full view of the window. *Surely, they would have fired by now. Killed her. Why haven't they?* But then he remembered his plea to Father Chandler as they unloaded the guns from the car, and his promise that he would not fail.

Thank you, Father. Thank you.

"Theia, my darling, please, calm down," Asma said, attempting his best to sound sincere. "Why don't you give me the gun?" He stretched his hand out further.

Theia took another step back, then reached her arm directly behind her, dropping the gun to the floor. "You want it? Come get it," she goaded.

When Asma stepped closer, Theia slapped his face, crying out, "You're a monster. I can't believe I ever loved you!"

With both hands, Asma grabbed her wrists, taking another step closer. "Calm down, Theia. I don't want to hurt you." Now, Asma's body was between hers and the window.

No! Matthew replayed Father Chandler's words in his head. 'Do whatever it takes to get him in the window. We will be ready.' This time, he knew they would have no choice but to take the shot. But Theia was too close. He couldn't risk her being hit. He wouldn't.

Summoning every remaining ounce of energy, he sprang from his seat, wrists still tied in front, hurling his body like a bowling ball at Theia and Asma. Asma's guards surged forward to stop him. But by then, it was too late.

As Matthew's body flattened Theia and Asma to the ground, a hole cracked through the east wing window. Immediately, the guards took cover, their guns drawn, honed on the window.

At first, there was silence.

"Sir!" a guard yelled from a covered position. "Sir! Are you hit?"

No response.

CHAPTER 61

Metempsychosis

Theia slowly roused from the impact. Her head spinning, she took account of what had just happened. Next to her, Asma lifted his head from the floor to glance at his chest, his hands probing for a wound. Finding none, he rolled onto his side, staring up to the window, as did Theia.

Near its edge was a small hole fracturing out like a spider's web.

Asma crawled out of sight of the window, slowly standing, continuing to check himself. "I'm not hit," he called to his men. Then he barked, "It's those damn monks. Get them. Send everyone! I want them dead! All of them… dead!"

Both ducking low, the guards made for the door while one bellowed into his radio, "Snipers on the front lawn by the east wing. Everyone, proceed to that location."

Now, Theia looked over at Matthew next to her. He was lying face down. Motionless.

"Matthew!" she cried, scrambling over to his body. "Matthew!"

FATHER CHANDLER WATCHED as Asma's men poured from the building. Spreading into a line, they advanced on their position. The exterior patrol guards also joined them from around the sides of the building. The men in suits doubled their grip on their 9mm pistols, the military-attired guards bringing their SA80 stocks into their shoulders.

Recognizing they had little time, Father Chandler spoke quickly, "Save your rounds. Make every shot count. Wait until they're close. You won't hit unless they're close. Godspeed, brother."

Father Huckabay gulped; their dire reality kicking in.

Father Chandler shuffled on his chest to face the advancing army. He peered down his scope, took another deep breath, then squeezed the trigger.

His first shot hit center mass, hurling the guard backwards, right off his feet. With trained speed, he jolted the bolt action, loading a fresh round. He pivoted his aim. Another breath. *Clap.* The second shot was another direct hit. This time, the guards dove into the grass and opened fire. Bullets from the automatic weapons drilled the earth just ahead of the monks, exploding soil high into the air. The monks ducked, shielding their heads with their hands.

In the middle of this open field, they were sitting ducks.

"Come on!" Father Chandler screamed to Huck over the gunfire. He grabbed his pal by the shoulder. "Pull back to the tree. Let's go!" Launching to their feet, he aimed at a guard firing the automatic bursts. He missed, but it afforded a momentary ceasefire. They took off running, back toward the large elm. Huck pointed his pistol behind him, firing randomly as he ran.

A hail of retaliatory bullets followed.

The elm tree was close. Twenty yards. Fifteen. Ten. Five.

Thud.

Huck groaned, tumbling to the ground. Just ahead of him, almost reaching the tree, Father Chandler skidded on his heels. "Huck!" he hollered behind him. Through the barrage of bullets, he raced back to aid his friend. A bullet clipped his arm, sending his rifle to the dirt.

He paused, considering retrieving it, but then took a running dive in Huck's direction. He landed close and sniper-crawled the remaining distance. "Huck, are you hurt bad?"

"My leg!" Huck rolled in agony, hands clasped around his thigh. "Shit. I'm sorry, brother."

Father Chandler removed his belt and fashioned a tourniquet around his pal's thigh. Huck grimaced as it tightened. Then he grabbed the pistol from the grass, releasing the magazine. Eight, maybe nine rounds he counted. It wasn't enough. Not nearly enough. Huddling next to his friend, he affectionately squeezed his arm, smiling as gunfire ripped through the air around them.

"It's okay, brother. It's okay."

ON REACHING MATTHEW, Theia laid a gentle hand on his back. "Matthew?" Feeling the damp warmth, she twisted her palm, finding it soaked red. She gasped. "No!" Carefully, she rolled him over onto his back. Blood trickled from his mouth, running down his cheek, and his eyes were agaze, one barely able to open.

He half blinked. *He's alive!*

"Matthew! Can you hear me?" Theia cried, fighting back tears.

From the corner of the room, Asma stepped closer, forming his Cheshire Cat grin as he neatened his tie, pulling on his cuff. "Matthew, my dear boy, you have just saved my life! Though, I can't imagine that was your intention." He chuckled at the irony, then addressed Theia. "Don't you see, my dear? What is written must be fulfilled. Nothing can stop it. I know you have feelings for this mortal but in time…"

As Asma proudly raved, Matthew's eyes slowly lowered, staring beyond his feet, to the devil himself. On the flight over, he vowed to help Theia—even if it was the last thing he did. Now was his chance. What Theia and Asma had failed to realize was Matthew was holding the gun in his tied hands. As fate would have it, he landed on it as his body hit the floor. He lifted his head, raising the gun, pointing it at Asma. Asma's confident speech shushed in an instant.

His jaw dropped, the nauseating grin dissolving off his face.

Matthew wasted no time. *Bang, bang… bang, bang!*

Asma's chest shuddered with each round. In disbelief, he glanced down at his bloodstained shirt and dropped to his knees. A second later, he collapsed forward, initially landing on Matthew's leg and rolling off onto his back.

He coughed, blood gurgling in his throat as he fought for breath.

Theia was shocked but immediately refocused on Matthew. Remembering her years as a field surgeon, she went to work. "Where does it hurt? Where are you hit?"

Matthew whispered, "I can't feel my legs."

Theia paused. *Not a good first sign.* Ripping open his shirt, she located the gushing wound. Finding it, she inhaled sharply and stared into Matthew's eyes.

The bullet had entered his sternum, almost dead center, in line with his spine.

"Oh, Matthew, no!" she cried.

Matthew reached for Theia's hair with both hands, the plastic ties still tearing into his flesh like wire. "You're safe," he whispered. "No more running."

Theia gently cupped his hands, kissing them before holding them against her cheek. "Oh, Matthew, what have I done?"

"Don't cry." The words were so soft they drifted like a breath of wind.

Once more, the haunting vision of Matthew dying in her arms flashed through her mind. As she squeezed his hands, she sensed his aura. It dimmed, fading rapidly.

"No! We should have left when I said." Her voice was a mix of self-blame and heartfelt regret. "Why wouldn't you listen? Oh, Matthew."

"No… you're… you're…" His words faded into a whisper, then into silence. As his heavy eyelids closed, his lips shaped the word *'free.'*

"Matthew? Don't go. I can't live without you. I love you. I love you so much. Please, Matthew, please don't…"

But her words froze in her mouth as she gazed at his stilled face. To her utter horror, she knew he was dead.

OUTSIDE, THE GUARDS had formed a semi-circle wall, closing in on the monks, who huddled exposed in the open field. Father Chandler heaved his friend onto his lap.

"Did ye get him?" Huck asked, lying there, staring up. "Did ye get De Atta?"

"Aye, I got him. We did it, brother."

Knowing the end was near, he saw no reason to tell him the truth now. That Matthew had launched into his frame just as the bullet fired. They had failed. And failed big.

Father Huckabay beamed his crooked teeth, patting his friend's arm. "We're heroes, brother! We're fuckin' heroes! We saved the world."

Father Chandler relished his friend's salvation. Until now, he had never understood why a fellow like Huck ever chose the Church. If anything, he was the anti-stereotype for the part, his whole life one long string of mistakes. Alcohol. Drugs. Stealing. A disappointment to his family. To his friends. To his daughter. And although his family would never learn of the sacrifice he had made tonight, he could tell from Huck's glimmering eyes that it didn't matter.

He'd become a monk to find redemption and peace from his sins. And tonight, on this freezing lawn under a beautiful starlit sky, he had found it.

Father Chandler repeated, "Heroes, brother. Saved the world," then he aimed his gun toward the castle and fired the remaining rounds.

THE EAST WING room was eerily quiet, apart from the occasional splutter emanating from Asma's dying lips. Theia knelt by Matthew, pressing his hands to her cheek, rocking back and forth. She reached for his face, already gray and frozen into a lifeless stare, and closed his lids. Then in a flood of tears, she collapsed over his chest.

Sorrow turned to disbelief.

She whimpered, "No, no, no, no…" Her streaming tears turned to sobs, her sobs to wails. "No, no, no…" Gaining volume on each crying word, her head fell back as she gazed up to the heavens, screaming an almighty, "*No!*" Louder than any mortal, her voice echoed through every room in the castle.

She slammed her hand onto Matthew's chest. Her back straightened and stiffened. After a moment, light began to glow from behind her chest armor. The intense brilliance radiated to her neck, spilling into the room in beams of silvery white that sparkled as if glitter carried with it.

Asma was clinging to life, wheezing his last breaths. He reached a curious hand to the dancing lights streaking in lines above his head. His hand fluoresced almost transparently, like an X-ray. As the energy intensified, Theia's hair flowed in waves as if standing against a fierce wind. Pulses of light surged down her arm, intensifying as they flowed into her hand, growing increasingly bright.

Soon, its radiance fully enveloped Matthew's chest. Theia closed her eyelids and pushed every ounce of her life force into Matthew. However, in her weakened state, her energy drained rapidly. She feared it would not be enough. Not to heal death. Not even at the cost of her own life.

Seemingly having no effect, her light energy flickered and dimmed; the words from the medium resonated through her mind.

"The man you love more than life itself will die in your arms, and *you* cannot save him."

'*You*' cannot save him, she repeated to herself. Only now did she understand what that meant.

You *alone* cannot save him.

Despite her eyes being closed, she sensed Asma's arm grasping at the miraculous light above him. She snatched his wrist.

There was no struggling free from her grip.

Asma began to writhe, his legs twitching. Then, beneath Theia's grip, his wrist shone with a brilliant light traveling the length of his arm. Like

Matthew, his chest also began to glow. As Theia guzzled his life-force, his arms and legs shuddered violently as if electricity ran through them.

Her entire body beamed so incredibly bright that the sun's rays paled by comparison.

The room's every lightbulb simultaneously burst, raining down incandescent particles. As energy surged through her, an unimaginable pain thrust out her chest and threw back her head. The ensuing ghostly scream thundered through the castle, beyond its walls.

THE BLINDING LIGHT beamed from the east wing window, illuminating the lawn like a shimmering golden sunrise. Along with it, Theia's unsettling scream sent chills through the guards who cowered into frightened stoops, shielding their eyes with outstretched hands.

Perhaps fearing an audience with God or assuming their master was no more, Asma's men cowardly fled to the shadows of the surrounding forest.

The monks perched from their huddled embrace, staring in awe, savoring the warming rays on their frozen faces. Father Huckabay laughed with excitement, squeezing his friend's arms as if to say, *we did it!*

"Mother Mary!" Father Chandler gasped, crossing himself.

BACK INSIDE THE east wing room, Asma released a bloodcurdling cry before death finally seized his breath rendering his body limp. In unison, the dazzling white light emanating from Theia seemed to implode back into her, casting the room into near darkness. Alongside it, her once-deafening cry transformed into an angelic silence as she collapsed over Matthew's body.

For a while, the room was still. A heavenly calm as though time had stopped.

Slowly, Theia sat back on her heels. Her eyes still closed, she heaved a long inhale as if finally breaching the surface after nearly drowning. Head back, she opened her eyes. Though it was dark, faint reflections of moonlight eerily defined the room in magical whispers of misty blue.

Her eyes fell to Matthew's face.

His wounds were gone. As too were his swollen eye and blood-stained mouth. His skin, now a healthy shade of pink, radiated warmth even in the muted beams of blue.

Just then, the two monks shuffled through the parlor toward the east wing. Huck was limping, his arm draped across Father Chandler's shoulder for support. They paused in the doorway, tensing from the charge of electricity raising the hair on their arms.

Shivers ran through their spines.

Except for a ray of light coming from the window, the room was pitch dark and hauntingly silent. After only a few steps they stopped, awed by what they saw. Through the window, cerulean moonlight rained over Theia in a transcendent beam. A targeted beam as if shone directly from heaven and only on her. Divine orbs like showering snowflakes descended inside the light, each absorbed by her shimmering halo. She knelt over Matthew, her head bowed and profiled to the side, appearing humbled yet otherworldly. Angelic.

Matthew lay still.

Next to him, Asma's suit and bloodstained shirt slowly collapsed like a deflating balloon. Now ash, the former body inside crumbled under the weight of the fabric.

"Matthew," Theia called out in a soft, motherlike voice. "Wake up, my love."

Matthew's eyes slowly opened, staring first at the ceiling and then drifting to hers. She smiled lovingly, her eyes welling.

"It's a miracle," Father Chandler gasped.

Wasting no time, he hit the quick dial on his phone. An impatient voice answered.

"Reverend," Father Chandler reported, "it's over. It's finally over. De Atta is dead. The prophecy is broken."

CHAPTER 62

Lincoln Hospital

One Week Later.

Knock! Knock!

Theia opened the door to Audree's room just enough to poke her head in. No longer hidden behind her emerald contacts, her sapphire-blue eyes peered inside as she beamed her beautiful smile. "Hey, you! Is it okay if I come in?"

Audree lay in her bed, inclined at a comfortable forty-five degrees, with Bill seated at her side, holding her hand. His other arm hung across his chest, supported by a pale blue medical sling.

"Well, that depends," Audree chirped sassily. "Did you bring me any of that English chocolate back?"

Through the narrow door opening, Theia brandished a gorgeous ensemble of yellow flowers: Gerber daisies, carnations, and roses. "Um, no, but I brought you these!"

"I can't exactly eat those, can I?" Audree complained. "The food in here is atrocious."

"It can't be worse than your cooking," Bill joked.

Audree playfully withdrew her hand from his caressing clutch. "Just because we're getting married, it doesn't mean you're free to insult me, you know."

"You're getting married?" Theia exclaimed from behind the door. "Wow. I *have* missed a lot."

"Oh, come on in, girl." Audree waved. "Stop loitering in the hall. Besides, you remembered what my favorite flowers are." Theia entered. "Just lay them on the counter, hun, next to those." She pointed at an enormous bouquet on the chest of drawers, opposite her bed. "I'll get the nurse to put them in a vase."

"Wow!" Theia was impressed by the stunning arrangement that barely left room for hers. She read the message on the tag and raised a brow at Audree. "Who's Mrs. Faraday?"

"From work. She's the... *district... attorney,*" she answered, slow and pronounced, while jiggling her head as if saying *His Majesty, the King of England.* "At least *someone* loves me," she added with a scornful eye at Bill.

"I've been by your side, day and night, for almost a week, woman!" Bill protested. "When did I have time to buy flowers?"

"You've got a phone, haven't you? You could have ordered some in the bathroom."

Bill sighed.

"He *has* just been shot, Audree," Theia pointed out. "Give him a break."

"So, you're on his side now. I see how it is. Mm-hm. First, I'm stabbed in the stomach by some kidnapping devil worshiper, now I'm stabbed in the back by my best friend. It's like Julius Caesar around here!"

Theia giggled as she pulled a chair to sit opposite Bill.

She squeezed Audree's hand, then shook it. "You're the best friend anyone could ever wish for. I'll never forget what you did for me and David and Sheila. I am so, so very sorry for everything I put you both through."

Audree's face softened with a tear, then instantly hardened. "Oh, stop it, girl. You're gonna make me cry."

But Theia continued, her eyes sad, "I don't know what I'd have done if either of you—"

"Oh, phooey! We're still here aren't we, sugarplum?" Then gently rubbing her stomach, Audree added, "Anyway, it's just a scrape."

"A scrape!" Theia almost fell off her chair. "Audree, your intestine was severed. Sepsis had set in. You nearly died!"

"Rubbish!" Audree waved a dismissive hand. "I'm saving the dying part for when they give me the hospital bill. And as for this one," she said as she thumbed at Bill, "it's going to take more than a few bullets to stop *this* tough bastard. Plenty have tried. The thought crossed my mind once or twice!"

Theia chuckled. "I hear she saved your life."

Bill opened his mouth, but Audree beat him to it. "You're damn right I did. He can't do anything without me."

Bill closed his mouth.

Audree turned to Theia, a serious face forming. "Okay, hun, now you're back. Let's have it. I want my answer."

"Answer?"

"Uh hm. Don't you remember? The last time I saw you before you left for England, I said I'd ask you this the next time I saw you. Surely you remember?"

Theia's eyes moved to the corner. "Um, nope. What did you ask me?"

"What did I ask you? Ugh. Seriously, girl! What I asked was…" She paused. "Wait a sec. I need to get comfortable first." Using both hands, she pushed herself farther up the bed, wincing.

"Easy, now," Bill griped, jumping from his seat to help her. Then with one hand, he adjusted her pillows, carefully easing her back.

Now comfortable, Audree asked, "Okay. After a thousand years of searching, did you finally find what you were looking for? *That* was the question."

Theia's head dipped. Deep in thought, she gazed into her lap where she rolled a diamond ring on the third finger of her left hand. It glistened, separating the LED light from the bedside lamp into a rainbow of color.

Audree asked again, softer this time. "Well, sugarplum, did you? Did you find what you were looking for?"

Theia raised her head slowly, gazing at her best friend. Holding back tears of joy, her flushing cheeks stretched a heartfelt smile, then finally, she said, "Yes!"

The Legacy

One Year Later.

The Christmas tree must have stood sixteen feet tall, its twinkling star almost reaching the coffered ceiling. An oversized red silk ribbon, intertwined with gold, wrapped around it like one of those old-fashioned barber poles. Although the eye-catching tree drew the most attention, the surrounding room appeared no less festooned. Every window, every picture frame hanging on the wall, the mantel, and even the new puppy kennel were swathed in glittering tinsel as if a giant party popper had exploded.

At the foot of the towering tree, a pile of newly opened presents were neatly stacked, with the floor around them bearing the torn remnants of odd scraps of red and blue wrapping paper.

Sheila had missed them during her tidying.

The front doorbell chimed with its two-tone gong. Sheila bolted from the kitchen to answer it, wearing her bright red reindeer apron and matching slippers—a gift set from her sister and husband visiting from out of town.

"Merry Christmas!" Audree and Bill sang in unison as she opened the door. Bill jiggled a bottle of red wine adorned with a red bow, and Audree balanced several wrapped gifts stacked in a pyramid atop her arms.

"Merry Christmas! Everyone's early today. Please, please, come on in," Sheila beckoned using her clasped oven mitts paired in one hand. "Make yourselves at home."

As Bill stepped inside the opulent hallway, he held up the cabernet. "Where d'ya want this, sweetheart?"

"Um…" Her mind was balancing tasks like spinning plates: check on the roast; the veggies simmering on the stove; finish preparing the hors d'oeuvres; tend to guests. "Um, I don't know. Do we need to decant it or something? I'm not really a wine person."

Bill shrugged. "I normally just pull, pour, and drink."

Bill's equal lack of etiquette instantly calmed her. She dropped her shoulders. "Why don't you put it on the dining table?" She pointed through the opened double doors of the large dining room behind him.

The dining table was gorgeously decorated. Each of the twelve place settings held white china plates edged in silver, christened with red Christmas crackers.

Audree followed Sheila to the formal living room, resting her presents on the arm of an easy chair. She grabbed the one on top, holding it against her bosom with both hands as she scanned the room. Her eyes sparkled at the sight of the glitzy decorations.

"Mighty me, Sheila! You went all out." But her compliment went unheard. Sheila's scurrying feet had already whisked her back to the kitchen.

Then she found him. Beyond the crackling fire, in the room's corner, David knelt by the Christmas tree, patiently assembling his latest figurine. As soon as he saw her, his face lit up. He scrambled to his toes, sprinting across the room and nearly knocking her off her feet when he slammed into her.

With tiny arms barely reaching the width of her generous hips, he pressed his cheek into the softness of her waist.

She chuckled, hugging him. "I'm happy to see you too, David. Did Santa find your new address okay?"

David's voice screeched with excitement, speaking a million miles per hour. "Yes, yes. Come see what I got." Grabbing her by the hand, he dragged her through the den toward the Christmas tree. Even her heavy-set frame couldn't resist the power of his tug. He pointed randomly. "I got a PlayStation! Look! And I got puzzles, I got coloring books, I got, I got…"

Audree giggled. "Oh my, you are a lucky boy!" She handed him her gift. "Merry Christmas, David." Taking it, he sank into a nearby chair, unwrapping it on his lap.

Audree stood and watched, a smile stretching across her face.

With only the corner peeled, he instantly recognized what it was. He gasped. "An iPad!" His peeling turned to frenzied ripping, shedding the remaining paper then holding it high like a first-place trophy. A second later, he placed it back down and plunged into Audree for another tight hug. "Thank you! Thank you, Aunty!"

She loved it when he called her that. "You're welcome, dumpling!"

Sheila sprang from the kitchen holding a fresh plate of hors d'oeuvres. David screamed over the guest's chatting, "Mommy, Mommy, look what Aunt Audree got me!"

"Yes, I know, sweety. It's very expensive and a tad extravagant. But there's no talking your Aunt Audree out of anything." She finally looked over at him. "Be *very* careful with it, okay?"

"I will, Mommy. I promise."

Audree ruffled David's hair and turned to join the other guests.

TAKING A RESPITE from the gossipmongering, Theia relaxed alone in a comfy armchair. The two couches beside her sat vacant.

Bill approached. "There you are. How ya doing, doll?"

Theia leaned forward to stand.

"Don't get up. You're fine. I'll come around." He circled the couch then sat diagonally on the nearside from her.

"I'm doing well!" she replied, easing back into her chair. She unscrewed the cap to her Fiji water, taking a sip. "I heard Zac got promoted, P.I. Partner, no less."

"Yup. I figured I'd start slowing down, ya know. I'm not getting any younger. Plus, he's a good kid, full of energy. Kinda like me thirty years ago." He thought on that, then said. "Maybe, not *exactly* like me. He's… more refined, I think."

Theia almost choked on her water. "Maybe just a little, Bill!"

"Hey, hun!" Theia recognized the voice chirping behind her. Before she could turn, she felt a gentle embrace on her shoulders, soft lips pressing into the top of her head followed by a long, "Mmmwah!" Then, "Mmm, your hair smells like apples. And I love the new color, hun. What is that? Auburn? Black? Does it have a touch of red? Or is that just my eyes?"

"It does," Theia replied, pulling on the ends drooping around her neckline. "It's new, *La couleur de Theia!* I figured no one's chasing me anymore so I may as well stop dyeing it."

Audree repositioned behind Bill for a better view. Like an artist examining their finished masterpiece, she leaned away. "Oh, girl, that is definitely your color. Brings out those gorgeous blue eyes of yours. Mm, mm. Looking *mighty* fine."

"I don't feel mighty fine." Theia pushed out her chest, her hand massaging the small of her back. She grimaced. "Damn back's been aching all morning."

"Welcome to the *mortal* world, sugarplum!" Then scouting the room, Audree asked, "Where's Matthew at? Is he here?"

Theia thumbed over her shoulder. "He's in the kitchen, playing chef! Sit, sit." She patted the arm of the couch next to her then pointed at the space next to Bill. "Keep me company."

Just then, Sheila raced by with another round of hors d'oeuvres. "Sheila," Theia shouted. "You come sit, too. You've been at it all morning, girl."

Though she tried to argue, Theia insisted.

As Sheila collapsed onto the couch along with Audree, she let out a never-ending sigh.

"The place looks wonderful," Audree complimented. "Love all the decorations."

"Thank you! We're still unpacking! But Christmas stuff was first, of course! Plus, with all this space, I had to buy a lot more. Don't think I overdid it, do you?"

For once, Bill beat Audree to the punch. "Nah. It looks... very... colorful." He shifted his stout frame as best he could, surveying the room. "Certainly gotta lotta space."

"It's more than we're used to, that's for sure." Sheila shook her head. "I still can't believe we were awarded all that money. Eight and a half *million* dollars. Phew! But I'd give it all back in a heartbeat if I could have my Ben back." She leaned forward, eyeing Theia from the far side of the couch. "I'm so grateful. Thank you, Theia. If it weren't for you..."

If it weren't for me? Theia cringed inwardly. *I'm the reason she and David went through all that suffering.* Of course, she could never tell her that. Her secret would remain between herself, Matthew, Audree, and Bill.

"It was Bill's investigative skills that made our case," Theia said, deflecting Sheila's gratitude. "He's the one you should be thanking. I just presented the argument. Besides, you and David have been through so much; you deserve an easier road."

Sheila passed Bill an endearing smile. Theia continued, "Anyways, I rather enjoyed practicing law again. It felt... good. Especially winning and making them pay." She perched proudly rubbing her hands together. "It's certainly more gratifying than drilling a root canal!" The comment received unanimous laughter—except from Sheila. *Her* thoughts were fixed in the past.

"Ben loved the docks. He made a lot of friends there. It's nice to know it will be a safer place now. He'd be happy with that." Sheila turned to Bill, her voice jittery and nervous, "They *will* implement all those training requirements and safety measures, won't they?"

"Hell yeah, they will," Bill chuffed. "Trust me, they won't be wanting to lose another 'wrongful death' suit anytime soon." His reassuring words relaxed her.

For just a moment, the conversation fell flat.

Theia shifted forward, gripping her lower back again. "Ugh. Which brings me to a decision I've made. When I return to work, it won't be as a dentist. I'm opening my own law firm! I'm going to practice again." Theia squared with Bill. "I could use a good investigator."

Bill puffed his cheeks and his eyes flared. "We're pretty slammed, but um…"

Audree punched his leg. "Of course, hun. He'd love to help." Then she wiggled her shoulders, as if back at the nightclub, jiving to the rhythm. Her words sang in soprano, "I can't believe it! We're going to be a team, fighting crime." Palms pressed firmly together, she briskly clapped her fingertips in front of her face. "I can't wait! It's going to be so much fun."

"Calm down, Audree." Theia chuckled. "It's only corporate law—not *that* thrilling."

But obviously, it was to Audree. Excitement grew, and her mind raced as did her jaw. "Can I sit with you in the courtroom like, as your assistant? You know I never lose an argument. I could teach you my tricks."

"Audree, I don't think whining and stamping your feet counts in court!"

Bill chuckled but instantly hushed when he received a much firmer thump to the leg. Massaging his thigh, he asked Sheila, "How's your young David coming along? He seems to be doing well."

"He is. He's really come out of his shell these last few months." Sheila glanced over her shoulder where David was quietly playing with his new action figure by the Christmas tree. She smiled lovingly, her head listing. "He finally got what he always wanted."

All eyes joined Sheila's.

Audree looked puzzled. "A Captain Universe action figure with X-ray vision?"

"No, silly! A big family." Sheila sent a heartfelt look to each of them. "Speaking of family." Sheila turned her attention to Theia. "What about you? How long to go?"

Theia rubbed her swollen belly with both hands and pushed out a gasp. "Three more weeks!"

"I wish I knew whether to buy blues or pinks," Audree complained, her pout forming. "Everything I've got so far is whites and yellows."

Theia smiled. "Matthew and I want it to be a surprise. It doesn't matter to us as long as he or she is healthy. And white and yellow are fine, Audree. Thank you!"

Suddenly, Sheila jolted to her feet. "The roast!!"

Audree yelled at her, "You sit down, Miss Busybody." She gave Bill an elbow. "Bill will sort it. You hang with us girls. Take a load off." Reluctantly, Sheila sat while Bill dragged himself off the couch and headed to the kitchen, just as ordered.

MATTHEW WAS CHOPPING carrots for the third round of hors d'oeuvres when Bill entered. "Hey, Bill!"

"Hey, Matthew. Merry Christmas!"

"Merry Christmas!" Returning to his carrots, Matthew sniggered. "Let me guess. Audree sent you in to help?"

"Yup! Got it in one!"

"Already lugging the old ball and chain, eh Bill?"

"Just you wait, sunshine," Bill griped. "You'll be under the thumb, before you can say 'happily ever after.'"

"Happily ever after!" Matthew beamed proudly.

Bill made his way to the double oven, snagging a pair of Christmas tea towels on the way.

When he opened the lower oven, a plume of smoke billowed out. He dodged clear of the searing heat, wafting with both tea towels. Carefully, he removed the roast and placed it on the counter. "Goddamn. Looks a bit crusty." He prodded it with his finger and searched the counter space around him. "Where are the knives at?"

Matthew pointed with his knife. "First drawer, under the toaster." He resumed his chopping. A few chops later, Matthew flinched, dropping the knife.

He clenched a tight fist around his finger. "Damn it!" he cursed, rushing to the sink.

Using the back of his hand, he twisted the tap lever, releasing a stream of water. As he pried open his fingers, a torrent of blood gushed out, sending a wave of nausea churning through his stomach, threatening to disrupt his early morning cornflakes and coffee.

"Is everything okay?" Bill asked. "You cut yourself?"

Matthew positioned his gashed finger by the running water and braced. *Damn, this is going to sting.*

He grimaced, averted his face, and plunged his hand into the warm stream. Surprisingly, there was no pain, not even the faintest twinge. As he relaxed his face, and also his hunched shoulders that had unwittingly tensed, he peered into the sink.

The cranberry red swirling around the drain soon ran clear.

He lifted his finger, examining it closely.

No cut, only a faded pink line, already returning to a normal skin tone.

Wow… That's so cool!

"Matthew, are you okay?" Bill inquired for a second time.

For some inexplicable reason, that question grated on Matthew's nerves, sending his blood boiling. In his mind's eye, he envisioned grabbing the chopping knife from the midst of half-chopped carrots and driving it into Bill's face. A chuckle escaped him at the thought. *That would be so awesome!*

Wait! What?

Matthew cast aside the dark image, dispelling the unsettling thoughts. The violent and hateful nature of these mental outbursts, becoming ever more frequent, gnawed at Matthew. It was as if, at times, he were a different person.

As he dried his hand on a towel, he turned to face Bill. "Yes, my dear boy," he declared, rather pompously. "I'm fine!" With a cheesy Cheshire Cat grin stretching across his face, he added, "Now, how about those hors d'oeuvres? My wife is feeding for two; I wouldn't want to keep a hungry child waiting!"

Thank you for reading my book!

As an indie author, your support means the world to me.
If you enjoyed it, I kindly ask that you consider leaving a review on
the platform where you purchased it.
Your feedback not only helps other readers discover this story but
also encourages and motivates me to continue writing.
I look forward to sharing more stories with you in the future.

— Dean

ACKNOWLEDGMENTS

When I first envisioned the life of a writer, my thoughts invariably turned to Paul Sheldon, the renowned author depicted in Stephen King's classic novel, Misery. He would isolate himself in a secluded cabin, surrounded only by his typewriter and stacks of pristine white long grain Mimeo paper. No interruptions. No ties to the outside world. No internet (let me say that again—no internet!)

After weeks of solitary writing, he would meet his editor for a coffee, eagerly awaiting her praise as she declared his novel the best to date, swiftly sending it for printing the next day.

Voila, the novel would be complete.

But in reality, nothing could be further from the truth.

Throughout the process of writing a book, I have come to understand that it is a collective effort that demands extensive research, meticulous structural feedback, and seemingly endless rounds of editing (let me say that again—endless rounds of editing!) It is with deep gratitude that I acknowledge the individuals who have played an integral role in shaping and refining this book.

First and foremost, I wish to express my heartfelt thanks to my sister, Angela, who has always stood by me, even when the towering school bully tried to trip my feet! Your support and expert guidance as a teacher and editor have been instrumental in shaping my writing style.

A shout out to Keith Evans, a GR8! pilot, whose insightful suggestion helped fine-tune the final line of the book. I would also like to extend my appreciation to Doug Chandler, my boss and friend, whose wit and resilience have been a true inspiration.

I was doing alright, but then I got over it!

I would be remiss if I didn't acknowledge the administration staff at 'The Church of Satan' for their prompt correspondence and information during my research, although it is important to note that I do not subscribe to their beliefs. Additionally, their portrayal in my story should not be misconstrued as a true representation of the organization.

A huge thank you to my exceptional editor, Annie Jenkinson, and her sub-editor, Brad Reynolds, whose keen eyes and incredible talent helped refine this book into its best possible form.

To the countless beta readers and proofreaders, specifically Haley Friary-Schenk and Donna Griffin, I am eternally grateful for your contributions. Your feedback and advice have breathed life into this book.

Lastly, but certainly not least, I want to express my sincere appreciation to my beloved wife, Amy, and our two children, Devan and Ryan. Amy, you possess the patience of a saint. My obsessive writing process owes you a lifetime supply of tea and sanity-saving chocolate. Thank you for believing in me, even when the words weren't flowing, and the plot resembled a tangled ball of yarn. Your editorial insights are always on point and have helped enormously to improve the narrative. And to my children, thank you for reminding me of the wonders and surprises that life holds. Your love and encouragement have been a constant source of inspiration throughout this journey.

Cheers!

ABOUT THE AUTHOR

Dean Corbyn is a professional pilot with over 25 years of experience, flying for high-profile individuals and celebrities. Originally from Sunderland, England, he has traveled extensively, residing in four countries on three continents.

When he is not crafting new stories in his home office or soaring the skies at near sonic speeds, Dean can be found hammering away in his garage workshop or indulging his inner geek with science and the quantum world.

Dean currently lives in the Texas Hill Country with his wife, two not-so-small children, and two not-so-smart mutts (plus herds of deer, wild boar, and everything trying to kill you from poisonous insects and snakes to mountain lions and coyotes! Oh my!)

Printed in Great Britain
by Amazon